say

you

will

Also by N. Gemini Sasson:

The Faderville Novels
Say No More
Say That Again
Say Something
Say When

The Sam and Bump Misadventures
Memories and Matchsticks
Lies and Letters
Threats and Threads

The Bruce Trilogy
The Crown in the Heather (Book I)
Worth Dying For (Book II)
The Honor Due a King (Book III)

The Isabella Books
Isabeau: A Novel of Queen Isabella
and Sir Roger Mortimer (Book I)

The King Must Die:
A Novel of Edward III (Book II)

Standalones
Uneasy Lies the Crown:
A Novel of Owain Glyndwr

In the Time of Kings

say

you

will

A FADERVILLE NOVEL
#5

N. GEMINI SASSON

cader idris press

SAY YOU WILL
Copyright © 2021 N. Gemini Sasson

ISBN 978-1-939344-17-5 (paperback)
Library of Congress Control No. 2021911408

For more details about N. Gemini Sasson and her books, go to:
www.ngeminisasson.com

Or become a 'fan' at:
www.facebook.com/NGeminiSasson

You can also sign up to learn about new releases via e-mail at:
http://eepurl.com/vSA6z

Editing by Lawrence Editing
Cover art by Ebook Launch

To all those struggling to fit in or to find purpose.

SAY YOU WILL

Everyone has a story. Even the dog.

Shadowed by a stray he names Fantasma, five-year-old Mateo Sandoval flees the poverty and crime of his homeland with his mother in search of the American dream. Shortly after arriving at his grandmother's house in Kentucky, however, his mother unexpectedly abandons them. For years, Mateo struggles to fit in—until he discovers running.

When the high school cross country coach dies unexpectedly, Grayson Darling steps in to fill the void. But for Mateo, the gravelly voice that inspired him is gone and the threat of deportation is all too real.

It's not until Grayson loans him his dog, Sooner, that Mateo's love of running returns. Meanwhile, Mateo discovers that the bully who taunts him daily is not as tough as he seems.

During the day, Sooner accompanies Grayson's girlfriend, Brandy Anders, to her new job as an assistant to small-town lawyer, Rex Franzen. With Sooner's help, Brandy finds new purpose.

Say You Will is about how we're often more alike than we're different and how our differences can actually be our strengths.

Note to Readers

While most of the Faderville Novels can be read independently, this story is a continuation of the lives of the characters as begun in the book, *Say When*. If you happened to have picked up *Say You Will* first, there is enough backstory woven in to make it understandable; however, you will get the most satisfaction by reading these two books in their intended order. Well, also because this book is one giant spoiler if you haven't already read *Say When*.

prologue

Rex

They say I'm a storyteller. Like it's some sort of affliction, not a gift. Folks that spew garbage like that are impatient listeners, I say. Stories are just snapshots of life, arranged in a logical order, but spiced up with snippets of hyperbole and a rainbow of adjectives. Ever gone to someone's house and they hauled out the photo album? Yep, sure you have. That's what I do—except with words. And we've all got words. People, anyways. Nowadays, though, everyone's got a phone with pictures on it, but who wants to search through thousands of pictures to share an anecdote when you can just tell a story?

So, what am I getting at? Let me cut to the chase, for those of you with busy-busy lives and better things to do.

We all think we're somehow different from each other. Unique. Special, even. Maybe 'better than' those others. But we really aren't. Not when you scrape back the layers. In our need to get ahead in life, or sometimes just to survive, we look for someone to blame when life robs us of our rewards. Let me tell you, I've dealt with a lot of people in my career who ain't happy no matter what. They think in

1

order to feel satisfied, to get their due, someone else has to suffer. Forget helping each other.

Lots of folks think I work for money. Me, Rex Franzen, a simple country lawyer. If that were true, I sure as heck wouldn't be doing business in Faderville. I do what I do to *help* people. To make one tiny aspect of their messy lives a little less miserable.

There are lots of ways to help people, though. I witness it every day. And I've never seen it more evident than in the example of a certain dog that showed up in these parts, oh, about a year ago. Her name was Sooner. I'm a tad foggy on how the moniker got bestowed upon her. Something about always being in a hurry when she was a pup. But ain't we all wanting to get somewhere fast? Like there's no value in the journey. Folks need to slow down, I say. Even the dog figured that out.

I'd like to think I learn a little something new every day from all these people I work for with all their legal problems, complicated lives, and family drama. But I never learned more than I did from that busy red dog and the two people whose family she completed. Let me skip to the middle, though, where it becomes not just about them, but about everyone around them and how one human being connects with another, who connects with another, and so on. One young man in particular.

So listen up. Everyone has a story. Even the dog.

chapter 1

Sooner

The drawn-out mewl pierced the air.

I hated that sound. Hated the memories it stirred. Memories of the night Brandy's van veered from the highway. The world had turned upside down again and again and again. Everything inside the van had flown from side to top to side to bottom. The bang and crunch of metal on rock. The eerie groan as it settled into a twisted heap at the bottom of the ravine. Brandy's broken body dangling from the harness of her seat belt.

I'd tried to revive her, licked at the parts of her I could reach, but she'd been too hurt to respond. Confused and afraid, I'd gone for help. Scrabbling up the craggy slope, I'd emerged at road's edge just as the vehicles with the spinning lights had come screaming down the highway.

That sound again.

The wail rose in volume as the vehicle topped a hill, then lowered before pitching high. Slowing, I glanced back. The leash tautened, tugging at my collar. Oblivious, my human, Grayson Darling—or one of them, to be exact, because I had two now—continued forward in his plodding rhythm as we ran. His toes scuffed over the asphalt, sending gravel skittering in all directions. I slowed more, hoping to send him a signal. We should get out of the way. Far off the road.

"What are you doing?" Grayson popped the leash lightly. "Don't lag, Sooner. We're almost done. Keep up the pace."

Panic shot through my spine, long tendrils of fear wrapping around my ribs and tightening. As the vehicle closed in on us, I twisted backward, inadvertently spinning away into the ditch. Grayson stumbled, barely hanging on.

"Whoaaaa!" He reeled me in as he came to a stop. Crouching down, he pulled me to him. "It's just an ambulance, girl. They're not coming to get us, promise. And I have my phone with me." He tapped the little box strapped to his upper arm. "If it was something going on at the farm, Loretta or Clayton would've called me by now. It's okay. Just sit here with me while—"

His soothing tone did nothing to calm my racing heart. Terrible memories flashed through my mind: the mechanical bird that had lifted Brandy into the sky, the people who'd tried to capture me, the endless days running alone and scared, the coyotes—

"—go past *all* the time." He stroked the fur along my neck, ran his fingers over the top of my head and behind my ears. "Well, not so much here like they did in New York City. There it was several times an hour sometimes, what with all those people crammed into a few square miles. Anyway, probably just some older person who fell and hurt their hip, or some kid tumbled out of a tree, or—"

A big square white truck with symbols on it bore down on us. It was so close now I could see the intense face of the woman driving it and a man sitting beside her. I trembled as the terrible sound rent the air again.

"It's okay, it's okay." Grayson hugged me to him, hiding my eyes until it had passed. "It's just an ambulance."

Gradually, its cries diminished as it sped away... until it was nothing more than a fading speck on the horizon, like some pesky deerfly that had tired of assaulting us and moved on in search of another target.

Grayson laid his chin on the top of my skull, his fingers stroking my neck, my chest, the ridge of my spine. His comforting embrace stirred another memory—of the day I'd thought was my last. The day I could no longer go on. Had given up hope of ever finding Brandy again. Chance had delivered me to Grayson. In his care, I'd discovered a new love—running.

Which was what we'd been doing on this warm sunny morning before the siren had flung me back in time.

My heartbeat slowed, my breathing deepened. Eventually, my tremors ceased.

"You okay now, girl?" he murmured into my ear. "See, I kept you safe. We're fine."

I licked his fingers, then his wrist. Grayson understood the sound had frightened me, although I was certain he had no idea of all the things I'd been through before he found me, just that I was in a sorry state, although he hadn't seemed all that well himself when we'd met. He pressed his face to mine and I licked his cheek.

Laughing, he ruffled my fur. "Hey, that tickles."

He stood to survey the road, now empty of vehicles as far as the eye could see, then the land around us, green hills rolling far and wide, great swaths of dew-laden grass broken only by the occasional tree line or stretch of fence. His eyes took on a serious look. "You know, there aren't that many people who live out this way. I hope it's not anyone we know. Or that it's not too serious. Like a car accident."

Our eyes met for a moment. He shrugged. "No sense worrying about it. Not like we can do anything." Taking a deep breath, he tapped my snout. "You good now? Can we finish our run? I promised Brandy I'd have you back by noon. Daytime lunch date, you know—and yes, you're invited."

We turned back toward the farm and resumed our run. "We're stopping at the root beer stand. Nothing fancy, I know, just a burger and fries, but the wait staff brings out your food on a tray while wearing roller skates and... Anyway, I thought it would be memorable. Brandy takes delight in the simplest things. That's what I enjoy about her. I mean, I've gone past that place a hundred times in the last year and—"

This was how it was every time he talked about Brandy, which was a *lot*. He'd say her name and his eyes would brighten and then he'd start babbling about stuff that had nothing to do with running or biscuits or balls. Even though I didn't understand most of the words, I got the meaning behind them—that he loved her in the same way I loved both of them.

"—swing by Rex's afterward to sign those papers. I can't believe how long it's taken to get it all in order. Who knew when I came here last year that it was all going to end up so involved, so... permanent?"

He slowed his stride and sniffed his armpit. "Whewee! Boy, could I use a shower. You dogs don't know how good you have it, not having sweat glands."

Even though I had no idea what he was talking about most of the time, I just loved the sound of his voice. Loved being with him and running. Just like I used to love doing agility and obedience with Brandy. It was sad she couldn't do those things anymore. In fact, even though she tried to hide it, I could tell she was still sad about how much harder things were for her now. But at least we all had each other. The next time I saw her, I planned to let her know just how much I'd missed her.

I still couldn't understand, though, why Brandy and Grayson lived in separate houses when they spent so much time together.

Maybe they just liked having their own things and their own beds to lie in. I was like that. Who wants to share their toys if they can have them all to themselves? Or maybe they liked car rides as much as I did and going to see each other was their excuse—although we could've all done that together. People made so little sense sometimes. Always so busy, too.

That was why they needed dogs, apparently. To remind them what was important—love.

And to listen. People were in constant need of being listened to. Probably because they liked to talk so much.

Me? I just liked *being* with someone. That was enough for me.

chapter 2
Brandy

Prickles of sweat jabbed at Brandy Ander's back and the underside of her legs. She tried to shift her weight in the wheelchair as her boyfriend, Grayson Darling, pushed it over the uneven sidewalk, but no matter how she positioned herself, the Kentucky humidity made her horribly uncomfortable. How much breezier it would feel if she could be up on her own two feet, walking hand in hand with Grayson along the main street of Faderville. Thank goodness it was only half a block from the parking lot to the front entrance of Rex Franzen's law firm.

They'd come here after a leisurely lunch at the root beer stand consisting of foam-topped mugs, thick greasy hamburgers, and beer-battered onion rings—all of which had sounded tasty beforehand, but she now regretted. Normally, after his morning run, Grayson would get some carryout and bring it to Brandy's apartment when he dropped Sooner off there, but working from home had become boring and Brandy had wanted to get out and about today.

Even though her arrangement with her employer had seemed ideal when she accepted it after being released from the hospital last year, she hadn't realized how much she missed her office companions. Without their banter and camaraderie, work was… well, just work. So whenever Grayson had errands to run, she was more than eager to come along. Besides, Sooner had become quite the celebrity in Faderville and the dog seemed to enjoy the attention as much as Brandy did the change in routine.

Grayson paused before the wood-framed glass door with its gold-etched lettering, a relic of the past century. "Do you need a pillow, hon? Can I adjust something for you?"

He was such a caring man. Still, she hated being treated like a toddler who couldn't tie her own shoes. She barely could, actually, now that she thought about it. Not without a lot of fuss and a few grunts, anyway. Even the simplest of tasks were hard. Sometimes, she wasn't sure why he took such great pains to accommodate her. They hadn't met until after the accident. He could've chosen to part ways as friends, in which case, she would've gone to live with her brother. Or learned to cope on her own.

Yet he'd sought a relationship. Chosen to stay beside her. Brought unexpected joy to her otherwise mundane and now challenging life. She couldn't imagine life without him—or Sooner.

To think that for a time she'd thought she might have to give both of them up.

As if sensing her thoughts, the red tri Australian Shepherd gazed up at her from the left side of her chair, one copper eyebrow lifted in concern. Brandy rubbed Sooner's ear affectionately. "I'm fine, Grayson."

He leaned sideways to meet her eyes more directly. "Really? Because you seem uncomfortable."

"No, I'm—" She stopped herself from telling a lie. "It's just so dang hot out here. It's like sitting on a vinyl car seat with the windows rolled up." She stopped there, not wanting to whine incessantly about things she couldn't change. Even though she often wanted to.

9

"Hmm, it is July, you know. The easy solution would be to go inside in the air conditioning, don't you think? Knowing Rex, we'll be lucky to get out of there in less than an hour, so plenty of time to cool off. I bet I could even wrangle some ice-cold root beers out of him." He looked at the dog. "What do you say, Sooner? Shall we go inside, see if he has any leftover bits of sandwich for you?"

Sooner yawned.

"She says she doesn't have an opinion on the matter," Brandy said. "Besides, you already snuck her plenty of fries. I saw."

"But how could she not want a sandwich?"

"She probably does. But remember, she's a dog. Her vocabulary is that of a two-year-old." Brandy tapped Sooner on the muzzle. The dog blinked at her. "Want to see if Rex has a biscuit for you?"

Sooner's ears perked. She cocked her head.

"You like biscuits, Sooner? Good dogs get biscuits, don't they? Big biscuits, little biscuits…"

Sooner lurched toward the door, all four feet dancing, her short nub wagging. Despite the characteristic short bobtail of her breed, she could still be very expressive with it.

After a gentle reminder from Brandy for Sooner to return to heel position, Grayson opened the door and they all went inside. Brandy cringed at the chaos around her. Manila envelopes and folders sat in teetering stacks atop a row of filing cabinets. Papers extruded from barely closed drawers. Law books had been pulled from the shelves, leaving gaps in the lineup wide enough that some of the books had fallen completely over. A half dozen more were stacked on what was once the secretary's desk. Grayson had told Brandy how Rex's receptionist, Martina, had skipped town with Magnus Jorgensen, the local accountant. Brandy thought Rex would've hired someone else by now, but as she recalled Grayson mentioning, he'd tried a few and not been satisfied with any of them, seeing as how none of them were Martina.

"That you, Darling?" a drawling voice from the back room called.

"Me, the dog, and"—Grayson winked at Brandy—"my *gorgeous* girlfriend."

A rush of warmth welled inside her chest. The way he looked at her in random moments like this, complimented her—she felt like a teenage girl who'd scored a prom date with the best-looking guy in high school.

A tall man in his sixties dressed in fancy cowboy attire braced a hand on the doorway. "In that case, just send the gals on back. You can scram. They're not only better looking than you, they're better company."

He disappeared back into his office.

Brandy glanced up at Grayson and shook her head. She'd met the country lawyer on a couple of occasions at the farm. He was a long-winded fellow and tended to balloon a two-minute explanation into a story-time that went on for an hour.

She waved Grayson on. "Go on. I'll wait out here, catch up on my emails, maybe do some people-watching while you sign papers."

"Sure you don't want to know how rich I'm going to be?" Grayson had unexpectedly inherited his uncle's farm last year where he now lived. "According to Rex, everything's been settled. Soon as I sign on the dotted line, the money will get transferred to my—"

"A summary over dinner will do just fine. Besides, the only way I'm going to back out on this relationship is if you tell me you've only been pretending to be a dog lover all along. That's a deal-breaker."

"You two going to chitchat all day?" Rex barked above a frantic shuffle of papers. "Or are we going to do business?"

"Coming!" Grayson leaned over and kissed Brandy. Then he whispered, "I'll try to make it quick."

"Good luck with that."

Sooner began to follow Grayson into Rex's office but stopped when Brandy didn't go, too. Before Grayson had shut the door, she'd already returned to Brandy's side.

After Brandy maneuvered her wheelchair over to the bookshelves, she began uprighting the fallen books and returning the ones that had been pulled out. A few minutes later, she'd filled in all the holes on the middle and lower shelves. About half a dozen books needed to go on the top two rows, but she'd ask for Grayson's help when he emerged—whenever that might be.

The phone rang. Brandy had the urge to pick up, but what would she say? No, not her job. Not like she could answer any questions, anyway.

As she leafed through a stack of loose papers, Sooner sniffed around. Short whiffs at first, but soon she was inhaling deeply, rooting behind the trash can with determination.

"Find something?" Brandy asked.

The dog plunged her face between the wall and trash can, toppling its contents.

"Sooner, bad dog."

The dog raised her head, a broken piece of tortilla chip clenched between her teeth. Before Brandy could move toward her, Sooner downed the chip in a single gulp.

"Right, better to ask for forgiveness than to ask and be denied. Heaven knows how old that was."

Wheeling over to the mess, Brandy plucked up the balls of paper and returned them to the trash can. Her mind began to wander as she moved about the waiting area, tidying odds and ends. Life had changed so drastically the day of her accident. Since then, her limits had been tested beyond what she thought was possible. She and Sooner had been on their way home from an obedience trial, a collection of ribbons arranged on the dashboard of her van, a testament to their teamwork and dedication to dog sport. She'd been barely an hour from home when she nodded off for a few seconds.

The van had hit a pothole and careened toward the guardrail, tearing through the length of metal. The van had plunged down the rocky hillside and into a dry ravine. Hours later, a rescue crew had airlifted her unconscious body to the hospital in Lexington.

Thankfully, she had very little recollection of the immediate aftermath. Painkillers had provided her with little more than watercolor memories of those days. There were surgeries, multiple ones, each time leaving her more drained, even as her caretakers promised her they were putting back together the broken pieces of her body.

The worst part about that time had been that Sooner had gone missing. Friends had searched for the dog. Shelters and vet clinics had been put on alert. Still, weeks went by with no indication her dog had survived the horrific accident that had left Brandy partially paralyzed.

With her father fighting his own battles and unable to come to her side after a stroke, she'd been largely alone those many weeks she was laid up in the hospital. Occasional visits from her out-of-town brother and friends from the dog club had broken up the monotony, but the reprieve was only ever fleeting. Sometimes, in fact, it had left her feeling even more depressed than before. Sad she was dependent on so many. Sad she couldn't get up and walk out herself. Sad that easy tasks were now hard. Mostly, though, sad she didn't have the unconditional love of her dog to comfort her.

The day Grayson came to visit her in the hospital with Sooner was like being rescued from deep beneath the rubble of a collapsed building. Darkness gave way to light. Her body felt buoyed up. Stronger. Her heart full again.

Yet, she'd recognized the bond Grayson had with Sooner almost immediately. She also knew how difficult caring for a dog would be in her condition. She'd resigned herself to giving the dog up to Grayson—especially after she learned about his own battle with

13

depression. It had been the hardest decision she'd ever made. In the deepest recesses of her heart, she'd known it was the right thing to do.

How fortunate that things had worked out as they had between her and Grayson. Despite the unusual circumstances, they'd fallen in love. Often, during quiet moments, she would wonder how it was that she was so lucky to have found him. She'd say that life couldn't have been more perfect for her, but...

She looked down at her legs. Focused hard on flexing the muscles at her hip. Suddenly self-conscious, she glanced around to make sure no one was looking. Then, she mustered all her energy—and lifted her knee. Two inches. It was all she could manage. She extended her foot. Four inches. Six, maybe.

Whimpering, Sooner rushed to sit in front of her and, with childlike curiosity, watched Brandy lift her foot again.

With a shudder, Brandy's foot dropped. She'd spent that morning in physical therapy. She both looked forward to and dreaded it. If she looked back over months, she could see how far she'd come. But there was so far yet to go.

She remembered how easy it had once been to run alongside Sooner through the agility course or perform intricate footwork in obedience. Now, even the most basic of movements were taxing. Her therapists often praised her, but Brandy felt—in a word—clumsy. Like a floppy rag doll.

It was a good thing her work depended on her brain.

Work. More and more she found it uninspiring. She was beginning to wonder if there might be something that would suit her better. Something more engaging.

Across the street, Hank Mays was pushing his little daughter Claire in her stroller while his wife, Becca, walked beside them, their infant son cradled against her chest. They owned the Apple Orchard, a thriving family restaurant close to the interstate where Brandy and

Grayson often dined. They seemed like such a nice family. People she'd like to know better. She had half a thought to hail them and have a chat out on the sidewalk to pass the time while she waited, but she didn't know them *that* well. She wished she did. She wanted to.

Clearly, she needed to get out more. Join a club. Volunteer. Something. She couldn't always rely on Grayson to provide her with entertainment. Fox Hollow, the residence facility where her apartment was, had busses that ran on a regular schedule to nearby shopping centers. No, that wasn't enough. She wasn't much of a shopper, anyway. And her place didn't have much storage space for extra stuff. They did take groups on daytrips to Lexington and elsewhere. A couple of weeks ago, the group had gone to a pro-duction of *Cats*. Granted it was mostly the seventy-five and over crowd, but there were a handful of others in assisted living closer to her age who she could strike up a casual friendship with. She'd look into things and talk one of the younger residents into going along next time. Maybe. Or not. It might pass an afternoon, but would it do much for her malaise in the long run?

"Pardon me." A woman in business attire, perhaps in her fifties, cracked the front door open.

Startled, Brandy nearly dropped the dirty coffee mug she meant to place in the bathroom sink for cleaning.

The woman's hard eyes settled on Sooner, sitting, as always, at Brandy's left. She and the dog regarded each other with cautious curiosity. After a few seconds, however, the woman relaxed, as if she perceived the dog to be of little concern.

Brandy had long ago learned that Sooner was an especially good judge of people. She'd apparently adopted a neutral opinion of this particular woman, whose business clothes seemed more than a little out of place in Faderville, a small town about thirty years behind the times and with very few professionals.

"Oh, hello," Brandy said. "Are you looking for Rex?"

15

"I am." The woman stepped inside, but only a few feet. "Is he in?"

"He is." Brandy set the mug back where she'd found it. A glimpse at the loudly ticking clock on the wall revealed Grayson and Rex had been in the back office for well over half an hour now— much longer than he'd promised her it would take. "He should be done with his current client by now. Do you want me to let him know you're here, Miss…?"

She wasn't anyone's receptionist, but it was the perfect excuse to interrupt and snatch Grayson from being subjected to another one of Rex's pointless stories.

"No, I…" The woman peered inside the messenger bag she was carrying and produced a manila envelope. After a pause, she slid it back in. "Sorry, it's been a harrowing morning. Actually, yes. If you could, that would be helpful. I'm Ms. LaCrosse… Stephanie LaCrosse, the principal at Faderville High School. I was going to drop off some papers from the school board, but I have a few questions. Shouldn't take more than five minutes of his time."

Something told Brandy there was more on Ms. LaCrosse's mind than legal papers, but she couldn't quite put her finger on it. Maybe it was the heaviness in the woman's voice or the way her forced smile didn't quite reach her eyes.

Brandy could've told her she didn't work here, but at that moment she felt a peculiar need to respond to this complete stranger in a more sympathetic way.

"My name's Brandy. Why don't you have a seat"—she indicated a row of leather chairs along the front wall backing up to the window—"and I'll see when he'll be free."

As Brandy pivoted her wheelchair, she watched Ms. LaCrosse slog toward the seating. The principal's low-heeled black pumps scuffed over the worn green tiles. She sloughed off her jacket like an unwelcome weight and folded it neatly before sitting and taking the envelope back out.

Several seconds passed before she looked up and met Brandy's eyes.

Brandy wasn't quite sure how to ask more. The best she could come up with was: "I hope nobody's suing the school district, are they?"

Ms. LaCrosse flapped her eyelashes a few times. "What? Oh... no. Nothing like that. Just some standard waivers to pass out to the students at the start of the school year. Trying to make sure we have all our 'T's crossed, so to speak." She touched the flap of the envelope, her mouth twisting, as if she fought to hold something back.

"Okay, good, because you looked... I don't know, not worried, really..." Brandy's thoughts trailed off before the right word finally came to her. "Troubled?" Then she quickly added, "I'm sorry. I don't mean to pry. It's just that I have this 'sense' when something's off with people. Even people I don't know."

"You're very perceptive."

"Kind of a curse, actually... always noticing expressions and gestures and tone. I probably should've gone into a different line of work, come to think of it."

"I'd say you're fine doing what you're doing. A little more compassion in the world would go a long way."

A long pause settled between them.

Just as Brandy was about to go knock on Rex's door, Ms. LaCrosse spoke again. "The cross country coach... he died suddenly this morning. Well, not suddenly, really. There were indications he'd had some heart trouble recently, that he wasn't as healthy as he used to be, but the man was close to seventy. Still, we all assumed he had a lot of years left. Hoped he would, anyway. He's been such a fixture at the school that it seems odd he won't be there anymore. I know the kids are going to take it hard."

17

"Sounds like he was well respected and admired."

"Those kids looked up to him, yes, but loved is probably a better word. A lot of our students don't come from the best of circumstances. So many people aren't aware of that. They think in a small town everything's fine. But it's not always."

By now, Brandy was intrigued. She'd existed in an insular world in her small but clean apartment, only getting to know the people directly around her on a superficial level while she'd been wrapped up in her own set of challenges and adjustments. Moving here from the Lexington suburbs, she'd assumed it to be a relatively boring existence, protected from the larger world. If she'd thought a little more about it, she would've recognized that lives everywhere were complicated.

"How so?" she asked.

Ms. LaCrosse folded her hands in her lap. "It varies a lot: poverty, alcoholism, drug addiction, health problems and lack of accessible medical and mental health care... Problems like that in a family are hard to overcome when you're a dependent with no income of your own. Add to that the distractions of modern life and you have a recipe for dysfunction. When I went into teaching almost thirty years ago, I thought I'd be able to save every child who walked through my classroom door. I learned almost immediately that the best you can do is give them a few short hours a day away from all those troubles—but too often the trauma of what they bring with them is so much bigger than their capacity to deal with it that... I'm sorry, that was probably more than you wanted to hear.

"Anyway, Coach Tervo... he was like a father figure to his kids. I don't know how he did it, but it was a rare gift."

"Don't worry about it. I understand. Sounds like he'll be greatly missed."

"More than missed, I'm afraid. Coach Tervo will be irreplaceable." A crimp formed between Ms. LaCrosse's eyebrows.

"Oh, dear. I just realized… I'm going to have to find a replacement for him—and quick. Summer practice is set to begin on Monday. I could put it off for a few weeks, a month even, but not much longer. The team made it to state last year. I'm sure they're eager to get started."

"There's no assistant coach who can take over?" Brandy had gone to a big high school in the suburbs of Lexington. Coaching staffs often consisted of a team of multiple coaches and volunteers, necessary to corral and direct large groups of active adolescents. There was always another in line, prepped to step in immediately.

"Assistant?" Ms. LaCrosse scoffed. "We're one of the poorest districts in the region, if not state. What we pay a single high school coach is what some of the bigger schools pay their assistant junior high coaches. No, he certainly didn't do it for love of money. He did it because he cared about the kids and was passionate about the sport."

"Maybe with such a successful record, someone who knows running well enough will be able to do the program justice. The talent is obviously there. I'm sure once you post the position—"

"You're not from around here, are you?"

"Excuse me?"

"Where are you from?"

"Lexington, but—"

"If we were in Lexington or anywhere within half an hour, that might be the case. But how many people do you see out running on the roads or sidewalks here every day?"

She waited for Brandy to answer. But Brandy got the point. Still, it seemed like a pessimistic view of things.

Sooner laid her head on Brandy's knee, a sleepy look in her green eyes.

"I know, girl. Probably tired from your…" She looked back up at Ms. LaCrosse. "Hey, I know someone who—"

The door to Rex's office flew open and the two men filed out. Sooner popped up and trotted to Grayson, her hind end gyrating like they'd just been reunited after a month-long absence.

"Lookie there!" Rex said. "If it ain't the finest principal this side of the Ohio River."

Ms. LaCrosse stood and presented him with the envelope. "We looked it over and it's all—"

"Boiler plate stuff. I just plagiarized from the Somerset crew." When she shot him a reproachful look, he flapped a hand. "I'm joshing, of course. Standard language. Any complaints?"

"None, but it covers the potential situations we discussed, correct?"

"And then some. I can come to the next board meeting if you need me to go over any details."

"That won't be necessary."

"Good, but the offer stands." He tossed the envelope on top of the filing cabinet closest to his office door.

Brandy resisted the urge to retrieve it and file it appropriately. No wonder his office looked like a tornado had hit. It was a reflection of his scattered brain.

Ms. LaCrosse and Grayson exchanged polite smiles.

"Where are my manners?" Rex said. "Have you met these two lovely people, Stephanie?"

"I didn't catch the name, but I've been talking to your new receptionist for about—"

"Receptionist? Brandy here? She's not my receptionist, although she's a far sight more presentable than the last gal who took the job and showed up in her track suit and sliders."

"Paralegal, then," Ms. LaCrosse said apologetically. "Anyway, I—"

"She doesn't work here at all. Somehow she got herself hooked up with this goon." With a lopsided smile, he tipped his head at

Grayson. "Not officially, yet, though. Apparently, every church and reception hall around is booked up for years." He elbowed Grayson in the ribs.

"Oh. I just assumed…" She turned to Brandy. "He really ought to hire you. Martina was efficient, but she had the personality of a German Shepherd."

Brandy stifled a laugh.

"Grayson Darling." Grayson extended his hand. "This is my girlfriend, Brandy Anders."

"You're a lucky man, Mr. Darling." Ms. LaCrosse arched an eyebrow. "You look vaguely familiar, but I can't recall where I've seen you. Is your family from around here?"

"My uncle… was. Skip Dalton. He owned the horse farm on Troutwine. I inherited it when he passed last year."

"I feel like I've seen you about town. Do you work somewhere here now?"

"From home. Financial planning, taxes. Whatever gets dropped in my lap. Sporadic work, but I like the one-on-one. Much more laid-back than my old job in New York City. Different pace of life here."

"Glacial in comparison, I'd imagine—on the surface, at least." She slipped a glance at Brandy, as if swearing her to secrecy. "I suppose I should be on my way now. It will probably hit me later where I've seen you, but I'm sure I have. Good day, gentlemen. Miss Anders."

She was halfway to the door before Brandy called out, "Excuse me, but you said you had a position at the school that needed filled?"

Ms. LaCrosse shook her head. Sadness filled her eyes. "It's much too soon, now that I think about it."

"Someone quit, retire, having a baby?" Rex asked as he held the door for her. "Decided on a career change?"

"I wish that were so, Mr. Franzen."

"They died? Who?" He was genuinely perplexed.

21

"Coach Tervo."

"Nooo. That feisty old goat? Last time I saw him he was pedaling his bicycle up the hill on Red Maple Road. When'd this happen?"

"Early this morning. His wife found him. He'd gone out to the mailbox to get the newspaper and collapsed on the front steps. Heart attack, apparently."

"A crying shame. Faderville High School has lost a legend. Do let me know when the viewing is. A lot of his former runners are clients of mine."

"I will. I'll see you then, if not before." She looked at Grayson one more time before leaving.

A few seconds elapsed before Grayson blurted out, "I know what you're thinking, Brandy. The answer is no."

"No to what? I don't have any idea what you're talking about."

"Yes, you do." Grayson placed a small box of papers in Brandy's lap, then wheeled her toward the door. "Thanks for everything, Rex. I'll call if I need you."

"Likewise, my friend. Likewise." Rex saluted him with two fingers, winked at Brandy, then returned to his office, grabbing the envelope Ms. LaCrosse had left.

They made it all the way out to Grayson's car and had Brandy and Sooner loaded up before Grayson spoke again as he turned the key. "You suggested me as a coach, didn't you?"

"I was going to, but I didn't have a chance. You and Windbag walked out just as I was about to mention that you were a pretty successful runner in your day."

"Which doesn't necessarily mean I'm good coaching material, Brandy. Actually, I don't think I'm the type at all. It's sort of some-thing you're called to—and those who don't have the energy to share their passion with a bunch of adolescents shouldn't take on a role like that. No, it's not me. I'm too…"

"Shy?"

"Pffft. I don't think so. How could you even call me that? Not like I'm afraid to talk to people."

"You were *afraid* to talk to me at first."

"Well, yeah. I was sure you were too good for me. Someone as smart and pretty as you. Figured I didn't stand a chance. I mean, why would you choose me? After all, I did have some baggage."

For a couple miles, Brandy didn't say anything. Sooner poked her snout forward from behind, then rested her chin on the top edge of Grayson's seat. She snorted contentedly, then licked at the rim of Grayson's ear. Scrunching his shoulder up, he laughed softly, then commanded her to lie down in the back. After a drawn-out sigh, she complied.

"That," Brandy said.

"Huh?"

"That's why I chose you. It's the way you love that dog for who she is. The way you laugh at her antics and watch her from the couch when she's stalking the squirrels or cats through the living room window. The way you remind her to be patient when you're getting your shoes on to go for a run. The way you sit on the porch steps with her afterward and massage her back and shoulders, then hold the water bowl for her as she laps it up and drools on your shoes. They say you can judge a man's character by how he treats animals. All I had to do was watch you with her. Your gentleness, your patience, your concern. How could I resist that?"

He shrugged his shoulders. "You must've overheard Rex tell me how much I was worth now."

"Billions?"

"Not quite."

"Hundreds of millions? Tens?"

"Enough to take care of us until the end. Maybe not lavishly— we'll have to stick to a reasonable budget—but enough."

"I didn't hear a word of it. I was busy talking to Ms. LaCrosse. That was terrible news about Coach Tervo." She saw a cloud pass over Grayson's face. "Did you know him? I never thought to ask."

"A little. I talked to him after the state meet last year. He asked me if I'd be interested in volunteering to help out with the team."

"What'd you say?"

"Told him I'd think about it. But I never followed through. There was so much to do on the farm."

"You have done a lot to get it ready as a training and boarding facility for the 4H kids."

"With Clayton and Loretta's help. It was their dream."

"True. But now what? The work is all done in that regard. Clayton and Loretta take care of most of the day-to-day operations. You have what—a dozen financial clients?"

"Eighteen. About every other week I pick up another one or two. It's growing."

"But your work hours are flexible, right?"

"Your point is?"

"Just that you have the time. Those kids are going to need someone who—"

"No."

"It would only be until—"

"I said no. Kids are not my thing. I can be polite enough to the ones who come by the farm for riding lessons with Loretta. In fact, it's been good for my business. I've gotten a couple of jobs that way when their parents learn what I do. And I'm sure word-of-mouth will lead to more. I'm just not into managing large groups of children. I don't have the patience to explain the physiology of training to them or the public speaking skills to inspire them to race from the gut."

"You're patient with Sooner—and you love running. Besides, you probably have more running experience than…"

Grayson glared at her.

"Okay, sorry. It was just a thought. I'll drop it."

Brandy zipped her lips tight. She might not mention it again, but still, she couldn't help but think it would be good not just for Grayson, but the kids, as well. If there was one thing she'd learned today, it was that reaching out to others had a way of lifting you up. She hadn't solved Ms. LaCrosse's long list of problems, let alone her immediate dilemma, but just by listening she'd formed a connection. And connections often led to other connections.

Sometimes, surprisingly, a stranger could lead you to learn new things. Even about yourself.

chapter 3
Mateo

If Mateo Sandoval had learned anything in his seventeen years, it was that he'd been born to run. When he was small, his mother used to tell him that he was standing by himself at seven months of age, walking by eight, and running by nine. When he wasn't running, he felt restless—and when he was, like today, he felt utterly and thrillingly alive. He was, admittedly, addicted to it.

The longer and more grueling the run, the better. It wasn't enough to churn out a few lazily plodded miles and call the day done. He adhered to a carefully laid out plan in which pace and distance were strictly dictated. When he ran, he was free of his worries. He was in control of the path he would take.

Today was a long, easy run on a loop that plunged deep into the forest and ran along the river for a few miles before turning uphill and continuing over narrowing trails. He enjoyed the remoteness of it, the challenge of choosing his steps carefully to avoid roots and stones. Mostly, the quiet. He could focus on his own breathing. The robust cadence of his heart. The drum of his footfalls on soft earth.

In the woods, alone, he'd found solace, peace, and oddly...

strength. A superpower, of sorts.

Since arriving in Faderville, Kentucky, twelve years ago, he'd been taunted for his dark skin, his race, his religion even. He was the only Catholic Mexican in his school. The only of either, really. From the beginning, the other kids made that achingly apparent to him. They also picked on him for being thin and quiet. But he was thin because he ran and he ran, in part, because he was thin. He was quiet because he'd learned not to call attention to himself in a setting where he was obviously different.

His grandmother often told him that bullies made fun of others in order to feel better about themselves. Still, Mateo could conjure no sympathy for them. No matter how hard he tried. The one thing he did notice, however, was how they banded together over their jabs. Sometimes, even kids who had been nice to him fell in with the group that lobbed insults at him. Just so they could belong.

Mateo decided it was better to be alone.

So he ran. To be alone. To be free. To be in command. He ran to the bus stop. He even ran all the way home when school let out. Better than riding the bus. All of which gave them more reasons to tease him.

"What's the matter, Speedy Gonzales? Mess your pants? Gotta run home for a new pair?"

"Run, Stick Boy, run!"

"Family ain't got a car, huh? Did your donkey die, too?"

"You better run, fence hopper! Border patrol's gonna bust your ass."

It happened so often that Mateo came to expect it. He'd hardened to the derision. Learned not to respond outwardly. Inside, however, was a different story.

On the third to last day of school last year, Mateo had gone back to his locker to retrieve his final paper for government class when the period bell rang. He sprinted for the stairs to the second level. If he was only a minute late and Mr. Sutherland was still getting organized, he could slip in unnoticed.

"Who do you think you are—Usain Bolt?" Jed Delaney mocked.

Mateo stopped, one foot on the first stair. Turned around. Came back to where Jed was standing by a row of lockers. He should've gone on, but he could no longer keep quiet. It was the third time in as many days that Jed had needled him in some manner. "Bolt is a sprinter. I bet you don't even know what events he runs?"

"Ooo, smarty pants, huh?" Jed cornered him in an alcove where the drinking fountains were. Out of the line of sight of anyone walking farther down the hallway. He was a head taller than Mateo and a good fifty pounds heavier. He played football and baseball and boasted incessantly about the conquests of every game. As if those were the only sports that mattered. He sneered. "Like anyone cares."

"A lot of people care. It's called the Olympics. Bolt won eight gold medals over the course of three Olympics and broke world records in the one hundred and two hundred meters. He has numerous world championship titles. His top speed is over twenty-seven miles per hour. The average human being can only manage fifteen. You, a pig could outrun you."

Jed scoffed. "You'd know."

It was a lame comeback. They both knew it. For the first time in his life, Mateo felt emboldened. So he went on. Tossed out every fact that came to mind.

"Do you even know how long a marathon is? Twenty-six point two miles. Do you have any idea why that particular length? It began when a Greek messenger named—"

He hadn't meant to say so much. In fact, he rarely talked out loud in school at all. The more silent he remained, the less he'd be noticed. He'd tried hard to keep all trace of an accent out of his speech, but he was always afraid it would creep in. Except for a few English phrases, his grandmother only spoke Spanish. It was all he heard at home except for the TV. He'd been five years old when he came to this country from Mexico with his mother and was fluent in both languages, but outside his home he never spoke Spanish. Ever. He didn't want anyone at school to know he knew how.

When he wasn't running, he was reading—about foreign countries and long-ago history and made-up lands with mythical creatures. He even kept a copy of the Constitution in his pocket and studied it when he had extra time on his hands. It contained all the Amendments and the Bill of Rights and he knew them better than anyone else in his government class—better than the teacher, Mr. Sutherland, even. Probably because he didn't take their meaning for granted. But on that particular day, he barraged the muscle-head before him with facts about running. "—women's world record in the marathon is two hours and fourteen minutes, which is five minutes and seven seconds per mile, on average. I've seen you in gym class. You can't even run one lap around the track at that pace."

"Sure, I can."

"No. You can't. Coach Tervo timed you. I saw the results in his grade book. It took you ninety-seven seconds. For one lap. One. Lap. A whole quarter mile. Do you even know what that works out to for a whole mile—if you could even keep that pace, which I doubt."

The math was easy, but Jed blinked dumbly. He rammed his palm at Mateo's chest, pushing him up against the cement block wall. "Who cares? No one, that's who."

Mateo braced his feet and straightened, for once unafraid, despite their difference in size. "Ah, so you can't. It's six minutes and twenty-eight seconds per mile, a minute and twenty seconds slower per mile than the *women's* world record. For a marathon. And in case you've already forgotten because your brain can't hold that much information, a marathon is twenty-six point two miles."

"So what? Maybe I wasn't trying. It's just gym class."

Another student crossed the hallway two doors down. Mateo

29

seized the opportunity and slipped past Jed, ready to make a break for it once he got a few more jabs in. "What's your GPA, Delaney?"

His lip twitched. "My what?"

"Grade point average. I think you—"

Jed poked Mateo in the sternum. Hard. "Maybe *you* oughta shut up, Stick Boy. Ever think of that?"

Before Mateo could conjure a reply, Jed's scarred hand came at his face and slammed it hard against a metal locker. The dulled ridges of the slotted vents pressed into his cheek. Mateo tried to push himself away, but Jed gave him another shove. A small, jagged edge of metal caught Mateo's skin, cutting a cold line across his cheek.

The library door, maybe fifty feet away, swung open.

As if nothing had happened, Jed stepped away and began rifling through his locker.

Feet padded down the hallway toward them. Mateo pivoted away from Jed to see who it was. Two girls, laughing, passed by the bay of lockers where they were. One of them slowed, glanced at Mateo, then continued on to join her friend. It was one of the girls from the cross country team. Her name, if he remembered correctly, was Louisa, or sometimes just Lou. He didn't know the other's name. Mateo flushed with embarrassment. He wiped the blood from his cheek with the end of his sleeve.

It was like that a lot, Mateo learned. Even the kids who knew it was wrong to bully someone else usually looked the other way. In some regard, he could understand. Why take sides in a fight that wasn't yours? In other ways, he couldn't. How could you ignore one person inflicting harm on another, whether it was throwing punches or insults? Both did damage. Except physical wounds healed. A spirit, once broken, was forever fragile.

The two girls went up the stairs and into a classroom, neither pausing to look back.

Only after they were gone did Mateo realize he'd missed his

chance to escape Jed's abuses. He could've simply said hello to them and followed, clinging to them as unwitting rescuers—or potential witnesses, should Jed not relent in his assault.

Instead, he'd remained, a willing victim.

Why hadn't he said or done *something*? Did he think he deserved Jed's treatment?

The metallic clink of a locker door shutting was followed by wry laughter. "Did you think those girls were going to save you, Matty?"

Mateo turned. Faced him. Stared hard, trying to figure what sort of human being took delight in such cruelty.

A figure emerged from the boys' restroom about thirty feet away on the other side of the hallway. It was Brogan, a defensive end on the football team and one of Jed's lackeys, part of the group that sat with him at the cool kids' table at the far end of the cafeteria. Jed was big, but mostly muscle. Brogan was just big. Really, *really* big.

Brogan swaggered up to Jed to stand just behind him. "Problem with the taco here?"

Even though Mateo had gotten used to the racial slurs, he was tired of hearing them. They more annoyed him than hurt his feelings. When were guys like this going to notice he worked hard, didn't get in trouble, and wasn't out to cause them any harm?

Slinging an over-stuffed backpack over his bulky shoulder, Jed sneered at Mateo. "Damn illegals. Stealing from the system. Why don't you all go back where you came from?"

Brogan laughed. "Yeah. Start now, why don't you? Good luck outrunning ICE."

There was so much wrong with what they'd said, Mateo didn't even know where to begin. First, he'd been five when his mother brought him here. Not because he'd had any say in the matter, but because she'd wanted the chance at a better life. If not for her, then for him and his descendants. The same as Jed's and Brogan's ancestors had wanted. So many like them chose to boil it down to something as simple as standing in line and filling out some papers. In reality, it was a drawn-out legal process with no guarantees that the outcome would be favorable.

Secondly, exactly what was it he was stealing? Mateo desperately wanted to say something. To correct Jed. To lead him to understand that he, Mateo, was no threat to him. But that would take… hours? Days? A lifetime? How could he overcome the prejudices of another in one brief interaction when for the rest of the time Jed's friends and parents filled his heart with lies, anger, and hatred?

In the end, all Mateo could think of saying was, "It must be exhausting."

Jed blinked. Brogan grunted a chuckle.

"To generate so much anger toward someone you barely know," Mateo explained. "That takes a lot of energy."

"I know enough about you and your kind to form an opinion," Jed said.

It was almost too much trouble to explain, but some things needed said. Besides, Mateo was already five minutes late to class. One more minute wouldn't matter at this point. "No, you don't. Not any more than I know about you. And yet… I don't hate you. I pity you. There must be something not right in your life for you to blame your troubles on someone whose circumstances you don't even know the details of." He'd tried so hard to get inside Jed's thoughts, but there wasn't enough to go on. There wasn't anything. Nothing he knew of, anyway. Still, there had to be a reason. *Had* to be. "Whatever it is that causes you so much pain, I am sorry for that."

Where such sympathy came from, Mateo wasn't even certain. His first instinct had been to fight back, defend himself, maybe even hurt Jed in the same way he'd been hurt. But something bigger had welled up inside him. Bigger than this one petty incident between himself and a small-town bully named Jed Delaney. A belief that there was *some* good inside everyone. Why couldn't Jed believe the same about him?

For a few moments, Mateo's appeal seemed to have the intended effect—of knocking Jed off center, making him stop and *think* about his actions for once.

And then... it became clear it had all gone right over his head.

"You know who's sorry, Matty boy?" Jed leaned in close, his broad nose inches from Mateo's. "Your people."

All the air went out of Mateo. Futility took the place of hope. Hardness replaced empathy. Why show kindness toward Jed when he only ever lashed out? What had ever happened in his life to make him so mean? If anyone should feel hardened to the world, it should be him, not Jed.

Still, he wouldn't treat Jed the way Jed treated him. He didn't have the energy for it. There were better uses of his time. Like getting back to class, for one.

Heedless of what Jed or Brogan might do, Mateo turned his back and went up the same stairs the two girls had. Jed said something behind him, but Mateo let the precise words bounce off him. All he heard was the tone—contempt.

What he didn't understand was what he, personally, had ever done to deserve it.

—o0Oo—

For a brief time in his life, a dog had been Mateo's shadow. It was what the people around Faderville called a 'cur'. Just a different word for a mutt. The dog had tan fur with black tips, darker on its back and around its face. Almost like the dog was wearing a mask and a saddle. Mateo had named the dog *El Fantasma*, Spanish for 'ghost' or 'phantom', because of the way it lurked in the shadows, just out of reach.

When Mateo was that young, frightened, starving boy tromping through the desert with his mother, the dog had begun following them and their small group—a handful of people from the most southern reaches of Mexico on their way to join relatives in the States and look for work, either to earn money to send home or start a new life entirely. He'd only been able to coax the dog close enough to pet twice, but the dog had always darted out of reach at the last second. Still, the bond had been undeniable.

The dog had watched them for weeks, pleading, hopeful. At first, his mother was certain the dog was a coyote, but the old man who served as their guide had laughed.

"That is no coyote," he'd said in Spanish, his tongue flicking behind a missing front tooth as he spoke. "Even if it was, the only one small enough for a coyote to take is your boy." He smiled eerily, revealing more missing teeth.

Mateo's mother had clung even tighter to him then, never allowing him to leave her sight. In fact, whenever they hid beneath rock overhangs, shielded not only from the sun, but also the planes and helicopters flying overhead to look for people like them, Mateo would often stir from a long, exhausted slumber to see his mother still wide-awake, a protective eye on him.

Still, the dog followed them, eating from the scraps of food they left behind, which was never much. The dog was so lean and gaunt it resembled a skeleton with fur. Often, Mateo would find the dog studying him from a distance, a pleading look in its soft brown eyes. It was as if he were looking into a mirror—into his own eyes. It was the look of hunger and loneliness and fear. Of not knowing what tomorrow might bring or where they would eventually find themselves.

Or if there would even be a tomorrow.

Mateo couldn't recall how many weeks or months they journeyed on foot or how many nights he slept beneath the stars, blanketed in cold, a coat of dust and grime covering his entire body, his underpants reeking of urine because he'd been too frightened to ask to pee behind a bush for fear of coyotes and snakes. He remembered not so much the bigger picture, but random details of smells and snatches of feelings.

Mostly, he remembered the dog, Fantasma. His fear of it passed and he began to regard it with pity. So many times he wanted to offer the dog some of his food, just enough to earn its trust, but he knew his mother would scold him for wasting even a single pinto bean from the cans she shared with him. So he did it in secret, scooping a few cold beans from the can and dropping them on the ground when she wasn't looking, making sure to hide them from plain sight. He knew the dog would be able to smell them and it did. More than once as they left a campsite, he would look back into the distance and observe the dog rooting for the life-giving morsels he'd left behind.

He'd often watched the dog trotting in their path, the dark claws of its hare-like feet digging into the gritty sand, its fine-boned legs swinging in an automatic rhythm, its back level and strong, head low. It went on like that for miles, often pausing as their dwindling group struggled over rough terrain or up a loosely soiled hill. The dog moved so much more easily than the humans did. Mateo envied it. He didn't want to be traveling through the desert; it was too hard for him, a young boy. But the dog seemed to never tire.

Although his mother often insisted on carrying him, after a couple weeks of watching the dog, he wouldn't let her. If the dog could trot all those miles, so would he. Mateo fell often. His hands and knees became scuffed and bloody. But he vowed to move on his own two feet, if only to relieve his mother of the burden.

Then came a day when their journey on foot ended. He hadn't seen the dog in days, which was concerning. They and three other families, some with children younger than him, were herded into the back of a small box truck. They were commanded to be quiet, no matter what. There was barely enough room to stand, let alone sit as the truck trundled noisily down the highway, toxic fumes leaking into the cramped, dark space. More than one person vomited. Mateo had to pee, but the truck didn't stop. It grew hotter and hotter inside. An older woman began to moan, then wail. Her male companion, an older son, maybe, pounded on the partition between the box and the cab of the truck. Everyone else cringed in terror. Still, the truck went on. In time, the woman dropped to the floor with a thud, unconscious. Except for a tiny slat of light from the front of the truck, they could see very little. Mateo's mother shielded his face from the sight as the man shook the woman and cried as he held her.

Mateo slipped in and out of wakefulness. In his dreams, he saw the dog, gliding over green hillsides, its paws churning over a grassy trail, eyes bright with freedom.

Even as much as he had disliked his small house in the village back home with its leaky roof and how the sewage had run in an exposed gutter just outside their front door and on down the street, making the whole neighborhood reek of human waste, even as much as the sporadic sound of gunshots sounded there, he wanted to go back. Yes, neighbors had been murdered, friends and family died because they couldn't afford medicine or doctors, but there was always a chance of survival. He couldn't understand why his mother had inflicted an even worse hell on them like this when there he'd had a bed and a little food. He loved her dearly, but still, he couldn't understand how their life was any better now than it had been.

Their suffering did not end suddenly. There were more rides in other trucks, more long, endless walks at night. There were days hiding in strangers' homes or decrepit sheds. Sometimes while on their terrible journey, his mother left him for a few hours. She told him not to go anywhere or talk to anyone. He did as she asked, although he didn't understand why or where she went or what she was doing. Sometimes she'd come back crying with a vacant look in her big brown eyes. But she came back with money and that meant food or a new pair of shoes and on very rare occasions a toy to keep him busy. So little made sense in those awful days. Even now, he struggled to understand.

Months went by before they finally arrived at his grandmother's house here in Kentucky. Her name was Ynez and she cleaned hotel rooms during the day and offices at night. While Mateo's mother, Anarosa, was still very young, Ynez had left her daughter with a cousin to come north to work in the vegetable fields, hoping to fetch her daughter later. The requirements to apply for citizenship, and even to maintain her work visa, had been complex and drawn-out. Several times she'd been rejected due to a technicality like an improperly authorized document. The fees to reapply regularly had been expensive, not to mention confusing. Over time, the backbreaking labor of crouching and stooping for hours took their toll on her and she had to find different work in a canning factory and then as a hotel maid, but through it all she'd been able to get enough money to send to Anarosa, who now had a young son of her own. But Anarosa wasn't satisfied with the low-paying, demeaning jobs available near Faderville where Ynez had a small house. She wanted to move to a bigger city and complained bitterly about how they were little better off than they'd been in Mexico.

"At least here your life is not in danger," Ynez had reminded her.

"My life? What does it matter when I am looked at as less here? When people I pass will not even meet my eyes, much less greet me with a smile? When I am followed by security guards when I go into a store? When I walk down the street and am cursed at and told to go home? I don't know where home is, but it is not here."

Mateo still remembered that fight between his mother and grandmother when he was just shy of eight years old. It had lasted into the night. Their words had been sharp, hurtful. It was hard to escape anything in that tiny house with its paper-thin walls. In the morning, he awoke to find his mother gone, the house strangely quiet. Since then, he'd lived alone with his grandmother.

Her one-bedroom house in the woods was little more than a shack, but it was surrounded by the peace and beauty of nature. There it was that Mateo grew to be a young man, his youth spent running through the wooded hills and along the creek down in the valley, imagining that Fantasma was close on his heels, running free still.

For years and years, he'd waited for his mother to come home, clung to the promises she'd uttered regularly during her phone calls, which had begun as weekly occurrences, slipped to monthly, and had since become rarities. When they did speak now, it never lasted more than a few minutes. Mateo found it hard to contain his disappointment. He wasn't even sure why he still took her calls, other than the fact his grandmother handed him the phone. He'd long ago given up hope of his mother's return or that they would all reunite in some other place.

This was his life now. Just the two of them—he and his grandmother.

And it was enough.

Someday, though, he would make his grandmother's sacrifices mean something. He would make her proud.

—o00o—

Sweat pouring down his back, Mateo pushed the mower along the row of crepe myrtles. There was still mulch to spread and weeds to pull, but if he did a good job, Mrs. Ballentine would usually tip him an extra five dollars. According to this morning's news program, it was supposed to hit ninety-three degrees by three o'clock. He would've preferred to be lazing at home in front of the fan sipping ice-cold lemonade today, but he took jobs when they were available and Mrs. Ballentine had called that morning to see if he could spruce up the yard before her relatives arrived in two days. He'd just gotten home from his morning five-mile run and still hadn't showered, since he knew he'd be bathed in sweat all day working outside. Of course, Mrs. Ballentine had been trying to stretch her money, so the lawn hadn't been mowed or the garden weeded in weeks. Still, Mateo was expected to finish the job in the same amount of time as if he'd been doing it weekly.

He was parched. Hadn't had a drink in nearly two hours. If he went to the door to ask for a drink now, she'd insist he sit down and rest, then begin a conversation about nothing, which would only make his day drag on longer.

So he pushed the mower quicker. Wondered if there was enough gas to even finish the yard. He'd forgotten to check.

With a twist of his arms, Mateo reversed direction, going down the last row of uncut grass along the road. A car turned the corner and began his way. A wide gravel shoulder lay between the yard and the road, but he paused in his mowing out of caution to watch the car.

The driver looked familiar. Their eyes met.

It was Jed.

Why was he out here, anyway? He lived in town.

Hurt. Fear. Anger. Mateo felt all of them at once. He hadn't forgotten their run-in at the end of the school year.

Jed stopped his car ten feet from Mateo. "Hey, Matty boy!" he yelled over the rumble of the mower and car engines. "You Mrs. Ballentine's lawn boy now?"

"Go away, Jed." Mateo turned away from him and pushed the mower again. Maybe Mrs. Ballentine would come out and chase Jed off. Or another car would come down the road. They were far out in the country, but there was always a chance.

The car door slammed. Wheeling around, Mateo let go of the lever bar that kept the mower running and found himself face to face with Jed. He could easily outrun the half-witted giant. If he wanted to. But that would scream weakness and fear, and Mateo was tired of yielding to this bully. So he stood his ground. Waited for a fist to smash into his jaw or a hand to shove him to the ground.

But Jed just stood there chest to chest with him. Looking down at him. Laughter bubbling from his barreled ribs. "Did you hear, Matty?"

"Hear what?"

"About them laborers at the slaughterhouse up in Harrodsburg. Bunch of bean-eaters, just like you. They was here without legal papers. Taking jobs from good, honest Americans. The authorities rounded 'em up in a bus. Sent half of 'em home. And I ain't talking the next town over. I mean dumped 'em at the border. Damn roaches probably just swam back across the Rio Grande next day."

Mateo was familiar with the story. He'd been watching the news that morning right before Mrs. Ballentine called. A meat-packing plant had hired undocumented workers. Dozens of them. They did so because the immigrants were willing to do the type of work locals would not, for very long hours at very little pay. Immigration authorities, having been informed, had finally shown up. The employers, of course, were given a perfunctory warning, but no fines were levied, nor were the owners charged with any wrongdoing. Many of the workers, however, had been taken into custody, their fates hanging in the balance. The raid had been conducted while their children were at school. Some of the workers, it was reported, would be sent back to their home countries. There was no word on what would become of their children—whether they would be left behind or sent back, as well. To Mateo it all seemed out of balance. The immigrants were the ones who paid the hefty price. The employers were not.

"Why are you telling me this, Jed?"

A gloating grin lifted Jed's broad cheeks. "Watch yourself, Matty

40

boy. Never know when someone could hammer down your door in the middle of the night and haul *you* off. If they got wind of where you were holed up, that is."

With that, Jed thumped his palm against Mateo's chest and swaggered away, back into his souped up muscle car. He revved the engine four times, then laid rubber as he sped recklessly down the curving road.

Even though it had long since shut off, Mateo clenched the lawnmower handle to steady his hands. His heart raced, fueled by the adrenaline that had bid him to run from danger. Instead, he'd stood his ground—and regretted it.

Next time, he'd slug the bastard. He would.

A dozen times, Mateo jerked at the cord to revive the mower. When he finally got the mower started again to push it along the last strip of grass, he noticed Mrs. Ballentine hiding at the edge of the drapes in her living room window. She'd watched the whole exchange. Said and done nothing.

Which made Mateo wonder if she would've remained mute had Jed actually shoved him to the ground. If Mateo had done that to Jed, there probably would've been a quick call to the sheriff.

As he released the power bar on the mower, letting the engine shut down again, and pushed it up the driveway, he raised a hand to wave at Mrs. Ballentine, thinking if he got her attention, he could request a glass of water now.

Instead, she slipped back into the shadows, pretending not to have been there at all.

—o0Oo—

The day after his run-in with Jed, Mateo heard an ambulance in the distance. It was early morning, late July. He was out running, as Coach Tervo would've expected of him. When he returned home, he

41

jumped in the shower before checking his phone to see if Mrs. Ballentine needed him to do any more work. There were no voicemails, but there was one text. From a teammate informing him that it was Coach Tervo who'd been in that ambulance. Efforts to revive him had been unsuccessful. He'd been found too late.

Laying his phone aside, Mateo took off running. No destination in mind. No watch on his wrist. Not even the right clothes for running—he was in a pair of cut-off jeans and a secondhand soccer jersey. He just… ran.

Again, he was the little boy in the desert, trailed by a ghost dog. He wasn't alone so much in the world out there by himself as he was *of* the world. One with the sky and trees and water and hills. And in all those things, he felt the presence of Tervo, whose gravelly voice carried on the wind:

Move your arms, Sandoval! You won't get anywhere if you don't move your arms faster. Focus on that. Your feet'll have to keep up.

And so he ran. Ran over trails and through woods and beside creek beds shallow with summer drought. Along roads he didn't know. Through pastures knee deep with tall grass that cut his shins and patches of burrs that stuck to his clothes. Floated above the earth, sailed beneath the sky. Until darkness fell and stars pricked the black umbrella overhead and he stood on top of a hill looking down on a country road, beyond which the first light of dawn parted the dark curtain of night.

There, he saw a man and dog running. Their mismatched strides were somehow synchronized in pace, as if theirs was a familiar routine. A leash was looped lightly between them, one end tucked into the man's waistband. The man was perhaps middle-age. Not as old as Tervo had been, but old enough to have a slight hitch in his stride. The dog, however, gaited smoothly, its head low, its shoulders barely moving as it flicked each paw forward over the rough country road.

As he watched them crest a low hill, then disappear into a shallow valley, Mateo finally lowered himself to the ground. It would not be the same without Tervo this year. Nothing would ever be the same again.

The others on the team—not quite friends, but not enemies, either—they would grieve for Tervo, too. Each in their own way. There was a sort of dependence among them. An accountability. An unspoken bond, like that of military brothers. No matter how different their background, on the field of battle—or on the race course—they looked out for one another. They did their part. Always. Their loyalty was to Tervo first, each other second, and themselves last. Whatever Tervo asked, they did. Because no one wanted to disappoint Coach Tervo, even though he would've never said aloud that you had let the team down. No one wanted that terrible weight on their conscience.

Without Tervo, though, did it matter anymore? Did anything matter?

Mateo only knew he felt more adrift now than he ever had. Like he was lost in that desert of his youth without a guide or companion—even without the ghost dog whose presence he so often felt.

He never told anyone about the dog. Not even his grandmother. But he sensed it beside him now, as if its purpose were to watch over him. To somehow protect or guide him.

For a moment, he wondered what it would be like to have a dog always at his side. Maybe then, he wouldn't feel so alone.

43

chapter 4
Brandy

Funny, Brandy thought as she lay in bed gazing at the light fixture on her bedroom ceiling, how you could feel alone even when surrounded by other people. If she remembered the layout of her Fox Hollow apartment correctly, the person in the next unit was probably asleep less than twenty feet from her.

A lump on the far corner of the bed stirred. Sooner stretched her legs and yawned, twisting her head around to gaze at Brandy.

Her heart warmed from the inside out. That dog—she meant so much to her. She'd often wondered what Sooner had endured in those days while wandering lost after the accident. It was a miracle the dog had survived at all. A bigger miracle yet that she'd ended up in Grayson's stables, just as he was at his darkest hour. Months had passed before he'd confessed to Brandy the full extent of his depression, but she felt beyond blessed that events, even as horrible as they'd been, had brought them all together. How differently it might all have panned out if Sooner had wound up in someone else's barn—or worse yet, dead on the side of the road.

Every day, Brandy counted her blessings. There were so many:

Grayson, Sooner, the therapists and workers here at Fox Hollow, this small but tidy apartment with all its customized conveniences...

Still, she was too often reminded of her disability. How many times had she been out with Grayson and had to go to the bathroom, only to find the stalls unable to accommodate wheelchairs? Or been faced with stairs, rather than a ramp? Or doorways or halls so narrow her elbows banged against them as she pushed at the rims of her chair. Since pushing the wheels was the only exercise she got some days, she'd foregone a motorized wheelchair. She wanted to retain as much independence and capability as she could. She had a stubborn resolve that way and had worked incredibly hard at physical therapy. Just last week, she'd hauled herself up into a stand at the kitchen sink when she'd lost a metal measuring spoon down the drain and wanted to see if she could somehow fish it out without calling a plumber. It had taken every bit of strength in her well-muscled arms and her wobbly legs to stand there and dangle a magnet on a string, but she'd gotten that spoon out before collapsing back onto the padded seat of her wheelchair. Every day since then, she'd practiced the move on her own. She knew it was dangerous to do without her therapist there to help her, but she had a goal in mind—that was, if Grayson ever popped the question. They hadn't even broached the subject of marriage. Or living together, for that matter. The exclusivity of their current situation was not in question. The future, however, was another matter.

Sooner sneezed.

"I know, girl. I may be an independent woman, but I still think it's romantic if the guy asks the girl. I mean, I could drop hints, but I don't want to be one of *those* women, you know? The kind who guilts her boyfriend into a commitment. I'm not even sure how I feel about it. Maybe I should just ask him about our future. See where it goes. I mean, if he's going to freak out, I'd rather he do it now. What do you think, princess?"

The dog would've loved for them all to be living together under one roof and not having her time split like the fought-over child in a heated divorce settlement. At any rate, a year wasn't *that* long to be dating. She and Grayson were both used to living on their own and maybe it was best if they didn't rush the status of their relationship.

Fifteen minutes passed. Brandy was still looking up at the ceiling, as if there was an answer written there. She couldn't sleep. Wasn't really sure what was troubling her. It took effort, but she rolled over onto her side to be closer to the dog. With hard work, she'd gained some independence, but there was still a lot she couldn't do, like drive.

"When Grayson picks you up in the morning for your run, I'm going to ask if he can drop me off downtown for a bit. I need to stop at the bank. Maybe I'll visit that donut shop he's always raving about."

The errands weren't really anything she needed to do right away. She was merely inventing an excuse again to get out... somewhere. Talk to people. Form connections. She was perfectly capable of navigating the sidewalks of a small town like Faderville. Having Grayson to push her or open doors certainly made life easier, but she could do it all on her own once she got there. There was usually someone willing to help when she absolutely needed it—and help was something she'd had to learn to accept. She'd discovered that if she responded with a smile and genuine gratitude, people were instantly at ease. She had to stop thinking of her situation as some sort of shameful affliction worthy of pity and instead treat it like she just had an armful of groceries and someone was holding the door for her. It was that simple.

Sooner's lips fluttered in a gentle snore. Before the accident, Brandy insisted the dog sleep in her own bed—on the floor. She'd given up on that rule when Sooner came back to her. She wanted to know her best friend was little more than an arm's reach away.

"I'll drop your name to Gertie, the donut lady, so maybe she'll give me some biscuits for you."

In the dim glow cast by a nightlight in the bathroom, Brandy thought she saw Sooner's eyelids twitch at the word 'biscuit'. Perhaps she was dreaming of dog bones raining down from the sky or rabbits bounding through tall grass or endless piles of squeaky toys—whatever it was that dogs dreamed about. Brandy sometimes dreamed she was running. Which was odd, because she'd never had the slightest urge to run before. Right now, she'd settle for being able to walk a few steps, however clumsily.

—o00o—

His arms hooked under hers, Grayson helped pull her from his SUV. She sometimes worried he might hurt his back, but he never complained or gave any indication it was hard. At least she'd grown strong enough to brace herself with the car door, turn, and lower herself into the wheelchair. To others it might have appeared to be a simple maneuver, but to Brandy it was like launching herself from an alpine ski ramp, doing an aerial triple twist, and landing face down in the snow with a smile plastered on her face. Okay, maybe not that hard, but it was a lot more complex than it looked.

More than being a nursemaid to her, Grayson had made her laugh when she most needed it. He'd brought her flowers when the skies were gray and her spirits flagging. He'd taken her to New York City last December and shown her all the sites, from the Rockettes to the Christmas tree at Rockefeller Center. Granted, half their time had been spent going through his belongings and deciding what to take back to Kentucky and what to re-purpose or dispose of, but they'd talked a lot—about both their pasts, their present situations…

What they hadn't yet talked about much were their years ahead. Whether they would spend them together or not. It might have bothered Brandy more, except she wasn't sure what her life would be like in a year or two even, let alone twenty.

"You sure you want me to leave you here for two whole hours?" Grayson shut the car door and locked it. He'd parked behind a row of buildings on the main street of Faderville at half past eight in the morning. Their normal routine had been for Grayson to pick Sooner up for a morning run, then deliver her back to Brandy's when they met for either lunch or dinner, depending on their schedules that day. Grayson met with financial clients on a varying basis at the farm he'd inherited from his uncle Skip and Brandy kept fairly regular hours as an information technology specialist working from home at her apartment.

Brandy turned her wheelchair and aimed it toward the street out front. "Absolutely. It gets old being cooped up in that apartment. People think working from home is something wonderful. Let me tell you, it can be incredibly boring. The scenery never changes from the time you wake up until your head hits the pillow. No one to talk to. It's not all it's cracked up to be."

"But isn't there a residents' center there, with activities and classes and… I don't know, people to talk to?"

"You forget the average age at Fox Hollow." Although it had begun as a retirement community with transitional living, Fox Hollow had recently expanded its apartment offerings to those with physical disabilities. It was an unusual establishment for a rural community like Faderville, but a much needed one.

"Right. I see your point." Grayson had followed her all the way out to the street.

Turning the corner, Brandy stopped, glanced back at the car. "Your dog is waiting."

Sooner's snout poked out over the edge of the window Grayson had left down a few inches.

"Oh, right. She gets antsy if we don't get at least three miles in.

I promised her six today, but maybe we could just—"

"That should take you about an hour, right? By the time you drive there and back, take a shower, change… Perfect timing." She checked the time on her watch. "See you in two."

"Are you su—"

"Yes, Grayson. I'm sure. I'll be fine. If I need anything, I can always call. Go take your dog running before it gets any hotter." The temperatures that day were headed toward the upper eighties, but it was still a good twenty degrees less.

Partway to his car, he turned back. "Brandy?"

"Yes?"

"I love you."

"I love you, too, Grayson." As he moved away, she added, "More than the sun and the moon and the stars."

Sooner barked in response. That had been their saying every night at bedtime since the day Brandy had brought her dog home from the breeder, having already been through two homes. Now it belonged to all of them.

—o0Oo—

A small bell tinkled above as Brandy pulled the door to Kerry's Donuts and More back. She pushed it open wide and wheeled into the store, a rush of air at her back as the door drifted shut behind her. A tempting display of baked goods were arrayed before her in tall glass cases on yellow trays. Cookies, cakes, and pies filled the case to the right. She skipped those and went to the case on the left. Each delectable was labeled: chocolate croissants, crème horns, walnut orange cranberry scones, raspberry pecan muffins, lemon poppy seed muffins… There was no calorie count indicator on the labels, but then if you came here looking for pastries it wasn't because it was good for your diet.

49

"Be right out," a voice called from the back room.

Brandy inhaled the aroma of freshly brewed coffee. A warm cup of java and a couple of donuts would be perfect, she thought. Overwhelmed by the choices, she wedged herself into the left-hand corner of the U-shaped display cases.

"Hello, can I...?" The voice trailed away. A plump face peered straight ahead from above the counter. "Damn it. What is it with people these days? Can't wait thirty seconds for a—"

"I'm right here." Brandy raised her hand in the air, then rolled back a few feet. "I wasn't hiding, really. Just admiring your handiwork."

"My apologies. I was expecting one of my regulars. He's, uh... tall. Sort of."

"Upright, you mean?"

"That, too." The woman grinned. "Knock next time and I'll get the door for you. That's a heavy beast. I'm always afraid it's gonna squish some of the lightweights."

"I like your candor. I'm Brandy."

"Gertie. What can I get you?"

"How about a cup of your wonderful coffee that Grayson always raves about?"

Gertie's smile widened. "Ah, I thought the name sounded familiar. You must be his girlfriend."

"The one and only... At least I hope I'm his *only* girlfriend. You don't know of any others, do you?"

"Oh, he has a whole harem." Gertie winked. "But he says you're the only one he's going to marry."

Going to marry? Had Grayson really said that to Gertie or was she just going along with the banter? Before Brandy could tease more information out of her, Gertie spoke again.

"Decaf or regular?"

"The real stuff, please. What's the point of coffee if it doesn't wake you up?"

"My sentiments exactly." Gertie went about pouring her a cup while Brandy tortured herself over too many irresistible choices. "What else would you like?"

"I can't make up my mind. What would you recommend?"

"Why not try Grayson's favorites first?"

"What would that be?"

"A chocolate covered Bismarck and a raspberry muffin. That's this month's favorite, anyway. The Bismarck never changes, but the second choice does."

Brandy gave her the okay signal and fished in her purse for some bills. After setting the donut bag beside her coffee on the counter, Gertie waved at her to put the money away.

"First purchase is on the house. Just let me know what you think when you come back next time."

"Are you sure? Seems like you could lose a lot of income that way."

"It's a tradition and... it's actually been great for business. I put a biscuit in the bottom for Sooner. Grayson have the dog with him today?"

"They're out running right now." Brandy took a bite of the scrumptious muffin, then sipped from the coffee cup. "Gertie, how did you come to own this place? Did you buy it from someone and decide not to change the name?"

The corners of Gertie's mouth drooped. "Now there's a story..."

And she proceeded to tell Brandy about her life with her husband, Kerry, who'd died a few years ago, an ex-marine, a little crusty around the edges, but the kind of guy who would've stopped on a torrentially stormy night to help you change a tire next to a busy highway. After his retirement from the service, they'd decided to open this store, simply because they figured Faderville needed such a

51

place. It wasn't a luxurious life, but it gave them both purpose and a sense of community.

In turn, Gertie asked whether the wheelchair was a temporary or permanent thing—something Brandy herself still wasn't sure about. Still, she was relieved someone in town *had* actually asked. It was more awkward when they didn't.

Sharing certain parts of yourself, Brandy knew, wasn't easy for everyone. Feelings were complicated and hard to understand. Which was why some people kept their pain closely guarded. As if they could just stuff their feelings inside a jar, screw the lid on tight, and deny the existence of their emotions. Last year, however, she'd learned it was better to own them. So had Grayson.

To feel—sadness, loss, anger, hope, joy—was to be human. And *that* was what connected people.

—oO0o—

Thirty minutes and two cups of coffee later, Brandy left the donut shop with a bag full of goodies and continued down the street. Frankly, she was already having a sugar crash and could use a nap, but as long as she kept moving or found someone else to talk to, she knew she could push through it and catch a second wind.

Unsure exactly where she was going, she stopped to gaze into every shop and read the signs on every business, including the hours of operation. There was an empty office across the street that read 'Jorgensen Accounting Services'. When Magnus Jorgensen skipped town with Rex Franzen's assistant Martina, it had left a void in the community that had gone unfilled until Grayson arrived. He'd picked up a fair number of Jorgensen's clients and was constantly adding more.

Three blocks later, which was the end of downtown, she came upon the local bank and decided it was as good a time as any to order new checks. She knew it would've been more convenient to do it online, but the internet made it too easy not to ever talk to people. For the better part of a year, she'd done most of her work online— e-mailing coworkers, sending and receiving files, backing up her work, running system checks… Only occasionally did she call someone at work to clarify matters more expediently. She'd started off taking a shuttle to Lexington once a month and then, a few transfers later, ended up at work for a meeting that rarely lasted more than a couple of hours. After four months of that, she and her boss decided she could teleconference. It saved her more than half a day sitting in a stranger's van and all the awkward getting in and out of each vehicle. The only bonus about the long commute had been seeing her work friends again. The first time it was like a reunion. But each time thereafter, there was less and less to talk about. Amazing, Brandy mused, how when you saw someone almost every day you had so much to share, but when you went longer in between there was less to say.

One thing about having a dog—whether you'd been weeks apart from one another or simply hours, every greeting was filled with boundless joy. Knowing there was someone in the world that loved you *that* much… it eased all the loneliness and sorrow, softened all the disappointments, and took the edge off any traces of anger.

There was actually a line at the bank for the teller. It was a small bank, with a single drive-thru window and three places for tellers inside. To the left were two desks, one with a lady explaining a home loan to an eager young couple. At the other desk, a man stamped papers and shuffled them from one stack to another. On the opposite side of the bank was an old-fashioned bank vault, the metal of the cogs polished to a sheen.

As Brandy waited her turn, a man in overalls entered and got in line behind her.

He smiled at her. "Nice day, ain't it?"

"Very." She was about to turn back around, when she noticed his name badge: Tucker. "Oh, I know you."

"You do? I'm sorry, but I think if I knew you, I'd remember." He pulled his chin back, studied her. "Have you been to the feed store? I work there. Maybe after five? I go home at five."

"No, I haven't. Grayson Darling, my boyfriend, goes to your store all the time. He's mentioned your name." She knew about a lot of the townspeople because Grayson so often spoke about them, and Tucker was one. This was her chance to get to know him firsthand. "So how long have you worked there?"

And thus began Tucker's story. About how he'd once had been in construction until a work accident sidelined him for months and he lost his job. How he'd struggled financially since then. How all his kids had grown up and moved away and then his wife had died two years ago. With that last revelation he went tellingly quiet.

The customer before her stepped away and the teller motioned Brandy forward.

Brandy hesitated. She wanted to offer her sympathies, but sorry didn't seem like enough. So she tried to imagine what she would've felt in his shoes. "That must be very lonely at times."

Looking down at the floor, he dug his hands into his pockets. Nodded. "I work a lot of hours, so I'm not alone all that much, but yeah... lonely about sums it up."

"Say," Brandy began, shifting her tone, "have you been to the donut store downtown?"

Tucker squinted at her for a few moments, like he couldn't quite figure out what donuts had to do with what they'd been talking about. "Not lately, no."

"You should. Tell Gertie I recommended her raspberry pecan muffins. World's best."

His eyebrows lifted with interest. "That good, huh?"

"Better than you can imagine." She wasn't exactly trying to set them up, but maybe they'd become friends. If togetherness was the cure for loneliness, why not give the two of them a nudge?

"You know"—he patted his stomach—"who says you can't have fancy muffins for lunch? I might just head there after this."

Mission accomplished.

chapter 5
Sooner

When Grayson and I ran together, it wasn't so much about the running—although that was wonderful—as it was about just being *together*. During those times, I was sure I was the luckiest dog in the world.

That morning, we ran longer than we ever had before. It was getting hot and Grayson was beginning to drag his feet. We stopped twice so he could pour a drink from the bottle he carried into his cupped palm. I lapped the water up. After he took a few sips from the bottle, we resumed our run. We ran up a long hill and down a steep one. Over gravelly roads and smooth ones. Past old wooden barns and gleaming metal barns, small house trailers and stately mansions, hay fields and patches of woods.

On and on we ran. Side by side in silence. Together.

It was as close to a perfect day as it could ever be.

Then I saw movement out of the corner of my eye. A dark shadow on the crest of a hill, skulking along the horizon there. I swung my head that way to look, but it was gone.

"Eyes straight ahead, Sooner." Grayson held his arm out away from his body to guide me with the leash. "You're weaving."

All I heard was my name and a tone that indicated I hadn't quite done something right. I focused on the line at the edge of the road, caught the swing of his leg in my peripheral vision, our steps timed to match speeds.

On one side of the road, cows meandered, chewing cud and watching us with lazy curiosity. Noisy birds with dark, glittery feathers squabbled in the power lines ahead of us. In the pasture on the other side, a rabbit poked its head above a clump of weeds. The urge to dart after it gripped me for a moment, but then I felt the clip of my leash bobbing and was reminded that my job, for now, was to be Grayson's running buddy. My favorite job in the whole world. Next to snuggling in the mornings with Brandy.

Grayson had arrived at the usual time to pick me up for a run, but this morning Brandy had gotten in the car with us. This was a little puzzling to me, but I liked surprises. Maybe Brandy was going to come with us, or maybe we were going to go somewhere different, like the park for a picnic. Maybe we were going to visit Gertie and Rex and all the other places where they gave me biscuits and petted me.

Then we left Brandy there in town. By herself. Without us. Without *me*. I was horrified! Why wasn't she coming with us? Why weren't we going with her? What was the point of picking her up and taking her somewhere else entirely?

By the time we got back to the farm and Grayson had clipped my running leash on me, I'd calmed a little. But I was still worried he might forget her.

Then I saw it again. A dog, clearly it was another dog. Or maybe…

Cold fear filled me. I slowed to look, the pull of the leash tightening. It had been a year since the coyotes had pursued me down the highway. I'd been so weak, so scared, I was sure they were going to kill me. Whatever it was now looked a lot like a coyote. The color and size were right. And yet... its face was a little too square, its ears more floppy than upright. Not far from it, atop the same hill, was a boy. An older boy with brown skin and hair that fell in waves above his shoulders. He sat holding his shins, his forehead resting upon his knees.

I wasn't even sure when it had happened or how, but we were standing there, no longer running, both of us staring at the boy on top of the hill.

Grayson wiped the sweat from his brow with a small bit of sleeve that barely covered the top of his arm. "Normally, I'd just go about my business, but..."

He shook his head and left the road, me in tow. We scrambled down into the ditch, deep with weeds, then up onto a thin stretch of land abutting a fence. The field was empty but for the boy... and the dog. I watched it with keenness, but Grayson seemed to pay no attention to it. Like he couldn't see it at all. He was only interested in the boy.

"Hey there," Grayson called. "Everything okay?"

The boy wasn't much farther away than Grayson could toss a tennis ball. Yet the boy didn't respond. The strange dog disappeared behind the hill.

"Hello?" he called more loudly. "I said is everything okay?"

Several breaths later, the boy lifted his head. "Yeah, sure. Fine." Then he laid his head back down.

"You, uh... live in that last house? Or the next road over, maybe?"

"I'm not lost, thanks," the boy said from beneath his elbows.

"Does he look all right to you, Sooner?" Grayson said quietly to me. "Because he doesn't look all right to me."

I was about to tug Grayson back toward the road to continue our run when the coyote-looking dog appeared on the other side of the boy, closer to him. How had it gotten there? I poked my head through a wire square of fence and whimpered. This merited investigation. I couldn't recall ever seeing the dog around here before. I sniffed the air, but couldn't catch its scent. Odd.

"I couldn't live with myself if I went on and later learned he…" A visible shudder rippled through Grayson. "No, something's wrong. We have to at least try, right, girl?"

Dropping my leash, he commanded me to stay. Then he clambered ungracefully over the fence and landed with a heavy thud on the other side. Before he could even bend over to lift up the bottom string of wire up for me, I found a gap beneath the fence and plunged under.

"You were supposed to stay," he reprimanded.

With Brandy, 'stay' meant don't move ever, not even if your butt is on fire, until she said it was okay. With Grayson, I was pretty sure it was only enforceable after about the third or fourth time. He was so inconsistent. Sometimes I just had to remind him who was in charge.

Anyway, there was that dog I had to check out.

Grayson barely had his fingers looped around the leash handle when I took off up the hill. I would've gotten there before the dog disappeared again had his dead weight not been dragging behind me.

"Whoooa! Slow down, girl!"

Spurred on by his encouragement, I pulled harder.

"Slow… down!"

I inhaled deeply. Smelled only grass and old piles of cow manure and the faded trace of a rabbit or two and the boy—salty sweat now dried on his sun-warm skin. But no dog. Why could I not smell the dog that had just been here, that had to be hiding just behind this very hill?

Now close to the boy, I stopped. Grayson pounded to a halt beside me, his breathing deep, but steady. Before Grayson could get a word out, the boy stood.

"Don't worry. I'm going."

"No, don't." Grayson stretched a hand out as if to grab his arm.

"This must be your land. I didn't mean to trespass." The boy—who was really more man than boy now that I got a better look—turned and started down the backside of the hill.

I crept that way, looked some more. No dog.

"Wait, no," Grayson said. "I know you."

The boy paused in his steps and turned pleading eyes on Grayson. "Don't call the sheriff, okay? I really didn't mean to trespass." He lowered his gaze. "I was just looking for someplace to... to think."

Grayson nodded then, as if he understood everything. "You're Mateo Sandoval. The boy who won the state cross country meet last year."

Mateo shrugged. "Maybe."

"I was there, remember? I talked to you before the race. Grayson Darling." He thrust his hand out. "That was such a thrill. You're a... were a junior, right? I can't wait to watch you this year again."

Mateo regarded his outstretched hand a few seconds before shaking it briefly.

"When's your first race? Maybe I'll come."

"No idea. Not sure I'll run again this year."

"What? I don't under—" The brightness in Grayson's face faded. "Oh, that's right. I heard yesterday about your coach. I'm really sorry."

"Thanks," Mateo muttered.

Even I noticed the silence stretching between them. Dogs were perfectly comfortable just being in another's presence, but for people it was sometimes awkward. Like now. This boy, Mateo, he wasn't just sad. He was lonely and... lost. Not lost like he didn't know his way home. But lost like he didn't know what to do or who to turn to.

Which was a terrible state to leave someone alone in.

"Well, bye." Mateo turned to go again.

He'd gone only a few steps when Grayson hurried after him. "No, stop. Please."

Mateo wheeled around, his arms flung wide. "What do you want?"

"You're upset about Coach Tervo. I get it. He was a great guy. I only talked to him the one time, after state. He told me—"

"Once? You talked to him *once*? How would you know anything about him?"

"Okay, okay. You're right. That was just my impression. Besides, other people have said it. Again, I understand. I do. But don't *not* run because he's gone. That's the exact reason you should."

Mateo squinted at him, opened his mouth. Closed it. Then he left.

We stood watching the boy go down the hill, around the next one. Watched him get smaller and smaller. Only when he was very far away, too far to hear us anymore, did I see the coyote-dog padding after him. Mateo never looked at the dog or called it to him. He simply continued on as if he didn't even know it was there.

Grayson scoffed. "Right. Who am I to talk? I never ran a day after Justin died. Not until I met you, anyway."

When I first encountered Grayson, I could sense a dark cloud hovering over him. A heaviness in his soul. I'd felt it myself, too. That loss of hope. The giving up. I honestly think the only thing that kept us going then was each other.

We returned to the road to finish our run. Grayson was unusually somber, the toes of his shoes scuffing over the asphalt, his pace slower than before.

As we turned onto the long driveway to Grayson's farm and passed the place where Loretta was turning the horses out, Grayson said, "He'll run again. He has to. It's who he is."

61

Run? Yes, I love to run!

I quickened the pace, forging ahead, my loping stride breaking uncontrollably into a gallop.

Grayson chuckled. "Easy, girl. Six miles with you has kind of tuckered me out. Let me hop in the shower and we'll go get Brandy, okay?"

Brandy, yes! I barked. *Brandy, Brandy, Brandy!*

chapter 6
Brandy

The last block was a slog. In addition to the blisters forming on Brandy's hands, she was already working up a sweat. The day was warming quickly. She checked her phone. No messages or missed calls. Odd. She'd half expected Grayson to call or text at some point to see if she wanted picked up early, but he hadn't.

While she loved that he wanted to spend so much time with her, she still wanted to do things on her own. Mostly, she wanted him to trust that she *could* do things on her own. Not everything, maybe, but a lot of things.

When he picked her up, they'd have to talk about—

"Miss Anders!"

Brandy cringed. *No, just no.*

"Brandy Anders, right?"

She turned her chair partway around. "Yes, that's right. Hello, Mr. Franzen."

"Good heavens, sweetheart, nobody calls me that. Except Judge Turnbull, but that's just 'cause she's still miffed at me for how I handled the Paulsen case." He stepped all the way out onto the sidewalk, holding the door of his office open. He waved her inside. "Come on in. I have a proposition for you."

"Oh… great." She said it almost as a question, then muttered under her breath as she wheeled through the doorway, "Can't wait to hear what it is."

It wasn't that she disliked Rex—he was an interesting character and Grayson had certainly struck up an easy friendship with him. He was just so… loud? No, that wasn't what bothered her. Talkative? Hmm, not that either. Brandy enjoyed talking to others. You could learn so much about a person just by listening and it was always great when they let you share. She'd noticed Rex picking up on tidbits as he yakked with Grayson or others. The guy was observant. He had a quick mind. She couldn't quite tease apart exactly what it was that—

And then she saw it. Bold as day. Although for Rex, it had probably become status quo. Loose papers had already begun to creep out of their files and land haphazardly upon any solid surface in the place. A few more law books had been pulled from their shelves and were sitting atop a filing cabinet. Not one, but two half full coffee mugs sat on the reception desk. The trash bin was overflowing.

Wasn't it just yesterday that she'd tidied it all up—and without a word of thanks, to boot?

"How can you operate like this?" She hadn't meant to blurt it out, but somebody had to say it. Maybe it was the fact that she'd begun to tire after close to two hours of pushing herself around and pulling open heavy doors installed long before the Americans with Disabilities Act was passed to accommodate people with handicaps. She'd even been prevented from going into a secondhand clothing shop and a local artisans' store due to the fact there were steps in front of the doors and no ramps. Not that she'd needed to go into either place, but it had irritated her and drained a little of her usually bubbly disposition.

Instead of taking offense to her comment, Rex laughed heartily. "See, that's what I like about you. You aren't afraid to jump in and take command when things are"—he flapped both hands at the disarray—"a little out of place."

"A little?" She picked up a mug. Inside, curdled milk floated atop the cold remains of unfinished coffee. Or it could've been tea, except she didn't peg Rex for a tea kind of guy. She didn't want to smell it to find out. "Looks like a cyclone hit."

"My momma used to say that exact same thing."

"I can't imagine how your house looks."

"You'd be surprised. My beloved runs a tight ship. I can't so much as set a drink down without a coaster or she's all over me. I admit it's a tad disheveled around here—I know, understatement of the century, you're probably thinking."

Brandy raised her eyebrows. She didn't need to say anything.

"I've always been a little... What's the word? Fidgety? Chatty? Antsy?"

"ADHD," Brandy offered. Because it was accurate.

"Sure, that, too. See, I always figured everyone's mind churned that fast. It's like I'm riding a bicycle downhill without any brakes, so I keep pedaling until the ground flattens out and I can coast a bit. When I'm face to face conversing with someone, if there's a pause, I fill it with words. Then one thought leads to another and another, until... Like now, I suppose. I know where I'm going when I start out. It's just there are a thousand ways to get there. Eventually, I do get to the point."

Brandy rolled her eyes.

"Bear with me now. You probably want to know why I asked you in here. You hadn't been in here a minute and you figured it out."

"I did, huh? Fill me in. Please." It was now a few minutes past when Grayson was supposed to be back. She wondered if he was sitting out back in the parking lot, waiting.

"I'm getting there, honest. See, while I'm talking to folks on the phone, I tend to pick objects up with the intention of putting them away, but then they say something worth listening to and there goes my attention. Being able to jump tracks makes it easy not to get perturbed by distractions, but later you look around and… Well, you can see for yourself."

He took a couple breaths, but Brandy could see he wasn't anywhere done with his monologue. If Grayson showed up soon and didn't find her at the corner where he'd left her, he'd call. Meanwhile, she might as well take advantage of the air conditioning in here.

"Things haven't been quite the same here since Martina skipped town with her paramour. She used to grumble at me that she didn't feel appreciated. Let me tell you, I sure do appreciate everything she used to do around here now. She could pull up a file in a heartbeat. She knew the names of all the clients' kids, what neighborhood they lived in, what their jobs were, their family story, medical history… At the end of the day, she'd stay an extra fifteen minutes making sure everything was back in its place. Hell, I can barely find my own car keys around here now, let alone where all the important stuff is. I do eventually, but I lose a lot of precious time in the process."

He stopped talking then. Stared straight at her like she was supposed to know what he was getting at. She didn't.

"Sooo…" She checked her phone again, glanced at the clock, trying to give hints she had somewhere else to be—in the car with Grayson on her way back home. "Do you want a recommendation on a cleaning service? Because I don't really know—"

He slapped his palms on his thighs. "Aw, come on! I already have someone who dusts and scrubs the toilet. Nice older Mexican gal who lets herself in on Friday evenings. Does a fine job, too."

Today was Friday and if the cleaning lady hadn't been in since a week ago, that would explain some of the mess. "You might want to think about having her come twice a week, at the least."

"Naw, I want *you*, dag nab it."

"Excuse me? I don't... I'm an IT specialist. I work with databases, the storage and transmission of information. Basically, that means making sure one computer can talk to another, so someone at a hospital in San Diego, for example, can transmit records to an insurance company in—"

"I don't mean to run the vacuum. I meant to keep this place operating more smoothly. Eugene Oldman—Old Man, as he's known around these parts—retired unexpectedly a month ago. Eighty-two and still practicing law, can you believe? He was the other lawyer in town. Word was his wife wanted to travel the world while they could still get around. Sunbathe in the French Riviera. Cruise the Rhine. Safari in the Serengeti. Anyway, he tossed most of his business my way and I've been swamped ever since. Can't keep my head above water now. In the last year, I've taken on four different people to try to fill Martina's shoes and, well, those that didn't leave for personal reasons just weren't up to snuff. You're perfect for the job."

"Seeing as how I already have a job—which has nothing to do with running an office, by the way—how is it I'm 'perfect for the job'?"

"It was the way you handled the principal. You care about people, Brandy. Filing, legal terminology, coordinating with the courts... all that can be learned. But people skills like yours—they don't come naturally to most. What I like best is that you're honest with me. And I need that, although sometimes I don't like to hear the truth. Who does? But at least I'm humble enough to know when someone smarter than me has pointed out my flaws and mistakes." He grabbed a chair and scooted it across the floor to sit directly in front of her. His hands were clasped together, begging her. "Say you'll take it. Please... say you will."

"Look, I'm not sure I—"

"Name a figure. I'll make it worth your while."

"Money's not the—"

"Brandy?" Grayson stepped in from the street, shutting the door softy behind him. "Rex... hi."

Sooner darted past his knee and ran to Brandy's side. She gave Brandy's fingers a few quick licks before turning her puppy dog eyes on Rex.

"Give me a minute, girl," the lawyer said to the dog. "You know which drawer the biscuits are in. Not like I carry them around in my pocket all day."

Sooner had a way of speaking with her eyes. Brandy loved that about her. She was the most communicative dog she'd ever known. But you had to be paying attention to those subtle twitches of her eyebrows and the way her eyes darted to a biscuit tin or her toy box.

"Grayson, have you been waiting long?" Brandy was ready to go. The conversation with Rex had been a little on the awkward side and she wasn't sure how to wiggle out of it gracefully.

"No, I just pulled up. But when I didn't see you, I thought I'd check in here, seeing as how it's just around the corner. Well, that and Sooner dragged me this way. Not sure if she was trailing your scent or just remembered Rex always keeps dog biscuits on hand."

Sooner circled around Rex and nudged at the back of his knees.

"Your dog is pushy, Grayson," Rex said. Then to Sooner, "Hang on, will you?"

As Rex disappeared into the back room and rummaged through his drawers, Grayson leaned in toward Brandy. "He been talking your ear off, I take it?"

"You could say that." Brandy glanced toward the door as Rex continued to make noise in the back. "He offered me a job."

"Here? Why? I thought you liked being able to work from home at your old job."

"Trust me, I didn't have you drop me off downtown so I could fill out applications. But I'm starting to question if—"

"Ah! Found them," Rex called through the doorway.

"We'll talk on the way home," Brandy told Grayson.

Already, though, she was wondering if maybe, just maybe, the universe had been leading her in this direction all along. She hadn't woken up today hating her job. But for a long time now, it had felt like something was lacking. That somehow she could be more helpful, more useful to others. Even working in the office of a small-town lawyer. Even as she was now.

—oO0o—

"He asked you to come work for him?" Grayson flipped the turn signal on, waited for another car to pass, then pulled onto the state highway.

"He did," Brandy replied.

"Why?"

"I don't know why exactly. He said it had something to do with being good with people."

"You are that. I wish I could be as at ease with total strangers as you are. Back in New York, if it hadn't been for my job, I could've gone all day without talking to anyone. Yet you, and people like you, they can talk to anyone—about anything. That's probably one of the main reasons I was attracted to you. I saw this gorgeous woman for the first time and all I could think of was I didn't know what to say that wouldn't come across as... dorky."

"I love that you're dorky."

"You make me feel less dorky." He smiled adoringly at Brandy, then glanced in his rearview mirror to check on the dog, who, familiar with the route back to Brandy's, was already curled into a ball in her crate. "So does Sooner, for that matter. When I started taking her around town, people would come right up to pet her and start talking

69

to me. But if I went out alone... yeah, not so much."

Brandy shrugged. "I never thought it was any sort of special gift. You just have to be curious about other people, see them as interesting and unique, and trust them. Anyway, what Rex really needs is someone to put that place in order. The chaos in there would drive a normal person insane. Talk about sensory overload. I don't see how he can even function. I mean, how does he not lose important papers?"

"I know what you mean. I've often thought that when I went in there, but I wasn't about to say anything. It's not my office. Did you tell him it was a mess?"

"I couldn't help myself. I probably shouldn't have."

"Maybe it was about time someone did."

"Was his old receptionist—the one he keeps talking about— good with people, or just good at keeping him in line?"

"The infamous Martina? I can't say for sure how she was with clients. I never met her. But the way he talks about her, it was certainly the latter. Anyway, are you actually considering it? Seems like it would be a huge pay cut."

"He said he'd make it worth my while."

"I doubt he has any idea what your current pay rate is."

"You're right. It might be a moot point anyway. But... my work now... I don't mind it, but..."

"You're considering it, aren't you? I don't get it. What's the attraction? Rex is a character, to put it nicely. Great guy in small doses, but set in his ways. He's a project that'd never be finished."

"Everyone thinks working from home is such a great gig. In a lot of ways, it is. But there's no one you can turn to and talk about how your day is going. No one to joke with or share pictures of your weekend mini vacation with or... You get the drift, right?"

"Sounds ideal."

Brandy reached over the center console and smacked his thigh.

"To me," he added. "But I can see where you'd get bored with no one to talk to. Any way you could give it a whirl while still keeping your current job? See if it works out before quitting entirely?"

"I've been thinking about that. There might be. It would mean a lot of hours until I get a feel for things." They were both quiet for a while. The prospect of working with real life people was tempting, but Brandy still wasn't sure she wanted to give up a steady job with benefits. Besides, Rex had already lost a few assistants in the past year. She set the question aside to focus on Grayson. "Anyway, how was your run? Did you go all six?"

"We did. Slow, but I wanted to make sure I was going to make it to the end. Wasn't too worried about Sooner. She could probably run a full marathon right now if she had to. That was our longest run so far."

"Wonderful! I'm glad she's found a new purpose with you. I miss the agility and obedience trials, but she never cared about ribbons. That was for my ego. Like I had to prove we were somehow more in step, more polished than everyone else. Running with you is just as good to her—and it's good for *you*."

"No argument there." He tightened his grip on the wheel as the car took a curve. "When I was younger, running was who I was. It was my reason for getting up in the morning, for eating right and getting plenty of sleep. My closest friends—my *only* friends—were other runners." A minute of silence followed as he worked the next thought up to the surface. "Did I ever tell you about my friend, Justin?"

"The name doesn't sound familiar." Brandy couldn't help but notice how sad he looked right then. "Why?"

"He was my best friend in college. A very accomplished runner in his own right. We often went on long runs together. Mostly just to talk. You know, like guys do—in that blunt, understated way. He was a good listener. Very direct, but with a good sense of humor."

71

"So what happened? You two drift apart after college? Did you ever think of looking him up, giving him a call?"

A pained look transformed Grayson's features. "I wish I could. He died."

"Oh. How?"

"We were out running. Car came around the corner, crossed the center line…"

Brandy touched his arm. "I'm sorry."

"It was over in a second. He didn't suffer."

Brandy understood how an accident like that could transform the way you looked at life. She could barely imagine, though, how it might have been to lose someone close to you in an instant. Right before your eyes. How it must have brought a cascade of emotions down on Grayson's shoulders—shock, grief, self-blame.

"I didn't run for almost three decades after that," he finally said.

She waited a while to see if he was going to say more about it, but he didn't. "Was that the accident you hurt your knee in?"

He nodded.

"So when you found Sooner and first took her running… how did that feel?"

"At first? Painful. Difficult. A hundred levels of horrible. But I made myself do it. For the dog, of course. Doc Hunter said she needed to get stronger, so we started walking and built up from there. Somehow… it healed *me*. From the inside out."

A couple more miles passed in silence. They'd long since passed the stage in their relationship where they felt compelled to talk every moment they were together. Now they could say something and just let the profoundness of the moment solidify between.

"So…" Grayson's mouth twisted as he wrestled with another topic. "So, you know how you're giving some thought to working at Rex's law firm, just to get out and talk to people? I've been thinking—"

"About Principal LaCrosse's offer?"

"How did you know?"

"I could tell something had changed. That you had something serious on your mind."

"How could you tell?"

She truly didn't know how. The signs were so subtle even she couldn't say what they were. "Just a sense. It's my superpower."

"I believe that. Anyway, while we were about a mile from home, I noticed someone sitting on a hill out there by Dickerson's old dairy farm."

"The place with the big white barn?"

"Yes, that one."

"And why was the person sitting on the hill?"

"That's what I wondered. So Sooner and I went to check it out. Turns out it was the star runner from the Faderville cross country team."

"The one we saw win the whole shebang last year?" Now it made sense why the boy would've been sitting there alone. "He was pretty torn up about his coach, huh?"

"You do have superpowers—more than one. You can even tell what people are feeling who aren't anywhere around."

"It just makes sense. Did you two talk?"

"Just long enough for him to say he was thinking of quitting the team."

"And you feel like you need to convince him not to?"

They made the last turn into the apartment complex. "When I spoke to Coach Tervo after the meet and commented how remarkable Mateo's talents were, he hinted that Mateo's family didn't have much money. I really think running could be his ticket, Brandy."

Grayson parked the car in Brandy's reserved parking spot in front of her apartment. She didn't have her own car anymore. Didn't need one, seeing as how she couldn't drive. After the accident, the van had been nothing more than a heap of mangled metal. She'd seen the pictures. Hadn't been able to recognize her own vehicle. Wondered how she'd managed to survive at all. It was a blessing that Sooner hadn't been hurt or killed and had gotten free. An even bigger blessing the dog had wandered into Grayson's barn.

Funny how all the plans she'd laid out for her life had taken such unexpected turns—and yet she wouldn't want it otherwise. If overcoming her current limitations was the price she had to pay, then so be it.

One of these days she was going to show Grayson what she'd been working herself up to. She wanted to wait for the big reveal, though. Wanted to see the surprise on his face. He'd be so proud…

"Hey." Grayson waved a hand in front of her face. He was standing at the open passenger side door. Brandy had barely been aware of him getting out of the car. Hadn't heard him open the door at all. He unclipped her seat belt for her. Not that she couldn't do that on her own. "Did you hear me? What time do you want me to pick you up for supper?"

"I thought maybe I could make something for us. Here."

Grayson retrieved her wheelchair from the back. "Well, I mentioned having that roast yesterday and you said how good it sounded, so I put it in the slow cooker when I got out of the shower. I hope that's okay—I used that special sage rub I told you about. I even thought I'd whip up some garlic mashed potatoes and sautéed Brussels sprouts. Those are your favorite sides, right?"

"Uh, yeah. Sounds good then." Brandy swallowed her disappointment. She'd wanted to show Grayson she was capable of doing a lot of ordinary things. It would have to wait until another day. "What time?"

He helped her into her wheelchair. "Six-thirty."

"That's later than we normally eat."

"I know." He released Sooner from her crate in the back, then handed her leash to Brandy. "I have an interview with Ms. LaCrosse. She said it's a formality, but we also have to go over a few things."

After a short trek up the sidewalk, Brandy unlocked the front door. Inside, she unclipped Sooner. The dog immediately trotted to her water dish by the kitchen sink and half emptied it.

"You're taking this coaching pretty seriously." At the small desk Brandy had set up in front of her big living room window, she turned her computer on and waited for it to boot up. She wasn't looking forward to an afternoon alone with her keyboard. "Yesterday you were dead set against it—when it was *my* idea."

"Turns out you may know what's better for me than I do myself." His breath tickled her neck as he leaned over to kiss the rim of her ear. "See you later. I can't wait to spend the evening alone with you."

Just as Brandy turned her head to meet Grayson's lips, a cold nose wedged between them.

Brandy sighed. "We're never *really* alone, are we?"

With a polite ruffle of Sooner's mane, Grayson nudged the dog off, then leaned back in and kissed her. "We should do something about that."

"Like how?"

He stood, smiled. "Give me time. I'll come up with an answer. Or a question, maybe."

Before she could ask what he meant, Grayson let himself out.

"What do you suppose he meant by that, Sooner?"

With a groan, the dog lay down, staring at the door.

"Yeah, I thought it was mean, too. Teasing his girlfriend like that. What's that about?"

The computer made soft little clicks and whirs in its hard drive, reminding Brandy that work called. She opened the program she'd been working on earlier. But instead of resuming where she'd left off, she reached for the tattered tennis ball next to her monitor. Sooner,

75

however, was already asleep, spent from her morning run, her copper legs kicking as she dreamed, her soft woofs muffled by closed lips.

Oh, to be a dog, Brandy thought. No worries about the future. The past quickly forgotten. Existing in the moment.

She stared at her screen for several minutes. Thought about making herself lunch. Took one more look at Sooner—and decided a nap would be ideal. She had to sleep on Rex's job offer. Take her time. An extra day or two wouldn't hurt. A major life move like that was nothing to be impulsive about.

chapter 7
Mateo

When Mateo awoke from his long slumber, he wasn't sure what time it was. He wasn't even sure of the day.

Summer had a way of blurring together like that. Long days heated by a blazing sun. Muggy starlit nights. Miles upon miles of road laid behind him. Yesterday—or was it the day before?—had been as if he were racing toward a finish line he would never reach.

He'd spent his whole life running. He'd had enough.

Tervo's promises had been a lie. Filled him with dreams he could never wholly own. Because in a day, it could all evaporate. In a moment, vanish.

Everyone believed Mateo ran for some sort of glory. For the praise. For the thrill of victory.

Yet the truth was something entirely the opposite. He ran because if he stood still, they would find him. They would take everything away. They would send him back to a place he could barely remember. A place that, according to his grandmother and mother, was an even worse hell than the limbo he lived in. A place where no one was safe.

He ran because he was afraid. Because he thought he could outrun the shadow that was chasing him. In truth, it had brought him closer to being discovered. To being cast out. He saw it all so clearly now.

Mateo sat up at the edge of his bed and looked through the letters one more time. There were more than twenty of them. One had arrived just yesterday. Before he heard the news about Tervo.

He'd wanted to go to him when it came in the mail. Ask him what to do. How to answer. Knew that Tervo would be proud and excited for him.

And then, with a few words in a text from his teammate Dusty, Tervo was gone. Mateo's abdomen had clenched as if he'd been punched in the gut by a professional boxer, stealing his breath, dropping him to his knees.

He'd taken off running then, simply because he didn't know what to do. The hope Tervo had instilled in him had been snuffed out. Lost forever.

When he first arrived home that morning after his endless run, he'd tossed all the letters into a pile behind the shed and lit a match. Just like his hope, the wind had blown it out before he could touch the tiny flame to the first corner. Four more times, the same thing. Until there were no more matches.

The day had been warm, but he'd felt a sudden chill, glimpsed an animal out of the corner of his eye, seen it dart from behind a trash can next to their dilapidated house and into the bushes at the edge of the yard. The chickens in his grandmother's small, dusty pen flapped and retreated to their hen houses, which were nothing more than a pair of old dog houses left out for the garbage collector that they'd reclaimed from the side of the road.

A few minutes later, he'd seen it again—or its shadow, rather. Too fast for a possum. Too big for a cat. Bigger than a fox, even. Dog? Coyote, maybe? It was gone, anyway. The chickens had settled, safe in their cramped, straw-filled space.

After straightening the letters and stuffing them into his gym bag, he'd ducked inside the enclosure, then lifted the tops off the houses to collect the eggs, which he took inside and placed in the refrigerator.

His grandmother hadn't been home. She seldom was. Yet she still cooked and left the food in containers in the fridge for him.

You need to eat, she always said in Spanish, because she knew very little English, just enough to know what rooms to clean in other people's houses and offices. *You're too skinny. A breeze will blow you away and then what will I do? Who will I come home to?*

He loved her, but she was like any grandmother, always treating him like a five-year-old. But he ate her food because he didn't want to upset her. And because it was good.

The soft snick of the front door latch sounded and he knew his grandmother was home early for once. Quickly, quietly, he stuffed the letters beneath his mattress and took out his little blue copy of the Constitution. If she knew about the letters, she'd insist he answer. Before she discovered them, though, he intended to get rid of them. Even though he wasn't sure why he felt the need to. She couldn't read them anyway. But she would ask what they were and then he would have to tell her. He was unable to lie to her. He'd tried a couple of times when he was younger. She'd seen right through it.

Lies. So many lies. Even the promises of free college tuition— all lies. Which was why he was so angry at Tervo. For lying about his future and then leaving so suddenly. What was he supposed to do now?

Lost for an answer, he skirted over the amendments—the abolition of slavery, women's right to vote, prohibition and later its repeal, presidential succession... So many details, so much to understand.

"Mateo! I made this food for you. Come eat. Don't let it spoil."

Her voice was high-pitched, like that of a young girl. It was also stern. Not to be defied.

He went into the room that was both living room, dining area, and kitchen. The couch, its rips mended by color-coordinated duct tape, constituted the living room. It was also where his grandmother slept. On the bookcase was a small TV Mateo had salvaged from someone's trash by the roadside when he was thirteen. Their sole source of entertainment, it got just four channels over the air and two of those were grainy if the weather was bad. The coffee table, or rather the discarded door atop two wooden orchard crates, served as their dining table. The kitchen spanned a whole eight feet: an electric cooktop next to the sink with a few cabinets below and two above. The oven was either a microwave or a crockpot, depending on the meal. Their refrigerator was beyond the back door in an unheated, enclosed porch where the washer and dryer also were. The house, basically, was two rooms and a bathroom. Three if you included the porch, where a plastic lawn chair and a lamp provided Mateo with a change of scenery when studying on his bed became tiresome.

They had no internet. He had to go to the library if he needed it for homework or use the computers at school. With planning, he managed. He was grateful, at least, for the flip phones his grandmother had invested in. She needed one for work, so clients could reach her, and had given him one, in case of an emergency. They were more of a necessity than a luxury, since there had never been phone lines on their remote, hilly road in the woods. Which made Mateo wonder what the people who lived here before them had done for communication.

In the winter, the drafts in the house were bone-chilling. In the spring sometimes Mateo had to place a tarp on the roof while it was raining and wait until there was a stretch of a few dry days so he could patch the roof with a bucket of tar. In the summer, like now, it was stifling hot because the windows were so tiny. The two fans they owned were not enough to cool even the miniscule square footage of their home.

Yet his home it was. A retreat from the taunts and judgmental eyes of the outside world. A place filled with the rich smells of his grandmother's cooking. In rare hours, holidays or a Sunday evening, she would sit on their lumpy couch and by the light of a single bulb, repair their clothes with a needle and thread.

His grandmother was at the kitchen counter, her back to him, taking groceries from a sack. While she rambled on in Spanish about her day, he put his dinner in the microwave. Its whir drowned out her words until the countdown timer beeped zero.

"Everyone was so shocked to hear it," she said, still not looking at him.

Even though he'd missed most of what she'd been talking about, he knew who she meant.

"He was old, yes," she went on, "but not *that* old. Did he ever seem ill to you, Mateo? Did he talk about his chest hurting or seem short of breath?"

"No, *abuela*. He did not." Although he did remember once, maybe twice, Coach Tervo placing a hand over his chest after returning from a bicycle ride. Whenever the team went out for a long run on the country roads beyond town, Tervo would ride behind on his old ten-speed bike, making sure everyone was safe and accounted for. He was always red-faced and sweaty afterward. But never short of breath, never complaining that anything hurt, besides his knees.

After pouring himself a glass of water, Mateo grabbed his plate from the microwave and headed for the back door.

"No, sit!" His grandmother waved him toward the couch. "I'm home for once. We'll eat together. Like a family."

He couldn't say he had to study. It was summer. So he sat, stared at his cooling plate of food. Waited for her to prepare her own meal from leftovers in the fridge and join him. When she settled on the couch, light as a bird since she weighed little more, they said a prayer together. She clicked the TV on, but put the sound on mute. Spanish subtitles flashed on the lower portion of the screen.

"You should keep the sound on, *abuela*," he told her in between shoveled bites. He hadn't realized how empty his stomach had been. Now that he thought about it, he hadn't eaten since the night before. "If you concentrate on the words they say, you'll start to understand. Your English will get better. I can help."

"Easy for you to say. You are young. I am not."

"But if you don't learn, who can you talk to—besides Tomas and Carlos, and maybe Gabriella?" The last was a woman who had come from Puerto Rico decades ago when she married a former marine. She still had a slight accent, despite twenty years working at the local grocery store and raising six children who spoke with a distinct Southern twang. The other two were brothers who lived in town and owned a contracting business, laying tile and putting up drywall. Mateo sometimes helped them at jobs. They did good work, but they got paid very little. He could've worked full-time for them and made more money, but not as much as he would if he went to college and got an even better job. *If* he went to college. "I will teach you to say the words right. We can take our time."

"No. I know enough."

They ate in silence for a while—Mateo packing his food into an empty stomach, his grandmother taking small bites of hers.

Even though it wasn't true, he let it go. She was a proud and intelligent woman, but stubborn. Afraid of making mistakes, that's what she was. Also afraid that if she learned more, more would be expected of her. Mateo understood that. When he was very young and first in school, he soon came to learn that if he had no answers to the teachers' questions, they would ask him none. In time, though, he became frustrated. He was curious about many things. Wanted to know how mountains were made, how rain fell from the sky, why leaves fell in autumn, how planes flew, televisions worked... He concentrated hard on his English, on making the sounds right, bought his own dictionary so he could learn new words. He'd used that dictionary so much that by the time he was ten, the spine had broken and pages were falling out.

"You could get more work, *abuela*," he said in English, testing her. "Maybe even better work."

She arched an eyebrow at him and replied in Spanish. "What I do is fine. It's honorable work. Important work. It feeds you. You eat a lot."

She picked up her unfinished plate and placed it in the fridge out back, then busied herself cleaning their tiny kitchen.

He'd wounded her pride. He had to make amends. TV light flickered in the dim light. It was dark inside not because it was after sundown—it wasn't—but because the windows were so small. For several minutes as he pretended to watch TV, he stole glances at her. She'd done so much for him. Sent the money that he and his mother had used to come north. He owed her so much.

"I can work," he said.

"No."

And that was the end of the discussion.

He hadn't told her yet about his decision not to run. He had a month until school started. Plenty of time to find work. To make money. He'd show her how much he could earn. How much he could help. She was almost seventy. A woman her age deserved to not work so much.

"Where were you last night?" she finally asked, blocking the TV.

"Running."

"All night? You were not in bed this morning when I left."

"Most of it."

"You lie. Why do you lie to me? You never have before."

"It's the truth, *abuela*."

"Why were you not wearing your running clothes? Where did you go?" Her arms were firmly crossed. "I do not like that you are lying to me. It makes me wonder what you have done that you have to hide it from me. Where did I go wrong, Mateo Xavier Sandoval? Where?"

Hot tears pricked at the backs of his eyelids. He swallowed them back. Bit the inside of his lip. Deep roiling rage welled up inside him. He clenched his fists. Wanted to pound them at the wall until they were bloody and broken. Anything to take his mind off these feelings he didn't understand.

"Is it because of Coach Tervo?" She moved to sit beside him again.

Anger crashed against the tide wall of his grief. Broke inside him. Carried him down into a bottomless well.

He nodded. Sat very still. Locked his gaze on a water stain on the coffee table. Breathed shallowly.

Her small, bird-like hand covered his.

"He was a good man. Like a father to you... yes?"

Mateo hadn't thought about it that way, but... Again, he nodded.

"You were lucky to have found him then. Even if he left too soon. You may not understand yet, but he was fortunate to not have to suffer when his time came. It is not so for most."

The moment she wrapped her frail arms around him, he collapsed against her chest. The tears came like spring raindrops at first, gentle and cool. Soon, they were a torrent. Her words had reminded him of a father he could not remember. Who he'd once been told was in a Mexican jail—for reasons he, Mateo, did not understand. A father who, if he were still alive, was many thousands of miles away.

His mother, too, had abandoned him to work in a faraway city. As much as he wanted to hope she would return, he no longer counted on it. When he asked his grandmother why they couldn't go live with her, she told him all the reasons why she didn't want to live in a big city. She felt safer in their little house in the woods, she'd said. There was more she wasn't telling him, Mateo knew, but he chose not to ask. He was afraid of what he might learn. Better not to know.

As he sat with her, his grief subsiding, soothed away by the gentleness of her hands stroking his back, he felt many things all at once. He pitied how small her world was. Wished she would learn more English so he could take her places and show her all there was to see and do.

And yet... he knew there could be no greater love than someone who would leave their world behind in search of a better life for her child and grandchild, for all it had cost her. He owed her so much.

Yesterday morning, he thought he'd seen the way forward. Toward an even better life for them. But now... Now everything had changed.

Not only was Tervo, his greatest champion and supporter, now gone, but he'd heard many things in the news lately. Things that made his every tomorrow uncertain. Paths to citizenship, he'd heard, were being restricted or even eliminated. People like him were being sent away. *Far* away. Jed Delaney had made sure he was aware of it.

He no longer trusted his future would be as bright as he'd once hoped. He only knew his responsibility was toward his grandmother now. He would do what was best for her.

chapter 8
Sooner

As Grayson drove down the lane along the pasture, the horses all raised their heads simultaneously. Spark, the spotted one, snorted in alert, her tail flicking. Heedless of the warning, Clifford trotted to the corner of the field closest to the house to greet us. The big one, Goliath, stood his ground, while Persephone retreated to a safe distance. I barked at them from inside the car, just to let them know how fierce I *could* be... if I wanted to.

Just before supper, Grayson had picked us up again. I loved supper—every meal, really—but ones spent with Grayson and Brandy at the farm were extra special. In the warmer months, they'd sit on the porch afterward and sometimes I could pester Grayson into throwing my ball or Frisbee for me until it got too dark to see where it landed. When it turned colder, he'd give me a bone and I'd lie in front of the blazing fireplace with it for hours, while Grayson and Brandy talked or... well, let me just say they were 'snuggling'.

Today when we arrived at the farm, Loretta raised a hand in greeting as she was filling the water trough. Her new barn cat, Felicity—a calico, Loretta called her—sat by the corner of the barn, her tail curled around her. We locked eyes and Felicity glared smugly back at me. If I'd thought that cat and I might become friends, she'd settled that with a hiss and swipe of her claws at our first meeting. I detested the day Loretta's husband, Clayton, had found her by the roadside and brought her here to keep the mice down in the hay loft. She was forever taunting me.

The horses Grayson had first cared for when I came to the farm were now largely tended to by Loretta and Clayton. Children, some very young, some older, came at intervals for riding lessons. Some of the kids brought me biscuits or threw my ball for me, so I got excited every time I saw them, but today was what Grayson called 'Friday', so there were no children here this evening.

A few new horses—boarders, Loretta referred to them as—had joined the herd and their owners came and went regularly to muck out stalls and groom them. I still kept my distance from the horses. They were monstrously large creatures with powerful muscles and solid hooves that could strike an object hard. It was better to keep a respectful distance than risk getting hurt.

After Grayson helped Brandy out of the car and into her wheelchair, Brandy said something about catching up with Loretta.

"Want me to walk you to the barn?" He checked his watch and glanced toward the house. "We've got a little time yet before dinner's ready, but I'm expecting Ms. LaCrosse at any moment."

"Go ahead. The trough isn't that far off the driveway. I'll be fine. If I start spinning my wheels on the crushed limestone by the barn, I'm sure Loretta or Clayton will rescue me."

Brandy pivoted her wheelchair and started for the barn without calling me along, which was a huge relief. I never relished being anywhere close to the horses, fence or not—never mind the cat. So I scurried after Grayson before she could change her mind on that account.

We were only halfway up the sidewalk to the front porch when another vehicle turned into the driveway. Grayson waited. The car was unfamiliar to me, so I woofed at it, but the moment the woman got out I remembered her. She had on a button-up blouse, a close-fitting dark skirt, and shoes not meant for tromping around the farm. Obviously, she was here to visit Grayson, seeing as how she couldn't ride a horse or shovel manure in that outfit.

Her heels clacked on the cement sidewalk. "Mr. Darling, so pleased you could accommodate my request." She extended her hand. "When I looked at the address on your résumé, I realized we lived only two miles apart. And all this time I never knew."

I got in a few more woofs before Grayson shushed me. It was hard to unwind once a visitor's arrival got me excited. I took my watchdog responsibilities seriously.

Grayson shook her hand and motioned for her to follow us. "I appreciate it, Ms. LaCrosse. Not that I couldn't have come to the school, but I did have a few client appointments this afternoon and—"

"No need to apologize, Mr. Darling."

"Please, call me Grayson."

We went inside and he indicated for her to sit on the new couch while he fetched them some drinks from the kitchen. The couch was a U-shaped one, so there was plenty of room for all three of us— Brandy, Grayson, and me. Grayson had made a lot of changes in the last year to accommodate Brandy, like a ramp up to the side of the porch, rails in the bathroom, and furniture that was easier for Brandy to use. We were spending more and more time here together, sometimes entire weekends, which made me hopeful that eventually we'd all stay here *all* the time.

Ms. LaCrosse sat in Brandy's place, so I jumped up on the couch and stared at her to let her know she ought to move somewhere else. It must've worked, because she scooted farther away. Satisfied she wasn't here to do any harm, I wagged my nub and moved closer, waiting to get petted, but she kept her palms pressed against the tops of her legs.

Grayson came back and handed Ms. LaCrosse her drink, then swatted in my general direction. "Sooner, off."

He'd delivered the command more sternly than usual, so I knew he meant business this time. Flattening my ears, I slid to the floor. On second thought, Ms. LaCrosse didn't seem like the sort of person who appreciated a warm nose rooting at her armpit or a tongue in her ear. Not that I was going to do any of that to a relative stranger, but you could tell whether someone was a dog person or not in pretty short order. She was not. I could smell cats on her. Figured. I made my way to Grayson and sat at his feet by the armchair.

"Sorry about her manners. That's where Brandy sits when she's here. We bought that couch together on a trip to Louisville."

Taking a sip of her tea, she peered at him over the rim of her glasses. "You and Miss Anders are engaged, I take it?"

His eyes widened momentarily. "Um, not... yet? Sorry again, I'm not sure how to answer that. We're serious, but, well... I got divorced a couple of years ago after a long marriage. We're not rushing into anything."

"My apologies. I shouldn't have pried. It's just that people who buy furniture together..." She set the glass on a coaster on the side table. "Let me just say you're lucky to have found her. Don't let her slip away. She's charming and very bright."

"Thanks. I think so, too."

"Now"—she took a small collection of papers from her oversized handbag—"the coaching matter. Your background in the sport speaks well for your chances that the board will approve you, but I do have a couple of... concerns. Not huge matters, mind you. I just wanted to go over them with you before I bring your name up at the school board meeting in a few days."

"Go ahead."

"Most of our coaches are people employed by the school system: mainly teachers, but also an assistant principal, a librarian... Those people have already been through a background check and training in first aid and CPR. You'd have to cram those in before taking on the role, but they can all be done online nowadays."

"No problem. Let me know what I need and I'll get to it as soon as I can."

"Good. I'll email you a list. Once completed, you can return them to our athletic director. I do the hiring, but she keeps track of those records. Next, I see there was a gap in your employment."

Grayson sat silently for several breaths. At length, he nodded.

"You look a bit young to have retired, but..."

"I... I couldn't find work. Not the same kind, anyway. I was downsized and foolishly thought I'd be able to get another job at the same level I'd had before. Turned out everyone else was doing the same thing. I lived off my savings during that time. By the time an offer came through, a lucrative one, I was already here. And by then Brandy—and Sooner here—had become part of my life. I'd say things turned out all right."

"Yes, of course. Some things are more important than money." She straightened her stack of papers. Set them on the cushion beside her. Laced her fingers together. "Which brings me to the next matter. You're aware of the salary that goes with this job? We're a small school system. It's not much."

"You mentioned it over the phone, yes."

"So why are you interested? Usually, I'd just be happy to have found someone decently qualified. But I'm always curious as to why anyone would take on a job that requires so many hours in return for so little pay. I know Coach Tervo built quite a program, but some of these kids... Working with young people has its challenges."

"I love running, Ms. LaCrosse. I know what it can do for young people."

90

"It takes more than just a passion for a sport to be an effective coach. Interpersonal skills are of primary importance. I don't mean to lecture you, but adolescents can test someone new in a role of authority. You have to convey leadership while displaying a caring nature. And some of them may come with, shall we say, baggage? Troubles at home, school... hormones. That can add up to unpredictable behavior. Ultimately, it doesn't matter how much you know about running or how successful you were as a runner. If you can't convince them to show up every day and work hard for rewards that may be, to them, far in the future, it won't matter how many trophies or medals you have to your credit."

"I'm fully aware of that."

"And?"

Air leaked out of him. It wasn't so much that he was breathing out before speaking. More like he had to let go of something he'd been holding back.

"I met Mateo Sandoval this morning. He seemed to indicate that since Coach Tervo wasn't around anymore, he didn't want to run."

"I'd venture to guess he was very upset. That's understandable. He'll come around."

"I'm not so sure. I kept wondering if there wasn't more to it than just Tervo's passing."

"And you want to be the one to talk him back into it?"

"I do. See, I gave up running once. A friend was hit by a car while running... I was with him. I didn't take a step for nearly thirty years. I should have. I think it would've helped me a lot."

"I see." She gathered her things and rose. "I'll present your résumé to the board on Monday. I'll send you the list of requirements for the position then, along with the team roster, complete with contact information for all the athletes."

Grayson escorted her all the way out to her car. Loretta and Brandy were still talking by the watering trough. Judging by the sound of a shovel hitting the edge of a wheelbarrow, Clayton was inside the barn, shoveling manure.

After Ms. LaCrosse got into her car, she lowered the window. "Mateo Sandoval's grades are impressive, especially given his situation. Between his studies, his running, and the occasional odd job, he doesn't have time to get into trouble—or for friends."

"What do you mean by situation?"

"He lives with his grandmother on Rockhill Road. More shack than house, really. She cleans and by what I hear barely speaks English. His mother's address is listed as Chicago. His father's— unknown. He has a bright future, if he decides to set his goals high enough. Good day, Mr. Darling... Grayson. And good luck."

Her shiny black car rolled down the lane and out onto the road. Grayson and I stood in the driveway a long time, the sun beaming down on us, the birds singing in the trees.

Grayson rubbed the back of his neck. "Would you like some friends to run with, Sooner?"

Run? I barked. *Yes, run!*

He laughed. "Sorry, girl. I didn't mean run right now. We already did that this morning. Six miles, remember? I'm going to pay for it, come tomorrow. You, on the other hand, will be raring to go again, I'm sure." He plucked my Frisbee off the porch railing and tossed it for me a few times before Brandy came back toward the house. We waited at the door while he scratched me behind the ears. "You ready for supper, Sooner?"

Supper, yes! I barked loudly.

"Shhh." He tapped me on the muzzle. "Right. I'm not even sure why I asked."

—o0Oo—

The park! The park! I barked. *I LOVE the park!*

"Sooner, hush!"

Three sleeps later, Grayson had driven the two of us to the big park for our morning run and we'd just pulled into the parking lot. All runs were exciting to me, but a car ride *and* a run at the park— I couldn't contain myself.

Run! Run! Run! Run—

Grayson clamped a hand over my muzzle. "I know you're excited, girl, but geesh, give it a rest. We'll run, promise. First, we have to meet the group."

Usually, Grayson made me ride in the crate like Brandy insisted, but the park wasn't very far from our house, so sometimes Grayson would let me ride in the back seat. I loved being able to go from one window to another to look out, especially when he rolled them down far enough so I could take in all the scents. I poked my nose above the glass while he gathered his notebook and papers.

People. I smelled people. Lots of them.

I squinted at a place beyond the parking lot where picnic benches were clustered. Skinny, a little on the short side… Ah, kids. Maybe they had food. Or a ball to throw. Did Grayson bring my ball?

When he finally opened the door to clip my leash on, I was spinning in circles. He told me to sit. I sat, then popped up. It was so hard to be still. I tried to be a good dog, I really did, but sometimes it was impossible. I wanted to meet the new people and he was taking *forever.*

He'd barely stepped away from the door before I bounded out, yanking him with me. He pulled back. Hard.

"No, Sooner! Easy, *easy*," he said in an unusually harsh voice.

I sank to the ground, my head between my paws. I wasn't used to Grayson being so… authoritative. My feelings were hurt. Sulking, I'd discovered, was a good way to let him know he needn't be so mean. I wanted to please him, desperately, but I was also *very* excited. Why did humans think it was necessary to be so subdued about your feelings? Why not just let it all out? If you were happy, you should let the world know.

He crouched down in front of me to stroke the top of my head and neck. "I'm sorry, girl. I know you want to meet everyone. I think you're going to like being part of the team—and they're going to like having you around. It'll be helpful for me, too. I don't always know what to say to people when I first meet them. You make that easier. Now, show them what a good dog you are, okay? Do what I ask you to, be on your best behavior—or you can't come to practice, okay?"

Okay? That word meant I didn't have to stay any longer. But I was confused. When had he told me to stay?

Clearly, he was worried about meeting those kids and needed something to take his mind off it. Just as he stood, I flopped onto my back.

Bang?

"Sooner, what are you doing? This isn't time for parlor tricks and I'm not dragging you across the parking lot like that. Now up on your feet. Let's go introduce ourselves, shall we?"

Except for my name, I didn't understand the rest. Humans had so *many* words. They really needed to speak more simply.

I sprang to my feet, bowed. Grinning, he cocked his head at me. I sat up, crossed my paws.

Sit pretty?

He laughed. "Come on. Let's say hi. I'm sure they'll all enjoy the entertainment."

Bouncing beside him, I did my best heads-up heeling. Brandy used to love it when I did this, but Grayson didn't have quite the same appreciation for it. I was determined to convince him anyway. Trying to stay even with his left leg as he strode forward, I gazed up at his face and pranced along. The notebook was tucked under his opposite arm. He wore a nervous smile, swallowing often as he glanced from the ground to the group clustered by the tables. They'd been talking, but as we approached, their conversation dropped off. They were all wearing running clothes and shoes and were what Grayson called 'teenagers'. Too big to be children, but not quite adults.

They didn't look as excited to see us as I was to see them.

"Hello!" Grayson said a little too loudly. As if the kids were much farther away. Then more softly, "I'm Grayson Darling, your new coach."

A girl with reddish-brown hair raised her hand. "Excuse me. Is that your full name? Grayson *Darling?*"

"Yes, Darling is my last name."

"What do we call you?"

"Coach Darling, I suppose."

One of the boys stepped forward. He had sandy-colored hair cut so short you could see his scalp. "But we called Tervo... Tervo. Sometimes Coach Tervo, but mostly just Tervo."

"Yeah," another boy added, "Tervo was his first name."

"Oh," Grayson said, bewildered. "What was his last name, then?"

They all looked at each other.

"Hanky, I think," another girl said, "although I'm not sure how to spell it."

"Heineken," the second boy corrected. Several of them snickered.

"You know the answer, Cruz." The sandy-haired boy, who appeared to be their leader, shook his head. "Heikkinen. Tervo Heikkinen. His parents were from Finland. They brought him here as a baby. You guys really need to listen better."

"Um, okay..." Setting his notebook on a table, Grayson flipped it open. "What would you like to call me? I'd prefer something besides 'Hey, you!'"

The girl giggled. But no one else laughed.

95

"Can we call you Coach Grayson?" she asked.

"Sure, that's fine."

Cruz kicked a stick on the ground. "Good, 'cause it might be kind of strange if we all called you 'darling'."

Some of the boys laughed.

"I'm Dusty," the leader said, stepping past him. "Team captain."

Grayson placed a finger on a page of his notebook, then looked up at Dusty. "Dustin Hamilton?"

He nodded.

"So we have Dusty and Cruz…" Grayson read through the names one by one. A few got no response, but he quickly went on to the next one, until—"Mateo Sandoval? Where's Mateo?"

"Not here," the one called Keen said.

"Hasn't been here for over a week," another in the back added.

Grayson stepped to the side to get a better look at him. "And you are?"

"Real name's Beckett, but I answer to Bucket. There's a story to it. Don't ask."

"I'm not sure I want to know." Then to Dusty, "You've all been coming here since… I mean, even though you didn't have a coach? Every day?"

"Except Sunday," Dusty replied. "We take that day off or run on our own then. Sometimes we run twice a day—those of us who are putting in more miles, anyway. But yeah, every day. Just like normal."

"Wow, okay. I'm surprised, but that's good."

"We did it for Tervo," Keen said.

"For Tervo," several repeated.

They all got very quiet and sad then. It was the same way I'd felt after the accident and didn't know where home was or what had happened to Brandy.

Grayson read off several more names, a few of which got no

response. By the time he reached the last one, his nervous anticipation had been replaced by a sort of barely concealed disappointment. He rifled through some more pages in his notebook before gently closing it.

Some of the boys had broken off into a small group and were gathered by a huge tree outside the circle of picnic tables. They were talking lowly, occasionally glancing our way.

"Look," Grayson began, "I have no intention of replacing Coach Tervo. I didn't know him well, but from what I hear, he was one in a million. I know that…" He paused to stare at the group of boys who'd separated themselves and were now talking more loudly. When his silence got no attention, he raised his voice. "Hey, why don't you guys join the group?"

They went on talking.

"Over here," Grayson said.

"We're good," one of them said. It was Cruz.

"You can't hear me if you're talking to each other. Come here." Then louder, "Now!"

They stopped. Looked at him. Not in surprise or embarrassment. But like he'd interrupted *their* conversation.

I'd learned to pay close attention to a person's tone, their face, their eyes. I didn't need words to know when, between two people, there was love, indifference, or conflict. This was one of the latter. A subtle, underlying tension. One that said Cruz didn't yet accept Grayson's leadership. Kind of like how Loretta's new barn cat, Felicity, didn't respect my natural superiority as a canine. We'd spend our days staring at each other, defying the other to make the first move. It was a perpetual standoff. Looked like that could be the case with Cruz.

"Now," Grayson repeated more softly, but just as tersely.

With a roll of his eyes, Cruz came closer, but stalled several feet short of the main group. His friends followed suit, shuffling along, taking their time.

"Anyway," Grayson began again, "I'm not here to replace him, so let's just start fresh, okay? Do the best we can. I know it's going to seem strange until we get to know each other, but I need you all to participate like you normally would. Call your friends who stopped coming and tell them practice is back on, same schedule. I count twenty-five on the roster, but we've barely got a dozen here. We need to do better if we're going to repeat as regional champs, maybe even make it to state as a team. First meet is in three weeks. We have a lot of time to make up for."

A couple of them nodded, but no one said anything.

Until Cruz spoke up. "Can we run now?"

"Don't be in such a hurry, Cruz," Dusty said. "Maybe Coach Grayson here has more to say."

"It's okay, Dusty." Grayson addressed the group then. "Five miles. But stay on the main trail. Got it, Cruz?" He looked at him directly.

"Sure... Coach." His upper lip twitched, almost like he was holding back a snarl.

"I'll bring up the rear. We'll convene back here when you're all done and do a group stretch."

"What're you going to do with the dog if you're running?" Bucket asked.

"She runs with me." He looked down at me. "Don't you, Sooner? Want to go running?"

Go running? I popped up from my sit, bounced a few times, whirled around. *Yes, run!*

The reddish-haired girl, whose name I'd learned was Louisa—or Lou, I wasn't sure which because she answered to either—giggled. "Oh my gosh, I love that dog!"

The girls moved off together, except for Lou, who lingered behind to pet me. "That is sooo cool that she runs with you. Can she be our mascot?"

"Sure," Grayson said.

Lou joined the other girls.

We'd already started jogging toward the path that led down into the wooded valley when Grayson called out, "Dusty... hold up a sec!"

Dusty circled back. "Yeah, Coach?"

"Can you get in touch with Mateo, tell him I hope to see him here tomorrow and that I understand? I don't want him or anyone else to think they're in trouble, but the best thing we can do is move forward and get back to regular life."

Scratching at his neck, Dusty hesitated before answering. "Well, I know that and most of the ones here get it, but... I'm not sure how to put this. Some of these guys, they'd love running no matter what. Some, they just did it for Tervo, you know?"

"No, I... I understand what you mean. But maybe they should give me a chance before they hang it up. So you'll call him?"

"Believe me, I've already tried. He won't answer. But I'll give it one more shot. I'll even put in a good word for you."

"Thanks. I'd appreciate it."

"No problem." Dusty turned and ran a few steps, then came back. "By the way, don't pay any attention to Cruz. He gave Tervo a hard time, too."

"And what did Tervo do?"

Dusty grinned. "Let's just say Tervo knew when to lay down the law and when to let it go."

After the kids had all taken off down the trail, Grayson and I followed, not far behind a pack of girls and one of the slower boys. Far enough away, though, that Grayson felt free to talk to me.

"Darn kids. Testing me just like you did at first. Remember that, Sooner?" He glanced at me, smiled. "Probably not. But I'll make a confession—you taught me to be a benevolent leader, instead of an

99

autocrat. A shower of praises, a few biscuits every now and then… they go a much longer way in fostering loyalty and cooperation than all the threats in the world."

Whatever he said, he seemed pretty pleased with himself. All I heard was one of my favorite words—biscuits.

After our run, the kids stood in a circle and stretched. Lou asked if she could hold my leash and as Grayson stood in the middle and explained each exercise, I did my play bow and rolled onto my back to show Lou I could stretch, too. The kids laughed, which made me happy. Most of the kids seemed happy, too. Except Cruz. Some things you couldn't force, though. Like convincing a cat you weren't out to eat her.

The longer practice went on, the more relaxed Grayson became. I was disappointed when it ended, but Lou and a couple of the other girls gave me lots of pats before leaving.

Lou, whose mother was waiting in a car nearby, gave me a big smooch on top of the head. "See you tomorrow, Sooner."

I licked her face, making her giggle.

She looked at Grayson. "You have the coolest dog in the world."

"Thanks." After she left and Grayson and I were alone, we walked to the car. He opened the rear door and I leaped inside. "Not a bad start, huh, Sooner?"

I folded down, feeling the first tug of exhaustion, and closed my eyes. Contentment filled me. Peace and pure joy. Just when I thought life couldn't get any better—it had.

chapter 9
Brandy

The prospect of where to start that morning had overwhelmed Brandy nearly to the point of tears. It was almost too much. She didn't know where to begin. So she turned to what was right in front of her—the receptionist's desk. But even that presented a snow-balling set of distractions. A week's worth of dust had accumulated on top. She wasn't sure where to put all the random paraphernalia that cluttered her view. No sooner had she placed a handful of paperclips in the center drawer than she found another stash in the lower right hand drawer, and yet more in a plastic container with a magnetized top on a shelf behind the desk.

In his office, Rex ended a phone call. She thought about asking him where he wanted her to put the office supplies, then immediately realized she'd spend all day interrupting him. Besides, he obviously didn't have a system anyway, so it might as well be hers from now on.

From now on? Brandy checked herself. She was a long way from making a decision about this job—she'd made it clear to Rex she was doing this on a trial basis. At any rate, she couldn't even begin to actually function in any sort of professional capacity until she had this place straightened out and there was no telling how long that was going to take.

The number of decisions Brandy had to make about minutia was staggering. She could understand why Rex hadn't tackled it. Then again, if he'd simply paused occasionally to put things back in their proper place, it wouldn't have gotten like this to begin with. She knew the cleaning lady came by after five on Fridays, so Brandy was determined to give her a slightly less daunting task to show up to.

"How's it going?" Rex popped his head out the door.

"Fantastic." Her sarcasm was barely subdued.

Nodding, he poured himself a cup of coffee from the pot Brandy had made for herself.

"Excuse me." When he didn't so much as look her way, she intercepted him in the doorway. A doorway barely wide enough for her wheelchair. "Excuse me, Rex, but... that was mine."

"Oh." He looked at the cup with genuine shock. "I'd, uh, offer it back to you, but I've already used this mug today. Anyway, I just assumed it was for me."

"You would."

"Pardon?"

A tall man, he towered over her even more in his cowboy boots. It was in moments like this that Brandy was reminded of her diminished physical stature. If she'd simply been sitting in a regular chair with two good legs, she would've stood up to face him eye to eye, or nearly so. As it was, she had to rely on her wit.

"Look, the coffee maker hadn't been used in ages. My assumption was that since any third grader can figure out how to fire up an automatic coffee pot that you didn't drink the stuff, so I made some for me. I cleaned it out first thing this morning when I got here and trucked over to Gertie's for some coffee grounds. If you want to include barista in my duties, we probably ought to renegotiate."

"You've been to Gertie's?" Hopeful, he looked around. "Didn't happen to fetch an extra glazed or two, did you? I ran out the door this morning with nothing more than a burnt piece of toast and the last swig of grapefruit juice on my stomach."

That was all he got out of her speech—where were the donuts?

At her old office, everyone got their own breakfast and coffee, even the bosses. On Fridays they took turns bringing in bagels from the local deli. That was as communal as they got. "I didn't realize I needed to take bakery orders."

"Would you mind?" He fished through all his pockets and eventually produced a twenty.

Brandy let her gaze pan the room as a hint. "I have a lot of work to do, I'm afraid."

"No problem-o. Let me know next time you go."

As much as she wanted to fling more sarcasm at him—sarcasm that would probably slide right off his Teflon ego—she resisted. The better thing to do, if she wanted to foster some mutual reciprocity, was offer to bring in donuts or bagels if he occasionally got them lunch.

The moment Rex returned to his office and closed the door, Brandy stuck out her tongue. Sure it was juvenile, but that was precisely how she felt right now. He wasn't a complete jerk. Just oblivious. And inconsiderate. And presumptuous.

Already she was beginning to rethink her decision. Thank goodness she'd agreed to it on a part-time only basis of three days a week. She'd need the days in between to give her patience a break. The way things were going on her first day, however, she'd have to have a heart-to-heart with him soon. First, though, she needed to plow a path through this junkyard. Now what had she been doing last?

The front door opened and Grayson walked in with Sooner. Letting the leash drop, he set a grocery sack on one of the chairs.

"Is it lunchtime already? How?" In a panic, Brandy checked her watch. "I've barely gotten started."

"Hello to you, too, sweetheart." Grayson pecked her on the cheek. "And no, it's not lunch yet. We dropped you off just over an hour ago. Already done with our run. I had to swing by the feed store to get some emergency horse wormer paste for Loretta—for one of the boarders, a horse, I mean, not Loretta—so I thought you might want a little company on your first day at your new job. Say hi to the dog. She missed you."

After a quick lap around the office, Sooner sniffed Brandy in greeting. Brandy gave her a quick pat on the head, then went back to surveying the chaos around her. It didn't seem like she'd gotten anything accomplished yet.

Grayson hopped onto the desk, right on top of the papers she'd been sorting earlier. "Going that well, huh?"

She blew out a puff of air. "How have you put up with him for a year?"

"To be honest, I didn't see him every day. Sometimes I was able to go a couple of weeks without even hearing his voice. He's easier to take in small doses."

"To be honest myself, if I only knew him in passing, I'd think he was a really friendly, helpful guy. But up close…" She showed her teeth and made her hands into cat claws.

Grayson burst out laughing. "Sorry." He sobered. "I was going to warn you, but you seemed pretty excited about the prospect of getting out of your apartment, so—"

"Someone there, darling?" Rex called through the door. "Walk-in client?"

"Just Grayson, Rex. And do not call me 'darling'! That's Grayson's last name."

"Roger that," he replied.

"Ohhh, can I hang out here for a while just for the show?"

Grayson chuckled. "You two are better than an episode of *The Real Housewives of Beverly Hills.*"

"If you stick around, I'll have to put you to work. Pick your poison—paper cuts or dust allergies?"

"Neither. I have an appointment back at the farm in forty-five minutes. Just enough time to get there, shower, and change." Retrieving his grocery sack, he pulled out a multicolored bouquet. "I hope this brightens your day."

"Ohhh, Grayson, thank you." She took the flowers from him and inhaled. "They smell wonderful, too."

"Better than the musty odor of old books?"

"Times a million. Could you dump the pens out of that old coffee can, fill it with some water, and put them... I don't know, wherever you can find a clear spot. So no lunch today?"

"It'll have to wait until Monday." He placed the flowers in their improvised vase on the corner of her desk. "I promise to keep my calendar clear for you."

"Okay. Just as well. I'd like to get a big chunk done today. Can I call you when I'm ready to go home?"

"Sure thing." He kissed her goodbye, then leaned over and gave Sooner a smooch on top of the head. Brandy loved how much he loved that dog. Her life was complete as long as she had the two of them.

Grayson had only been gone five minutes when the first client of the day walked in.

"Good morning!" Brandy chimed. The second she blurted it out, she realized her chipper tone had been overkill. She took it down a few notches. "Do you have an appointment?"

The woman, a few years younger than Brandy, nodded. Her eyes were slightly puffy and red-rimmed, but Brandy couldn't tell if it was from crying or allergies. She sometimes had a problem herself with the latter.

105

"Zelda FitzHugh. Ten o'clock. I'm a little early. Sorry." Claiming the closest chair, she shed her denim jacket. Her lower lip quivered ever so slightly. "Rex and I are going over my final divorce papers."

"Oh, dear. I'm so sorry. That's got to be hard." She hadn't meant to blurt that out. It was just her natural reaction to be sympathetic. Yes, the woman had been crying. For days, most likely. Remembering some tissues in one of the drawers, she got them out and offered her one.

Zelda blew her nose several times, then dabbed at her eyes.

Concerned, Sooner approached Zelda slowly, then laid her chin on her knee.

Stroking the dog's ears and neck, Zelda smiled. "She must be a therapy dog."

"Not officially, but I suppose that's one of her jobs. She just likes attention. She is a certified service dog, though. If I drop something, she can pick it up and bring it to me." Brandy dropped a pencil on the floor, then commanded Sooner to fetch it. "See?"

Then Brandy showed her how Sooner could flip a light switch and drop a piece of paper in the trash can.

"She reminds me so much of Goldie." At which Zelda broke out in tears again.

Half a box of tissues later, Brandy learned that Goldie was the Golden Retriever that Zelda's husband had taken as part of the settlement. She'd needed the house more, but it had been a tough call.

"I know it seems silly to say it, but that dog was like my only child."

"No, I get it. I feel that way, too."

"It was three months before I put her bowls up in a cupboard and her toy basket in the closet. Eventually, I dropped them off at a friend's to give back to my ex. Do you have any idea what it's like to be without her?"

"I do, actually."

Before Brandy could tell the story of how Sooner got lost after the accident, Rex emerged from his office.

"Zelda, dear heart! Right on time. Come on back, won't you?"

After that, Brandy didn't have more than fifteen uninterrupted minutes to herself the rest of the day. She'd meant to get started reorganizing files, with the intent of scanning them all at some point so everything could be pulled up on the computer, but a steady stream of clients dropping in and phone calls prevented her from doing half of what she wanted.

Miraculously, however, the day had flown by. She'd quickly developed a knack for greeting clients, old and new, and even had most of their files ready by the time they arrived. Working from home had been so mundane, so predictable. So… lonely.

Today had been anything but. She was even getting used to Rex.

"You handled it all like a charm," he reassured her as he readied to leave. "Sure you'll be all right here by yourself?"

"I won't stay more than an hour, I promise. Besides, is there anything to worry about here in Faderville? Bank robberies, drive-by shootings, muggings?"

"The area's not completely crime-free or I'd be out a chunk of business. So keep an eye out. Last week someone threw a brick through the auto mechanic's front window. Didn't steal anything, but you never know. You remember how to lock up?"

"Um, turn the key, check the knob?"

"Smart as a whip! Oh, hey, Ynez should be by anytime. She has her own key, though. There's an envelope on my desk with her pay, so if you see her walking out of here with it, don't worry."

"Ynez?"

"Cleaning lady. And just so you know, no sense trying to carry on a conversation with her. I don't think she understands more than a dozen words of English. Have a good weekend, Brandy. Same starting time Monday—if I haven't scared you away already."

"Verdict is still out on that one."

"You keep that sense of humor. It makes up for your obsessively tidy nature. Bye now."

Rex had his hand out to push the door open when Sooner blocked him.

"Sooner, come," Brandy commanded.

"No, no. She was just reminding me I forgot something." He produced a biscuit from his pants pocket. Pointed at the dog. "You know this isn't free, right?"

She sneezed, sat back.

"What do good dogs do?" he asked her.

Sooner pushed her paws off the floor to balance upright.

"I didn't know she knew how to beg," Brandy said.

"Watch this." Then to the dog, "What do *really* good dogs do?"

After returning to a sit, Sooner looked away, yawned. Then she lay down and rolled over onto her back, legs in the air.

Rex released her and tossed the dog biscuit into the air. She snapped it up.

"You taught her that? When?"

"As much as I'd like to take credit, it was Grayson who taught her that. Before you came into the picture, if I recall. Anywho, we have this little routine, the dog and me. No payday without work. Which reminds me—you keep track of your hours."

Hours? Brandy checked her watch as Rex left. She'd been here nine hours already. What was one more? She shot Grayson a short text to pick her up at six.

She may have started the day feeling overwhelmed, but at least she'd accomplished a lot. What satisfied her the most, however, was the smiles and thank-yous she'd received from clients today. Paychecks were nice, but it was even better to be appreciated.

—o0Oo—

It was a quarter till six when the lock on the front door turned. Back in Rex's office, Brandy froze. She was setting the files for Monday's clients on his desk. Surely, Grayson didn't have a key. Had Rex forgotten something?

There was the soft whoosh of an opening door, followed by the brief intrusion of the hum of cars going down the main street. Sooner, who'd been lying beneath Rex's desk half-asleep while Brandy finished up, raised her head abruptly. The moment the lock clicked shut, she was on her feet and charging into the front room, barking viciously.

Brandy moved far enough into the doorway to spy a petite, Hispanic-looking woman.

Now she remembered.

"Sooner, come," Brandy called.

The dog halted halfway between them. The woman was backed up to the front door, one hand over her heart.

"Come!"

Reluctantly, Sooner backed away several feet, then turned and trotted back to Brandy, who clipped the leash on her.

"Sorry about that. Let me get something for you."

Brandy retrieved the envelope lying in the center of Rex's desk. The flap was open. Carefully, she flipped the envelope over to see if anything was written on front. Two ten-dollar bills landed on the desk. She quickly stuffed them back inside and took note of the name on front: Ynez.

The envelope in her lap, Brandy wheeled herself to the doorway, Sooner in tow. "Ynez? Hello."

Terrified brown eyes met hers. The woman was small, not even five feet and probably less than a hundred pounds. She was all bone and sinew. The creases of her skin and the graying at her temples

109

indicated she was upward of sixty, possibly close to seventy.

"*Hola.*" Flashing a nervous smile, Ynez quickly averted her eyes and set a laundry basket full of cleaning supplies off to the side.

The envelope extended, Brandy moved forward. "Rex left this for you. I presume it's for an hour's work, although if you can make a noticeable headway in that time, I'll proclaim you a miracle worker—and if you can't, just leave me a note and I'll make sure Rex makes up the difference next week."

Ynez nodded, her expression unchanging, and busied herself with taking out a bottle of glass cleaner and going to work erasing the fingerprints on the plate glass of the front door.

Brandy wasn't certain if she'd understood, so she tested her. "Approximately what time do you anticipate finishing?"

Ynez nodded more vigorously.

So Brandy reached into the far corners of her memory and pieced the question together in broken Spanish.

After a brief pause, Ynez glanced at the dog, then at Brandy. Sooner had adopted a friendlier disposition and it seemed to put her more at ease. "I clean… one hour."

"Is that how long it… usually takes?" It took a while for Brandy to think of the words. It had been almost two decades since she'd last used the language regularly. After three years of high school Spanish, she'd followed up with two more courses in college, thinking it would make good sense for her future employment prospects to be fluent in a second language. But other course requirements had gotten in the way and since then, the most she'd used her knowledge had been flipping through channels on cable TV.

Chuckling, Ynez shrugged. "As far as Mr. Franzen knows, yes."

"But it takes… more hours?"

"Two. Sometimes three. If I work fast."

"You tell him that, yes? He pays more sometimes?"

Ynez scoffed. Clearly, she found the notion humorous. "If I ask

110

for more, he will hire someone else."

"Did he say that?"

"He would have to know." She shook a thin finger at Brandy. "Say nothing. I need every job I can get. My grandson eats twice his weight every day. Who are you, anyway?"

"Excuse me?" Brandy was getting lost in the rapidness of the woman's speech. She'd caught something about needing work, a grandson eating, and—

"Your name?"

"Oh, I'm sorry. I forgot. Brandy Anders. I'm Rex's..." She couldn't think of the words for office manager, receptionist, or secretary. Eventually 'assistant' came to her.

"I wish you luck, Señorita Anders... Señora?"

Sooner watched Ynez's every movement intensely, her gaze following Ynez's hands as she spritzed the glass and wiped in rapid circles.

"Señorita. For now." Brandy wasn't sure she could quite explain that she and Grayson were exclusive. It seemed a bit too complicated and... *personal* to bring up the first time meeting someone.

Politely curious, Brandy asked Ynez more questions—about her family, what other jobs she did, where she lived. It was amazing how chatty Ynez was in Spanish. She'd come north nearly two decades ago after her husband died and had saved up money to send for her daughter and grandson. After a while, her daughter had gone on to Chicago, where she was able to earn more. She'd sent some back for Mateo's care, but lately that had dwindled to almost nothing. It was hard to tell if she was worried about her daughter or disappointed in the choices she'd made. A bit of both, Brandy guessed. At any rate, she couldn't imagine moving to another country for work and not knowing the language. It had to be very isolating.

Before Brandy knew it, Grayson arrived, ready to take her back to the farm for dinner. She sent him out to the car with Sooner, gathered her things, and then joined him.

They were a mile down the road when Grayson scanned her belongings. "Your flowers! Let me turn around and—"

"No, that's okay. I hope you don't mind, but I gave them to someone."

"Oh." He was quiet for a minute, but the situation was clearly bothering him. "You didn't like them? I mean, that's okay if you didn't. Just let me know what you—"

"They were perfect, Grayson. I gave them to someone who I'm pretty sure doesn't have someone as thoughtful as you in her life and probably can't spend the extra amount on herself."

"Oh," he said. But it was a different kind of 'oh' than the first one. An understanding one. "Who?"

"Ynez, the lady who was cleaning Rex's office. She works longer than what he pays her for and is afraid if she asks for more, he'll hire someone else."

"Rex is a lot of things, but cheapskate isn't one of them. You should tell him."

"I know. I'm going to, but I…" Her words trailed off as her thoughts jumped around. She clapped her hands together. "I know! I'll threaten to quit if he doesn't double her pay."

"That's a little severe, don't you think?"

"Not at all."

"All I'm saying is maybe you should save quitting until you're really desperate. He's not unreasonable, either. Just fill him in. See how it goes." He slowed before turning onto another road. "If that doesn't work, you can flounce those pretty copper curls of yours."

"That's not the kind of office relationship I was going for. Besides, he's married, right?"

"He is. And I take my suggestion back. You're spoken for. I don't want anyone getting ideas."

"Spoken for—is that what you call it?"

His mouth opened. Nothing came out. He closed it. Drove for what became an awkwardly long time.

Brandy hadn't been fishing for anything more solid. She'd only been taking a jab at his word selection. So what he said next took her completely off guard.

"Brandy, I've been doing some thinking lately and… I'm not sure how to say it, but… I think of you as my 'forever girl'."

"Forever, huh?" They were both staring at the road ahead. Mulling over that one word and all its implications. "That's a very long time."

He nodded. "Eternity."

"More than a life sentence."

Grayson reached across the space between them. She placed her hand in his.

Warmth spread up her arm. Poured into her heart. Floated her spirit so high it was like looking down from heaven.

"Anymore," he said, "I can't imagine a future without you. When I think of my life years—no, decades from now, I see myself as an old man, barely any hair, thick black glasses, and wearing some beat-up old cardigan I can't part with because it's comfortable. And I'm there on a park bench with my arm around you."

The picture came vividly to life in Brandy's mind.

He glanced at her, smiled. "What do you see?"

She wanted to ask if he saw her in a wheelchair or on the bench with him, but the way he'd looked at her, spoken to her… she knew it didn't matter to him either way. It didn't even matter to her.

"I see it, too."

chapter 10
Mateo

The way Mateo saw it, things would never be the same. Tervo's presence in Mateo's life had made all the difference in the world, coming at a time when the young man wavered in both direction and purpose.

Despite having lived in the same house in the same community for the last dozen years of his life, despite the constancy of his stern and industrious grandmother, Mateo had always felt adrift, denied the deeply anchored roots of his classmates. He'd never resented them for it. Instead, he focused on all the things he would—or could—do, if given the chance.

Look forward, he figured, if you can't bear to look back.

In the days following Tervo's unexpected demise, Mateo spent many hours roaming the very trails he'd logged countless miles on. Although the urge to break into a run often gripped him, he defied it. Running had no place in his life anymore. The trance of its allure had been broken. Gone with the absence of Coach Tervo's gravelly voice carrying across the expanse.

Move your arms, Sandoval! Blessed mother of... Move. Your. Arms!

His barking had once been Mateo's conscience. Driven him harder than his will alone ever could. Pushed him to shatter the self-imposed limits of his own self-doubt.

In short, Mateo might never have believed what was possible if Tervo hadn't first believed in him. It enlightened Mateo to the effect, both good and bad, that people could have on one another. He'd grown up wary, mistrustful of others, reliant only on himself and his grandmother. His hope in his mother had been shaken when she abandoned him. It was severed when the reality finally sank in that she was never coming back. He'd remained doubly guarded since then. Made no effort to make friends with the other kids at school. Outside of the team, experience had taught him that the only ones who sought to interact with him were the ones inflicting harm. Those that were neutral simply pretended he wasn't there. A non-person.

Even when he joined the team due to Tervo's persistence, he'd kept to himself, declining offers for after-practice get-togethers in lieu of study, odd jobs, or chores at home. Over time, his teammates accepted it. Although they were never unkind, it was often clear he was missing out. Frequently, he wondered how it might have gone if he'd accepted the invitations into their inner circle. But once would lead to twice, which would lead to more offers. He was not like them. It was just easier to maintain a safe distance.

Besides, Tervo was gone now. That distinctive voice would never reach across the distance to blast inside his ears and throttle any traces of his self-doubt. No more would his words appeal to a greater, yet uncultivated, calling in Mateo.

It's easy to be less, to be nothing, Mateo. All you have to do is fold to the ground and give up. To be more, to be greater... of course it's hard as hell. Only one runner can cross the line first. If it were easy, they'd all be doing it. You, Mateo... you can be exceptional—if you want to be.

He'd told Mateo that at the end of the most difficult workout he could ever remember. When everyone else had already run out of steam. Then Tervo made him run another hard mile. And he'd done it. Five seconds under the required time.

There had been no graveside funeral for Tervo. His wife, at his predetermined request, had donated his body to the nearest university medical school. Tervo didn't believe in ceremony. He showered praise readily when earned, yet sought none for himself. His only payment for all the hours he'd put in, he once said, was building character in those he coached. Often, he'd gone beyond his normal coaching obligations, doling out lunch money he never asked to be repaid, running shoes to those who sorely needed them, and rides to and from practice.

Last year when the topic of colleges came up, Tervo had broached the subject of Mateo's documentation status. At first, Mateo was reluctant to give his information to the government. But Tervo seemed to understand and assured him that if he wanted to remain in America and fulfill his dreams, it was a necessary step. Then, he'd patiently walked him through the application process, explaining how it would allow him to remain in school and even seek employment.

The day the paper came granting Mateo deferred action status— and soon after that his work authorization card—he'd been gripped with an uneasy mixture of joy and worry. Hope and fear.

It was everything to him. And yet it could so easily be taken away.

Now lost for purpose, Mateo called around, looking for work. He found some odd jobs mowing lawns and doing other yard work, but many of the opportunities had already been snapped up by others. He avoided calls from his teammates. No doubt they were asking him why he hadn't been to practice. Dusty, in particular, had been relentless.

8 a.m. tmrw at the park, Dusty had texted. *New coach. Seems cool.*

Mateo didn't reply. Dusty lived in a two-level brick house in a newer subdivision. By Mateo's standards, his family was well-off. He didn't understand what it was to live in fear that your freedom could be taken away with the stroke of a pen. That on any given night, you could go to sleep in your own bed and be dragged from it, then shipped off to a place your own parents had tried in desperation for their lives to flee.

There'd been a couple of calls from an unknown number, which he ignored. The third time the number appeared, it had been followed by a short message from the new coach in a forced, chipper voice.

Hello, Mateo. This is Coach Grayson. Practice is on again at the park, weekday mornings. Usual time. See you there.

Mateo deleted it. Even contemplated blocking the number, but decided not to.

Hey! You on vacation or sick? Dusty texted the next day.

Vacation? He'd never in his life had one.

When he didn't answer that one, two hours later came another text.

What the heck, Matty? You get kicked out of the country or what? (Kidding!)

Even the most innocent dig wounded him deeply. But he could never show it.

Anyway, he hated the nickname 'Matty'. Although Dusty rarely called him that, Jed used the name whenever he could. Mateo was never sure what the point of Anglicizing his name was, whether it was meant to make him seem more like them or to reject his heritage altogether.

Searching for money, Mateo turned his jeans pockets inside out. All four pairs. Each of them secondhand. Thankfully, holes in the knees were fashionable. None fit well. Also trendy. He rifled through his drawers and even checked in the two shoe boxes stored in the back of his closet—the only closet in the house. He tallied a grand total of thirty-seven dollars.

So far his efforts to save for the future and contribute to household expenses had failed miserably. He'd have to go into town, ask around, fill out some applications. The purpose of which would be to find more reliable work. Other kids from school had part-time jobs. A few had dropped out to work full-time. At the time, he'd thought it foolish. Now he understood the necessity.

The problem, Mateo soon figured out, was that town was a long ways off. Particularly the business section, where the jobs would be. Having vowed never to run again, he started off walking fifteen minutes after his grandmother had left to go clean at the motel just off the interstate. She also cleaned houses and offices, sometimes working as much as eighty hours a week. With that much time to himself, Mateo had learned to do a lot of things, but driving was not one of them. What was the point when there was only one car between them and his grandmother had it all the time? He'd figure out transportation once he had a job.

The sun was barely up, but being August, it was already getting humid. If he walked the whole way to the far side of town and back, by the time he filled out a dozen applications and came home, it would be past the time his grandmother was due to return. Plenty of time, though, to conjure up an explanation.

So wearing his cleanest jeans and his best polo shirt, he began to run. Not for exercise, but just to get where he needed to go faster. Every time he heard a car, he slowed to a walk. Sweat poured down his chest. His armpits were soaked. Even his underpants were damp with perspiration.

A blister was forming on the back of his left heel, too. The shoes he was wearing weren't made for running miles in. His shins were burning. His mouth was dry with thirst. And he was hungry. To the point of feeling faint. He'd been so intent on getting an early start, he'd forgotten to eat.

After Rockhill Road ended, he'd taken two other back roads, hoping to avoid traffic. Then he came upon the state highway. If he turned onto that, he could save himself a mile. But that risked someone he knew coming up on him in a car. Which could lead to questions he didn't want to answer.

For five minutes, Mateo waited until several vehicles had passed. He had a clear view either way from the hill where he stood. Finally, the last truck went by. He sprinted downhill and across the two-lane highway. A couple hundred yards later, he was about to slow to a jog when he heard another vehicle in the distance on the main road. So he ran fast to get farther out of view. It wasn't really running if he was only doing it for a minute to avoid being seen.

To his horror, the vehicle turned onto the country road he was on. For hundreds of acres around him, there was nothing but gently rolling pasture. The next house, with a barn and detached garage that might have given him somewhere to hide, was close to half a mile away.

He returned to a walk. Running in his street clothes would look too odd. He hoped it was nobody he knew. Worried that it was. Tried to conjure an explanation. Couldn't. The vehicle drew closer. Retreating to the gravel shoulder, he kept his head down. The car slowed. He avoided looking over his shoulder. Maybe it was only an older driver being cautious. Or maybe it was Jed.

A truck came abreast of him. Mateo kept his eyes forward.

"Need a ride, son?"

The voice, a mature one, was vaguely familiar, but Mateo couldn't piece together from where. Mateo slid his gaze to the truck's tires, its front end, and finally, the driver. The face was familiar, too, but no name came to mind. The man had a handlebar mustache and sideburns, as if he'd just stepped through a time portal from the '70s. He was well dressed, too, with a suit jacket, button-up shirt, and a bolero.

"No, but thanks," Mateo said with a weak smile.

"You sure? I thought maybe your car broke down."

"Yeah, sure. Just going down the road." He wanted the man, whoever he was, to go on.

The truck rolled along slowly beside him, the man quiet for a few seconds. "To where? That's old man Vinton's house ahead and I know he doesn't like company. Doesn't hire out help, either."

"I'm fine. Thank you for the offer, though." His grandmother had always taught him to be polite, even when he didn't want to be. The man was probably suspicious he was up to no good, seeing as how Mateo was the only Latino youth in town.

"All righty, then. Just trying to be a Good Samaritan. Have a nice day, son."

The man touched his fingertips to his brow in something of a salute and the truck gathered speed. Mateo exhaled in relief. He still couldn't place how he knew—

Fifty yards away, the brakes squeaked. The truck rocked backward, then began to roll in reverse back toward him.

"No," Mateo whispered. "No, no, no."

The truck stopped. Mateo stopped, too. It was hot. Very hot. He glanced down at his shoes. The blister on his left heel was bloody and there was another forming on the top of his right big toe. His stomach was so taut with hunger it was as painful as if he'd swallowed a stone. He had just enough money on him for a bag of chips and a large drink from the convenience store.

"Now I remember!" The man pointed at him. "You're Ynez's grandboy. Matthew, is it?"

"Close. Mateo." It had been years since he'd been introduced to the man. He'd been with his grandmother in town somewhere. At the grocery store, maybe? The encounter had been brief, whenever it had been.

"You don't remember me, do you?"

"Kind of. But not your name. Sorry."

"To be fair, it was a few years ago. You were half a foot shorter then. I'm Rex. Rex Franzen, lawyer. Your grandmother makes my office presentable. Does a damn fine job, too." He stretched his neck to get a better view of Mateo. "Look, I saw you gimping. Feet hurt?"

"Blister."

"Those things are the devil if they're in just the right spot. Why don't I give you a lift, however far it is you're going? If you're worried about accepting a ride from someone you don't know all that well, shoot your granny a message and tell her—"

"Are you"—he wasn't sure how to backtrack gracefully, so he just took the leap—"are you going to town?"

Rex didn't ask why he'd had a change of heart. "On my way to the office a hair early to look over files. Hop in."

Thankful to give his feet some relief, Mateo climbed into the truck. He buckled up and immediately turned his gaze to the scenery beyond his window. The truck gained speed and a welcome breeze poured in. If he clung to any hope that Rex would leave him in peace, it was soon crushed.

"Your grandmother's proud of you, son. You know that?"

Mateo shrugged.

"She doesn't say it, but I can tell. Every Friday—she comes more than that now, my new assistant demanded it—every Friday, I leave her any newspaper clippings I come across that have your name in them. Sometimes it's just the school honor roll listing. Your name is in the highest category every time. But mostly, it's in the sports section. All the team wins, your individual titles... Course, none of that attention would've happened if Coach Tervo hadn't created an empire of concrete skyscrapers out of a hill of sand over the past decade and a half... He was something, wasn't he? Never knew him personally, but it was easy to get a feel for him from all his quotes—and the man had some memorable ones. With his record, he could've gone to any of the big city schools around Lexington or Louisville. Maybe even a small college program. Yet he chose to stay in this Podunk town. That's—not sure what to call it. Dedication, I s'pose. He made cross country a bigger deal in this town than football or basketball. That ain't no easy task in these parts. Man was a miracle worker. Look what he's done. All those trophies and press coverage. More important, lots of his athletes have gone on to run in college. I bet you're getting a boatload of offers, am I right?"

Mateo forced a smile. "Some."

The truth was, most of those had come to him through Coach Tervo. He'd always informed Mateo which ones were worth paying attention to and which to politely decline. After his win at last year's state meet, the inquiries had poured in, even from places he'd never heard of. He had to look them up on the internet at school. Tervo would go over each letter or email with him, discussing not just the recent successes of the programs, but the academic offerings of the school, distance from home, and overall cost of tuition and room and board.

Lots of kids think just 'cause they get offered a scholarship to some big school, Tervo had said only a month ago, *it's a done deal, but you have to factor in how much of the bill they're willing to foot and how deep in debt you want to be after four years. A lot of places won't give you a full ride the first year. Too many rookies can't deal with the pressures of college classes and being away from home. They want you to prove that you're not going to flunk out. That's money they could've spent on some other kid who needed it. But some will take the gamble. Those are the ones you talk to.*

And remember this, Mateo—wherever you decide to go, you're there to learn. Got it? Running's just a vehicle to prepare you for the rest of your life. Don't forget that, kid. Seize the opportunity. Use it as a stepladder to haul yourself up.

That voice. It played over and over in his head like a movie clip on a loop. Would it grow fainter over the years? What would Tervo say of him now? Would he shake his head in disappointment that he was no longer running? Or would he touch his arm in sympathy and say some things were more important?

What did it even matter anymore? He had to do what *he* thought was right.

They rolled to a stop at an intersection at the edge of town. Old clapboard houses with crumbling roofs stood in crowded rows. Mateo figured this was close enough. "You can let me out here. Thank you."

"Not until you tell me which colleges you're seriously considering. So, have you narrowed it down?"

"I haven't, no. But I will."

"When?"

If there hadn't been a car in the lane to the right of them, Mateo would've just shoved the door open and jumped out. "Soon."

The car beside them turned right, but another immediately took its place. The light still hadn't changed.

"Just thought I might have something to talk to your grandmother about next time I saw her." The light turned green. After the intersection, Rex switched lanes, then came to a halt at the curb. "Not that I can talk directly to her. I've got a new assistant now who knows enough Spanish to, though. I'll mention that I gave you a ride, just so she knows we've met."

Panic surged in Mateo's chest. He didn't know what Tervo might have thought about what he was doing, but he was sure about his grandmother. "Please, say nothing. I'm not supposed to accept rides from... people."

It was true. But the scolding for hitching a ride would have been slight in comparison to the interrogation he would face about why he was going to town, never mind missing practice.

Tapping his fingers on the steering wheel, Rex gave him a sidelong glance. "She didn't know you were coming here, did she?"

Lying was hard for Mateo, so he said nothing.

123

"Want to share why you came to town?"

"Looking for work. For… money. To help my grandmother."

"Ah." He fished a business card from his wallet. "Come by my office at noon. Center of town. Can't miss it. I usually pick up sandwiches for myself and Brandy. You look like you could use some calories." He reached in front of Mateo to open the glove compartment and produced a couple of granola bars and a can of soda. "This should get you through until then."

"I can't accept. It's not—"

"You know, it'd be a darn shame if someone happened to mention to your grandmother they saw you in town today."

It wasn't hard to figure out who that 'someone' might be. He took the food and got out. "Thank you."

The lawyer broke out in a huge smile. "Well-mannered, hardworking young man like you—shouldn't be too hard to find a job. Good luck."

Mateo hadn't gone ten steps when Rex pulled up to him again. It took a lot of self-restraint not to roll his eyes at him. Or run the other way.

Rex raised a finger. "Say, if you do find a job in town, have you thought about how you're going to get to and from work every day?"

Mateo turned away. Started walking.

"Right. One problem at a time. See you later." Rex pulled away without another word, leaving Mateo to gimp along.

Unwilling to concede, head held high, the canvas of his sneakers rubbing at the raw skin of his feet, he headed toward the first business he saw—a muffler shop. He knew nothing about cars, he admitted when the manager asked about his experience, but he said he'd be willing to clean. They told him to come back in another month or two, but didn't offer to take his name and number.

At the ice cream shop, he was told they had no openings and wouldn't until next spring. At the convenience store, when asked his age, he was told he was too young. At the hair salon, they giggled and suggested he try the gaming store on the other side of town. He knew without going there that one would be a waste of his time. At the computer store, they asked if he knew how to run a diagnostic. No, he said, he didn't. Apply online, they told him. He was sure that even if he did, he'd never hear back from them.

Mateo's hand drifted to the lump in his back pocket—his worn copy of the Constitution, inside which was tucked his work authorization card. Little good either did him today. Instead of memorizing Articles, Amendments, and the Bill of Rights, he should've been taking apart old computers and putting them back together again.

Deflated, Mateo continued down the main street, stopping at every business he came to. The more he inquired, the clearer it became—it wasn't that there weren't any jobs to be had. There just weren't any for him.

Then, he saw the center crossroads of town. There, diagonal from where he stood, the lettering on the front window said 'Rex Franzen, Attorney at Law'.

His stomach clenched in hunger. It was fourteen minutes past noon. He was late.

chapter 11
Brandy

"Why didn't you tell me I was late, Brandy? What good are you?" Rex checked his pockets. He had a habit of tossing his personal items in random places, which frequently led to furious searches.

"Looking for these?" Brandy held his keys up, rattling them. With her other hand, she pushed his wallet across the desk. "Or this?"

"Why do you have those?"

"I didn't steal them, if that's what you're implying. You left them on the sink in the restroom. I collected them before some sneaky client committed grand theft auto and ran up all your credit cards."

"If you're practicing to be a standup comedian, you might not want to give up your day job." He retrieved his things and marched for the door. "You want the brisket and Monterey Jack today or the ham and Swiss?"

"Ham and Swiss. I'm feeling traditional. But remember—Dijon mustard, not yellow. And spinach. None of that tasteless iceberg lettuce."

"Usual drink and chips?"

"Sure."

The door swung shut behind him. Ten seconds later, he was back. "I've got a young friend stopping by to join us for lunch. If he shows up, keep him entertained until I get back." He looked at this watch, shook his head. "Huh. I suspect at this point he might've taken a pass. Anyway, be on the lookout."

"Will do."

Her boss had been gone less than a minute when Brandy noticed something. "Hear that, Sooner?"

The dog, tucked under her desk, lifted an eyebrow, then returned to her early mid afternoon nap.

"That's right, girl. Peace and quiet. Glorious, isn't it?" Brandy scooted her wheelchair around her desk, noticing for the first time the soft squish of the wheels over the carpet and padding. It was so much easier to maneuver around on the vinyl flooring in her apartment or the hardwood floors of Grayson's farmhouse. The small details other people didn't have to think about. At least there were already handrails in the restroom here.

On her way for a bathroom break, she glimpsed a law book that had been sitting on top of a filing cabinet for two days. She recalled that Rex had pulled it out, flipped through it, and set it aside when his cell phone rang. Stretching her arm, she pulled the heavy volume down and took it to the shelves. There, on the top row, was the space it belonged in. She could wait until Rex returned and ask him to put it back... or she could just do it herself. Which would require standing on her own two feet.

It took a minute for her to think it through. First, she set the book on one of the leather chairs so it would be within easy reach. Next, she situated her body so she could lever herself up using one of the arms of the visitor's chairs. Locking her brakes, she leaned forward and pulled herself up.

For what seemed like forever, she remained in a half-crouched, half-standing position, the weight of her upper body pressing down into her hands. Gradually, she straightened her back. Her legs shook with effort. She'd done this many times at physical therapy, only there were sturdy bars instead of chair arms. Her muscles were unfamiliar with the request and complied reluctantly. She'd come so far from a year ago when all she could do was lie in her hospital bed, slipping in and out of consciousness. It had taken weeks to learn to sit up again, to use her arms. Months to be able to lift her foot while sitting. To any other person, what she was doing could be done without thinking, without strain. To her, it was like scaling the Matterhorn. Even the slightest movement had to be done with great care.

She noticed Sooner moving toward her with curious concern—as if the dog was aware she was witnessing something quite out of the ordinary.

Gradually, the wobbling in Brandy's legs stopped. It was more nerves than weakness, she realized. Still, she couldn't do this all day. Sooner or later her legs would give out.

The book seemed so far away. After moving her right hand to clutch a middle shelf for support, she let go of the visitor's chair and picked up the book. Her arms, she marveled, were strong—in relative terms, anyway. She'd gotten used to hoisting her own body weight with them. Jamal, her physical therapist, had insisted on an intense regimen of dumbbells and therapy bands. While she could sense the shift in her balance from lifting the book, she was surprisingly in control. She extended her arm slightly above her head and slid the book in.

Giddiness rushed over her. She grabbed the arm chair, then plopped herself ungracefully into her wheelchair. This was monumental. Squealing, she clapped her hands.

Sooner barked twice. But not at her. Someone had just come in the door.

Brandy clamped her hands over her mouth.

The boy… young man looked down at the ground, his hands shoved deep in his pockets. His skin was brown from the sun and his dark hair was damp with sweat, as if he'd just run a mile or more out in the torrid heat.

"Is Mr. Franzen here?" he asked softly.

Lowering her hands, Brandy patted her leg to get Sooner's attention. The dog trotted dutifully to Brandy's side and sat. "I apologize. She usually doesn't bark when people come in here, but I was… putting a book away and…"

"I saw." He glanced at her in a way that conveyed he wanted to ask questions, but was too polite to do so.

"I was in an accident last year. My van went off the highway into a ravine." She'd learned there were times when it was better to explain her situation up front. "I'm having to relearn a lot of things like standing on my own. That's a pretty big deal these days. I'd love to train for a marathon someday, but right now I'd settle for walking across the street."

The young man looked uncomfortable, so she changed the subject. "Rex should be back soon. I'm Brandy Anders, his executive assistant." The title had popped into her head that very moment. She liked the sound of it. "And you are…?"

"Mateo."

"Do you have an appointment? I don't remember anything on the schedule." Returning to her desk, she pulled up the hourly schedule.

"No, I… he said something about lunch, but that's okay. He probably already ate." He turned to leave.

"Wait, no." Brandy indicated the visitors' chairs. "Please, sit. He *was* expecting you, come to think of it. He's running a bit behind. He actually just stepped out to get lunch. It's only a few doors down. Shouldn't take him more than ten minutes."

Almost reluctantly, Mateo sat in the farthest of the leather chairs, his back to the large window looking out onto the street, as if he needed a safe corner from which to view the world. He kept his body slightly forward, hands braced on either side of his legs like he might spring forward and bolt out the door at any moment.

As curious as Brandy was as to why he was here, she figured she'd find out in short order. Maybe he'd gotten in trouble with the law or at school and Rex had volunteered his services as a favor to a friend. Plausible, but this kid didn't look like the troublesome kind. Still, since starting here, she'd been surprised by the stories she'd heard, both from the clients and from Rex. Life was complicated. People you saw on the streets or met face to face who appeared like they had it all together were often plagued by family drama, addiction, legal issues, financial problems, and sometimes just poor choices. She'd never judge another human being again.

Yet there was something about Mateo that made her heart go out to him without even knowing a thing about him.

"Can I get you something to drink?" she asked.

"No, thank you." A few seconds later, he said, "Water, maybe? If you have any."

"Sure. Stay right there. Rex keeps a fully stocked refrigerator in his office. We've got all kinds of drinks, if you want anything else."

"Water's fine, thank you."

She took her time in Rex's office, rearranging the rows of bottled water and scattered cans inside the fridge to give Mateo time to settle in before getting out a drink for him. Then she took some papers out of several files she'd pulled earlier for Rex. Realizing he'd be back at any moment, she started for the front room, but stopped short of the doorway where she could view the young man at an angle. Sooner had sidled up to him and was sitting a couple of feet away. The two were gazing at each other fondly, like old friends.

"*Hola*," Mateo said to Sooner.

The dog crept forward, her head low in a submissive gesture. He held out the back of his hand for her to sniff and she inhaled the scents on his fingers and clothing. She rooted at his hand until his fingers found the top of her skull and moved to her ears, scratching to her delight. Soon, her chin was in his lap.

In perfect Spanish, she could hear Mateo talking to Sooner. "... what I have to do. I don't know if she'll understand, but..." He was speaking so softly, it was hard to hear every word. "Jed said it was true and I checked... sending people back. Whole families. Showing up at... It is what I have to do, yes?" His fingers dug deep into the fur at Sooner's neck and she groaned. "I knew you'd understand."

That dog had the ability to speak to people's souls in a way no human being could.

Brandy cleared her throat and went through the doorway, holding the bottle up. "Here you go."

He flashed a friendly grin at her as he took the water. The edginess had melted from him.

At her computer, Brandy surfed the internet. She desperately wanted to say something about Mateo speaking fluent Spanish, but thought better of it.

"You made it!" Rex pushed the door open wider with his hip. He held the bag of sandwiches up. "Come on in back, both of you. We can dig in at the fancy conference table. I've got half an hour before the next appointment. Just enough time to hear how your day's going, son."

Mateo looked like he was having second thoughts, so after Rex went in back, Brandy took the long way around her desk and intercepted Mateo.

"Don't worry. He does ninety percent of the talking. There isn't always a point to his stories, though, so just smile and nod."

At the conference table, Rex already had the food distributed. He indicated the seat across from him for Mateo. "I took the liberty

131

of ordering you a meatball sub, Mateo. Hope you don't mind. It had the most calories. You'll need every one of them for all the miles you put in."

He thanked Rex, but hesitated to dive in.

"You're a runner?" Brandy was trying to make a connection. His name had sounded vaguely familiar.

Mateo hurriedly unwrapped the sandwich and took a bite.

Then she remembered. "Grayson and I saw you at the state meet last year. You won!"

His hands froze just as he was poised to take another bite. Swallowing, he began to wrap the sandwich back up and stood. "I just remembered—I was supposed to check back at this one place after twelve. Thank you for the food, but I... I need to go."

Rex slapped his palm on the table. "Sit down, son. This is Faderville, Kentucky, not New York City. Nobody around here's gonna give a hoot if you show up at twelve or twelve-thirty. Now, have you tried the oil change place?"

Poor Mateo looked like a deer in the headlights as he sank down, nodding. Rex threw out more suggestions and Mateo acknowledged all but two. Faderville was only so big. Opportunities were limited. Brandy felt lucky to have this job, even if she did have to put up with a messy, overly talkative attorney. Anyway, he was starting to grow on her.

"Might as well eat, then. Fast kid like you can't be skipping meals." Rex poured his chips onto the open half of his sandwich wrapper and popped one in his mouth. "Brandy's boyfriend is the new cross country coach. Small world, ain't it, Mateo?"

Chewing his food slower now, Mateo said nothing.

Brandy saw an opening and took it. "Grayson just started a few days ago. Not anything he planned to do. It just happened when he ran into Principal LaCrosse here last week. We were so sorry to hear about Coach Tervo. I'll have to tell Grayson I saw you. We've both been so busy the last couple of days, we haven't talked much."

Rex pointed at Mateo. "Did you know, Brandy, that this is Ynez's grandson?"

"Really? Now that you mention it, I can see the resemblance. She was telling me about you last week, Mateo."

Mateo lowered his sandwich. "She... told you?"

"In Spanish, yes. Mine is a little rusty, but I was better at understanding her than I was at saying things. She's so gracious, though. She never laughs at me, although heaven knows I deserve it. I was surprised at how she's grown her business. She's such a hard worker and..." Noticing the look on Mateo's face, she paused. "What is it, Mateo?"

"When will she be here again?"

"This afternoon," Brandy said. "Usually about a quarter after five. Why?"

"Please, don't tell her I was here... in town. She doesn't know."

Before Rex could hijack the conversation, Brandy asked, "Why wouldn't you want to tell her, Mateo?"

He stared at his hands so long, Brandy wondered if he'd heard her.

"Why, Mateo? You came to find a part-time job, right? Lots of kids your age do that. I'm sure Grayson would work around it with you. Have you told him you're looking yet? I'd understand if you hadn't, since I'm guessing you don't have anything solid yet."

"I... I haven't been to practice since... since before Tervo..."

A heavy silence settled in the room.

Brandy understood grief. Better than she wished. She'd lost her father last year and still missed him. She understood how it changed a person.

Still, Mateo had been the best in the state. Garnered national attention. And, Brandy suspected, was one of the key reasons why Grayson had taken the position. Working with an athlete like Mateo was a once in a lifetime opportunity. "I still don't understand, though. Why haven't you been to practice since then?"

"I need more than part-time work. I need money. In case."

"In case what?" Rex prodded. "You in some kind of trouble?"

"No." Mateo swung his head toward him, his eyes flashing defensively. "I haven't done anything wrong—ever!"

"Whoa, turn down the volume, son. I wasn't accusing you of anything. I'm here to help. Look, if you need money, there has to be a good reason. Is your grandmother in debt? Need medical care? Car repairs, new roof?" Rex planted his hands on the table and, standing, leaned across it. "Is somebody trying to extort you? I have friends in law enforcement. Just say the word and—"

"Do you know immigration law?"

As if he'd been slugged with a baseball bat, Rex sat abruptly. "Not very well, no. It's not in my wheelhouse. But I s'pose I could look around. Find you someone." He drummed his fingers on the table, thinking. "I'll make some calls, but it may take me several days. Is this an urgent matter?"

"No, but..." Mateo pulled something from his back pocket and laid it on the table—an address book or a thick pamphlet of some kind. "I want to know my rights in case something does happen."

While Rex scribbled some notes, Brandy asked Mateo, "So you haven't lived here all your life, have you?"

"I wasn't born here, no. My mother brought me here when I was five so we could join *mi abuela*."

It all made a lot of sense to Brandy now. "You're a Dreamer, then?"

"That's what they call it, yes. A couple of years ago, I thought it would be possible to become a citizen. Coach Tervo helped me get my DACA papers and work authorization card. I've studied hard, too, so I could qualify for the best schools." He pressed his fingers on the embossed lettering of the booklet he'd placed before him.

Brandy could just make out on the cover, in gold print, an eagle holding a sheath of arrows in its clutches—the Great Seal of the United States. "I even memorized the Constitution. I wanted to make my mother and grandmother proud. Show them that everything they did for me—it meant something. I got good grades, worked for extra money, ran hard... Even though I didn't have many friends, my teachers noticed my efforts. Tervo noticed. Some of the kids, they began to accept me. I started to believe that here"—he pointed to the floor, but it was clear he meant a bigger place—"here, you can become anything if you work hard enough and stay out of trouble."

His chin lowered then. His voice softened. As if someone had stolen that dream and he realized the impossibility of getting it back. "But lately, I don't know if that's true anymore. I've seen stories on TV and the internet... Some kids at school, they feel it's okay now to tell me I don't belong here. That I'm only stealing what should be theirs. The funny thing is most of the time it's kids who have more than they'll ever need. Kids who don't know what it is to go to bed with not enough food in your stomach, or see someone you love get sick and not be able to afford medicine. They don't know what it's like to travel across the desert on foot, your belongings nothing more than what you can carry in a small backpack, in search of a new home in a better land. They don't know what it's like to walk into a store where your grandmother has sent you to buy tomatoes and peppers and have a security officer shadow you down every aisle. They don't know what it's like to be followed into an empty locker room and be shoved against a wall. They will never feel the cut of being called names. They believe their cruelty is justified. As if they're protecting themselves from some evil. But the evil is only inside them. More and more, I see this everywhere. And I know that I'm not wanted here. A land that took Tervo and his parents in not so long ago." His voice, by now, was shaking with both rage and passion. "But he was white and I... am not. It's not so hard to see.

135

"So you understand why I no longer feel safe? If I knew for sure nothing was going to change, that laws would be finalized and one day I could become just as American as the rest of them, I'd run in college as Tervo wanted me to." He shoved his booklet back in his pocket. "But why bother, when it could all change in an instant?"

Pushing his sandwich away, he rose and turned for the door.

"Hold on, Mateo!" Rex called.

But Mateo didn't heed him.

Rex hurried after him and blocked him at the front door. "Check at Mac Kendrick's used car lot at the end of town. They were looking for someone to detail cars just a few days ago—assuming you can use a vacuum and wax the exterior." When Mateo didn't answer, Rex added, "Take a right out the front door. Follow the main drag until you get to Lexington Avenue. That becomes the state highway. The dealership is about a mile past the edge of town."

Mateo nodded, then squeezed past him. After he'd gone out the front door, Rex leaned out and shouted. "Show up here at five, if you need a ride home!"

When he came back in, Brandy said, "Are they really looking for an auto detailer?"

Rex marched past her, pulling his phone out. "They will be in about five minutes after I talk to Mac. Sometimes you gotta call in favors. Just need to save them up for things that really matter."

chapter 12
Mateo

Apparently, Rex Franzen didn't have a solid grasp on how far a mile was.

Mateo stopped at the crest of a low hill. Sighed. After thirty minutes of walking, the car lot was less than half a mile away now, yet it may as well have been a thousand miles. Sunlight glinted off waxed hoods and chrome trim. Pennants of red, yellow, and blue, strung from light pole to light pole, drooped in the breezeless air.

Five minutes passed. Five minutes during which sweat streamed from every pore of Mateo's weary body. He couldn't muster the will to move one more step. Rejection had worn him down. Flattened him. He'd started off the day determined to get a job. Anywhere. Doing anything. So he could pay for an immigration attorney and help with expenses at home. Whatever it took to lighten his grandmother's burden and ensure their future was to remain here.

Well, maybe not 'here' as in Faderville, but here in America.

Salty perspiration stung at Mateo's eyes. He squinted into the distance. There, at the edge of the used car lot between two trucks, a blurry figure stood—a brawny man dressed in a white button-up shirt, looking his way. Almost as if he were waiting for him.

Head down, Mateo forced his feet to move. Every step brought a fresh stab of pain. Nobody ever died from blisters, he reminded himself. Still, they hurt. A lot.

When he was maybe a hundred yards away, he raised his eyes. The man was gone. All the same, he made a conscious effort not to limp. The office was to the left. He veered toward it, wending his way between a group of brightly-colored hatchbacks and sedans in muted shades of gray and taupe. Slowing between rows, he looked back at where he'd come from. He couldn't even see the town anymore.

Don't you dare look back, Mateo, Tervo's voice echoed in his memory. *Ever! If they know you're fading, that you're hurting as much or more than they are, that will shatter the illusion that you're invincible. Don't ever let them think otherwise. Let them think that nothing fazes you. Nothing!*

"Can I help you?"

A jolt of panic seized Mateo's heart. He whipped around, his eyes settling on a bulky figure.

The man, neither old nor young, smiled at him. "Looking to purchase your first set of wheels?"

It took a few seconds, but Mateo found his tongue. "Uh, no."

Before Mateo could explain himself, the man stuck out his hand. "Mac Kendrick. And you are...?"

"Mateo."

Mac shook his hand, then tugged his tie loose and stretched his neck. A rather broad neck. With shoulders to match. "Hotter than blazes out here, isn't it?"

Suddenly aware of the sweat staining his shirt, Mateo nodded. Maybe he'd come back some other day when he looked more presentable.

"Just window shopping then?" Mac asked. "Used to do that when I was your age myself, about a decade ago. Had my eyes on a sleek red Mustang with racing stripes, but Pa wouldn't have it. Said I had to drive something more practical until I was old enough to have some sense. Turned out he was right. I wrecked the clunker he gave me. He told me I'd have to pay for the next vehicle out of my own pocket. That's when I started working here. Of course, Pa owned the place, but... Ah, never mind."

He surveyed Mateo from head to foot, making Mateo wish he could somehow hide the bloodstains on the toes of his shoes. Clearly this day had been a total waste of time and energy. He should've gone to the library and filled out applications online, then waited for a call that was probably never going to come.

Mac rubbed at the stubble on his chin. "Say, smart-looking kid like you wouldn't be looking for work, would you? I just had a no good drunk get booted because he failed to show up for the third time, so I could use another hand. You interested?"

The impulse to shout yes gripped Mateo, but he quickly tamped it down. Not wanting to appear desperate, he shrugged and looked nonchalantly around the lot. "Depends. Doing what?"

"Oh, cleaning out the trade-ins, washing, waxing, that sort of thing. Think you could handle that?"

"Well, I've never done that before, but... yeah, probably." Then to make sure what he might be signing up for, he added, "What kind of hours are we talking about?"

"I'm flexible on that, as long as you show up when you say you will. Just to warn you, though, sometimes I'm swamped with cars that need cleaned up, other times it's a bit slow."

For the first time that day, for the first time in many days, Mateo felt the tiniest spark of hope. Still, he wanted to convey a certain air of confidence. "I'm interested, yes. How much does it pay?"

Mac gave him a surprisingly light tap in the sternum with his fingertip. "You could have a future in sales, Mateo. How's four bucks an hour over minimum sound?"

Mateo couldn't help himself then. He offered his hand. "When can I start?"

"How about now?"

They shook on it.

—oO0o—

Throughout the afternoon, Mateo couldn't shake the feeling that Mac Kendrick had been the overly eager one. Who offers someone a job without references or a completed application? The interview, if it could be called that, had lasted mere minutes. Mateo was so used to people regarding him as unqualified or untrustworthy that he couldn't, at first, truly believe he'd succeeded. But the longer he vacuumed and wiped and rinsed and waxed, the more real it became. He had a job. A regular job. At good pay—which made him more than a little suspicious.

How oddly coincidental it had been that Rex directed him to Mac's car lot and Mac was there waiting for him.

The more Mateo thought about it, the surer he was that it wasn't a coincidence. That steely armor of pride he'd inherited from his grandmother bade him to march into Mac's office and say that he'd reconsidered. Charity was charity, no matter what form it came in. He wanted to make his own way in the world, not have favors handed to him.

On the other hand, he'd already tried by himself with dismal results. If Rex had put in a good word for him because of his grandmother, so what? Who was he to question his kindness or his pity, whatever the case? It was just a menial labor job, sucking up other people's dust and pebbles, scrubbing away bug guts, and spraying off road grime.

He was, however, determined to do a better job cleaning cars than anyone before him. Connecting the narrow nozzle to the vacuum hose, he attacked the dark recesses beneath the driver's seat of an older model minivan that had seen a long and useful life. Undaunted, he reached under and cleared out some loose change, two barrettes, and bits of partially melted candy. When he was confident he'd gotten all the larger objects, he started vacuuming again. Pieces of gravel dinged against the inside of the vacuum canister. He adjusted his angle, probing deeper. He'd make this car so clean that—

A tap on his shoulder startled him. He spiraled backward, dropping the nozzle. It was Mac. His mouth was moving, but all Mateo could hear was the hungry roar of the vacuum.

"Huh?" he said, barely loud enough to hear himself.

Mac hit the off button. "I said, 'Go home.'"

Dismay crushed Mateo's chest. Had he done something wrong? Not worked fast enough? "I'll finish this one, I promise. I can even stay longer and do that—"

"No, no, you're fine, Mateo, just fine. The Chevy can wait. It's four-thirty already. We're zealots about getting out of here at five sharp on Fridays. Almost forgot—I need you to stop in at the office and fill out some paperwork Cara has for you."

His heart took another leap. "Paperwork?"

"Yes, to make it official. Do you have ID on you?"

Then Mateo remembered. "I have my work authorization card."

"Good, good. That'll work perfectly."

His heart settling, Mateo slid from the back seat. "I still need to finish this one, though."

"While I admire your work ethic, it's not an emergency. It'll still be here when you come back. Tomorrow morning?"

Mateo nodded. "What time?"

Once they settled on tomorrow's hours, Mateo went and filled out the paperwork. After he'd double-checked all his information, he glanced at the clock: two minutes till five. He wouldn't make it back to town in time to hitch a ride from Rex. He'd have to walk home. If he ran, he could definitely make it home before his grandmother was done for the day with her work. But… blisters.

He didn't want Mac or Cara to know he didn't have a way home. Or a way back in the morning, for that matter. The mechanic had already left for the day, as had the other salesman.

He was sitting on the curb at the side of the office when Mac came up to him. "Need a ride, Mateo?"

He shook his head. "No, I'm good. Thanks, though."

"You sure? Maybe Cara or I are headed your way."

"Thank you, but no. They'll be along in a bit."

Mac regarded him skeptically, then after a pause said goodbye and left. Cara locked up and departed a minute later.

The most surprising part to Mateo was that they'd left him alone there. He could've busted out a window and stolen some tools, for all they knew. Then again, there were probably security cameras everywhere. And they knew where he lived.

He pushed himself up and started walking. Slowly. Painfully. His knees wobbly. Hunger like a heavy stone in his gut. So parched he felt like a sponge wrung dry. Despite the food Rex had given him that day, he hadn't had enough. Especially liquids. Between the heat and the walking, he'd become dehydrated. Why hadn't he gotten a water from the fridge before he left? Mac had told him he could have all he needed. Yet he'd been so intent on completing his work he'd even skipped the breaks he'd been afforded.

Cars whizzed past on the two-lane highway, blasting him with hot air and the stench of gasoline fumes. Nausea made his stomach churn. He focused on the horizon where another road crossed. He didn't know these roads well, never ran here. If he had to guess, though, since that road ran east-west, it should take him back to the quickest route home. Unless it curved north or south somewhere along its path. He didn't know. Had no one to ask.

The patter of light feet sounded behind him. He whipped

around. Squinted hard. Saw nothing. Probably just some gravel he'd loosened as he'd tread over it, sliding down into the ditch.

He forced himself on, watching the approaching cars out of habit. He'd learned to never trust them. More than once, some insane driver had tried to play a game of chicken with him. Better to leap into a patch of burdock than risk getting clipped by the bumper of a truck going sixty miles an hour.

A cop ahead. Highway patrol? No, sheriff's deputy, coming his way, slowing. Mateo quickly lowered his eyes. Fear rippled down his spine. But why? He'd done nothing wrong. Still, he'd been stopped twice while out running. Questioned. Been followed in the store, even out into the parking lot with his grandmother. He knew why.

The patrol car passed him and he let out a breath he hadn't realized he'd been holding. In the distance, he glimpsed a low form, skulking through a stand of tangled saplings. A stray dog, perhaps? He stared harder, but whatever it was had disappeared into the undergrowth of thicker woods back off the road. A minute later, his attention was diverted when he thought he heard a car coming from behind, decelerating. Maybe the patrol car had turned around, come back to question him. Maybe it was Jed Delaney... No, he wouldn't look. Didn't want to know.

He could smell diesel. A truck. Mateo looked. It was Rex.

"Get in." Rex nodded toward the shoulder ahead. "Unless you want to end up hobbling on bloody stumps by the time you make it home. If you do, that is."

He had a point.

Rex crossed the opposing lane and pulled onto the shoulder. Not enough energy to argue, Mateo got in. Besides, he didn't want to suffer his grandmother's wrath. It was going to be bad enough when she found out eventually. He just didn't want to deal with it today.

For a good five minutes, they rode in silence. What Mateo really wanted to do, though, was lie down and sleep. Maybe eat first, but definitely sleep. And then—

"Mac told me you stayed until closing."

Inwardly, Mateo groaned. He'd hoped this encounter would be a quiet one. But this was Rex Franzen. That wasn't possible. Rather than avoid the obvious, he jumped straight to it. "Thanks for putting in a good word for me."

"What makes you think I had anything to do with you getting that job?"

Mateo rolled his eyes.

"Okay, so what if I did? You picked a rotten time to go looking for a job, what with summer more than half over. Most kids start that process in the spring sometime."

Mateo looked at him directly then. "I told you why I needed work now. Besides"—he returned his gaze to the passing scenery—"things have changed recently."

"Right. I get that." Rex drew a stick of gum from his pocket and popped it in his mouth. It smelled of licorice. "Anyway, when you didn't show up back at the office, I did call Mac and he said you were still there, apparently waiting on a ride. I figured you probably hadn't told your grandma about the gig just yet, so I came looking. Found you about where I expected."

"Thanks for the ride home."

"No problem. But that's not the only reason I swung out this way. I wanted to let you know I found you an immigration lawyer. Gal named Valentina Gutierrez, up in Frankfort. I told her about your case and she's willing to take it on, *pro bono*."

"For free?"

"Technically, yes. She wouldn't charge you for her services. She gets reimbursed through a foundation set up specifically for folks in the same boat as you. Catch is you have to do some volunteer work. Something charitable in your community. Picking up trash in the park, exercising dogs at the shelter, tutoring, that sort of thing. Ten hours a month, that's all. See, down the road, you'll have to report in numerous times before they'll make you a citizen. Not only do you have to stay out of trouble, but you have to show you're an upstanding citizen—stay in school, hold an honest job, that sort of thing. And if you give back to society in some way, that'll work even more in your favor."

He made it sound like Mateo had been sprung from prison and had to report to a parole officer. He hadn't done anything wrong. Ever. All he wanted were the same rights and chances everyone else got.

Turning his head away to gather his thoughts, Mateo caught sight of a stray dog out in a pasture, much like the one he'd seen earlier. He focused hard on it. It reminded him of… Fantasma? How strange that it could look so much like the dog of his childhood. In fact, he could've sworn he'd seen that dog more than once lately.

"You see"—Rex went on, interrupting his thoughts—"she was an immigrant, too. From Columbia or Venezuela, can't remember which. Super smart gal. Graduated from one of those Ivy League schools up north. Better résumé than mine, that's for darn sure. She understands the process isn't as simple as some people reckon it to be. She knows what your best bet is, all the pitfalls you can run up against. Knows the disappointments and the successes. We had a long talk. It was eye-opening, I tell you. A lot of folks don't want to hear what it's really like, and if they do they cast those people in a, shall we say, less than flattering light? Then again, why am I telling you this? You know better than anybody the willful ignorance that goes on out there. It's enough to make my blood boil."

No matter how hard Mateo looked now, he couldn't see the dog. Its presence left him with a surreal feeling—that somehow he was being watched.

Or guarded over.

Rex blabbered on until the last half mile before reaching Mateo's house about how this Gutierrez lady was going to work with him, draw up papers, and file them. Mateo understood the gist of it, but the details held little meaning just yet.

After stopping his truck in Mateo's driveway, Rex pulled a piece of scrap paper from his pocket and handed it to Mateo. "I didn't have your phone number to give her, but she said you can call her anytime, weekends or evenings. She even said she'd be willing to meet you at my office next time she's down this way, which should be a few weeks from today. So if you don't object, I'll tell her you'll meet with her then—sound good?"

Nodding, Mateo took the paper. Studied it as if it held some magical secret he couldn't quite decipher. Just like he couldn't understand why he was the object of Jed's derision, he couldn't comprehend why he deserved this... What was it, really? Charity? A favor? So he asked. "Why?"

It took a few moments for Rex to answer. "Because..." He shifted in his seat, discomfort twisting his lips beneath his exquisitely groomed mustache. "Because in my line of work, you see a whole spectrum of people: the good, the bad, the in-between. You're one of the good guys, Mateo. I figure people like you, if you get just one good break, it can make all the difference. Then you can go out into the world and, maybe, someday pay it forward yourself. But if the world keeps beating you down, if guys like me who have it good cling to the false belief that it serves them to keep stomping on the unfortunate, well, eventually people like you learn there's nothing but meanness in the world. And that, son, only begets more meanness, which begets more." He flashed a smile. "*Ad infinitum.*"

In a moment of panic, Mateo felt for his copy of the Constitution. It was still there, shoved deep in his back pocket, probably damp from the day's humidity and his own sweat. He was about to get out of the truck when one more question came to him.

"What does it take to get a legal degree?"

Rex snorted. "What brought that on? I kinda figured a chatterbox like me'd have driven you away by now."

"You help people, right? I mean, in different ways, but you do. Just wondering if it takes a lot of years of college and money. I haven't looked into it."

"Lotta years, yep. And a crap ton of moola. But if you feel called to a particular vocation, to *be* something, you can't obsess too much about money. Purpose is your reward. Don't ask how many years it took me to pay off school loans, though." He smoothed down his mustache a few times. "As for helping people—I suppose I do. Laws, contracts, legal papers... the language is convoluted. You can recognize it as English, yet still not understand it unless some blowhard like me parses it out for you. Lots of folk hate lawyers and I suspect there are some shady ones. But they—*we* play an important role, don't we? Laws are there for a reason. To protect the weak and underprivileged, to keep all of us on a level playing field. Without 'em the whole darn civilized world would fall apart. It'd be absolute chaos."

Although what Rex had said was true, it wasn't the whole truth. "But sometimes the people who make or interpret the laws... skew them toward their own interests, yes?"

Raising an eyebrow, Rex nodded. "Seventeen and you already get that everyone sees the world through their own lens. You're damn smart, kid. An old soul, my momma would've called you. You'd make a good lawyer."

Mateo grinned. "Actually, I was thinking judge or legislator." He got out and shut the door.

"Even better," Rex said to him through the open window. "Take care now—and let your grandma in on your new employment soon. Better she hear it from you than someone else. As for not showing up to cross country practice—you're on your own there. I'm staying out of that."

For lots of reasons, Mateo was starting to like Rex Franzen, when only that morning he'd regretted running into him. Funny how one chance meeting could change the trajectory of your life.

Halfway to the door, Mateo heard Rex thump his palm against the side of the truck. He turned around and saw Rex leaning out the driver's side window.

"You working tomorrow?"

"Yeah, why?"

"How you gonna get there?"

That was a problem Mateo hadn't solved yet. He shrugged.

"I saw about a mile back someone was having a yard sale. Looked like they had a bicycle in good condition. Want me to go back and barter with them?"

As great an idea as it was, Mateo didn't have the money for a new bike. He also didn't have a way to get back to Mac's. Walking and running were out of the question. There wasn't enough Vaseline in the world to ease his pain. He'd end up crawling.

"I'll cap it at fifty bucks," Rex offered. "Just pay me back when you can. I'll be back in a jiffy. If I'm not here by six, assume they wouldn't budge. Sound okay?"

"Sure." He was too tired to argue. Twenty minutes later, his belly full of reheated beans and rice, he had a sleek, black, twenty-speed bike. Rex told him he'd wrestled the owner down to forty bucks, but somehow Mateo doubted he was telling the truth.

—o00o—

"Whose bicycle is that?" his grandmother asked.

Mateo sat up straighter in the lawn chair. He'd been holed up on the back porch, reading a book about the fall of the Roman Empire that he'd bought at a dollar sale at the library last year. He'd read it three times already, but each time old details took on new meaning for him.

"Mine," he admitted sheepishly. It was propped outside by the screen door, not too far from where he sat. "Nice, yes?"

She narrowed her dark eyes. Stared so long and so intently, he felt himself melting under her scrutiny.

"I started a job at Mr. Kendrick's car lot today. I clean out the trade-ins."

A pause. More scrutiny. "And this Mr. Kendrick... he paid you in cash the first day? Enough to buy a bicycle?"

"It's used, *abuela*. A neighbor was selling it." The answer was slightly evasive, he knew.

"Selling?"

The implication in that single word phrased as a question stung his heart. He decided to take Rex's advice and be honest with her. "The lawyer whose office you clean on Fridays, Mr. Franzen, he gave me a ride home. He paid for it, but I have to pay him back—and I will the first time I get paid, I swear."

Her eyes narrowed even further. "How do you know Mr. Franzen?"

He'd known she would ask. He'd thought through all the questions she might pose. Or tried to. "I went to town to look for work and ran into him. He learned I was your grandson. He was the one who suggested I go to—"

"The other jobs you do were not paying enough? Or did Mrs. Ballentine hire someone else?"

"No, I'm still—"

"How will this fit in with your running? There are only so many hours in a day, Mateo. If you do not do well this fall, it may hurt your chances of a scholarship and then you will not be able to afford college at all."

He'd known she would get around to that, too. Only the answer he'd prepared... He knew without saying it out loud that she wouldn't accept it. That to go against her wishes would summon forth an Ice Age between them.

It was an impossible situation. If he returned to running, she would be happy for now, but it could very well cost them both in the long haul. Injury could shatter that dream at any point, and then he wouldn't be able to afford college anyway. Precious income would've been lost. Dreams of championships and Olympic berths came to not just the gifted and driven, but the fortunate—those who could afford not to work while they spent precious hours training. How many talented runners had been sidelined for lack of decent shoes or parents who could afford the time and money to drive them to high-profile contests where the best coaches gathered to scout the next generation they would cultivate into fame? Tervo had mentioned qualifying for a national invitational, but travel to that was paid for privately, not by the school, he'd told him. There were so many factors that went into it. His coach had not only instilled confidence in him, but a pragmatic outlook. Nothing could be taken for granted.

But a job… He could work a job and save his money for him and his grandmother. For the day when legal fees were required—because he knew they would be and that this Gutierrez lady could not incur all those. He could also save his money for the day when his grandmother was too sick or too old to continue working. He could save to fix things on this house, for groceries, a roof, for a new used car for his grandmother—maybe even a car for himself so he could get to work when it was cold or rainy, or to go to a better job farther away.

If only he could make her understand all that.

Yet as he met her eyes, in his heart he knew there was only one answer he could give her.

He looked down at the floor. Heard his voice as if it belonged to someone else. "I'll talk to the new coach about it. I'm hoping he'll let me work something out."

Even as he said it, though, he didn't truly know. Not how the new coach, Grayson Darling, would react, or if his new boss would be flexible.

Things had been much simpler when there was only running in his life. But now there was so much more to consider—and with every day that passed, securing his citizenship and caring for his grandmother, those things seemed more important and pressing than ever.

"You will find a way, Mateo, or else the job will have to go." His grandmother turned to leave, but paused in the doorway. "Next time, you must talk to me about these things first, you understand?"

"Yes, *abuela*," he said.

"Before I forget…" She turned around fully, the muted evening light painting dark streaks in the creases and folds of her skin. "Before I forget, day after tomorrow at five, Sunday… we are invited for dinner. Wear your best clothes. I will drive us there."

"With who? Where?" They'd never been invited to dinner anywhere. His grandmother didn't like to socialize. At all. Even with the handful of people in town she counted as friends.

"At Grayson Darling's farm. His girlfriend, Brandy, she works at Mr. Franzen's office. She's very kind to me. I couldn't say no."

Then she left. There had been no question in the announcement. Not could he or would he like to. But that they were going because she wanted to. Wanted *him* to go. To talk to the new coach.

No matter how strong his reasoning or desire, he couldn't go against her wishes. Not because he feared her, but because he loved her.

chapter 13

Sooner

It was a special day called Sunday—a day that neither Brandy nor Grayson worked. Today, we were at the park on a blanket in the shade of a big tree. Grayson, as usual, fed me bits of sandwich while Brandy scowled at him.

He grinned. "What?"

"I saw that—along with the five times before it." Brandy was sitting with her back against the trunk of a tree, sipping from a bottle of water. "She gets fed twice a day, you know. If you want to give her a snack, there are carrot sticks in the cooler somewhere."

"Aw, honey, it's only a little ham. Can't hurt her."

Ham? I loved ham. It was right up there with peanut butter and pizza crust and chicken and… any human food, really. As much as I enjoyed my kibble, variety was wonderful. I lay down in front of Grayson, offering up my best tricks: roll over, bang, crawl. Laughing, he tore off another strip of ham, but when Brandy cleared her throat, he stuffed it in his own mouth.

Noooo! I lowered my chin to the ground, right between my paws, and gave him the saddest puppy dog eyes I could manage. *I am a good dog,* I whimpered, wagging my nub. *See how happy I make you?*

Smiling, he patted me on the head—as if that were sufficient consolation. "Sorry, girl. The deli is closed."

What did *that* mean?

A chipmunk raced across the grass and darted into a weedy patch bordering the woods. I leaped to my feet, alert.

"No, Sooner," Brandy said. "Leave it."

But, but, but—

"Brandy?" Grayson swatted at a pesky fly. "Can you take out that red container from the basket for me?"

She peeked inside and dug around, then pulled out a plastic bowl. "Sure. What's in here?"

"Open it."

Shrugging, she popped the lid. "Some of Gertie's special white chocolate raspberry muff—" Her jaw dropped. Slowly, she pulled out a silver chain. Dangling from it was something shiny. She held it up. "Grayson, it's beautiful."

He helped her put it on. "A heart with a tree inside. I saw it and thought of you."

"Why?"

"Well, a heart because I love you. And a tree because you're strong. So it's probably some really stout tree, like an oak." He put it around her neck. "Or maybe a horse chestnut or a catalpa with those pretty flowers. But it can be whatever kind of tree you want it to be. It's just that… every day I look at you and I'm amazed at how you make the hard things look easy and… I'm so inspired that… I just realize how lucky—"

"Grayson."

He stopped babbling. Looked into her eyes. "Yes?"

"Shut up and kiss me."

They did that thing where they smash mouths. Looked like fun to me, so I tried to join in, jamming my snout in close and getting in a couple of big sloppy licks before Grayson fell on his back.

Brandy burst out laughing. When she'd recovered from the hilarity, she reached inside the picnic basket and brought out... the Frisbee! She handed it to Grayson.

I leaped to my feet and barked. *Frisbee, Frisbee, Frisbee!* I backed up and spun in circles to generate speed for the anticipated launch. *Throw it, Grayson! Throw it!*

After downing the last of his sandwich, Grayson got to his feet and moved out a ways from the blanket. Toss after toss, I raced after the disc, vaulting high, snatching it just as it dipped in its arc, twirling midair. Then I'd land, sometimes deftly like a cat dropping from a low limb, sometimes with a graceful tumble as I re-oriented upon grassy earth. When I came back to Grayson to present my prize, it was always with tremendous joy and utmost speed. The faster I returned with the disc, I reasoned, the more times he could throw it before the sun went down.

I'd only brought it back to him ten times when his interest waned. He'd begun talking to Brandy and his attention slid to her. He flung it halfheartedly one more time before sinking down beside her.

"Let me get this straight." He was propped up on one elbow, studying her. "You actually like working for Rex *more* than your old job? How can that be?"

Panting, I spat the Frisbee between them to urge Grayson to return to our game of fetch.

"Don't act so surprised, Grayson. I get to meet new people, help them."

"Yeah, I get that. But working for Rex? I thought he drove you nuts."

"Well... he does, but—"

I flipped the disc at Brandy. *Play?*

"Not right now, Sooner." She picked it up and tossed it toward the edge of the blanket. "Like I was saying, he does, but—"

I brought it back. Stared at her.

"He's kind of growing on—"

Dropped it in her lap.

Her mouth twisted. "There is no way I'm touching that, Sooner." She dug around in the picnic basket, found a plastic bag, and wrapped my perfect, beloved, *precious* Frisbee in it. A second later it was buried in the depths of the basket, off-limits. "I'm not afraid of a few dog germs, but that thing's coated in slime."

She rinsed her hands with a splash of water and wiped them on the blanket. "What was I saying...? Oh, yes, right. Anyway, I've gotten used to him rambling. I've even figured out when to tune him out and just go about my business and when to pay attention. I'm learning a lot about all kinds of laws. Some days are more exciting than others, but every day is different. It's rewarding in ways I never imagined. I told my old boss to find a replacement for me and Rex is going to bring me on full-time. Know what else? I got him to double Ynez's pay!"

They were paying no attention to me. Fine, I could play that game and ignore them, too. This seemed like a good time to take a nap. I lay down and stretched out my legs, keeping one eye open in case of a chipmunk ambush.

"Ynez?" Grayson asked.

"The cleaning lady, remember? She's Mateo's grandmother."

"Oh, right."

"They're coming to dinner tonight," Brandy blurted out.

"Who?"

"Mateo—and his grandmother. And Clayton and Loretta, like usual."

"You're just now telling me? When did you decide this?"

"You're not happy? I can make up an excuse, say I'm sick. If you don't—"

155

"No, no, it's okay. It's just that… he hasn't been to practice yet."

"I know. That's why, when his grandmother showed up to clean this Friday, I insisted she come. It took some arm twisting, but I finally got her to agree. Anyway… I don't know if I should tell you this, but—" She slapped a hand over her mouth, mumbling a curse.

"Whatever it is, now you have to tell me. Out with it."

Her hand fell away. "He stopped by Rex's office at lunchtime on Friday. Seems he was in town trying to find work. Rex managed to set him up detailing cars at Mac Kendrick's lot. He's trying to save money. For a lawyer."

"A lawyer? That's why he was at Rex's? Why does he need a lawyer? Is he in some kind of trouble?"

"Not in the way you and I think of being in trouble with the law. He's looking for an immigration lawyer. Grayson, he's a Dreamer."

"Wow, really? I guess I didn't know. It never crossed my mind." He busied himself collecting the little plastic containers they'd brought their food in and putting them back in the basket. "What does any of that have to do with him not showing up to practice?"

"I think he's worried that if he doesn't get everything in order, he'll get sent back to Mexico."

"Could he? I thought that was all sorted. That the children brought here were safe for now."

"Turns out there are a lot of misconceptions about that. In reality, their status is in perpetual limbo. Congress always talks about reforming immigration, but never really does. The Latino community gets a lot of mixed messages. American businesses often hire them as seasonal work: agriculture, hospitality, landscaping, construction… or just to do the jobs that those born here aren't willing to do. If they're lucky, the job turns into something more permanent."

"Don't they worry about getting turned away or sent back?"

"Sure, but it's a risk they're willing to take. They don't see

156

breaking immigration law the same as, say, stealing. Who could blame them, considering the conflicting messages they get?"

His face turned upward, Grayson was quiet for a few moments. "All those things you never think about. In New York, I was surrounded by immigrants. The city would've ground to a halt without them. It's a little different here. They're there, you see them, but they're kind of off in their own little pockets." He shook his head. "Anyway, where did you learn all this?"

"Rex explained it to me after speaking to an attorney named Valentina Gutierrez. She came here from South America. Her story isn't much different from the rest. All any of them want is a job, a way to provide for their families. The same as you and me. But where they came from, there weren't many jobs. And what there is often doesn't pay much."

Grayson snapped the lid on a plastic bowl. "Okay, I follow you so far. But why don't they just apply to enter legally and wait until it's okay to come?"

A sigh leaked out of Brandy. "Because it usually takes years to get approved. Even then, they need money to go through the process. Something they don't have in the first place."

"Right, that makes sense."

She took the bowl from Grayson and put it away. He helped her into her wheelchair.

No, they couldn't be ready to go so soon. It was time for a diversion. I grabbed a stick and dropped it in Brandy's lap. Her fingers closed around it and she moved her hand to the side, but her gaze was distant, as if she'd forgotten she was about to throw it. I woofed softly to remind her, *Play?*

The stick fell from her grasp with a disappointing *plop* onto the ground.

I shrieked my devastation. Not that I'd intended to. It just came out. How else was I supposed to express my sheer and utter horror?

"Sooner, quiet!" Brandy said.

Grayson patted me on the head, then put my leash on. "I know, I know. You're not ready to go. But we'll come back tomorrow and run, I promise."

Run? I whined. I lurched toward the trail we usually took. The leash tightened, but he reeled me back in.

"Tomorrow, Sooner. Tomorrow."

I had no idea what this word 'tomorrow' meant, but I figured it was a polite way of saying no.

After folding the blanket and laying it in Brandy's lap, he pushed her over the grass to the parking lot. The basket was loaded into the middle seat and I was secured in my crate.

On the drive home, I heard them talking and fought the lull of a nap. You never knew when they might utter that one word that would hold some meaning for me: run, ball, supper, bone, play—

"It's all so tentative, don't you think, Grayson? Imagine, the only home you've ever known is here. You've done your level best to be a good citizen, to work hard and prove you deserve to stay... How would it feel to have all that taken away, to be ripped from your family, parted from friends?"

There was a long pause before Grayson answered. "Pretty horrible, I suppose."

"How can anyone be so heartless, so cruel? Why does everyone who's already here think that only *their* ancestors had a right to come here? I just... I don't get it."

She sounded so upset and I couldn't understand why. What was there to be upset about when you had everything and everyone you needed? My belly was full of kibble and sandwich bits, I'd gotten to play in the park, and I was with my two favorite people. I wanted to curl up in her lap and let her stroke my fur until she calmed.

Grayson reached across the space between them. "I know it's not fair. Sometimes people believe that in order to protect their way of life, it's necessary to turn others away."

"What's that supposed to mean?"

He drew his hand back to flick the turn signal on before slowing to make a turn. "I'm not defending it, but I lived in New York long enough to be around all sorts—those who still saw America as the great Melting Pot and those who, well, let's just say they view the world as a place of scarcity and threats, that there are only so many jobs to go around and inviting newcomers in not only shrinks that job pool, but changes things—culture, cuisine, religion, entertainment, commerce. And like it or not, some people are naturally cautious about what they don't understand." He glanced at her as he steered the car onto another road. "Am I making any sense?"

"Sort of."

"But...?"

"It's just wrong, that's all."

A minute went by during which I sank back down and almost went back to sleep, until—

"How can you be so calm about this?" Brandy said. "How can you even begin to see the other side of it? Before I met Ynez and Mateo, I never thought about the details of immigrating to America. To me, it was just some long ago story my dad used to tell about his grandparents at Ellis Island. Before a couple of weeks ago, I never thought much about why people would come here in this day and age. I also figured all you had to do was fill out some forms and wait your turn. I wasn't aware how complicated, drawn out, or expensive it could be. After Rex talked to the immigration specialist, he told me it could take a decade or more to become a citizen, that there were several steps to go through in the process, and that a simple mistake on a form could set you back years or even get you deported."

"And it's because you've heard Mateo's story, that you now see things differently—or more completely, to be accurate." Grayson

159

tapped at the brakes as we came to a stop and waited for another car to go through the intersection. "So, you know how I claim to be an introvert? At my former job, I got to meet a variety of people. Being the subdued, business-minded type, people tended to talk 'at' me a lot. Tell me their stories and opinions, whether I was interested or not. So I heard every angle and because I couldn't afford to lose clients, I had to listen. Even pretend to care when I didn't, sometimes. I heard from first generation immigrants, who just wanted to start a restaurant or send their kid to medical school. On the flip side, I also heard from those whose families had been here for countless generations already, who only wanted to protect and ensure their own future. They wanted things to stay as they were—or maybe even go back to the way things were when they were growing up—so their way of life didn't disappear. Some fear change. Others have no choice but to forge toward it."

Shrugging, Brandy looked out the window. "I hate it when you're logical."

"It doesn't mean I agree. I just try to make a point of understanding people. It helped me when I—"

An old truck rumbled by in the opposite direction, drowning out his words.

"I think," Brandy began as she turned her gaze on Grayson, "the only thing any of us can be sure of is that life *will* change. I mean… look at me."

And he did. Look at her. People don't always have to say a lot of words to convey what they're feeling.

"I know," he replied softly. "But what happened to you, it was an accident. There was no way you could've known how much your life would change in an instant."

"My point is—you can either choose to adjust and make the best of it, maybe even find the silver lining in it, or you can fight it and complain and generally be miserable."

"That right there, Brandy, is just one more thing I love about you."

chapter 14
Sooner

In the corner of the kitchen, a rotating fan pushed hot air around. Loretta opened the oven door wider. A wave of heat rolled over my fur and I nearly wilted, but I refused to back away. Food could fall on the floor at any moment.

With a pair of mitts, Loretta pulled a glass dish out and placed it on the counter. A ripple of cheesy aroma wafted down as she sliced into the food with a big knife. I scooted closer, waiting, hoping.

"My momma's lasagna recipe," Loretta said. "Ain't nothing better."

"It smells fantastic!" Brandy plinked the utensils onto the dining room table one by one.

"Who did you say was coming?"

"Ynez, the lady who cleans Rex's office, and her grandson."

"Where do they live?"

Brandy rolled into the kitchen and over to the cupboard where the glasses were kept. Shortly after she and Grayson had begun dating, he'd moved all the more frequently used items to the lower cabinets so Brandy could get to them. He even installed a ramp to the back kitchen door with handrails for the day when Brandy would walk again. Lately, I'd seen her pulling herself up to a stand in the apartment to work on her strength and balance. She was slowly getting stronger.

"I'm not entirely sure." Brandy set several glasses in her lap and headed back to the dining room.

"Just wondering if it was Ennis Baxter from church. Not really sure what she does for a living."

"Oh no, not Ennis. Ynez. Y-N-E-Z. I assume her last name's Sandoval."

Loretta, who'd started slicing a long loaf of bread, cocked her head. "Sandoval?"

"Yep." Brandy set the glasses next to each plate.

One brow arched, Loretta mumbled, "Sounds like someone fresh over the fence."

"What was that?"

"Nothing. Just asking the dog if she wants some fresh garlic bread." Loretta swept her hand across the counter, sending a spray of crumbs to the floor.

I lunged, sniffing and licking until I'd devoured every speck. Loretta placed the rest of the bread in a basket with a cloth on top. I scooted close enough to place my nose at the counter's edge to inhale.

"Sooner, leave it!" Brandy scolded from behind.

She joined Loretta at the sink to dry the bowls and utensils Loretta had begun washing.

Deterred but still diligent, I went to lie beneath the kitchen table. Maybe at dinner Clayton or Grayson would slip me some chunks of bread. They were better trained. All I had to do was place my chin on their knee and whimper softly.

The two men had just come in from the stables and sat on the couch. Since it looked as though no more food was going to fall on the kitchen floor anytime soon, I joined them.

Stretching his legs, Clayton scratched at his beard stubble with his prosthetic hand. "So this kid and his grandmother are coming?"

"Uh-huh." Grayson flipped through the TV channels. "Might be a little awkward, though."

"Why's that?"

"Last year's state champ. He quit running when Tervo died and hasn't been to practice since. Brandy invited them. Not sure if that was coincidence or devious planning on her part."

"Knowing Brandy, it was prob'ly her way of setting things straight. Kumbaya and all that. So you're gonna talk him into coming back out?"

"Nope."

"No? Why not?"

"Because it's better if it's his decision. Although I might ask what he's been up to, that sort of thing."

"Reverse psychology, huh?"

"Not really. Just want to let him know I care. Besides, maybe he needs a little time to, you know, mourn."

Clayton gave him a sideways look. "Sounds like some of that woo-woo talk. Me? I'd get straight to the point, tell him he has an obligation to the team."

"True as that is, I think it'll gain me more trust in the long run if I don't pressure him. First, I need to reach out, allow him his space, then—"

"If I were you—"

"Well, you're not, thank goodness."

They looked at each other, then burst out laughing.

Clayton rubbed the back of his sunburned neck. "Sorry, I only know football. Different culture."

"I'd imagine so."

They talked some more, but their words began to blend together in a low buzz. I was close to drifting off when I heard a car turn down the lane. I lifted my head, tuned in. It wasn't a car engine I recognized.

Shaking off the fuzz of sleep, I trotted to the front door and gazed out through the screen. A small white car pulled to a stop out front. My alarm bark kicked in.

"Must be them." Grayson joined me at the door.

I let out a few more woofs to alert the newcomers that I was on to them and my humans had been warned of their arrival.

"Sooner, hush."

I woofed softly twice more.

"Hush!" he said more sharply as two car doors slammed in quick succession.

Slinking off to the side, a tiny growl vibrated in my throat. I knew what he meant, but I wasn't going off duty that soon. I had to keep those strangers on their toes. Besides, I couldn't see that far and their scent wasn't strong enough yet for me to figure out who it was or if I knew them at all.

"Sooner, if you don't hush, I'm going to banish you to the crate in the office."

I didn't catch much except for the 'hush' and 'crate' part, but his tone was clear. I hung my head to let him know I got the message. I'd be quiet, but I'd watch their every move. Somebody had to protect my people.

A familiar voice reached my ears: rapid speech, words strange to me, coming from a small, but insistent person. Then the response: the same rhythm to the words, but a slower cadence. The first voice, I knew, but the second—I wasn't sure. It sounded vaguely familiar.

I peeked around the door corner. It was the lady from Rex's office who smelled of cleaning products: Ynez. With her was an older boy, on the skinny side.

"Ynez, hello." Grayson pushed the screen door open. "Mateo. Come on in."

I sniffed the backs of their legs for additional information as they passed. The woman came regularly to Rex's office. The boy… Yes, now I remembered him. I'd met him at the office once, but he was also the one who'd been sitting alone on the hill. I observed him closely as they were introduced to Clayton and Loretta. He seemed less sad this time, but a little… I wasn't sure, but I got the sense he wanted to be anywhere but here right now.

They sat at the table while Grayson and Loretta carried the food in from the kitchen. I followed them back and forth, just in case they dropped something. When they were finally all seated, I assumed my faithful spot under the table between Grayson and Brandy, as dishes of food were passed around and forks scraped across plates and the old wooden chairs creaked as the humans shifted in place.

It was the dullest supper ever. Nothing fell on the floor. Nobody snuck me a scrap of anything. No plates were set down for me to lick. The conversation had nothing to do with any of the important things in life like balls or walks.

Suddenly, Loretta stood up. "Pardon me, but I have a boatload of chores to finish up this evening. Riding lessons tomorrow. New boarder coming in, too."

"Ohhh." Brandy frowned. "Sure you can't sit with us another fifteen minutes or so?"

"Really, I can't. Like I said, a lot to get done before the sun goes down." She fixed Clayton with a stare. "Clayton?"

He groaned. "I thought we—"

"The bales?"

"But you said—"

"Never mind what I said earlier. Lots to do tomorrow and those bales aren't going to get stacked by themselves."

Grumbling under his breath, he wadded his napkin and followed Loretta into the kitchen where they set their dishes in the sink. On their way out, Clayton waved and said, "Sorry, folks. No arguing with the boss. See y'all later."

I ambled over to the picture window to watch them go and saw Felicity the cat sitting atop a fence post. They crossed the yard and disappeared into the barn while everyone else at the table continued eating and talking. Well, more eating than talking.

Since supper was so boring, I stayed where I was, alert for any move Felicity might make. When she finally budged, it was only to sink down and tuck her feet under her. Bathed in a sunbeam, she was as still as the statues in one of the parks Brandy and I used to visit in the big city, back before Grayson came into our lives. But after a while, even watching the cat got boring. I liked it when she hopped down from the post and trotted across the grass. When she did, I'd take off at a dead sprint and chase her up a tree. It was a great game, because it proved to Felicity that I was superior—she couldn't come down safely until I let her. Which was never. Then I'd bark at her and tell her to stay and never come down. That was usually when Grayson or Brandy would call me inside and spoil the fun, but that was beside the point.

I whined a little to see if anyone would let me out so I could provoke Felicity into a game of chase, but no one responded. Ever hopeful, I went to sit at Grayson's side. Unfortunately, even my most convincingly sad puppy dog eyes couldn't get his attention. I sank to the floor, sniffing for crumbs until my eyelids grew heavy.

When Mateo scooted his chair away from the table, I snapped to attention. He pulled his grandmother's chair back for her. She said something in her different words.

"*Mi abuela* says she is grateful for the meal," Mateo said, voice soft, chin lowered, "and she enjoyed your company."

As they headed for the door, Ynez elbowed him.

With a barely concealed sigh, Mateo added, "And she would like to repay the favor—maybe bring you lunch, some of her pork empanadas, or—"

"Don't worry about it," Grayson said, as he walked behind them. "No need to keep tabs. It was nice just having you over. I'm sure we'll do it again sometime."

Suddenly, Brandy was in front of them, blocking their path. It was amazing how fast she could maneuver those wheels of hers. Like a car without the noise or gas fumes.

"Ynez? Come to the kitchen with me. I want to ask you something about those churros you talked about Friday."

Ynez's forehead scrunched. "Churros?"

"*Sí*, churros." Brandy tipped her head toward the kitchen, then led her there.

Still standing by the door with Grayson, Mateo looked outside, then down at his feet.

"Why don't we wait on the porch?" Grayson said. "Nice breeze out there. This old house doesn't have AC."

After telling me to stay inside, Grayson opened the door and they went out to stand at the porch rail. Just as I was about to go check out things in the kitchen, Grayson spoke.

"I'm sorry about Coach Tervo. I really am."

Shrugging, Mateo dug his hands into his jeans pockets. "Thanks."

"Well"—Grayson moved away a couple of steps, as if to give Mateo space—"I just wanted to, you know, say it. Because I do understand what it's like to lose someone important to you unexpectedly."

A few seconds passed. Mateo glanced sideways at him. "Yeah, how?"

More seconds slipped by. It always took Grayson longer than Brandy, I'd noticed, to find the words he wanted. He inhaled deeply. "My best friend… He was hit by a car while we were out running together."

Now it was Grayson who looked down at his feet. "I'd say it was a mercy that he didn't suffer, since he died instantly, but… it doesn't matter. He was young. About to get engaged. We were in our final year of college. At the time, he meant more to me than anyone. I felt—I don't know—lost without him.'"

Plopping down on the top step, Mateo plucked a leaf from the hydrangea bush and twirled it between his fingers. "Did you go back to running after that?"

"No. Not until last year. And then I only ran because"—he looked at me, one eyebrow arched—"*that* dog was driving me insane. I had to run some energy out of her. I hadn't realized until then how much I missed running."

Something in Mateo stiffened then. Resisted. The leaf fell to the ground as he clenched his fist. "I'm going to wait in the car." He rose. Took a few steps. Turned around. Looked at Grayson directly for the first time that evening. "I'll be there."

Grayson blinked. "What?"

"Practice. Tomorrow."

"Oh… good. But I wasn't asking about—"

"My grandmother told me if I want to keep my job at the car lot, I have to keep running. That I should work something out with you. If it's possible."

"Sure. No problem. Should be easy to manage in the summer. School year will be a little trickier, but we can work something out."

Behind me, feet clacked across the old wooden planks of the dining room into the living room.

Mateo started to go.

"Hey, Mateo." Grayson waited until he turned back around. Which took a moment. "Eight a.m. at the park. See you there."

Brandy opened the door for Ynez then, and I rushed out, grabbing a Frisbee from under a bush next to the stairs. My prize held high, I raced over the sidewalk, veered around Mateo, and sat just as he reached for the car door handle.

169

He pulled his hand back. "You can't come with us. Move."

I sneezed. Wiggled. Nudged him with the disc.

"She just wants attention," Brandy called from the porch. "If you pet her, she'll be happy."

"Oh." Slowly—somewhat reluctantly, I sensed—Mateo stroked the top of my head. But not for long. "Okay, now move. I need to get in."

I bumped his hand with the disc. I couldn't make this any more obvious. He was sad. And a little mad. Although I didn't understand why.

"Sorry," Brandy said, "she's relentless. Sooner, come here, girl."

I purposefully ignored her. There were times when a person needed to love on a dog. Or just play. Not that I could make all their troubles go away, but this boy seemed to have more than his fair share.

He made a move like he was going to knee me out of the way. I jumped back, bowed. Rolled over. Leaped to my feet. Growled and thrashed my head from side to side, as if playing an invisible game of tug. It wasn't until I stopped, panting as I caught my breath, that I noticed Ynez reaching out for the disc. I hadn't paid attention to her approach. The moment her small, gnarled hand clamped the edge, I let go.

She said something I didn't understand, then pointed toward the open lawn beyond a row of shade trees. She drew her hand across her body and cocked it back.

I launched myself in the direction her shoulders were pointing. She flung her hand forward. Not gracefully, but she had the general motion right. The disc lofted. Not fast. Not far. But it had caught a burst of wind and for a moment seemed to float. I tracked its ascent. Judged its arc. Slowed, waited, watched. Jumped. Stretched my neck. Snapped my jaws.

As I landed on a cushion of grass and pivoted back, the disc in my mouth, Ynez clapped.

Mateo, I noticed, was smiling, too.

Not so much at me, maybe, as at his grandmother. It didn't matter why, anyway. Just that he had.

—o00o—

It was the perfect end to a perfect day—lying on the porch, the sun's fading rays warm on my face, my humans talking softly as the porch swing creaked. Brandy, I'd noticed, had been kicking her feet gently to help rock the swing. Not much, but she seemed to delight in it. Her legs were getting stronger.

"Hey, guess who's dating who?" Grayson said.

Brandy shook her head. "No idea. Who?"

"Tucker and Gertie."

"Seriously?!" Brandy slapped Grayson's thigh lightly. "I'm so happy for them!"

"Yeah, me, too. Nice, isn't it? Wonder how those two got together."

Brandy did a little dance with her upper body, making the swing wobble. "I might've told Tucker about the best muffins on the planet and suggested he get himself some."

"Well, that's your good deed for the year." He handed Brandy her lemonade. "May they have a happy and lasting relationship."

They clinked glasses and sipped.

Over by the barn, Clayton's truck roared to life. The truck doors slammed shut and he and Loretta left for their home.

"Say, did you notice anything different," Brandy said, "about Loretta tonight?"

"Not in particular. Why?"

"Well, after Ynez and Mateo first sat down at the table, Loretta was helping me in the kitchen and she asked if they were illegals."

"What did you say?"

"I asked her what difference it would make."

"And she said what?"

"She muttered something then about their kind taking money under the table and not paying taxes. I told her Ynez and I had actually had a discussion about that this week—how she keeps track of the income from all her jobs and has her friend Gabriella help her fill out her taxes every year and that since she's partially self-employed, she has to set money aside to pay those taxes. And that at her hotel job, they certainly do take out taxes—even though she's not entitled to any social security." Setting her glass aside, Brandy expelled a heavy sigh. "It just made me so mad. I had to set her straight. It was all I could do not to raise my voice. I didn't want Ynez or Mateo to overhear us."

"And did she say anything about it after that?"

"No."

"Good."

"I hate it when people assume things like that when they don't have their facts straight."

Grayson kissed her cheek. "Well, I love it that you came to Ynez's defense. Maybe Loretta didn't know any better."

Brandy shrugged. "Maybe. Sometimes, though, I think people just want easy answers. They want to blame someone for whatever they think isn't going right in their lives. Put them in a box they can clearly define so they don't have to stretch their imagination too far. So they resort to anger instead of compassion and grace."

"Sadly, there's probably a lot of truth to that."

They swung a while more before Brandy spoke again. "Grayson, I have to ask you something."

"Sounds serious. Do I want to hear it?"

"I think we *have* to talk about it. Your ex-wife…"

"Ah, yes. Fiona." He slid his arm around her and she leaned into

172

him. "You want to know what happened between us."

"I probably ought to, don't you think?"

"I suppose you deserve that much." He took a few breaths before continuing. The chains of the swing groaned as they swayed forward and back. "How do you think people judge you—as a woman?"

"What do you mean?"

"Like, how do you think other women define you as… worthy, successful, that sort of thing?"

"Oh. As a woman? I guess by what I'm wearing, whether I have good hair, if I have nice curves—but not too curvy. People probably wondered why, at over forty, I wasn't already married with kids. What are you getting at?"

"Do you judge yourself that way?"

"No!" Then, more gently, "Well… maybe a little. I guess that's why I immersed myself in competing with my dogs. I didn't have to think about any of those things if I kept busy. So how do guys judge each other?"

"By how much money we make, what our job is, how high up the ladder we've climbed… Those are the big things, but there are others."

"So, you immersed yourself in your work?"

"I did. To the detriment of my marriage. My work became my identity. Even when I came home, my mind was still in the office. I was in charge of multimillion-dollar loans and worked with some shrewd business people. There was a lot of pressure. I couldn't be bothered with whether or not I personally liked someone. No taking risks on someone who didn't have the capital to back it up. It was all about the bottom line." He placed his hand over hers. "But that's no excuse for what I did to Fee. I… I neglected her, plain and simple. Forgot to appreciate everything that had made me fall in love with her in the first place. I thought if I could secure one more deal, make

173

a little more money, set us up for a cozy retirement… Stupid of me, really. She deserved better."

There was a long silence. I almost fell asleep.

Then Brandy spoke barely above a whisper. "Do you still…? Do you ever…?"

"Do I ever what—think of her? Do I still love her? I care about her, yes. I wonder how she's doing. If she's healthy and happy. I'm grateful she was in my life—and for a short time we were happy together. Then, I changed. For selfish reasons. Not out of meanness. Just mindlessness, really. I had my reasons, however shortsighted they were. She kept trying to reel me back in, but I'd stopped listening, stopped making the effort. Stopped letting her know when I was worried or stressed or… a lot of things. In short, I put up a wall, trying to appear stronger than I was." They rocked back and forth some more. "She got remarried, did I tell you?"

"Yeah, I think so." Brandy sat up straighter. "So how did you eventually figure this all out?"

"Not by myself. I had… have a good therapist—Dr. Philipot. At first, I dreaded every session. Yet I knew I had to understand how I got where I was, so I could move on and learn how to do better."

"You still talk to him or her—your therapist?"

"Him, and yes. Just not as often these days. More of a check-in to make sure I'm still doing okay."

"And are you?"

"Yeah, I am. I really, really am." He lifted her hand and kissed her knuckles. "Mental health is highly underrated. If we all spent more time getting our heads in a better place, we could solve half the world's problems."

They snuggled closer and I knew all was right in my world. I had no more jobs to do today. Not even chasing Felicity the cat. She was probably asleep in the barn rafters. The crickets were chirping like crazy. Over by the pond, the bullfrogs were bellowing. And in the barn—

Thud, thud… thud.

"Goliath?" Brandy went still. "Or Clifford?"

Thud, thud.

"More likely Persephone, judging by the insistent frequency." Grayson dragged his feet over the planks to stop the swing. He listened some more. "Yep, that's her. Apparently, Loretta forgot to remove the feed bucket from her stall. I don't know why Persephone does that."

"She's hoping you'll fill it up again."

Grayson laughed. "I suppose so." He patted Brandy's knee. "Wait here. I'll take care of it. Back in a few."

I thought about following Grayson as he rose and started down the steps—after all, the cat probably needed reminding of where her place was just in case she was roaming the aisle between the stalls—but I was enjoying just lazing next to Brandy. So I shut my eyes, listening to the gentle creak of the swing as Brandy swayed to get it going again.

"Agh!"

My heart jumped. I sat up, peering into the silvery light of dusk.

Why was Grayson lying on the ground?

"Honey?" Brandy called. "Are you okay?"

Grayson groaned. He was flat on his back, fingers clawing at tufts of grass. "I'll live… I think."

Worried, I ran to him. Brandy would've had to somehow get herself into her wheelchair, then into the house and out the back door down the ramp. Even then, Grayson wasn't on the sidewalk or in the driveway. He'd taken the shortcut across the lawn toward the barn.

"Do you need help?" Brandy said from the porch swing. "Do I need to call Clayton and Loretta? They can't be more than a few miles down the road."

Grayson hadn't so much as moved. He was just circling one

foot, then the other, more slowly. Grimacing, he sucked in air. I stood over him, unsure of what to do.

Then, "No, I don't think so. Just tweaked my ankle. Give me a few."

"Are you sure?"

He didn't answer right away. So I snuffled at his ear.

"Stop it," he muttered angrily.

"What?!"

"Nothing! Just... Yeah, I'm sure."

I licked his face to encourage him to get up. Sputtering, he grabbed my jowls in both hands.

"All right, all right." After swatting me back, he wedged an elbow beneath him and sat up. A strained look on his face, he reached toward one ankle and probed it. "Well, crap. Just... crap."

"Grayson? I'm calling them."

"No, don't! I'm coming." He pulled one leg underneath him and pushed up with both hands. When he stood, though, all his weight was on one leg.

It took a long time for Grayson to hobble back to the porch. The moment he got to the top step and collapsed, I curled around him and slipped under his arm to hold him up. And so he could hug me.

Somehow, Brandy had managed to situate herself in her wheelchair. She joined us. "You don't look okay."

"I will be... eventually." His breath tickled the top of my head as he rested his chin there.

Brandy, in turn, ran her fingers through his fuzz of short, graying hair. "Sprained, you think?"

"Maybe. Probably."

"I did that once during an agility trial. Tripped over the end of the dog walk. Ankle swelled up like a cantaloupe. Turned a pretty shade of purple, then eventually greenish-yellow. Anyway, I'll bring

176

you some ice water—"

"Brandy? What about Sooner?"

"Sorry, I don't follow you. There's nothing wrong with her, is there? She was lying up here with me when you—"

"I won't be able to run for a few days. Maybe longer, even. I don't think I can wear her out enough just throwing a ball."

"Doesn't seem like it'll be a problem."

"Huh? But she—"

"Grayson, you coach a whole team of runners. Sooner loves to run; she loves kids. Figure it out."

chapter 15
Mateo

Mateo wasn't sure how he'd get through this season, let alone his first day back at practice.

The ride there had been stonily silent—his grandmother clenching the steering wheel, staring ahead. She'd said very little, except, "Do what your new coach tells you to, Mateo. It will be a good year. You'll see."

Inwardly, he scoffed. He'd show up. When he could. But his heart was no longer in it. He had more important matters to worry about. Far more important. Besides, Grayson Darling was nothing like Coach Tervo. It would never be the same.

"Hey, man." Dusty pounded him on the shoulder. "Glad to see you're over your senioritis. Welcome back."

Even though it was still five minutes until the start of practice, everyone was already there. Bucket and Keen waved in greeting. Cruz nodded.

Lou, leaning against the mottled trunk of a sycamore tree, smiled. "Mateo... hi."

As far as Mateo could recall, it was the first time she'd ever spoken to him. He hadn't realized until then how blue her eyes were.

For the first time in many days, his heart beat stronger. He looked away.

A small SUV entered the parking lot. Less than a minute later, Grayson got out. With a pair of crutches. And his dog. Or Brandy's dog. He wasn't clear on that.

Sooner, a little wary of the crutches, skulked alongside him as he hobbled toward the picnic tables.

"What happened, Coach?" Keen asked.

"I stepped in a hole, but in my defense, it was getting dark." Grinning, Grayson added, "Guess I should've come up with a better story on the way over."

They told him he was a klutz. That many of them had done worse. That it didn't look all that bad.

Lou brought her fists to her chest in a dramatic gesture. "You were rappelling on El Capitan and the lines snapped just as you were about to reach the summit, causing you to land on a cliff edge and have to wait eight hours for a chopper rescue, right?"

"Something like that." Grayson winked.

"Bet he robbed a liquor store," Cruz joked, "and tripped over his laces right before the po-po busted him. You got an ankle bracelet on?"

Laughter rippled through the team. Grayson dropped the dog's leash while he took attendance. Sooner made a beeline for Mateo. Curling behind his legs, she nudged at the back of his kneecaps with her nose. It was hard—she nearly knocked him off balance twice—but he ignored her. He just wanted to get this first run over with.

"Hey there, Sooner." Dusty squatted down to scratch behind Sooner's ears. Then to Grayson, "Regular loop twice?"

"Sure. Two quick loops for Groups A and B. C and D, just one." He called his dog to him. "Afterward, we'll throw some strides and core in. Get to it."

Mateo headed for the trail at the wood's edge.

"Mateo… wait," Grayson called.

He turned. His group was waiting nearby. Same guys, same routine. Just like always.

"Come here." Grayson beckoned.

Tentative, Mateo approached him.

Grayson held the dog's leash out. "Take her with you, will you?"

"Excuse me?" Mateo wasn't sure he understood. *Take the dog? Where?*

"On your run," Grayson said, as if reading his mind. "I can't run with her myself, obviously. Won't be able to for a couple of weeks, maybe. Brandy suggested I let one of you kids run some energy out of her."

"Maybe someone else could—"

"No, you. She likes you." He placed the leash in Mateo's hand and stepped back. Sooner took one look at Grayson, then ambled the few steps to sit at Mateo's feet. "See, she's ready to go."

"I've…" He stared at the leash handle as it lay across his palm. Nothing but a thin strip of nylon with a loop on one end and the dog on the other. "I've never run with a dog before. What if she trips me, or pulls away, or—"

"She won't. She knows better. She's an old pro at this. Now go on. You'll make her day."

The dog? He'd given him the dog to run with? Why? Was this some sort of punishment?

Softly, Mateo began, "I don't think I—"

But as Mateo looked up from his hand, Grayson had already moved away. He was over by the picnic tables now, talking to some of the girls, offering them encouragement, laughing with them.

"You coming?" Dusty asked.

Golden green eyes gazed up at Mateo, plied away the layers of his resistance. Tugged at his heart.

"Sure." And with that, they were off. Down the trail that led to the river. Dozens of shoes and four paws flying over rich earth. Arms swinging. A bobtail wagging. Hearts happy. All but Mateo's, which was still feeling the weight of having lost his mentor.

—oO0o—

Days became weeks. It wasn't so much that Coach Grayson had picked Mateo to exercise the dog. Or even that he, Mateo, had *asked* to run with the dog.

The dog had picked him.

The first few times, Mateo would try to hand the leash back to Grayson, but Sooner was mesmerized by him, as if only he could lead her to the portal that would take her on some fantastic journey. Always, at some point during their runs, he would look down at the dog and she would look up at him, and when their eyes met there was a spark, a connection… as if they had met a long time ago—not just weeks.

Her presence, however, brought with it a sense of normalcy. Peace, even. The summer that had been punctuated with Tervo's loss was unexpectedly transformed—at least for the couple of hours a day he was at practice, running with a borrowed dog. Anger and uncertainty retreated. Not entirely gone, but less of a constant. He began to look forward to their time together. Sooner didn't judge him for the color of his skin. Didn't care if he was popular or accomplished. It didn't matter to her if he was drowning in money or had none at all.

As the days blurred together toward summer's end, he arrived at practice one morning feeling more energized than he had in weeks. The air was abnormally cool and a brisk wind rattled the leaves overhead. Here and there, a few leaden clouds blotted the sky.

Grayson glanced up, then took out his phone and made a few

swipes. "Ack!" He beckoned to Dusty and to Lou, who he'd recently named the boys' and girls' captains. "It's looking dicey. There's a front coming in, but I think we have some time. One time round the river loop, okay? I know it's not our normal routine for this day of the week, but make sure everyone understands."

Nodding in agreement, they relayed the information to the different groups.

Three miles into their run, Mateo pulled away from his teammates. The cooler temperatures had invigorated both him and Sooner—her breathing hard but not labored—and he was having a hard time holding her back. He'd expected running with a dog to be awkward. That she would weave back and forth or bolt at every squirrel or bird within eyesight. While she was aware of the wildlife around them, she gave no indication that she was going to leave his side. Eventually, he'd tucked the leash into his waistband like he'd seen Grayson do. It was like running alongside his own shadow.

The dog looked happy. Deliriously happy.

"You like this running, eh?"

She glanced at him, a hint of a smile in her cheeks.

"Want to go faster?"

She sneezed and he took that as a yes.

With a thrust of his knees, Mateo charge up a short hill on the wooded path, veering away from the river. Her easy trot switched to a spirited gallop. His muscles burning from the effort, Mateo eased up on the downside of the hill. His heart banged inside his chest. When his breathing had slowed again and they came to another hill, he charged up it. Again, Sooner bounded after him. They did this game a few more times. Fartlek, Tervo had called it. Another word for speedplay. It wasn't part of today's workout plan, but a spontaneous exhilarating event.

A stiff wind blew at Mateo's face, pushed at his chest in resistance, and he slowed. The dog was finally looking tired. So was he. A good kind of tired.

To his right, the undergrowth stirred. Twigs cracked. A blurry shadow skulked behind tree trunks, then darted beneath the cover of a thorny bush, the ragged plume of its tail betraying its location. A wild animal of some sort. Watching, following. Mateo thought he glimpsed a pair of eyes, oddly familiar. When Sooner hopped over a low fallen branch, his own eyes swung back to the trail before him. He searched again for the animal, but found no sign. Still, he couldn't quite shake an uneasiness in his gut that warned him to remain vigilant. Maybe it was only a flood of adrenalin from running fast on a trail alone where footing was treacherous.

When he was very young and his spirit was plagued by the insults of bullies, he used to run hard like this. As fast as he could, as far as he could. No clock, no prescribed distance or sets of intervals at defined paces. Just ran to feel the earth fly beneath his feet, to sense his blood rushing through his veins, his muscles contracting to deliver their power, lungs drawing in precious air...

Just ahead, a narrow path veered away. He followed it, his pace now steady, not pressed.

"We can sit on the bluff for a few minutes, okay, Sooner? You can see forever from up there."

The trail was narrow. Too narrow for her to run beside him without a branch lashing at her eye. Mateo paused to unclip her leash. He would put her back on leash when they came down. It was no more than a couple hundred yards from where they stood. He tried to shoo her ahead of him, but she hesitated. So he went on ahead, glancing back and speaking to her in encouragement as she trailed after him.

"*¡Rápido! ¡Apúrate!*"

Although unsure why he'd spoken to the dog in Spanish, he shrugged it off. Usually, he only did so when with his grandmother. But for some reason, now, it seemed right. Running with Sooner, he could be entirely himself, no pretenses.

When he was at the top of the bluff, Mateo would always sit alone on the rocky overhang to take in the view. From there he could look down on the treetops, see the rolling hills interrupting a deep valley. Through the valley wound a shallow river with a stone-littered bed. At places, he could glimpse the reflection of the sky upon the water. Others knew about the bluff. He'd heard boyfriends and girlfriends sometimes came here to kiss, although he knew nothing of such things firsthand.

His mind jumped to Lou. The way the sun lit fire to the reddish-brown of her hair. The smattering of freckles on her nose. The way one eyebrow was higher than the other and her mouth tilted like she had a secret to tell. She'd been saying hi to him first thing every day. Heat spreading from his chest to his neck, he'd always look away. He wasn't sure what he thought of her. Why was he even thinking of her now?

He went partway up the trail. Slowed. Gazed into the emerald wilderness. Glowering clouds, heavy with the threat of rain, hovered above the treetops. The wind tangled his hair, tossed it across his eyes. All around, leaves rattled furiously, as if they might be stripped from their branches at any moment. He thought he heard—but wasn't sure—the faint rumble of thunder. If they were going to get to the top and back to base camp, they'd have to be quick.

Eager to beat the storm, he started up the trail again. The cool air scrubbing at his face was exhilarating, heightening his senses.

To him the bluff was a special place. Like sitting on top of the world. A place where words could do no harm. Where fear and prejudice were unknown. Where peace and beauty were one, indivisible. A place where he could dream of his future and imagine what could be. If he had the—

The sky flickered. Clouds bellowed. His bones jangled.

He glanced beside him, then behind. She was there. Hanging

back. As if warning him.

Time to turn back. They would have to perch upon the bluff some other day.

chapter 16
Sooner

I lifted my nose. Smelled earth and dampness and the looming threat of rain.

Ahead of me ran Mateo. His arms swung rhythmically, his shoes barely touching the ground. He glanced over his shoulder at me.

"*¡Rápido! ¡Apúrate!*"

I hurried to catch up, digging my claws into soft dirt, my speed increasing with each stride. We ran hard over the narrow trail beneath a tangled archway of tree limbs. The path had climbed and dipped over a series of hills and diverged several times, yet we were steadily going upward. I didn't know this trail, but I felt Mateo's excitement, his love for running.

This must be what it was like, I thought, to be a bird gliding across the sky or a deer bounding across a field, unhindered and free.

Just as we reached a place where the trees opened up, lightning flashed in the distance. The skin beneath my fur prickled. The air vibrated, rumbled. Something deep within me warned of a danger I didn't fully understand. Find safety, it commanded, but stay *with* him.

Go back, I wanted to tell him. *This isn't safe.*

He glanced my way, wheeled around, and started back. Urgency consumed me.

Faster and faster we went, down, down, down, loose earth sliding beneath us, branches whipping at us, the sky alternating light and dark.

Just as he veered onto the main trail, his eyes again met mine for the briefest of moments. Then his toes caught beneath a root. His chest continued forward. His hands flew out before him. His body hit the ground hard.

I rushed to him.

"*Basta, basta, basta.*" He swatted me away as he tried to raise himself up on an elbow. His face contorted in agony. Moaning in pain, he collapsed, then rolled to his side as he drew one arm in protectively.

Concern filled me. Nothing to offer but comfort, I licked his face.

"*Pronto, mi amigo. Pronto.*"

Again, my skin tingled. The fur lifted from my neck. I backed away from him.

The boom and the flash came as one.

The world around me faded.

—o0Oo—

Lean arms held me tight. I wasn't sure if it was another's heartbeat or mine I felt, just that when I opened my eyes, Mateo was gazing at me with grave concern.

"Coach! Coach!" Mateo called. "The lightning… I think it struck her."

Carrying me, he walked slowly now. I looked around. Saw nothing but fuzzy images—tree branches crisscrossing a gray sky, faces bobbing and blending. Every stride jarred me. My body buzzed from the inside out, from the tip of my nose to the nub of my tail. My thoughts were scattered, my attention darting, fading...

Mateo stumbled and winced, his hold on me slipping. I snapped to awareness, gripped back panic, even though my limbs were numb and limp. Mateo shifted my weight in his arms and clutched me tighter.

Footsteps slapped over the earth toward us.

His face dripping with rain, Grayson gazed down at me, stroked my cheek. "Is she okay?"

"I don't know, I don't know." Mateo's voice trembled. "Just stunned, I think."

Faraway, thunder rolled, the sound going on and on like the roar of a receding train. Like the one that had chased me over the bridge when I was lost and alone.

Is this all a terrible dream? A memory?

"Put her in the back of my car, Mateo," Grayson said, his voice muffled by the static in my ears. "We'll take her to Doc Hunter."

Other faces pressed inward, but Grayson muttered commands and they went away, piling into waiting cars.

His own face grimacing in pain, Mateo laid me on the back seat of Grayson's SUV.

The doors closed. The engine started. Wipers slapped at the front window.

Thwop-thwop-thwop.

Rain pounded on the car roof. I was sure it would cave in and I'd drown in the deluge.

I tried to keep my eyes open, but it was hard. So hard. My body felt light and heavy all at once. I focused on lifting my head, but couldn't. My legs were still attached—I could see my feet dangling over the edge of the seat, felt them tingling. So why couldn't I move them?

"Everyone else was back fifteen minutes ago." Grayson sounded so far away. "What took you so long?"

"We took the bluff spur." Mateo's voice was small, faint. He was in the passenger seat, but he, too, sounded distant. "She had so much energy today, it was cooler... I'm sorry. It was wrong to—"

"I was worried, that's all. It's just... you're supposed to keep to the route I tell you to take. That's for a reason."

"I know," Mateo said. Then in a whisper I could barely hear, "I'm sorry. Sorry."

"It's not your fault the storm came in faster than predicted. Maybe I should have canceled practice—or at least told you all to be back in thirty minutes."

"It *was* my fault. I went too far."

"It wasn't. I don't want to hear any more. You're okay. Sooner will be okay..." Then more softly, "I hope."

The wipers clubbed at the windshield.

Whack-whack-whack-whack.

"*Are* you all right?" Grayson asked. "You've been holding your arm protectively ever since you got in the car."

"I... fell."

"Hurt something?"

"My shoulder a little."

"After we take Sooner to Doc Hunter's, we can stop by the urgent care place just east of Faderville. They can take a look at you. Maybe do an X-ray, just to make sure nothing's broken, but speaking from experience, even a tendon or muscle tear can—"

"I'm fine. Really. It's just a little sore. Some ice at home, I'll be fine."

"We'll see how far you can move your arm when..."

They spoke more, but their words had blended together, voices indistinguishable as I drifted off to sleep. Took refuge in the soft, sweet darkness of my dreams.

—o00o—

In my dream—and I knew it was a dream, a very *real* dream, only because I woke up eventually—I ran free in a wide-open place beneath a startlingly blue sky. It was not a green land like the place we lived that Brandy always referred to as Kentucky. In Kentucky during the warm months, there was always birdsong and the buzz of insects. So many that they all overlapped. Here, the sounds were sparse. It was a land of browns and reds, of short, stubby plants with prickly thorns and clumps of dry grasses and thorny bushes with waxy leaves.

The earth was gritty and sharp beneath my paws as I ran, loping endlessly. My belly was taut, hunger stabbing at my insides. Between bare hills wound a river, and there the trees stood, huddled like thirsty cattle at a trough in summer. I ran toward it, not only to sate my own thirst, but because there was a group of people headed there on foot. I had learned in my wanderings that people often left food behind when they trekked through this barren land and eating their scraps was easier than hunting for my food. So I would follow one group a ways, then find another.

I was wary of people, though. Many had guns. I'd been shot at. Never hit, but I sensed the danger. Knew that guns could kill.

This time, however, was different. There was a young boy in the group. A boy with brown wavy hair and dark eyes. I could read something in those eyes. His soul calling to me. A plea. Fear.

And so I followed. Ever watchful. Alert.

There were men in the group I didn't trust. The ones with guns. But I didn't just fear them for that reason. I feared for the boy and his mother. That the men might hurt them. The men's voices were gruff and they laughed too loudly. Their eyes darted suspiciously, as if they didn't quite trust one another. They kept guard over the food and ate before the women and children. They told them what to do—

and not in a kind way.

Day after day I followed and watched. Night after night, too, because they often moved when the sun went down. I followed long after I would normally have left. The boy began to hide food. I knew he was leaving it for me because he would often sit near the edge of their camp whenever they stopped and watch me as he ate. But some of the food he always tucked into his pants pockets and I would later find it under a rock or in a hole after they had gone.

Finally one day, mechanical birds flew overhead with people inside. People obviously looking for the group I had been following. As soon as they heard the birds, the wanderers ran for a rocky ravine and hid, crammed elbow to elbow beneath low overhanging rocks.

All except for the boy and his mother. They had fallen behind because the boy had had to use the bathroom. A bearded man with a big stomach yanked them into a tangle of bushes in a low place.

My head low, I crept to where they were lying—the boy, his mother, and the man. The boy was crying. Not soft sniffles, but great wailing sobs. His mother shook in fright. She whispered frantically to her son, but he would not be consoled. The *thwop-thwop-thwop* of the mechanical bird's wings grew louder as it drifted their way, hovering then darting, like some giant hummingbird in search of nectar.

The bearded man drew a gun from his waistband, pressed it to the mother's temple, and muttered terse words. Eyes aghast, she shook her head and yanked the boy closer as she tried to shush him. But he went on crying.

A soft click sounded from the man's gun as he moved the aim of the barrel from her head to the boy's face.

She covered her son's mouth with one hand, the other pressing the underside of his jaw closed so he could not cry out. "He will kill you," she said. "And then he will kill me. Stop, Mateo. *Please... stop.*"

Mateo?

191

I moved closer to crouch behind a small rock. The boy must've seen my tail on the other side, because he glanced there, then at me.

I am here, I whimpered. *Be still. Quiet.*

Mateo sobbed once more, as if he couldn't hold it back. Then he went very still, his gaze now locked on my face. His tears slid down over her fingers, dropped onto the dirt to leave dark stains.

They lay like that a very long time. Until the big bird was gone and the rest of the group had begun to trickle from beneath their hiding place to search the sky. Mateo's mother watched them begin to move on. Her glance, questioning, flicked to the bearded man.

The bearded man muttered to her words I could not hear, but their message was clear: *Stay where you are.*

Closing her eyes, she trembled visibly, then drew her son closer to kiss the top of his head.

By now, I had crawled so far forward I was out in the open. But the man paid no attention to me. He waited until the rest of the group was long out of sight, then he got to his knees, stood, and, with his fingers wound in her long black hair, began to pull Mateo's mother to her feet. She let out a short shriek before the man kicked at her.

I bolted forward, overcome with purpose. Loose rocks skittered from beneath my paws as I dashed toward them. The man jerked his head my way.

In the moment his eyes met mine, I knew I had to risk it all. I went for the arm with which he held the gun. Leaped through the air. Opened my mouth wide.

"No!" he shouted.

I heard the pop of the gun. Smelled the tang of its metal. Saw a small object propelled from its narrow barrel.

Fire stabbed my chest.

My teeth connected with the meaty flesh of his arm, just below the elbow. My body impacted with his, taking us down in a frantic tumble. The gun fell from his grasp, clattered down a short slope. I

192

was still latched onto his arm as we rolled, vaguely aware of Mateo's mother snatching her small son by the waist and rushing away.

Somewhere in the scuffle, the bearded man shoved me away. I snapped at him, but when I tried to raise myself up to bite at his bulky calves, my legs gave way. Pain pierced my heart.

"Caesar!" Another voice called from atop a short mound not far away. "Enough! Let's go. The truck is waiting."

From then on, I recalled nothing but a gray watery image of Mateo in his mother's arms looking back at me as I lay there helpless, my life slowly bleeding onto the desert floor.

—o0Oo—

It was the strangest thing. I could see… but I couldn't see. There was a crack. A flash of light. My insides buzzing. All at once.

Everything was white. Like a blinding snowstorm without the snow. Or more like a thick, bright fog. I couldn't tell if I was upright or lying down. I only knew my feet were not touching earth. I was just… there, staring through the mist, waiting for it to clear, for the static in my brain to settle. And then… I was floating, surrounded by warmth, the sound of a racing heartbeat distant in my ears. Soon, voices buzzed faintly, as if coming to me through a long tunnel.

I don't know how long it went on like that—the whiteness, the sounds coming and going, the floating… It was being alive, but thoughtless. Still living, but outside my bodily form. I neither loved nor hated it. I was not afraid. I just… was.

Yet all the while that I was aware of my earthly form, I was also somewhere else. Sometime not that long ago.

Fuzzy shapes shifted, defined. I was looking down on them and yet I was everywhere. One shape drew my attention—that of a small boy, eyes overflowing with tears. He was sobbing, in that shuddery way small children do, crying out for comfort. His mother embraced

193

him from behind. They were lying on the rocky ground beneath the shade of an overhang.

Ah, I remembered now. I wish I hadn't. Because I died that day. But I didn't stop existing. Angels never did. They just took on different forms, showed up when they were needed.

They were everywhere. If you just knew what to look for.

—o0Oo—

The white light brightened. Buzzed. Struggled. Dimmed to a halo. The shadow of a human form hovered above me, outlined in a rainbow.

"She'll be all right," Doc Hunter said. I remembered him from when Grayson found me in the horse barn in the stall next to Goliath's. "Blood work was normal, vitals are... stable." Then to someone behind him. "You can bring them in now."

Footsteps. Two more forms. One, a grown boy, hanging back, heavy with guilt. Mateo. The other, dripping with relief. Grayson.

I drifted back to sleep. Returned to my dreams. Of running beneath a desert sun. Following a young boy with dark hair and fear-filled eyes. Watching him as he watched me.

Lying there, adrift in dreams, I came to understand... even the bad times can lead to good. If I kept searching. If I gave up resisting and simply allowed it to be.

And I knew, eventually, everything would be all right. In its own way.

Even if I had to wait a lifetime.

chapter 17
Mateo

Like the short clips in a movie trailer, the memory had returned in flashes. Snippets of moving pictures, snatches of spoken word, surges of terror. The longer Mateo stood there watching Sooner fight for her life, the more it all came back to him. He hadn't remembered any of it before, but he knew it was real, even though the details were still fuzzy. The man named Caesar had threatened to kill him if his mother didn't agree to go with him later. After coming to Kentucky, he'd heard his mother talking on the phone to someone named Caesar, but hadn't made the connection until now. Hadn't even remembered the man, really. He'd blocked it out to keep from reliving that day over and over.

He understood now why his mother had left and who she'd gone to. What he didn't understand was why, when she had her own mother here and a home. And him.

Mateo stood with his back to the wall as the veterinarian, Dr. Hunter McHugh, examined Sooner. The dog was lying on a shiny metal table, her eyes hazy with the pull of sleep, her breathing still shallow and rapid.

The vet pressed his stethoscope to her chest. Several seconds later, he shined a penlight into her pupils. She lifted her head and licked his hand. "Still stable. Just more than a bit stunned. I can't venture to guess how many volts of electricity shot through her body, but from what I can tell not enough to do any major damage. No burns, just a few singed hairs on her back. Her heart sounds strong, no arrhythmia... That's the most important thing."

"So she'll make a full recovery?" Grayson, standing on the near side of the table, squeezed her back paw lightly.

"She's practically there." Doc Hunter, as Grayson called him, nodded toward Mateo. "Good thing this young man was there to carry her back."

Shame flooded Mateo's chest. He hung his head. If he hadn't gone so far with her, if he'd been paying better attention to the skies, to the signals she was trying to send him—

"See, Mateo"—Grayson placed a hand on his shoulder—"she's going to be fine. Just fine."

"She..." Mateo thought back to his earliest memories of journeying through the desert, of the ghost dog that had saved him and his mother from death. He'd felt something inexplicable when he first met Sooner. Now he understood. "She saved me."

Grayson's brow scrunched. "You mean you saved *her*."

As he pushed away from the wall, Mateo's left arm throbbed from his shoulder to his elbow. He went to her. Lowered himself to his knees.

"I'm here," he whispered. "Be still."

Sooner closed her eyes, sneezed softly, her cheeks bunching into the vaguest of smiles.

He sensed it then—that connection of souls. A knowing. The same thing he'd felt toward Fantasma in the desert all those years ago. This time, however, she'd rescued him in a much less overt way. This time she'd returned his joy to him, his passion. Brought him back to the present and reminded him of all of life's gifts.

"I only wanted to see the view from the bluff… to show her. It was wrong. I shouldn't have…" He let his words trail away.

Grayson touched him once more between the shoulder blades. "Hey, everything turned out fine. You're both okay."

How was it that Grayson wasn't angry with him? Tervo probably would've been. He was with himself, anyway. Next time he'd be more careful. If there was a next time.

The weight of everything pressed down on him, tightened his chest. Mateo felt so many things all at once: ashamed, grateful, afraid, overwhelmed, hopeful… connected.

Connected. The past to the present. A father he never knew. His journey through the desert with his mother. A mother he barely had contact with now. What had happened to her? Why could she not come home and be with him and *abuela*? And more recently—Tervo, the coach who had made him believe he could be someone extraordinary, and now Grayson, who made him feel… he wasn't sure. But he'd give it some time. See what came of it.

—o0Oo—

When Grayson turned right instead of left out of the veterinary clinic parking lot, panic momentarily seized Mateo.

"My home's on Rockhill." He pointed behind them. "That way."

Rain was coming down lightly now, but water was still flowing across the road. The creeks would be full by sundown.

"I know." Glancing in the rearview mirror, Grayson checked his speed as they hit a puddle. Sooner was sitting up in her crate in the back, awake and alert, although wobbly. "The urgent care place is only a few miles away. We can get you checked out and home in time for supper."

Mateo never invited anyone to his house. For one, his

grandmother wasn't home much and he didn't like questions about where she or his parents were. Second, even if she'd been there, she didn't like visitors she couldn't talk with. And third, the place was practically falling down. He didn't want anyone looking down on them or pitying him because they were poor. He'd rather they just know about him based on his grades and his running accomplishments. He didn't want to be judged otherwise.

Besides, there was the matter of his citizenship—or lack thereof. He'd been to the doctor before, but that was before more recent changes. He didn't want to take the risk.

"I'm fine. Really. You can take me home."

Grayson arched a skeptical eyebrow at him. "The last hour and a half you haven't so much as raised your hand above hip level. I've seen you grimace more than once, Mateo. You're not as good at hiding it as you think."

"It's not broken." Mateo flexed his fingers, his wrist, his elbow—anything that didn't make him want to scream out in pain. "Just a little bruised. That's all."

"If you're injured we need to get it looked at. I don't want anything serious to go untreated. I need all my runners healthy. And I'm not just saying that because you're state champ. I'd tell you that if you were the slowest kid on the team."

As much as Mateo wanted to be thankful for his concern, he couldn't go anywhere there was paperwork to be filled out. He didn't want to call attention to himself. "Please, take me home. We don't have any way to pay for it."

He prayed that would be enough. Somehow it was easier to admit to than his legal status.

Several seconds passed. Seconds that dragged into a minute. Finally, Grayson pulled into a driveway. They sat there for a while. Then Grayson turned to him. "On one condition. If it gets bad, if later you think maybe it's worse than you thought… you'll let me know. There's a clinic over in Somerset that treats people for free. I offered to help with some of their accounting, for a nominal fee. It's my little contribution to goodwill in the world, kind of—if you can call crunching numbers for a nonprofit that. They can't do surgery or anything complicated like that, but they can at least take X-rays, give medications… the basics. I'll take you there anytime you need it. Your grandmother, too."

At that moment, Mateo's resistance ebbed. Just a little. He realized he'd assumed things about Grayson that weren't true. Misunderstood him. Just as all those bullies had once done to him.

Grayson didn't see a brown-skinned 'illegal'. He neither hated nor mistrusted Mateo because of where he came from. He only saw a boy who was meant to run—and in that way, they were more alike than different.

"All right," Mateo said. "If I… if we need to go there, either of us, I'll let you know."

"Good." Grayson backed the car out and headed back the way they'd come. To the little house on Rockhill Road where Mateo and his grandmother lived.

chapter 18

Brandy

Sooner lay stretched beneath Brandy's desk at Rex's office—which made it hard for Brandy to get to her computer. She didn't have the heart to ask the dog to move. Yesterday had been a rough day for the girl, getting struck by lightning. It was a wonder she wasn't even more zonked.

It was yet another miracle Sooner had survived. The dog had been through so much in her few short years. Surely, she had some special purpose beyond just bringing Brandy and Grayson together.

Brandy stared at her for a long time, admiring the rich liver red of her coat, the comical tan eyebrows that accentuated her every expression, the red freckles on her white feet... She loved that dog more than life itself. Just having her near made everything better. Even on the worst of days.

Today wasn't a bad day, however. Just a mind-numbingly boring one so far. Decluttering Rex's office and reorganizing his files had consumed most of her time the first month. It had almost become an obsession, causing her to put in more hours than she'd originally intended. That, in turn, had led her to resign from her previous job almost immediately. Rex, as promised, had paid her well for the trouble. The more organized everything became, the less time she spent looking for any one thing, which now left her with time to spare.

Rex, to put it mildly, was astounded with her efficiency. He'd proclaimed she was doing an even better job than Martina had, but Brandy was certain he was just saying that to keep her on board. He couldn't afford to lose another assistant.

Yesterday's thunderstorms had saturated the ground. Today's weather was less threatening, but the rain persisted. A steady, soaking rain with a trace of autumn's first chill to it.

Brandy retrieved her sweater from a peg on the wall. She made a second pot of coffee because she'd had a hard time getting to sleep last night, since she'd been so worried about Sooner.

According to Doc Hunter, the lightning had given Sooner's neural system quite a jolt, so she was still a little dazed and woozy on her feet, but otherwise she didn't seem any worse for wear. Still, it was like having a sick child. She felt the need to watch over her, make sure she was breathing whenever she drifted off to sleep, rub her back, and tell her everything was going to be okay.

Her phone dinged with a text. It was Grayson.

How is she?

Same as last time you asked just fifteen minutes ago, Brandy replied. *Asleep.*

Should I pick her up and take her back to the vet?

Brandy gazed out the window. Huge raindrops bounced off the sidewalk. *No. She was fine until she nodded off. Just sleepier than normal. A nice change, actually.*

Okay. Let me know if she does anything weird. Or doesn't want to wake up.

201

I think she'll be fine.

A minute later, Grayson texted, *I'm just worried about her.*

I know. But she's been through worse.

True.

The aroma of fresh coffee must've wafted beneath the crack under Rex's door, because he opened it partway and stuck his head out to inhale. "Ah, smells like heaven. Don't tell Gertie this, but I think you brew an even better pot than she does. And that's saying a helluva lot."

"Don't worry, Rex. I made enough for you."

Rex ambled out and poured his own cup—Brandy had trained him through positive reinforcement to do that much—but before disappearing back into his office, he told her to keep his next client entertained while he made a call.

"I do that more than you know, Rex," she told him. "You have a tendency to run over time on calls and appointments. If it weren't for the fact that the dog keeps your clients distracted while they're waiting, you'd be losing a lot of business."

Setting his mug aside momentarily, he put his hands on his knees and peered under the desk. Sooner opened one eye, then resumed napping.

"Looks like she's sleeping on the job today," he said.

"Hey, she came to work, didn't she? Give her some credit."

Straightening, he picked up his mug. "I'll do better than that. I'll pay her in extra biscuits this week for going beyond the call of duty for public relations. There was a short story in the paper today about how she's become the team mascot and took a zap yesterday. Dog's a celebrity in this town. I bet they make her grand marshal of the Fourth of July parade."

"She'd love that."

Minutes later, Sooner's legs were twitching as she dreamed. Muffled woofs puffed out her cheeks.

Brandy had just gotten reabsorbed in her work when the door opened and a man in his sixties stomped in. She greeted him in her normal cheery fashion, which earned her a grunted reply. The man plopped down in a seat and whipped out his phone.

Denver Keplinger, grump-in-chief. Every time he came in, Brandy tensed up. There was no making the man happy.

After reading a text, he let out a perturbed sigh and pounded a reply. This continued for several more minutes, the man growing more and more agitated with each exchange.

One of Brandy's tasks, even though it had never been discussed as one of her duties, was to familiarize herself with the clients' cases and personal history. Rex was fairly free with information, always swearing her to secrecy. Denny, as most knew him, was entangled in an inheritance dispute with two of his siblings. Their father had died without a will and matters had been tied up in probate for a seemingly, to him, interminable amount of time.

"How's your day going, Denny?" Brandy ventured, bracing herself for the tirade to come.

"How's it going?" He put his phone face down on the window ledge and sat. "Worst damn day of my life, that's how."

She was almost sorry she'd asked.

Moments later, a whiskered face was staring up at him with gentle green eyes. Patient. Concerned. Or maybe it was just that having a blast of electricity strip her neurons from the inside out had taken the edge off her, but she looked like she had the rest of her life to absorb all his troubles.

"Why's that?" Brandy asked.

He looked at Sooner a while, something in his façade hedging. His hand drifted out, touched the fuzzy top of the dog's head, stroked it a few times as she blinked her eyes shut.

"Hospital can't get their damn billing straight. As if I don't have enough to deal with."

"Enough? Something besides the probate issue?"

He scoffed. "Yeah, something."

"Oh?" It was best to gently ply the revelations out of people, Brandy had learned. Most just wanted someone to listen to their problems so they didn't have to suffer alone. Plus, Sooner was the best icebreaker there was. That dog could milk a confession out of a career criminal or heal a broken heart with those puppy dog eyes of hers.

In this case, however, Denny was a man's man and showing there was even the slightest crack in his bulletproof shell wasn't anything he relished.

"Something serious?" Brandy prompted. "Not with the kids, I hope."

Denny's five kids were all grown and living elsewhere, but it was a good place to start.

He shook his head slowly.

"Knees giving you problems?" She'd seen him in a knee brace recently and didn't know if it was anything to be concerned about.

"No, not my knees. I'm fine. Physically, anyway."

"Is Shelly okay?"

No reply. His jaw quivered the tiniest bit. And then... the dam broke. He covered his face with both hands and sobbed. Brandy brought him a box of tissues and waited it out. Meanwhile, Sooner had rested her chin on his thigh.

When he'd finally resumed normal breathing, he ran his hands over Sooner's mane while she swayed woozily. Then, leaning forward, he cupped her face in his calloused palms and whispered to her what a good dog she was. She licked his face, which elicited a faint smile from him.

"I miss my dog, Buddy," he said. "He was a good boy."

"Oh, you lost your dog recently? That is terrible. I can understand why you're having such a hard day."

"Not recently, no. I had him as a kid. He was my best friend. Used to follow me as I biked around town. Fetched my baseball when I wanted to practice batting and couldn't find a buddy to play with. Best dog in the whole world—except maybe for this one."

"Is it something with Shelly that has you so concerned?"

He nodded. "Been battling brain cancer for a better part of two years now. Just when we think she's got it licked, it comes back with a vengeance. And if that's not bad enough, insurance keeps giving us trouble. The doctors say she needs specific treatments and drugs, but some are considered experimental. Insurance says no, they aren't covered. Coldhearted bas—" He looked at Brandy. "What are you supposed to say when your wife's sick and the doctors say this or that could save her life, huh? So you do it and she gets better, but then the bill collectors are hunting you down... We burned through everything we were saving for retirement—not that I wouldn't give everything I own to save her, but..." He held up his hands. "I'm sorry. It's not your job to fix my problems."

"Don't apologize. I understand. Those sorts of issues just make a hard time in life even harder. It would wear anyone down."

"Sure does." As Denny reached toward Sooner again, she lifted her paw in a high five signal. Chuckling, he touched her paw. "Times like these make me think how good it would be for Shelly to have a pet she could love on. She's more of a cat person, though."

"Nothing wrong with cats. I hear they're often used at nursing homes for therapy. They're usually a few notches lower on the energy scale than dogs." Grinning, Brandy arched an eyebrow at Sooner. More than anything, she was amazed at how drastically Denny's mood had shifted since he'd first come in the door. Then, she remembered a short conversation she'd had with one of the nurses at Fox Hollow while walking Sooner last week. "Hey, someone I know took in a cat when one of the residents at Fox Hollow died. The relative the owner had designated to take it has health issues of

205

their own now and the nurse who's been caring for Midnight has a cat who doesn't like the new addition. It's an older cat, maybe nine or ten, but—"

"I'll ask Shelly as soon as I get home. Wait, no… Can you just give me a contact? If I give her time to think about it, she'll come up with a dozen reasons not to take the cat in."

Brandy jotted the nurse's name and number on a piece of paper.

"Say," Denny began, "you don't know of a good reliable cleaning person, do you? We could sure use the help these days."

"As a matter of fact, I do." Brandy added Ynez's name and number to the back of the paper and handed it to him. She'd recommended her to two other clients in the past week.

The door to Rex's office swung open. "Denver? Good to see you!" Rex motioned Denny on back. "This way, my good man. This way. I'm pleased to tell you things are finally moving along. Elliot has agreed to divvy the pot into thirds and Joanna's all in, too."

As if stunned, Denny splayed a hand over his heart, stopping at the door. "Wow. Joanna caved? Elliot, I can see, but Joanna? I don't get it. What's the catch?"

Rex held up both hands. "I wouldn't say she caved, exactly. But she may have been"—he winked—"persuaded to compromise. Seems they both figured some things are more important than money."

Sooner settled back into her usual spot beside Brandy's desk. Brandy gazed at the closed door, the buzz of their muffled voices drifting from the crack underneath. Gazed at it so long that Sooner rose and placed her chin on Brandy's knee, as if concerned she'd suddenly lapsed into a coma.

Her fingers smoothing the hair atop the dog's skull, a sense of calm and peace filled Brandy. "Rex is still a hot mess, Sooner, don't get me wrong. Gets under my skin some days. But he's not *all* bad. In fact, in some ways he's a pretty decent fellow."

Sooner's eyebrows twitched. Almost like she was urging Brandy to finish the thought.

"Yeah, I get it. There's some good in *all* people. Most, anyway. Or maybe it's more accurate to say everyone has a purpose—whether it's to lift us up or knock us down and teach us something. And the people who walk around in a rage? Maybe they're hurting inside. Just like the rest of us."

Gently, Brandy pushed back from her desk. She stretched her legs out. Lifted her feet one at a time, as if marching in place. That was what this year had felt like. Struggling and not getting much of anywhere. But as hard as it had been, she'd learned from it, challenged herself in unexpected ways. Her story may have been uniquely her own, but that was true for everyone.

Through it all, she'd grown. Part of life was pushing past the pain. Because without that pain, you could never truly appreciate the joys life brings.

The ringtone on her phone stirred her from her reverie. It was Grayson.

"Grayson, hi."

"Hey, babe. How's it going?"

"Great... *Really* great. I mean that."

He chuckled. "Good, I'm glad. Want me to bring you lunch? I made some wicked egg salad sandwiches and my special blackberry iced tea."

"You just want to check on the dog."

"Hmm, maybe."

"Sure, then. And noon would be good. Looks like a break between clients then." She heard Denny laughing. She'd never heard him laugh, never seen him smile before today. But then, she hadn't realized how difficult his life had been recently. "Grayson... thank you."

"Uh, okay. For what?"

"For everything." Brandy traced her fingertips over the heart-tree necklace. "For taking care of Sooner. For coming along in my life when I needed someone just like you. For loving me. Just... thanks for being you."

"Oh, you're welcome." After a pause, he added, "What brought this on?"

"Just that I realized today how lucky I am to have someone like you I can share my troubles with—and given what I've been through, that's a lot. Someone who just... listens. Without judgment. Someone who cares. To know you're always there for me... It makes me feel safe, cared for, and like I matter."

"I feel the same way about you."

"You do?" she asked.

"Yes. And do you know who I learned it all from?"

"Who?"

"Sooner. Sooner taught me what it means to have someone there for you, no matter how crummy you feel. We all hurt. We all get upset. We all have rough patches. But if you have someone who cares and loves you anyway, it helps you feel like you can make it through anything."

chapter 19
Mateo

The more time that went by, the more Mateo hurt. As soon as Grayson had dropped him off at home, Mateo rummaged in the medicine cabinet for pain relievers. Then, since his grandmother was not yet home, he emptied the two trays of ice cubes into a plastic grocery sack and iced his shoulder. The pain only grew worse. He hadn't fallen on his shoulder, but when he'd put his hand out, his elbow and shoulder had taken the impact, twisting as he rolled onto his side.

Although he didn't feel like eating, he ate anyway. Food in his stomach might take his mind off the discomfort. Halfway through the meal his grandmother had prepared for him early that morning, he contemplated dumping it in the trash. But he knew she'd find it and interrogate him. It was difficult, if not impossible, to keep things from her.

For an hour, he picked at the plate of chicken and spicy potatoes. They were even less appetizing when cold. Their smell, normally tempting to his always hungry stomach, made him nauseous. He flicked through channels, hoping to find something to take his mind off his troubles. Then, above the mindless banter of a sitcom, he heard the familiar rattle of the muffler on his grandmother's car.

Scooping the food up with his fingers, he shoveled it down, each bite making him feel sicker and sicker, but that at least distracted him from the screaming pain on his left side.

"Ah, good! You found the food I made." His grandmother shrugged off her purse and hid it behind the couch.

"Very good. The best." He swallowed the last few bites having barely chewed them. Picking up his plate and taking it to the kitchen sink, he rinsed and scrubbed it before setting it in the drying rack. Dishes were not allowed to sit out unwashed, ever. A dishwasher was not a luxury they could afford and there wasn't extra room on the counter for dirty plates and cups to accumulate. He stretched his good arm above his head, letting out an exaggerated yawn. "I think I'll go to bed now and get up early tomorrow to run. Good night, *abuela.*"

He was about to close his bedroom door behind him when his grandmother said, "Mateo…"

Slowly, he turned.

"I'm home an hour early. You're always awake until much later. Are you ill?"

Mateo shook his head. "Just tired."

"I don't think so." Her eyes shifted to the sack of melted ice in the sink. He'd forgotten to empty it. "Something is wrong—what?"

He had to tell her the truth. Some of it, anyway. She'd figure it out eventually. "I fell while running. My shoulder… it's a little bruised."

A minute later he was sitting next to her on the couch as she probed his arm and collarbone and tested his range of motion. He winced repeatedly, even as he tried to be stoic.

"I used to dream of being a nurse, did you know?"

"No."

"I did. When I was young. Before I had your mother. But where

210

we come from, those who have nothing to begin with stand very little chance of becoming something more. That's the way it was where I grew up. You could only go to university if your parents had money to send you. Otherwise you had to work. Sometimes very young. As a student, I was bright. There were a few scholarships for people like me, but not enough. I knew I had to do better for my own daughter. I had to give her opportunity. So I sent her to another village to be with relatives where, at the time, it was not as bad. And I came here to work. I meant to go somewhere else, a bigger city, but along the way I found a job here. Then that became another job and another… I never left. It was not a lot of money, but it was enough. More than I'd ever had before. Enough to send some home to fetch Anarosa and you. Enough to save for this small house."

After retrieving some balm from the bathroom, she rubbed it into his shoulder. "I know this place isn't much. Barely big enough for one person, let alone two. It needs work. But whenever I start to think it isn't good enough, I remember that I have a warm place to sleep in winter, that I have running water with which to shower, that I have electricity and a lamp to read by and a TV to watch. Then, I am grateful. Very grateful. Do you know why?"

Before he could respond, she continued, "Because when I first came to this country as I passed through a bigger city, a place I thought maybe I could stay, because with all those people surely there was work, I saw a man asleep under a bridge. It was raining and cold, so I sought shelter under the bridge, too. In time, he woke and saw me. We began to talk. He told me he was saving money to buy a tent so he could have a place of his own. A tent. I had only fifty dollars left. I gave him twenty. I was hungry. I could have used the money for many things—a room where it was safe, new clothes, a cheap phone. But I had more than he did. He was so grateful he began to cry. The next day I came that way again. He wasn't there."

"He bought his tent?"

"I don't know. Possibly. I told myself he did. That because he was rested and healthy, he found a job. To this day the story I wish to believe is that he only needed one person to help him begin to make his life better. And I'm grateful to be able to eat, to work, to have this." Smiling, she looked around at the sparse contents of their cramped home. "And I have made it my wish that in your life, you will be able to become what you want to be, what you are capable of. So one day maybe you can help others, just as I wanted to. That is why I push you so much, Mateo. Not so you can live in a bigger house and drive a better car. But so you can find a way to serve, to lessen others' suffering... There are many ways. Many. Here, it is possible. Where you were born, it is practically *im*possible. If poverty does not trap you, then lack of medicine and doctors will lead you to an early death... or the gangs will force you to join them. Or kill you. That is what they did to the men in your family. I didn't want that for you. Don't ask what they did to the women. So when I had enough money, I sent for you and your mother. But she thought she could earn more somewhere else. She was probably right."

She bit back her words then. Mateo had always sensed there was something about his mother she wasn't sharing. Or maybe something she only suspected, but didn't want to know. Perhaps he'd never learn the truth. Whenever he'd tried before, it had turned to this—a stony silence, a bitter set to her features. So he took the conversation elsewhere, albeit no less pleasant.

"Is it really so bad there, *abuela*—back home?" Although he hesitated to call where he was born 'home'. He barely remembered it. Besides, this was his home now.

"It is."

"I hear the kids at school talking. They think—"

"What they think is of no consequence."

"But they think that beyond the borders there is nothing but an empty wasteland and people without souls. They think—"

Shooing him away, she snapped out a blanket and laid it on the couch—her bed.

"Go out into the world, Mateo. See how others live. Don't just look at pictures on the internet or TV. Walk among them. Talk to them. See what they endure, what they value, what they fear… Most people, they only want to not be miserable. To live without illness or pain or hunger. To raise their children in peace. To have hope and security. There is value in every human life. When we close our eyes and hearts to it, we only prolong and increase the suffering. It doesn't go away simply because we aren't looking."

He wasn't sure what to say to her. It was like she'd dropped the weight of the world on his slight shoulders. He understood she was a devout woman, that she believed in doing unto others. But still, he felt she was naïve in many ways.

"Things are changing, *abuela*. They say I might never be able to become a citizen now."

"They call you an 'illegal', do they?"

"They have, yes."

"Then their ancestors were the same once, too. We all came from somewhere else, Mateo."

"But they're not in danger of being sent back to a place they can't even remember."

"Perhaps. But they're ignorant and they live in fear, when *they* have everything to be grateful for. They just choose not to be. Happiness"—she thumped a palm to her breastbone—"comes from inside."

He stood in his doorway, mulling over all she'd said. Most nights, she was too tired from a full day of work to say much. Usually, she nagged at him to study. There was very little time and no energy to share her thoughts. Yet as he gazed at her thin frame tucked beneath a worn blanket, the glow of the TV flickering in the room, he realized how very wise she was. She'd shared that wisdom with

213

him in small but blunt ways throughout the years. It just hadn't struck him until then.

"Go to bed, Mateo. Rest. It's what your body requires right now. You won't feel much like running in the morning. Or moving, even."

He did as she said. But he barely slept. Couldn't. The pain made it impossible.

So he lay awake thinking of all he had to be grateful for—his grandmother who provided for him every day, his mother who had brought him here at great risk to herself, Coach Tervo who had seen the runner in him, the potential… Even Coach Grayson, who refused to let him waste those talents.

But that night, as he tossed and turned, more than anything he was grateful for the little red dog that had reminded him what it was to run free again. A prayer for her seemed in order.

His room lit only by the silver glow of a half moon, he took the shoebox from beneath his bed in which he'd kept the most important letters from college coaches. There'd been so many he'd had to move the rest to a bigger box in the closet. From beneath a collection of medals won at races, he fished out the worn set of rosary beads his mother had given him before she left for Chicago.

There was a set sequence to the prayers, a bead for each one, days on which certain ones were to be said. It had been so long. Years since they'd attended a Mass. So he began with what he remembered and left out what he could not.

Kneeling beside his bed, he whispered, "*Creo en Dios, Padre todopoderoso, creador del Cielo y de la Tierra…*"

He uttered his prayers until his tongue stumbled and an irrepressible yawn interrupted the rote rhythm of his words. Unable to keep his eyes open, he lay down in bed. Yet sleep eluded him. It wasn't like some fast opponent he could overtake. In order to catch sleep, he had to surrender to it. His frustration only grew worse, his body more tired, the pain more intense. Whether on his back, side, or stomach, no position was comfortable. His entire arm throbbed. It was hard to move his fingers, let alone lift his hand in the air or reach for an object. He was doubtful that an X-ray would show any broken bones or displaced joints. Still, he'd never experienced anything quite so painful, so persistent.

Above all the discomfort was the inescapable worry of whether Sooner would be okay. If he'd kept to the path he was supposed to have taken, if he'd paid attention to the sky, if he'd returned to base camp sooner...

If, if, if...

How could he have been so careless?

Pay attention, Mateo! Tervo's voice resounded with authority. *Always, always, always pay attention to what's around you. Be aware of it. Don't take for granted that what was true yesterday, an hour ago, even a minute ago, is the same. You can be thirty seconds ahead of the next guy, then suddenly find he's hot on your heels. Things change! Be ready for them.*

It wasn't until the pink-gray dusk before dawn that his body found rest, although his mind drifted in a state of half-wakefulness, half-dreaming. In the pictures behind his eyelids, he was a young boy again, running barefoot—not through the desert, but through a wood dense with forest as rain poured. Fern-like leaves and sharp-edged sedges brushed his shins as he raced along the narrow trail, the footing slick. For all that he tried to blink away the rain, he could barely see where he was going.

Don't give up, Sandoval! Tervo shouted. *Don't you dare give up!*

Whenever he stole a glance behind him, there was nothing, no one. Ahead of him, he was only vaguely aware of the vegetation stirring with movement. But it could have been the wind.

As time went on, he had the sense not that he was being chased, but that he was chasing *something*. Trying desperately to catch up, but unable. No matter how hard he tried, he could run no faster.

Yet he ran and ran and ran. Not away from, but toward

215

something. Rain beating down on his bare arms and chest. The path dipping and twisting and rising again.

Finally, he caught a glimpse of the bushy plume of a tail and the back of a pair of upright, triangular ears.

Fantasma?

The harder he tried to catch the dog, the heavier his legs felt. Still, he wouldn't give up. Had to find where she—at least he'd always assumed it was a she—was leading him.

The crack of a gunshot sounded. Yet he felt no fear. Only exhilaration. His heart lightened.

So he ran faster... and faster...

Until the woods ended and the skies cleared and a sunny meadow appeared before him. Across which stretched a finish tape between two poles and beyond it a chute with a rainbow of pennants.

But... there was no dog. No one to witness him finishing. No Lou, no *abuela*, no Coach Grayson, no Tervo.

Arms raised high, the tape broke across his chest. With another step, he collapsed onto a bed of grass, drenched in the scent of rainfall and damp earth. He rolled over, heaving with breath, eyes shut as the sun warmed his face.

Then, he heard the stampede of paws—and a familiar bark.

His eyes flew open. He raised himself up on an elbow, peered toward the sound.

But all he saw was a sliver of light beneath his bedroom door. His grandmother's socked feet shuffled over the thin rug beside the couch as she rose and readied for the day. Pushing aside his blanket, he swung his feet over the side of the bed to sit up.

Gradually, his eyes adjusted to the dim glow of dawn emanating from beyond his window. The pale light caught the faint glimmer of his medals, hanging from a string between two nails. Gradually, the certificates of academic accomplishments, tacked above the medals, came into sharper focus—along with the pain in his shoulder.

216

chapter 20
Mateo

Mateo could barely hide his pain. But he had to. He didn't want anyone to know. Didn't want to see a doctor. He could endure this.

Hardest of all was keeping it from his grandmother. She already knew, yes, but he was determined not to let her know how *much* it bothered him. If she knew that, there would be appointments, X-rays, medicine—and bills they couldn't afford. They had no insurance. None. Even the simplest of treatments would take money away from their meager budget. Money that meant surviving. With enough money, they might be able to stay in America. Without it, there was a good chance they wouldn't.

Unless his life depended on it, he would grit his teeth and wait for the pain to fade. It would. In time.

As a small child, he had survived the desert. Weeks on the road. Being hunted by men with guns for reasons he didn't then understand. He had started school in an unfamiliar place where they spoke a language that to him was foreign. He had felt lost and dumb and undeserving of kindness or generosity. Although he no longer felt that way, it had ingrained in him a compassion far beyond that of others his age. His grandmother once called him an 'old soul'. Supposedly, she meant it as a compliment.

He did feel old that day as he showed up at practice and started his warm-up. Stiff in every joint, battered in every muscle. As if he'd plummeted ten floors and landed on concrete, rather than stumbling a few feet onto soft earth.

Today's practice was intervals on a grassy loop in the picnic area of the park. Orange cones had never looked so daunting. He was due at the car lot later for a six-hour shift. School started tomorrow, so he needed to squeeze in as many hours beforehand as he could.

Grayson—Mateo still had a hard time thinking of him as 'Coach'—tapped at the buttons on his watch.

Beep, beep... beep.

"Everyone ready?"

"Wait!" Lou shouted from the back of the pack. "I need to retie my shoes. They're too tight."

"Are those new?" Amelia asked. She was the new freshman who'd come on board a week ago.

"Yes. Got them at the outlet yesterday in the clearance section. Seventy-five percent off!"

"Do they have other—"

"We have a workout to do, ladies," Grayson said. "You can discuss your purchases during the water break. By the way, Amelia, that's my favorite brand. Now let's go. We have twelve of these."

A subdued groan went around. Grayson responded with a "Ready? Seeettt... Go!"

They took off in groups, ten seconds apart. Mateo was on the inside, but he was struggling before the first turn. His movements were jerky. His strides uneven. It wasn't so much his legs that were failing him, but his upper body. He felt twisted to one side, his left arm bound to his chest while his other arm swung wildly to compensate. His instincts had told him to slack off today. Maybe even take a few days off altogether to allow his body to heal. But Mateo had never quit a race or workout in his life. So he took a deep breath, forced the tension from his shoulders, and focused on his legs.

By the second turn, Cruz was ahead of him and Dusty was sitting on his shoulder. Every footfall sent shock waves of pain upward from the ground and into his shoulder. The more he tried to smooth out his movements, the more his body resisted. He shortened his stride and picked up his turnover. Better, but he still couldn't avoid the hitch in his arm swing.

As they turned the last corner, Dusty glanced at him. "You got this. Hang in there, Speedy Gonzales."

Mateo cringed. Talk about shallow stereotypes. Why did they always—

Dusty was barely breathing. Glancing at his watch only made Mateo more aware of how far off pace he was. Yet no matter how much he commanded his muscles to move faster, they wouldn't. Couldn't. The last time he'd felt this flattened, he'd been down with the flu two years ago.

No matter how hard he focused on pushing forward, his body refused. He could tell Dusty was easing up so as not to pull ahead of him. It was only when Keen edged past them that Dusty took off— but not until he'd given Mateo an apologetic look.

By the time he crossed the line, Mateo was the fifth man in. He stumbled off to the side, clutching his knees. It wasn't his lungs or heart that had failed him, but his bones. It was like they weren't hinged together properly. Like someone had taken a baseball bat to his skeleton during his sleep and rearranged it.

Pumping his arms in the air, Cruz circled back in an easy jog. "One down, eleven to go!"

The rest of the guys were circling the picnic tables, checking their watches to see how much time they had before they had to hit the line again. When the girls started filtering in, Mateo forced himself to shuffle along in a recovery jog. Rather than feeling rejuvenated by the break, he only became more aware of the pain, his legs more leaden, his chest tighter.

Too soon, the first wave regrouped. Mateo hobbled to the line, clearing his watch so he'd be ready to restart it. This time he'd focus on relaxing. If he loosened up, his strength would return. It might take a few, but he had to push through this.

"Not you."

It wasn't until Coach Grayson stepped in front of Mateo that he realized the instruction was for him.

He wanted to ask why, but he knew.

One by one, the groups set off. When the last was out of earshot, Grayson turned to Mateo. "Looks like you got roughed up worse than you let on."

"Just stiff today, that's all." Straightening himself, he shrugged. "Some bruises, maybe."

Grayson nodded. "Right."

"How's the dog?" Mateo asked, eager to change the subject.

"Aside from being a little woozy, she seems okay, but I left her with Brandy today. Just to be safe."

"I'm sorry. I shouldn't—"

"It's not your fault, okay?"

"It was stupid of me. I—"

"Stop. That storm came out of nowhere. You're not to blame. Sooner will be fine. The fact that you carried her all the way back here at a dead sprint... At any rate, don't let it bother you. When she comes back, I'll still need someone to wear her out. For some reason, she's drawn to you. Like you were some long lost friend she finally found."

They stood there awkwardly for a while longer, through the second set, then a third and fourth.

"What do you want me to do?" Mateo finally asked as the first group took off again.

"Oh." Grayson blinked rapidly, as if startled from his thoughts. He eyed Mateo. Folded his arms. "You icing? Taking anti-inflammatories?"

Mateo nodded. Neither had helped much, but he didn't say so.

A few seconds later, Grayson held his arms wide. "Do this."

Mateo mimicked him. It took effort. His injured shoulder was on fire.

Grayson brought his arms forward, then raised them above his head.

He did the first move, but the second... He couldn't. Looking down, he shook his head.

"Go run an easy mile and stretch. Emphasis on easy."

Stung, he looked up. "One mile? Just... one?"

"Sure. That'll give you three for today. That's enough."

Before Mateo could object again, Louisa Abrams came plodding up. She wiped her brow with the back of her hand. "Coach, I'm supposed to remind you I have that dentist appointment today. My mom should be here in about ten minutes."

"Perfect timing, Lou. Take Mateo on the cool-down loop with you."

"Okay!" she said enthusiastically.

Next thing he knew, Mateo was shuffling alongside her, his eyes fixed straight ahead.

"You all right?" she asked.

"Huh?"

"Your arm. I noticed you holding it kind of funny. Did you fall yesterday?"

"Yeah... Wait." He whipped his head in her direction. "You noticed? Is it that obvious?"

"Sort of. I mean, not if you didn't pay attention to how you usually swing your arms when you run… Oh, that sounded kind of creeper-ish, didn't it? I guess, well, you just have a distinctive stride. You don't run like the other guys—or they don't run like you, to be exact. You more or less kind of float. Almost like your feet barely touch the ground. You remind me of a gazelle. No, wait… that's not right. They bound. More like a wolf, loping along for miles and miles, never tiring. Have you ever been to the Lamar Valley in Yellowstone?"

He didn't have the guts to tell her he hadn't been outside Kentucky since he was five.

Evidently, she took his reluctance as a no, because she went on to describe it in awestruck detail: the broad expanse of open grassland embraced by rugged mountains, the glimmering river winding lazily through it, and how the pronghorn, bison, and elk came there in the summer, and how two summers ago she and her family got up before dawn to witness it all, and rows of photographers were there to capture a pursuit that unfolded before their eyes.

"It was incredible and yet sad all at once. These two wolves, one gray, one black, were trotting toward a lone elk calf from different directions. One of the photographers let me watch through his camera lens and then suddenly another one was saying, 'To the west… See the others?' Anyway, I had to give up my view and then these cameras were all clicking, clicking, clicking, and all you could see were these five or six long-legged specks swooping in and the calf darting frantically, left, then right, then forward, until… Well, you get it. Nature at work. Meanwhile, there are thousands—and I mean *thousands*—of bison ambling through the valley in a sort of wooly cloud, wading through the river, some crossing the road behind us… Now *that* was scary! When they got close enough that you could hear them snorting, we retreated to the car. On the way back, one was taking a dust bath. I got some pictures. Tons. Just a camera phone. But I should show you sometime. So if you ever get a chance to go—"

She stopped talking and slowed. They were almost done with their mile cool-down.

"I'm sorry. I haven't let you talk at all. I get excited when I think about it. Of all the places my family has been, I loved that one the most."

Mateo knew she had three younger siblings and her parents often brought the whole troop in tow to the meets. They were very involved in helping with the team and seemed like a very close family—all six of them. He imagined what it would be like to be part of a big family like that, traveling and having fun. He liked Lou in a way he didn't fully understand—for her joy, her enthusiasm, her… Well, just *her*.

"That's okay. I'd like to go there someday. You make it sound…" He searched for a word. Nothing did justice to the picture she'd painted. Finally, "Magical. You'd make a great travel writer."

She stopped dead then. The dappled shade of sunlight filtering through the leaves of a sycamore danced between them. "Thanks. You know, I've actually considered that." One hand bracing herself against the tree trunk, she grabbed an ankle from behind to stretch her quads. "My parents… they don't have a lot of money. I mean enough, just not a *lot*, you know. So we go camping. How else are you supposed to tote four kids halfway across the country on next to nothing? So even though we're not staying in posh hotels or dining at fine restaurants, and instead are sleeping in secondhand tents and grilling burgers over a campfire, it's so much fun. I figure I can roll everything I've learned from them into a blog on budget vacationing."

With a huff and an eye roll, she dropped her foot to the ground. "There I go again, not letting you get a word in edgewise."

"It's okay. Really." The next thing that came out of his mouth shocked him perhaps more than her. "Maybe we could get together later and you could tell me more about Yellowstone."

For the first time since they'd begun their cool-down, she was speechless. She bit her lip as if to suppress a smile. "Like… a date-date?"

"Oh… um…" Mateo was stuck. If he said no, she might be offended. But if he said yes, she might be repulsed. He'd lose either way. "I… I don't know. I just wanted to hear more, that's all."

"Oh." Lou looked down. Almost like she was disappointed he hadn't formally asked her out.

A car honked from the parking lot. Stealing a glance, she scowled. "She's early. She's always early." Then to Mateo, "When? Where?"

"Huh?"

"When do you want to get together? We could meet somewhere. Say, Founder's Park, on the north side of town? There are swings there. A walking path. Doesn't cost anything."

"Oh, sure. Sounds great. But I have to work until seven."

"Eight, then. Founder's Park." The car honked again and she waved in acknowledgment. "See you there."

And like that, Mateo had his first date with a girl. If it was a date. He wasn't sure.

It wasn't until Lou was in the car with her mom and they were pulling out of the parking lot that Mateo remembered the pain in his shoulder.

—o00o—

The note Mateo left his grandmother hadn't exactly been a lie. He *was* meeting a friend from the team. He'd even told her when he'd be back. If she asked later, he'd tell her where and with who, hoping she wouldn't question if Lou was a boy or a girl. As traditional as his grandmother was, he was afraid she wouldn't approve of him meeting a girl alone—even if it was in a public place.

Anyway, it wasn't a date—or so he thought until she showed up. Lou clearly had a different perception of their get-together.

She was dressed in a fitted black skirt with yellow daisies on it and a white off-the-shoulder blouse. But the most startling thing about her appearance was that her hair wasn't in a ponytail for once. It hung long and straight, swinging freely as she strode toward him. The orange light of a sinking sun cast it in cinnamon hues. He'd always thought it a ruddy brown before, pulled back tight by an elastic band and damp with sweat. At school, he'd never really looked at it. Not in this way.

As she came closer, he could see the dash of peach eyeshadow and the powdering of blush on her cheeks. She was pretty without the makeup, but—

Pretty? Why had he just now noticed?

As she came to stand before him, he saw her freckles—on the tip of her nose, the rims of her ears, the tops of her shoulders. The lines in her forehead that made her look permanently thoughtful. The way her eyes crinkled as she broke into a nervous smile. All of her imperfectly perfect.

"Hi." She looked around. "I thought I was early, but you beat me here."

He shrugged. Thrust his hands in the pockets of his good khaki shorts. The one pair he owned. "I came from work."

He had. He'd brought a change of clothes and freshened up in the employees' bathroom at Mac's before coming straight here on his bike. It had been challenging to clean cars with a bum shoulder, but somehow he'd managed, never mentioning it to Mac.

"You been here long?" she asked.

"I don't know—five minutes?" More like twenty-five, actually.

After an awkward pause, she thrust a bottle in his direction. "I brought you something. I don't know if you like it, but it's my

225

favorite."

He stared at the brown bottle, unsure what to make of it. The label was facing away from him. Had she brought… beer? What did she think this was going to turn into? Did she have cigarettes in her back pocket, too?

"It's birch beer." She rotated the bottle so he could see the label. "Kind of like… sarsaparilla? Or cream soda, maybe? It's a twist top."

Relieved it wasn't alcohol after all, he almost reached out with his left hand before remembering how limited his range of motion was. So he accepted it with the other hand and opened it. Took a swig. "It's good. I like it." After a couple more swallows, he lowered the bottle. "Sorry, I didn't bring anything."

"It's okay. I didn't expect you to."

Still, it was a thoughtful gesture. He felt he owed her something. A compliment, at least. "You look nice. *Really* nice."

Color rose in her cheeks. She let out a long breath. As if she'd been holding it for minutes. Then softly, "Thanks. I hoped you'd notice. Usually, I'm all sweaty when you see me. Oh, sorry, bad picture."

"Don't worry about it. That's usually how you see me, too." He chugged his drink. Noticed it was already half gone. Hadn't realized how thirsty he'd been. Or maybe his mouth was just dry because he was nervous. "So… what do you want to do? Swing? Teeter? I haven't done those in years."

Laughing, she tucked a rebellious strand of hair behind her ear. "Me neither. But wouldn't it be kind of hard for us to finish our drinks doing either one?"

"Yeah, I suppose." He surveyed the park, small by any standards. A triangular corner of two side streets, really. Three swings, a seesaw, and a couple of picnic tables beneath a row of maple trees. The picnic tables were already occupied. He pointed to the brick wall in the corner. "Want to sit there for a while?"

"Sure!"

Again, the enthusiasm behind her reply was a bit over the top, but it solidified to Mateo that this was more than just two friends meeting to chat.

They walked over to the wall. Slowly. Like it was a big decision. A binding commitment of some sort.

Mateo waited until she sat first on the hip-high brick wall. He almost reached out to help her, in the same way a gentleman would pull back a chair for his date, but the pain in his shoulder prevented him. Athletic, Lou hopped up with ease. He was relieved he hadn't had to lift her up and yet at the same time disappointed. Any excuse to be closer. He would've gritted his teeth through the pain. As they'd walked, he'd been compelled to let his hand brush hers. He hadn't, though. Didn't want to assume too much just yet.

"So... tomorrow..." Lou began.

He couldn't quite figure where she was headed, so he waited. Stuck in the now. Unaware of anything but this moment, this place, her...

"Are you ready for school?" she asked.

Looking away, he sucked in a sharp breath. As if she'd just punched him in the gut.

She touched his arm. Only for a moment. But it was enough for him to return his gaze to her. So much concern in those eyes. She tilted her head. Tucked her hair behind her ear. Listening intently. No judgment in her gaze. "What is it?"

His lip twitched as he warded off a snarl. "Truth? Jed Delaney, that's what. I haven't seen him in... weeks."

"Hmm, yeah, I get that. He's a total loser. A bully. If you ask me, he has plenty of his own issues to deal with."

"Issues?"

"He's gotten in trouble since his kindergarten days. Can't sit still. Smarts off so the other kids laugh at him. My aunt was his fifth grade

227

teacher and says he—" She covered her mouth. "Sorry, I shouldn't spread rumors."

"Were you going to say something true?"

After a pause, she nodded.

"Then it's not a rumor." Normally, he wasn't interested in other people's private lives, but something compelled him. He couldn't imagine what 'issues' Jed Delaney would have, other than a lower than average IQ.

One reddish eyebrow lifted, she glanced at him sideways. "Okay, but it seems… confidential."

"She told *you*, didn't she?"

Confronted with the facts, she let out a sigh. "All right, but you have to swear not to tell anyone."

"Done."

"He has ADHD. The school psychologist who tested him suggested medication and behavioral therapy, but his dad wouldn't let him have either. Said he was just lazy and needed to 'try harder', to put it kindly. My friend Amber lives next door to him. Apparently, his dad has a temper and has roughed Jed up a time or two when he got in trouble. One time, Amber's mom called the sheriff and Jed denied that his dad had ever touched him. Just explained away his bruises by saying he slipped and fell down a hill. Amber's mom says she thinks he inherited it from his dad. Dale Delaney hasn't kept a steady job for more than two years straight. I hear he's been hauled in a couple of times for getting in bar fights, too." As if she'd suddenly decided their evening had taken too dark a turn, she closed her eyes momentarily, threw her head back, and pulled in a deep breath. "Anyway, never mind. I get it. Hope he's not in any of your classes. He has it out for a lot of people, so don't take anything he says personally."

Mateo didn't want to ruin any more of this night talking about Jed, so he let it go.

Setting her barely touched bottle aside, Lou scooted closer to him. Close enough that their legs were touching and he could feel the warmth of her skin next to his. He forgot about school. Forgot about the fear of running into Jed Delaney every day. Somehow, he sensed, it wouldn't be so bad this year. Things would be better. Even as his shoulder ached and burned, he believed that.

Sitting there next to Lou, energy surged inside him. Buoyed him up and carried him along like the swell of high tide lifting a rudderless boat. He didn't want this night to end. Didn't want to leave here. Thought for sure he'd never need food or sleep again.

Still, he was vaguely aware of the stark realities of life. He'd eventually have to leave the park in order to get home before dark. He was dreading the moment he'd have to tear himself away. Counting the hours until he could see her again. Already.

The smile she gave him lassoed him from his thoughts and brought him squarely back into the moment.

"So," she said, "what should we talk about?"

"Tell me where you've been. With your family." In truth, she could've rambled on about her school supply list and he would've hung onto every word.

"That could take a while. I'm not sure where to start."

"Start anywhere. It's all new to me. I haven't been more than a couple of hours beyond right here in... well, since I came here."

She turned her torso to face him. "How about you talk, instead. Tell me about that."

"About what?"

"Coming here. Tell me what you remember from your life before here. Tell me how you got here. What it was like when you first came."

No one... *no one* had ever asked him those things before. It was so much a part of who he was—and yet before now, no one had ever cared to ask.

229

And so he told her his story. Even about the stray dog.

The wall upon which they sat was built in the shape of a V. On the side facing the street it said, 'Welcome to Faderville'. Nothing else. No population count. No 'City of Champions', 'Rose Town USA', or any such charming moniker. Faderville had no real claim to fame. It was just a place where people worked and lived. A crossroads of obscure origins that had brought together a white girl whose parents had little knowledge of their obscure heritage, but whose family had lived here for more than a century—and a first generation immigrant who'd fled his squalid origins on foot as a child and landed here unable to speak the language, but who hoped for a better future for his own descendants, if not himself.

They were just kids, starting out in life, and in their hopes and dreams, as they sat on the brick wall and talked while the sun sank— about Lou's travels and her love of books and Mateo's interests in law and government—they discovered that what they found most fascinating about each other… was that they *were* different.

And in their differences, the world somehow became richer and more complete than it would have been if they'd been the same in every way.

—o0Oo—

School would not be the same that year. Not only had Mateo's agitator, Jed, turned up in his first period class, but in two more. Three times too many. Tomorrow perhaps, he'd go to the guidance counselor, see if he could get his schedule rearranged. Even as he pondered how he could juggle his subjects, he knew he'd have a hard time making that happen. Faderville was a *very* small school. There weren't many options.

While Lou's revelations had shed new light on Jed's behavior, it did nothing to change the likelihood of a run-in happening again.

Mateo was so busy scanning the faces of taller, bigger bodies crowding the hallway that he'd gone a good thirty feet before a familiar, feminine voice beside him snatched him from his vigilance.

"Can I carry some of those for you?" Extending both hands, Lou smiled at him. At *him*. "I saw you before homeroom, trying to figure out how to carry everything for the day—I'm guessing so you wouldn't have to go back to your locker?"

Mateo shifted his backpack on his good shoulder. "It's okay, really. Besides, it weighs about fifty pounds."

"Which is what the feed sacks weigh that I throw in the back of my dad's pickup. Don't even ask how many bales of hay and straw I toss around. I show goats and sheep at the fair every summer. Did you know that? Try wrangling a mama ewe for sheering, or trimming the hooves on a yearling ram who's full of himself."

"I take it you don't live in town."

"Nope. We live on the same road as the veterinarian, Dr. McHugh. Do you know him?"

"Yeah." Mateo hung his head. He still felt somehow responsible for the incident. "I saw him earlier this week when… you know."

"Oh, sure. Well, the dog's going to be okay, right?" She reached for his hand, squeezing it a second before letting go.

His backpack slid and he slanted his shoulder toward his ear to stop it.

"Look," she said, "you've got one side hiked up like Quasimodo. I can tell it's bothering you, even if you can't, but if you want to act tough, be my guest. Just letting you know I'm here if you need me." Wearing a lopsided grin, she tossed her head back, her long auburn hair swishing. "Anyway, I figured it was a good excuse to walk with you."

Stopping next to a bulletin board of college posters, he set his backpack down and unzipped it. He handed her two textbooks. "That'll help. Seriously."

231

"What are these—a thousand pages each?" Books clutched to her chest, Lou scurried after him as he started forward.

Mateo didn't get far, though. Despite ducking to the side to avoid the hulking form that had appeared out of nowhere, his backpack clipped Jed Delaney's upper arm. Off-kilter, Mateo stumbled backward.

"Sorry, sorry," he said.

"Watch where you're going, Matty boy!" Jed bumped him one more time for good measure.

The brick wall impacting with Mateo's bad shoulder stopped him from going down. A fresh bolt of pain blasted through him. For a moment, he leaned his forehead against the rough surface of the bricks, muttering curse words in Spanish. If he'd had full use of his left arm... If Lou hadn't been right there... He pulled in three deep breaths, trying to calm himself and formulate a response.

"What is *wrong* with you?" Lou swung the textbooks flat against Jed's abdomen.

Jed grunted. His eyelids flapped.

"He said he was sorry!" Lou jabbed a thin finger at his sternum. "Get over yourself, will you?"

"Dude needs to look where he's going."

"You were on the other side of the hall thirty seconds ago. Maybe you're the one who needs to look where you're going."

"Lou." Mateo touched her arm, could barely resist grabbing it and pulling her away. Thankfully, she turned to him.

"I got this, Mateo." She waved him off, turning her fury back on Jed. "You think you own this hallway? Why don't you just learn to walk in a straight line?"

"Maybe I was going to look at some of these." He pointed to a random poster.

"That's for an Ivy League school. You don't even come close to meeting their—"

"Lou, stop," Mateo urged in her ear. "He's not worth it."

Jed's face reddened with anger. "Not worth—"

"Is there a problem?" Mr. Sutherland, the government teacher, strode from his doorway toward them. His was the sixth period class Mateo shared with Jed. Other students had slowed to watch the unfolding drama. A wide circle was forming around them. All of which made Mateo feel not only safer, but bolder.

Squinting, Mateo took a step toward the poster. "No problem, Mr. Sutherland. Jed was just asking if we knew whether Dartmouth College had a football team. Except he pronounced it Dart-Mouth. You have such a great sense of humor, Jed."

Apparently, Jed didn't get the burn, because he just nodded and chuckled with the onlookers.

"Say"—Mr. Sutherland turned his attention to Mateo—"it just occurred to me... I have a connection through a friend with the lady who heads the Government Department at Dartmouth. There's a scholarship for first generation immigrants. With your good grades and athletic accomplishments, it would certainly give you a leg up. Want me to hook you up, see if a campus visit could be arranged?"

Once again, Mateo was caught off-balance. He was uncomfortable with the attention, knowing it would only make Jed even more likely to exact his revenge the next time.

"Um, sure." He jerked his head toward the end of the hallway. "We should go, Lou. Don't want Mrs. Penewit to lock the cafeteria doors on us, do we?"

She pasted on a ridiculously fake smile. "Of course not." Pivoting on her heel, she took off down the hallway with Mateo's books.

They had both rounded the corner when Mateo finally caught up with her. She took one look at him and snorted with laughter.

"What?" he asked.

"Dart-Mouth? That was a good one."

They set Mateo's books on the bench of a far corner table and joined the lunch line.

Arms crossed, Lou grinned at him. "You know if he gets you cornered alone now—"

"Lou, he wants to pound my face in no matter what. Might as well get a few digs in." They shuffled forward a few steps at a time until they had their trays and were scooting them along the metal rail, making their requests to the cafeteria workers. By the time they'd finally sat down, Mateo had a different take. "You know, after what you told me yesterday… Do you suppose it's because he feels bad about himself that he lashes out at others?"

Her fish stick already slathered in tartar sauce, she set it back on her plate. "Mateo Sandoval, you can't be serious… can you?"

"I'm just saying, maybe it's people who hurt the most who want to hurt others."

"And maybe some people are just jerks." She popped the fish stick in her mouth. When her plate was clean, she propped her chin on her hands and gazed at Mateo.

"What?" Warmth spread from his chest to his face. He averted his gaze. Not because he didn't want to look into her eyes—he did —but because he was afraid someone would notice how much attention she was paying to him. How close they were sitting. That she was with him at all. He studied the clock intently, calculating how many minutes were left until they'd have to part ways.

Lou leaned far to the right, made faces, raised both hands up to block his view. Until his eyes returned to hers.

"I was just thinking," she said. "You're the humblest and smartest guy I know. And all this time I thought you were just a jock."

"I don't think cross country runners qualify as jocks." He downed the last of his orange juice.

"You're the best *athlete* in this school, Mateo. Even so, that's not even your best quality. I wish everyone else could see how much more there is to you." Before he could protest, she raised a finger to halt him. "That's a compliment. A very sincere compliment. My mom used to tell me when I was little and people complimented me on my hair, even if it embarrassed me, to just say 'thank you'."

The bell for fifth period rang. Everyone swarmed toward the doors and began spilling out into the hallway. Except them.

"Thank you." He thought his words were drowned out in the buzz of conversation around them, but she smiled, seeming to have heard.

They drifted back to the senior wing, stopping at Lou's locker just long enough to retrieve her books for the afternoon.

He stopped at the door to his math class, grateful there was no chance that Jed would be in his calculus class. He wasn't even sure Jed had made it to algebra.

The bell was going to ring at any moment. The hallway was almost clear of people. They both seemed to want it that way. He wasn't sure why, but—

Lou stood on her tiptoes and pecked him on the cheek. Her lips imprinted his skin with a ring of fire. He touched it with his fingertips. Had to resist dropping his backpack, pulling her to him, and kissing her back on the mouth, full-on. The urge was so strong it took all his willpower to stop himself.

Once she was settled firmly back on the flats of her feet, she said, "Same time tonight?"

The bell rang. Farther down the hallway, a few tardy students scurried into their classes. One door shut. Then another. They didn't move.

She slid his books off the top of her stack and handed them back to him. "It's okay if you don't—"

He kissed her. So quick and light he wondered if it even counted. "Tonight. Same time—and place," he added, as if she might forget.

Before he could even gauge her reaction, he ducked into his

classroom and claimed the closest seat.

"Glad you could join us, Mr. Sandoval." Ms. Uptegraph laid a syllabus on his desk. Leaning over, she peered at him over her glasses. "Next time, don't be late. I don't care how cute she is."

chapter 21
Brandy

"I don't care how cute you are." Brandy dipped the cracker in her roasted pepper humus and munched loudly. "You're not getting any this time."

One copper eyebrow arched, Sooner sat back on her haunches and blew out a sigh of indignation. When that didn't work, she lifted a paw to offer a high five.

"You can pull out every trick you know." Brandy wagged a finger at her. "You can even make up new ones. I. Don't. Care. You ate half a snack bag of my chips—and you stole them off the top of the filing cabinet while I was in the bathroom, you weasel. Lucky thing you didn't suffocate with your nose in the bag. You should be ashamed."

Sooner swiped a paw across the top of her muzzle, another trick Grayson had taught her when he asked if she was ashamed.

It was getting hard to be mad at the dog, even as terrified as Brandy had been to discover her with her snout shoved in the little foil bag, crunching away. Fortunately, she'd half ripped the bag down the side when she opened it and there had been little chance of

237

asphyxiation. All the same, she didn't want Sooner to think she could just help herself to whatever she wanted as soon as the human was out of the room. She'd heard the story from Grayson of how Sooner had gotten into the trash and kept him up all night while he waited for a dose of hydrogen peroxide to work its magic and make her vomit up a garbage smorgasbord. She certainly didn't want to let her think she could get away with shenanigans like that.

"Again, you're not getting—"

The door whooshed open and a middle-aged woman in turquoise capris and a loud floral print shirt strutted in. Brandy hadn't quite registered what the fuzz was poking out of the top of her oversized knockoff leather handbag when the woman pulled out a wiggly windup mop and set it on the floor. The toy dog rushed at Sooner, its silken tail stuck up in the air. As it neared her, it pogoed on stiff legs, announcing its presence in high-pitched yaps.

"Don't worry." The woman dropped her handbag in a chair, her voice barely audible over the stream of ear-piercing barks. "She's friendly."

Hackles up, Sooner sprang to her feet and bared her teeth, growling.

The woman gasped in horror and snatched her precious up. "Your beast was about to attack my baby!"

Cradled like an infant in its owner's arms, the dog barked even more ferociously than before.

That was when Brandy noticed the small blue vest the dog was wearing. The stitching on the side said 'Emotional Support Animal'. She'd read about websites where a person could get a fake certificate and vest so they could take their pet wherever they wanted. To become a real *service* animal required extensive training and a steady temperament in all situations. This dog clearly had neither.

Reminding herself she was at work, Brandy had to stop herself from lecturing the woman. Taking a deep breath, she commanded

Sooner to lie down behind her. Still tense, Sooner did as told, although she kept a close eye on the little tan and white dog cradled against the woman's bosom. Brandy couldn't identify the breed. Likely, it was some sort of terrier mix, possibly part poodle. Still, its behavior and the owner's irresponsibility rankled her.

"I'm sorry"—Brandy bit the inside of her lip, fully aware that she shouldn't have to be the one to apologize—"but my dog doesn't know yours. She was afraid, that's all."

"Afraid? Who could ever be afraid of Beebee? Besides, my little princess is super-duper friendly. She wouldn't harm a flea—not that she's ever had any, mind you. And I told you she was friendly, but you overreacted anyway."

"Overreacted?" Brandy pasted on a smile. "Let me explain. If you and I were two strangers passing on the street and you ran at me waving your arms in the air and screeching hysterically, I'd assume you were a lunatic and punch you if I couldn't run away. We shouldn't expect dogs to sit there idly when another dog rushes at them without a proper introduction. Better yet, maybe you could respect the fact that Sooner here is a working service dog and—"

"Beebee comforts me when I have anxiety. She loves everybody—people *and* dogs. Cats, even. She just wanted to say hi. Why is that such a big deal? Maybe if you wouldn't flip out and just let them sniff rear ends, they'd be wagging their tails in no time. You really need to calm down."

"Calm down? *I* need to calm down?!" Brandy could put up with a lot, but telling her to calm down about her dog's space being intruded upon was not a matter she was willing to budge on. It wasn't the first time she'd crossed paths with an irresponsible owner, but it was the last time she was going to let it slide, job or no job. "Your dog startled her. You haven't absorbed a—"

"Ladies, ladies... take a break." Hands waving, Rex burst forth from his office. He stepped between them. "Aster Holbrook, is that

239

you? I haven't seen you in what… four, five years?"

Aster sniffed. "Ten, actually."

"And you've had the same husband all this time?"

She glared at him, her acrylic nails scratching furiously at Beebee's neck. "Don't be ridiculous."

"What brings you here? I thought you were with Eugene Oldman last settlement. I figured you'd go to Somerset or Lexington for legal advice after he bowed out—that or you'd finally found 'the one'. Trouble in paradise?"

"Hell, more likely." She pulled her shoulders up, summoning her humility. "I need… representation."

"Ah, do you, now?" He turned toward Brandy and rolled his eyes. Aster couldn't see his expression from where she was, but the message was pretty clear. "Can you pull up my schedule, Brandy?" Returning his attention to Aster, he explained, "It's been a regular crazy town here ever since Eugene retired. Wasn't very considerate of him to do that without notice. Better yet, he could've trained up a replacement to take over his practice. Nice place for someone fresh out of law school to start out—established clientele, broad array of legal services needed. A new attorney can either make a lifelong business out of it or use it as a stepping stone. Ain't no shame in the latter. Let me get you a beverage while I check my availability. That cute li'l critter of yours need any water? I'd offer a biscuit, but she'd probably break a jaw on the size o' the ones I keep stashed away."

"I carry my own bottled water for Beebee. I don't want her getting an upset tummy. She has a sensitive digestive system." Aster marched to the chairs and took her time to choose which one to sit in. "And no refreshments for me, thank you. I'm on a cleanse. I don't want to ingest anything not on the plan."

He came around the backside of Brandy's desk to peer at the screen, making lots of 'aha' and 'hmm' sounds as Brandy clicked from page to page on the weekly calendar. "Yep, yep. Well, that doesn't look promising, does it, Brandy? I'm not seeing an opening until early December, are you?"

"That's correct." She'd let Rex steer this ship.

He approached Aster. "I am so, so terribly, awfully sorry, Ms. Holbrook. Is it Holbrook, still? S'pose I should've asked."

"Holbrook-Weatherford, to be precise. But December, you say?" She surveyed the office, empty of patrons. "How can you possibly be that booked up? I drive by here all the time. Can't say I've ever seen more than a couple of cars in the parking lot."

Hesitating, Rex scratched at the back of his neck.

"Court," Brandy interjected. "He's at the courthouse a lot. Criminal cases. Getting a load of those lately. He sometimes meets the clients—we don't like to call them defendants—at the jailhouse."

"Detention facility," Rex corrected in a low voice.

"Right, right." Brandy clicked the mouse a few more times. "Should I pencil you in for… say, December 9 at three p.m., Ms. Holbrook-Weatherford? Oh, wait… he *can* see you earlier. Looks like there's an opening same day at two."

Unable to hide her sneer, Aster stuffed Beebee back in her purse and gave Sooner a look of disdain. "That won't be necessary. I'll look up an attorney in Somerset. My sister knows a few. I'm sure they'll be happy to take my money."

"Have a nice day!" Brandy called as the door swung shut behind her. Then to Rex, "Sorry, I tried to be nice, wanted to help her, but…"

"Brandy, some people don't want to be helped." He opened the front door and peered out briefly, as if to make sure she wasn't coming back. "Did her little gremlin cannon out of her satchel straight at Sooner?"

"Yes, how'd you know?"

"That Tasmanian devil did it to my beloved in the waiting room at the dentist last year. She about drop-kicked the little monster right into the magazine rack. Aster claimed it was a designer dog—a teacup French bull-poo. With papers."

"A French *what?*"

"Bull-poo. That's when the daddy-dog is a French Bulldog and the mama's a teacup Poodle. If it's the other way around, they're a Poo-bull. Bragged she paid five grand for it."

"You're serious—five thousand dollars for a mutt?" Brandy shook her head. "Don't get me wrong, mixed breeds are fine. I've known some wonderful ones. My first obedience dog as a kid was a mixed breed. But geesh, I only paid a fraction of that for Sooner and she has a pedigree a dozen generations long with titled, health tested parents."

"Woman obviously has more money than sense."

"So you're not mad at me for ticking her off? I lost you what sounds like a big chunk of business."

Rex waved it off. "You did me a favor, Brandy. And Sooner there is a good judge of character." He winked at the dog. "I worked with Aster on her *first* divorce. Most difficult client I've ever had."

"How many times has she been married?"

He thought about it as he paused before his office door. "If I'm counting right, that'll be her fifth."

"I'm not surprised. Who'd want to stay with her once she shows her true colors. What I don't get is why anyone would marry her in the first place."

"That one's easy. Her granddad started out as a cattle farmer, owned thousands of acres on the north end of town. Prime pasture. Eventually sold it off parcel by parcel for all those housing developments you pass on the way here. She's the richest woman in Adair County."

"If she was born into money, then what's *her* story?"

"Her story?"

"Yeah, why is she so... so nasty?"

"I reckon because it's easier to blame someone else when things don't go her way. Anywho, some people just aren't worth the aggravation. She can throw her money around somewhere else. No skin off my back." He ripped open the wrapper on a mini candy bar he took from the candy bowl on Brandy's desk and popped it in his mouth. "Say, how long's it been since Sooner got zapped? A week now?"

"Ten days, I think. Grayson took her for a checkup a couple of days ago. Doc Hunter says she's doing great. No lasting effects that he can tell, aside from a few singed hairs."

"Ain't that something? You'd think she'd have superpowers now with that much voltage running through her."

"Nope, same old Sooner." Brandy patted her.

Rex went back to his office and Brandy returned her attention to the digital files she'd been searching just before Faderville's own Beverly Hills housewife had sashayed in. An email alert popped up and she opened it. "Hey, Rex!"

"Still here," he answered through the open door.

"That immigration attorney says she can be here at the end of the month to meet with Mateo."

"Valentina Gutierrez? Excellent!" He returned and read the email. "What time?"

"She only has a window from three to about five... Oh, he'd have to miss practice, but I think Fridays are pretty easy. Grayson would probably let him run on his own."

"Make it happen, then." He retreated to his office. "Let your fellow know the boy will be in a meeting that day, will you?"

A few moments later, Rex reappeared in the doorway. "Not meaning to shun you, dear heart, but excuse me while I make some calls." With an apologetic smile, he closed the door.

That meant he was going to shoot the breeze with some colleagues in the area or people at the courthouse to get the scoop on ongoing cases. Brandy had been amazed at the number of personal favors he was able to call in due to his ability to reach out to others.

There was also an email from Denny thanking Rex for bringing his family back together. He put in a good word for Brandy being such a welcoming presence at the office. And Shelly doted on the new cat. Apparently, it took her mind off of her physical ailments.

For years, Brandy had believed that success was about goals and plans: getting through college with good grades, landing a steady job at decent pay, saving for and buying her own house before the age of thirty, then her nearly obsessive training and titling of dogs. Before she knew it, two plus decades of adulthood had slipped by and what had she really done to contribute to society? She hadn't made anyone else's life worse, but she hadn't exactly made it better—unless you counted patiently walking a client through complex record-keeping software.

Yet here was Rex, small-town attorney, guiding average people through the intricacies of legal roadblocks and thus assisting them through some of the more difficult stages of life.

She'd hesitated to take this job. Change was always risky. At first, it had seemed like all she was here for was to sort through papers and assign items a place. But purpose had found her. Even in this most ordinary of jobs.

"How about you—do you like your job, Sooner?" she asked the dog. Yawning, Sooner lay down. "No comment, huh? Fine coworker you are."

—o00o—

"You are here late," Ynez said in halting English, carefully pronouncing each word, as Brandy had taught her. A look of concentration on her face, she set down her basket of cleaning supplies and raised a finger. *"You're* here late." She beamed with pride. "Better?"

"Much. Just waiting for Grayson to pick me up," Brandy replied in Spanish. A good fifteen minutes had already gone by since Rex had left. "Seems like practice is running a little late today." Speaking in alternate languages was a ritual they'd adopted to help each other learn faster. Brandy found she had to switch gears quickly, as an interpreter would. "What is it, Ynez?"

"I worry for Mateo," Ynez said, reverting to her first language as she collapsed into the chair next to her basket. "He has worked so hard for so long and... I cannot imagine how my heart will break if he is ever sent back to a place he barely remembers. I remember it, though. And while it was once my home, things have changed so much. It is not his home. There is no future for him in Mexico. His relatives there, even if they could take him in, what could they do for him? No, he is much better off here, whether in Faderville or some big city. Here, he can be safe. He has choices. So far, he has chosen well."

The tears came then. Brandy went to her and put her arms around her. As much as she wanted to tell her about the immigration lawyer, she'd leave that for Mateo to do. Ynez had lived in fear not only for her own well-being ever since she arrived here, but her family's as well. Which made Brandy wonder—

"Ynez, I don't mean to pry, but Mateo's mother... Where is she now? Does she have a job somewhere else? I only ask because, from the way you've talked about her, she didn't go back to Mexico. Yet I know it's just been you two for quite some time."

Ynez drew a tissue from her pocket and mopped at her eyes, then blew her nose. "She is in Chicago... I think."

"You don't know?"

"Not for certain. We haven't spoken for over a year."

"Why?"

Her mouth firmly set, Ynez shrugged.

"You don't have to tell me, Ynez." Brandy squeezed her hand. "It's okay."

Then, in very plain English, Ynez said, "Anarosa has *not* made good choices."

With that, Ynez rose and began cleaning. Brandy knew when not to force something. Whatever it was had been deeply hurtful to Ynez.

After returning some phone calls, Brandy checked the time. Grayson was due any minute, but there was still a little time to spare, so she decided to pay Ynez a compliment.

"You know what amazes me about you, Ynez?"

One eyebrow raised, Ynez glanced at her and went back to attacking the horizontal surfaces with a dust rag. "What?"

"How well you do what you do. Sometimes I don't even notice something's dirty until you start cleaning it. By the time you're done, the place looks so much more inviting. It has worked out so much better with you coming twice a week. I even referred you to, I don't know, a half dozen of our clients lately."

"Ah, that would explain why I have more business than I can handle now. I have to remind myself it's not a bad problem to have." She swapped her dirty dust cloth for a clean one. "But thank you. Last week I was able to purchase internet for our phones. It may not be the best, but it will help Mateo with his schoolwork so he doesn't always have to go to the library to use their computers to look things up."

"That's great! It's almost impossible these days to operate in the world without decent internet. I don't think most people who live in cities where it's ubiquitous realize how not everyone has it or can afford it. Maybe someday that'll change."

Although there was a generation between her and Ynez, they had become unexpectedly close. Their conversations, familiar and

246

easy, made Brandy think that this would've been what it was like to have a mother you were close with.

"What is it?" Ynez stood in front of her.

"Oh, nothing. I was just... thinking of my mother."

"She died?"

"Years ago." Looking down, Brandy shook her head. "Overdose. Prescription drugs."

This time it was Ynez's turn to hug Brandy. When she finally let go of her, she told her. "My daughter... I don't know if there are drugs involved. Possibly. But... her choices... She is with a man who... uses her." She didn't need to say how. They both understood.

"Why does she stay?"

She shrugged. "When I ask her, I don't get good answers. I think she believes she owes him. When she went to Chicago—to look for a job, she said—he let her stay with him. They have never married. But she is an adult. I cannot make her do anything. I just don't think... I don't think it is a healthy relationship, if you understand what I mean."

"Is she afraid he'll hurt her? Has he?"

"Maybe. I don't know. But I think she is also afraid to leave. That he'll turn her in. And then things will be worse for her. For now, she has a home, food, some nice things... If she is ever sent back, she won't have any of that." She took the vacuum from the closet and, after plugging it in, fully unraveled the cord. "People do not understand what it is like for women like us, women who have nothing, who come from nothing. Sometimes, women in that position, they feel that if a man makes promises, waves some money at them, they can swallow their dignity, if only for a little while. But then they become trapped. Men like Anarosa's—they know how to keep them... what is the word? Dependent. They break down their confidence, make them believe they are not smart enough or don't have any skills to make it on their own. They make the women believe

247

that they *need* them. For everything."

Without further explanation, Ynez hit the switch and began vacuuming. Brandy couldn't imagine what it was like to be so desperate and terrified that you stayed in a clearly dysfunctional relationship because that was the only way you felt your basic needs would be met and you wouldn't... *couldn't* survive otherwise. But then, her father had always supported her choices in life. Even encouraged her to be independent. And she had been. Had always known it was possible. Even when she'd doubted herself, he'd been there to cheer her on, let her know if anything fell through he'd help her out.

While Ynez vacuumed, Brandy pretended to straighten her desk. In reality, she was only moving things around, trying to get her head around it. And then... then she understood.

Ynez and her daughter hadn't come from the same background as her. Not anything remotely similar. For them it was different not only culturally, but economically. Despite the problems with Brandy's mother, her father had provided more than sufficiently for them. A high school diploma had been a given, a college degree the natural next step. Brandy's dad had even co-signed on her first car loan and guided her through the home buying process. None of that had existed for Ynez and Anarosa. Where they came from, leaving school to start a family or for a job had been the expectation. Even so, the kinds of jobs available for an uneducated woman were the low-paying kind. *If* jobs were even available.

During their conversations, Ynez had also mentioned the gangs that terrorized their neighborhood with guns. Guns made in America and bought on the black market. She'd hinted, too, that women— even girls in their early teens—were not safe from the unsolicited attentions of men.

At some point, Ynez had made the hard decision to send her daughter and grandson to relatives farther away from the city and come to America to work for money. When she had a home of her own and enough money to send for them, she did.

That was probably when things went awry for Anarosa. Brandy knew that the men—the 'coyotes' she learned they were called after talking with Ynez—were far from being upstanding human beings. They took money from desperate people and shipped them like cattle. Sometimes not even that humanely, packing them in box trucks without cooling, or herding them across the wilderness like errant sheep. Many died in the attempt.

An unfamiliar heaviness filled Brandy's chest. There were so many misconceptions about immigrants, so little understanding of their situations. If only people would—

A tap on the window startled Brandy. Grayson gazed in from out on the sidewalk, smiling. Beside him was Sooner, her liver-colored nose pressed to the glass. Brandy gathered her keys and purse, then waved at Ynez on the way out.

As soon as they were in the car, Grayson started talking, but Brandy was only half paying attention.

"So Mateo has started running with her again. They're both doing better, although Mateo's shoulder is still a little wonky. Maybe he tore something when he fell. Makes me wonder if he ought to seek a formal diagnosis or if it was something that will just take time to... Hey, are you listening?"

A couple of seconds went by before Brandy snapped out of her thoughts. "Yes... Well, sort of."

"What's on your mind?"

She shook her head. "Something Ynez told me. I'm not sure it's my place to share, though."

For a few moments, he was silent. Until, "Does it have to do with Mateo? I'm only asking because he's my athlete and I should probably know if something's wrong. Is there—something I should know, I mean?"

249

"Right now, no. I… I've just come to realize they've faced a lot of challenges that people like you and me don't know anything about."

"People like you and me, huh? That sounds pretty weighty."

"It is. I think… I hope Mateo will turn out okay. But if he does, it will be because of the sacrifices his grandmother made."

"You can say that again. I admire her. Her hard work is reflected in his."

Brandy watched the scenery drift by as they turned onto the road to Grayson's house. "You know, who you are isn't so much about your big successes in the world. It's about how you handle the everyday: the mundane chores, the interactions with people, your mindset. I see that in Ynez and Rex… even you."

"How do you mean?"

"Someone can be the most accomplished person in the world," Brandy elaborated, "and still not be worth admiring. Others can tackle ordinary jobs with pride and zeal, like Ynez. Or use their personal talents to pay it forward, like you. Or make every person they come across feel like they matter, like Rex does."

"Sounds a little like you're talking about yourself, too."

She narrowed her eyes at him, then grinned. "Actually, I wasn't. It's just that I think sometimes we admire the wrong people—the ones with freakish talent, or who got lucky, or had every advantage or loads of money. Maybe instead, we should herald the people who clean our offices and mow our lawns, the ones who pick our vegetables and drive the trucks that bring food to the grocery stores. We could do with a few less CEOs in the world. But the ordinary workers who make our lives easier? Yeah, not so much."

They pulled into Grayson's driveway. He turned the engine off. Sat there staring at her.

She searched his eyes, his face, but couldn't quite discern the mood behind them. "What is it? You look pensive. Like you're about to say something mind-blowingly profound."

His intense expression softened. "Just… thank you."

"For what?"

He leaned across the space between them and kissed her lovingly. "For reminding me I should never take anyone for granted. I did that once before. I won't do it again."

—o0oo—

They ate dinner on the front porch that evening, as crickets chirped their chorus and a crowd of sparrows quarreled in the nearby azalea bushes. The last of the summer's fireflies flickered yellow in the pastures like stars drifting on a cosmic wind.

"Did I tell you I ran into Loretta at the donut shop yesterday?" His plate clean, Grayson set it on the small round metal table between them and stretched his arms over his head.

Brandy was seated in the other Adirondack chair next to the steps, Sooner lying beside her, paws dangling over the top step, both eyes closed. Her stomach was so full from Grayson's chili and cornbread that she was close to falling asleep herself. "No, I don't think you did. Did she have anything new to say?"

Not that she really wanted to know. The easy friendship she'd once had with Loretta felt somehow tainted now. Whenever they met next, she'd be civil to her, but her opinion of her—

"She offered to make Thanksgiving dinner for us. I know it's a little ways off yet, but…"

Her spine stiffened. She wasn't sure she could be civil for *that* long—an entire holiday feast. Not even for Grayson's sake. "Don't they have family of their own?"

"They do, but her daughter is spending that holiday with their in-laws."

She could feel Grayson staring at her. There had to be a graceful way out of it. And then—

"Loretta wanted to know if it'd be all right to invite Ynez and Mateo, too."

The question took her totally by surprise. "What? Why?"

Grayson gazed out at the flickering landscape. "Guess she noticed you've hardly said two words to her since that evening." He turned his face toward hers, his features barely lit in the dimming glow of dusk. "She said she's sorry. About what she said. Wants to make it up to you. To them."

Brandy let that roll around in her mind. Tried to make sense of it. She was sure Grayson had left something out. "Was this your idea?"

"No!" Clenching the arms of his chair, he sat up straighter. Then, "Well... I may have gone on and on about how hard Mateo works. Harder than anyone else on the team. And how much I admired him for that. And said how he must've learned his work ethic from his grandmother. And mentioned how close you and Ynez have become..." A faint grin tilted his mouth. Like he desperately wanted for her to accept this olive branch. No matter whose idea it was. He sat back again. Relaxed. "Okay, sure, I may have led her there... maybe... but *she* was the one who suggested all of us gathering for the holiday—and she *did* say she was sorry. Brandy... please?"

Thanksgiving was more than a month away. Plenty of time to let go of her own disappointment and embrace hope. "Yes, I'd like that. And thank *you*."

"For...?"

"For being you. For caring enough to make things better."

"Well, not talking about things doesn't solve them, does it? Take it from me."

"So you're saying *I* should've told her how disappointed I was?"

"If it helps, I know it's not always easy to know what to say or how to ask something."

In that moment, she felt there was still more he was trying to get out, so she just waited it out. Waited what seemed like forever.

Finally, "Brandy?"

"I'm still here." Seconds plodded by, heavy with anticipation. "Did you have a question?"

"Oh, yeah, yeah. Actually, more like a statement, but I was wondering if you might agree."

"With what?"

"I could live like this forever. Right here. Dog asleep on the porch. A day's satisfying work done. A belly full of white chicken chili and cornbread. An old home full of history. A gorgeous piece of property—horses in the pasture, trees a hundred years old or more, the green hills, the woods, the winding country roads..." He went silent for a few breaths, the sounds of the night filling the space between his words. "Still, it wouldn't be heaven without you here."

In that moment, Brandy knew life couldn't get much better than it was now. Except for having the full use of her legs back, however. But she was working on that.

"Yeah, it *is* heaven."

She wished she could wake up to it every morning. But in an hour, he'd take her and Sooner back to her apartment. Tomorrow, he'd drive her to work, then pick the dog up in the afternoon for practice before returning to fetch her for dinner. It was a comfortable routine, but—

"I was thinking... Ah heck, I'll just blurt it out. Brandy, will you..." Rising, he crouched before her and took her hand. "Will you move in with me?"

Quickly, he added, "I talked to a guy who installs those chair lift things. He came out yesterday. Said the staircase is plenty wide enough and he could have a crew out here first thing next week. That way, we could be together every night. Every morning. I even have someone coming the week after to put down an asphalt path out to the barn, so you could go out there to talk to Loretta whenever you want. If there's anything else you can think of…"

He left it hanging there, his enthusiasm fading the longer it took her to reply. It wasn't that she didn't like the idea—she did. The idea of eliminating all the back and forth made a lot of sense, not to mention shuttling the dog around like a child of divorce. Plus, they could be together, instead of existing like bachelor and bachelorette, parting ways intermittently to return to solitude.

It was just that she'd thought when he began with 'Brandy, will you…?' that he was going to ask an altogether different question and her heart had taken a leap.

"Can you arrange for a live-in physical therapist?" she finally answered.

His smile faded. He lowered his head, his grip on her fingers loosening. "It's okay if you don't—"

"Grayson, you asked if there was anything else. I was only joking. It *is* convenient that they're right there in Fox Hollow, but I think I could manage it. I'm down to twice a week now."

He dared to meet her eyes. "So you're saying…?"

"If you think we're ready"—she placed her other hand on top of his and squeezed extra hard—"then yes."

chapter 22
Sooner

"You sure you're ready?" Jamal asked.

Brandy squinted at him. "Do you think I am?"

"You're the only one who knows."

We were in the physical therapy room at Fox Hollow. Brandy was learning something not new, but old.

She was learning to walk again.

"What about other patients you've had, Jamal? Did they ever... fail? Were some just never able to walk again?"

Jamal reached under the nearby table where I was lying. I flopped over so he could scratch my belly, just like I liked it. He was a dark-skinned younger guy with big shoulder muscles but a quiet, soothing voice. And he gave the best tummy rubs ever. "Everyone's different, Brandy. Different degree of injuries, different ages and backgrounds, different mindsets. I can't really compare."

"But did any of them try and then fall flat on their face?"

Leaning against the padded table behind him, he crossed his arms. "Sure, but you know what? They lived. Maybe a bruise or two, but no bones were broken."

"So they never walked again?"

"Some of them, no. Some, yes. A lot never try at all. But only those who do stand a chance of getting back on their feet."

"Damn your honesty. So what if I can't?"

"Why do you even ask that? You're usually so positive."

"I've never tried to walk on my own before. I mean since... you know. Stand holding onto something, sure. But today... I don't know. It just seems so daunting. And I hate that you're making so much damn sense."

"Swearing won't help, but if it makes you feel better—"

"Shut the hell up, Jamal. I'm trying to talk myself into this."

"Ouch. Keep at it, girlfriend. Go ahead and use every word you know. I never take it personally. I see it more as a reflection of your own inertia. I had an eighty-year-old man used to call me an SOB at the beginning of every session after his knee replacement. Had that dude doing laps around the flower garden within a month." He readjusted the walker before her, barely moving it an inch. "Now, let's put all the parts together, just like we practiced."

"We?"

"Work with me, will you? Let's pretend I'm the cheerleader and you're the star ball player. Now go ahead. Lean forward. Push yourself up."

She did. Smoothly. Threw one hand out. Clutched the walker. Then the other hand. Raised herself. Stood with her elbows locked.

"Look there! Steady as a rock." Jamal backed up a step.

"Oh, I got this part down pat. It's the moving part that scares me."

"Naw, nothing to it. You spent your whole life walking before last year. It's like riding a bike. You may be a bit rusty at first, but then—"

"A bit?"

"Just do it, okay? Now slide the walker forward a few inches and

256

at the same time step out with that left leg. On three. One, two—"

With a tentative jerk, Brandy scooted the walker forward. But her left leg lagged behind and she wobbled.

"Now lift yourself ever so slightly and rock forward. You can do this, c'mon. I already put a bet down on you."

"There's a pool on whether or not I can use this thing?"

"We do that with everyone. Now, come this way." He stepped backward.

"Don't walk backward, please. You make that look too easy."

"You're stalling."

Leaning her upper body forward, Brandy brought her right leg even with the other. For a few moments, she stood frozen in disbelief.

"Again," Jamal said.

She took another step, then another. Tiny steps, yet huge ones.

"You got it, girl. You got it," Jamal praised. He clapped and whooped. Gyrated his body around with his hands circling above his head. "That's what I'm talking about! Gonna have you running a marathon by next year."

I barked twice to celebrate with them. Nobody even told me to be quiet.

"Let's just settle for me getting around my house for now, can we?"

They did this a few more times, letting Brandy rest in between sets. Each time, she got a little more confident, a little quicker.

"You're going to let me take this home, right?"

"Of course," Jamal said as he helped Brandy back into her wheelchair. "I want you to practice at least once a day on your own—not more than twice yet, mind you—but always with someone there, okay?"

Her face, which only moments before had been bright and smiling, fell. "With someone. Oh. In case I fall. Right."

"Partly. It's pretty common to start to feel a little too confident and overdo it. But it's also to keep you accountable. Maybe your fiancé—"

"Boyfriend," Brandy corrected. "Although soon we'll be living together at Grayson's place. So I don't know what that makes us."

I perked up at the mention of Grayson's name. Was he here? On his way? I peered at the front door. No, no Grayson. Lately, he'd been at Brandy's place a lot, helping her pack her things into boxes, taking a few at a time back to his place. I knew it could only mean one thing—that we were all going to stay in one place together, at last. That meant all my toys and balls and my beloved Frisbee would be at Grayson's house. Content, I stretched my legs and yawned.

"Makes you two pretty serious, I'd say. Maybe he could help you. Is he coming to pick you up like usual?"

"No, actually. Rex is picking me up today." Pausing, she touched the pendant on her necklace and sniffed back tears. "Say, I'd appreciate it if, next time you do see Grayson, you don't tell him we're working on this, okay?"

"Whoa." Jamal handed her a tissue. "What are those for? Happy tears, I hope."

"I don't know what I feel, Jamal. Relieved, overwhelmed, sad… scared?"

"Scared? Why? Baby girl, you just did the equivalent of climbing Mt. Everest. Proud doesn't begin to describe how I feel about what you just did. I only wish you hadn't been the very first appointment of the day so there would've been an audience here to witness how amazing you were. And not only once, but what—five, six times?"

"You'd make a great cheerleader, Jamal."

"Thanks. I was."

"Huh?"

"A cheerleader. For the UK Wildcats. What, you pegged me for a football player?"

"Well, yeah. I mean, the muscles."

"Those are gymnast muscles, thank you. I can do ten backflips in a row."

"Why did I not know this about you?"

"Because my job is to focus on you. Now tell me, what's on your mind?"

Brandy seemed to draw into herself then. I went to her and rooted at her hand, sure that if she stroked my fur she'd remember how much I loved her and forget whatever was troubling her. Her hand flopped limply beside her wheelchair as I nudged it with my nose. Eventually, I began licking her fingers.

She grabbed my snout lightly. "Sooner, stop. That's annoying."

She said my name! But her tone...

I sat back and looked up at her face. She was sad. I didn't understand. What was there to be sad about today? She'd walked. I was here. We'd go to Brandy's work together soon. Later, Grayson would take me to practice and then we'd all have supper together. It was a good life. A very good life.

"For a long time," Brandy began, "I thought I knew how the rest of my life would be. I lived alone, but I wasn't lonely. I had friends to do things with, my dad and brother to talk to, my dog here to keep me busy. Life was... good. Then one day, it wasn't anymore. Just like that. Everything changed in an instant. Healing took all my energy. I hurt in places and to degrees I'd never experienced before. And I'd lost my dog. My dad fell ill, then eventually died. As for my friends, they did what they could, but they had their own lives to live. I understood.

"Then, Grayson showed up one day with Sooner. As dark as my days had been, there was suddenly a ray of hope. I can't say I've enjoyed depending on this contraption"—she tapped the arms of her wheelchair—"but it's better than being bedridden. And to have someone who cared enough about me to want to be with me, even as I am—I was blown away and skeptical all at the same time. I mean really, why? But I shoved all those doubts aside and focused on what I had to be grateful for. Which was a lot, considering.

"Still, you get used to how things are. Comfortable, even when they're not ideal. Someone once said we grow used to our own suffering and don't want to let go of it. Maybe because we're afraid of changing. Sort of better the devil you do know than the one you don't. And now, here I am, taking steps, *real* steps to walking again. It just seems like such an enormous undertaking, you know? I'm terrified by the thought of it. Afraid I'll fall flat on my bum. In front of people. Afraid I'll always have a limp. That I'll be so slow walking down the aisle in the grocery store that people will cuss under their breath at me." Her eyes unfocused, she paused. "I'm even afraid that Grayson will... I don't even know. See me differently. As someone he no longer has to rescue."

For a long time, Jamal didn't say anything. He refolded a towel and placed it under the bench he'd been leaning on. "I'm not sure that what you're afraid of is what you've actually said."

"Then what *am* I afraid of? I'm not even sure. I just feel so... so uncertain."

"Disappointing yourself. Afraid to accept that, while you will get stronger, you'll never quite be the same person you once were— physically, that is."

"Geesh, that's pretty sobering. Thanks for the pep talk," she said sarcastically.

"Brandy, you're not just your body. You're this." He thumped his chest, then tapped his temple. "And this."

Another patient and therapist entered the room. The therapist was Miranda, who I'd seen many times before in passing. The patient was a girl, half-grown, with two dark brown braids and thick glasses. She wobbled slightly when she walked, as if she had to steady herself with every step.

Miranda led her to one of the far tables. "You look like you're getting pretty used to those new legs of yours, Hope."

With a hop and a twist, Hope was sitting on the table. Clutching her knees, she swung her feet back and forth. Only they weren't feet, but curved pieces of... I'm not sure what they were. Something hard and shiny. That was when I noticed that her real legs ended just below the knee and those things like feet but not feet were somehow attached there.

"Sooo much better than the old prosthetics," Hope said, beaming. "Daddy says maybe I can do the Paralympics one day. I want to be a triathlete, just like him. I'm already pretty good at swimming. I can kind of bike, but I'd need a special bike. A fast one. If I run a lot, I can do it. I know I can. Tatiana McFadden is my hero." She saw Brandy then and waved at her. "Do *you* know who she is?"

"Sorry, I don't," Brandy answered.

"She's a track athlete. Wheelchair."

"Wow, sounds like it takes a lot of work."

"She's a professional! You should see her arm muscles." Making two fists, she curled her arms upward to show off her own muscles. "I'm working on mine. Daddy says I have to be a little older to start serious training, though." She made a frowny face.

"Don't worry, honey," Miranda told her. "You've got plenty of time for all that. Now, let's check your flexibility, then we'll get to our exercises, all right?"

Jamal wheeled Brandy out to the front lobby to wait for Rex.

"Jamal, what happened to Hope and how long has she been like that?"

"Since she was born. The umbilical cord got wrapped around her feet *in utero*, cutting off the circulation. They had to amputate when she was an infant."

"She just seems so..."

"Hopeful? Positive? If it's any consolation, she's never known anything else."

"So she doesn't see herself as having a disability?"

"I wouldn't go that far. She knows she has it harder. She just doesn't let that stop her from doing what's possible. Even from doing amazing things—and I'm pretty sure one day she will. In fact, I'm going to go ask for her autograph. She's going to win a gold medal someday, I bet."

Cool air blasting up through the vent by the front window, I lay over it. I was just drifting off for my second, or maybe third, nap of the day when Rex pulled up outside.

—o0Oo—

It was hard to sleep when Rex talked. Not because he talked a lot, which he did, but because he'd start talking at a normal volume, then get really loud and excited, then go back to normal, then back to loud. Every once in a while, he'd whistle or laugh or smack his palm against his thigh or 'knock on wood'. He certainly didn't know how to speak softly like Grayson or Brandy.

"Let me get this straight." Rex drummed his fingers on the steering wheel. "You're learning to use a walker, but you don't want Grayson to know?"

"That's right," Brandy said.

I was sitting between them in the truck. While I loved getting to sit up front where I could see so much, Rex made me a little nervous. He drove faster than Grayson, didn't leave much room between his bumper and the car ahead of him, and he tended to hit the brakes late when we came to a stop, then punch the gas really hard when he started again. If I hadn't had a strong stomach, I probably would've tossed my kibble on the dashboard a few times.

Rex fixed her with a hard stare. "Why?"

Gripping the armrest on the door, Brandy stole a glance at the speedometer. "You do realize you're doing sixty-eight in a fifty-five zone, right?"

"Right, sorry. Thanks for the reminder." He slowed down. "I have gotten a couple of tickets on this stretch. Sometimes I forget Bruce hides in his cruiser just the other side of that white barn ahead."

"Bruce? You know the highway patrolman by his first name?"

"Sure. Figured out a long time ago if you make an encounter like that casual, they're more likely to let you off the hook. Anyway, why wouldn't you let Grayson in on it, Brandy? Doggone it, that's a big deal. I know he'd be proud of you."

"He would. I agree."

"So then why the big secret?"

"You *can't* tell him, Rex."

"Why the hell not?"

"I'm saving it. As a surprise."

"Surprise for what?" Looking ahead, he squinted, like he was thinking extra hard. "Ohhh, oh, oh, oh. I get it now. You think he's gonna ask you?"

She shrugged. "Sometimes I think he's about to and then… sometimes I'm not sure he ever will."

"You two go together like honey and biscuits. I understand courting for a while before taking the leap, but there's no doubt in my mind he wants to be with you until you're a couple of geriatrics."

"I'm moving in with him."

"Ah, okay. Personally, I never understood the cohabitation thing myself, but I say whatever floats your boat. So what's the end game here? Trying to figure out if the way you brush your teeth or he leaves the toilet set up ruins the magic before you commit to forever?"

Leaning into me, Brandy hugged me lightly. "I'm not sure, Rex… Wait, why am I even talking to you about something so

263

personal? You're my boss!"

"First of all, I asked. Second, not like I don't care about you. So do you even know what *you* want?"

"Well, I know that Grayson's the one for me."

"Great! It's settled then. You just keep working on him and before you know it—"

"See, that's it, though. I don't know."

"You're two adults. You can talk about these things, you know."

"It's not that easy. He's been married before. I think... I think he has doubts about marriage."

"But you don't?"

"No, not really. I mean, everything that's happened this past year—the accident, Sooner getting lost and him finding her—I know it sounds cliché, but it's like we were meant to be together. Listen to me. I never thought I'd be one to talk about 'fate' and 'love at first sight', but that's exactly what it feels like. To me, anyway. I'm just not sure about Grayson. Not that I don't believe for a second he doesn't love me, mind you. But... I think he has doubts about himself. About being the person he'd need to be for me down the road—and I don't want him to feel like he has to commit to me for the rest of his life out of some sense of guilt or pity or even duty to the universe. Is this making any sense?"

"Not one iota." Shaking his head, he sighed wearily. "Everybody thinks marriage is a stroll in the rose garden. That if two folk are meant to be together, they're going to get along perfectly every day of their lives. Poppycock! Case in point—me. Ask my beloved what it's like to live with a man who can't find his car keys, wallet, or briefcase on a daily basis. Who shows up late to dinner and dominates every conversation when we have friends over for drinks—not that I do that on purpose, but my beloved has this telltale glare that says, 'Shut your trap, Rex. Let someone else speak for a change.' Anywho, I was saying... She ain't left me yet. Some'd say she has plenty of reason to. I don't claim to be perfect. In fact, I admit I can be a little challenging to live with."

"What? No! Really? I can't imagine." Brandy rolled her eyes. "You're the *perfect* boss."

"I must be if I let you talk to me like that." He smiled at her and they both laughed. "My point is—ah, hell, there wasn't any point. Just saying, none of us are perfect. Not Grayson, not you... certainly not me. Although my beloved is pretty dang close. And marriage is not a foolproof institution. It's a contract not to give up on each other. You let Grayson know that no matter what happens, no matter how dark things get for either of you or ugly between you, that you'll stick around and work it out because it'll make both of you better people and your relationship even stronger. I've seen enough divorces in my day—Aster Holbrook-Whatever, being a prime example—to know that too often people give up because working it out means admitting you played some part in it falling apart. Easier to blame the other person. Do you know what 'irreconcilable differences' really means? It doesn't mean anything except, 'I give up.'"

"I follow you, Rex. I really do." It got remarkably quiet. Like they'd said all there was to say. Just as we pulled into the parking lot behind the office, Brandy added, "But it's not really the piece of paper that determines the commitment, is it? Look at Oprah and Stedman."

Rex scratched his head. "Pardon? Should I know them? Can't say as I do."

"Oprah Winfrey and her significant other, Stedman Graham. They never married. Didn't feel it was necessary. And they've been together a long time. Or Kurt Russell and Goldie Hawn. Or Spencer Tracy and—"

"Is there a point to this?"

"Just thinking out loud. I don't want to be like some twenty-year-old girl who thinks her life's worth is determined by finding herself a good man to marry. Why not, you know, just be happy with how things are? With life as it is, right now?" Sighing, she put an arm over my vest and rested the bottom of her chin on my head. "No, I *know*—I really *am* happy with the way things are. I am. Thanks for listening, though."

"Anytime, my dear. Anytime."

"You know what else?" Brandy twisted sideways to gaze at him more directly. "Who says the guy has to be the one to do the asking, huh?"

Rex threw his hands up. "Don't look at me! I'm all for women doing whatever they want." He took the key from the ignition. "Time for another day at work. You up for it?"

"Always." As we waited for Rex to get Brandy's wheelchair out of the bed, she pressed her hands to my cheeks and said, "How about you, Sooner? You ready to go to work?"

I was always ready. But I licked her face, anyway.

She laughed, which was a happy sound, so I licked her nose and cheeks and eyelids and ears...

"All righty, you two." Rex held the door open for her. "Let's get to work then."

Yes! I barked. *Work!*

They laughed.

One of many jobs was to make my people happy. Which made *me* happy.

chapter 23
Mateo

Happy. That was how Mateo felt. Occasionally, he was still reminded of Tervo's absence, his passing a fresh thud in the cadence of his heart. But then he'd remember all that Tervo—and Coach Grayson—had entrusted him with.

As his injury improved, so had his confidence. This week was the first he'd sensed his legs more solidly beneath him. Curiously, running with the dog at first had made him forget his pain, until day after day it became so little that he was seldom aware of it at all. In the meantime, Sooner's joy at greeting him every day at practice for a run had been infectious. He rediscovered the delight of feeling the earth glide beneath him, the crunch of newly fallen leaves, the wind in his face. Even though Coach Grayson's ankle had recovered just fine, he seemed in no hurry to reclaim his running partner—and Mateo wasn't quite ready to hand her back, either.

By the time he was ready to race for the first time that season, his nearest competitor was Cruz—nearly forty seconds behind him. Since then, he'd only gotten stronger and faster. Still, even though Grayson's training produced faster times—not just for him, but everyone on the team—it was always Tervo's voice he heard, whether zoned out on a long run or sprinting toward the finish line at a meet.

Remember, Sandoval, that you have to take the risk. You have to dare to be great. Don't shy away from success. Be afraid of giving up in the final stretch, of never stepping up to the line. Just don't be afraid of failing. Very few people who succeeded in the end never failed at all.

—o00o—

At the end of practice one day, Mateo returned Sooner to Grayson and unlocked his bike from the tree where he'd left it. Grayson put the dog in her crate in the back of his car and then sat inside it, immersed in training plans.

At the edge of the parking lot stood Lou, waiting to speak to him. Everyone else had already left and it was just the two of them. That had been the case a lot lately.

"You're still here." He wheeled his bike up to her. "I'd give you a ride, but... then I wouldn't have one. I could run beside you."

She grinned. "I live on the other side of town."

"It's the thought that counts, right?"

"Sure. Anyway, I may have told my mom practice ends fifteen minutes later than it actually does today... just so I could stay and talk to you."

"Oh." He glanced around. The coach was sitting in the driver's seat of his car, tapping at his phone. "Well, talking is all we can do. You know he won't leave until we do, right?"

She frowned. "Ah, good point. Bummer."

"Was there something you wanted to talk about?"

"Yeah, actually there is." She zipped her hoodie up, straightening the hem. "Jed asked me to homecoming."

Mateo didn't say anything right away. It was so far out of left field, he didn't have the words. But he did feel something—a deep burning jealousy.

"What did you say to him?" he finally asked.

"Nothing yet." She'd turned her face away, but when she looked back at him, there was a grimace of disgust on it. "Although, 'Aw, hell no' came to mind."

She laughed then. Mateo still didn't find it funny. He wanted to punch Jed. But if he acted on that impulse, what then—run away?

"You know why he did it, right?" Lou said. "To provoke you. He's not really interested in me. He just wants to claim me, so you can't have me. Then when I tell him no, he's going to beat the snot out of you anyway."

"That won't happen."

"I wouldn't be so confident. He has it out for you."

"First, he'd have to catch me." Mateo grinned then. In truth, he knew Jed would likely corner him, just as he'd done before, but he was trying to appear braver than he actually was. For Lou.

Lou remained serious. "Maybe I shouldn't tell you this, but... I heard... I heard his friend, Brogan, started a rumor that you—"

Her mom's car pulled into the parking lot and came toward them.

"That I what?" Mateo prompted.

She bit her lip. "That you tried something with me. Something I didn't want you to. He said people will believe it... because you're"— her voice fell to a whisper with the last word—"Mexican."

It all struck Mateo hard in that moment. There were people who would believe this Brogan kid, even though Mateo had never even dated a girl before, let alone done anything remotely like that. Just because of where he'd come from. Because his skin was brown.

A strange sense of detachment overcame him. Others would have raged over the unfairness of it. But there had never been much fight in Mateo. Fighting would've been a fatal mistake when it came to Jed Delaney and his thugs. There wasn't even much of an option

269

in the way of flight. Where would he flee to? Back to Mexico? So like he usually did, Mateo froze—in both thought and action. He swallowed it back like a bitter pill he was forced to endure without ever even knowing why it was he had to be subjected to it.

Looking down at the ground, he simply uttered, "I would never..."

Just as her mother pulled abreast of them, Lou grabbed his hand. Squeezed it hard. "I know you wouldn't. I just thought you should know what they were up to."

Lou's mom got out of the car and walked around to the passenger's side, trying to stifle a smile. "Sorry to interrupt, but it's time to go home, Lou. Your grandparents are coming for dinner. You've got just enough time to shower before they show up."

"Okay, Mom. Got it." She made a face. Something her mom understood.

"Your turn to drive." Her mom got in the passenger's seat and pretended not to look at them.

"So," Lou began, "you were going to ask me something?"

Confused, he blinked. "I was?"

"Uh, yeah." She waited. Shifted on her feet. Waggled those chestnut eyebrows of hers. "It's a month away still, but..."

"Oh." Homecoming, of course. That was when Mateo realized she was still holding his hand. "Tell him you're going with me."

Squinting, Lou cocked her head. "So you *are* asking or not? Because I'm not really sure if I'm just supposed to use that as a lie to avoid Jed Delaney—or do you really want to go with me?"

"So you're asking *me* now?" he teased.

She blew out a puff of air. "Does it matter at this point? Still, I'd like it if you did."

"I would've asked you anyway," he said in defense. He wasn't sure if that was true or not. He still felt a bit awkward around her. Afraid she hadn't yet made up her mind to like him that way. But it seemed the smart thing to say. So just to make it formal, "Louisa Abrams, will you go to homecoming with me?"

"Yes!" she yelled. Then bouncing on the balls of her feet as she threw her arms around him, she added, "Yes, yes, yes!"

From his car, Grayson poked his head out the window. Her mom was smiling as Lou yanked open the door and jumped in.

"I told you he was going to ask me," she told her mom. Then she shut the door, put her seat belt on, and waved at Mateo as she pulled away slowly.

With a nod to the coach, he hopped on his bike and pedaled toward home. He forgot about rumors and being an outsider. Forgot about the dog. About being bullied. And never being sure if, on any give tomorrow, his home would still be his home.

For a little while, anyway.

Life, he was beginning to understand, was neither wholly good nor bad. Sometimes, it was both at once and many times over in the same day.

—o0Oo—

Mateo saw it too late. Heard the crunch of glass as he sped over the broken shards, lackluster beneath a cloud-choked sky. Hopeful his bicycle tires hadn't been cut, he kept going on the side street through the Bottlebrush Creek subdivision, but soon enough he could see his front tire going flat.

Barely two miles from home, he could've walked from here, but this was the last place in the county he wanted to take a stroll. Especially alone. Even in this neighborhood where the houses were crowded close to one another. Thankfully, a storm was threatening, so it appeared that everyone was inside. He'd taken this shortcut because the skies were darkening. Not that a little rain put him off, but he'd been apprehensive about lightning since Sooner's accident.

He still couldn't get over the fact that it had hit the dog and not him. He had no inclination to test his luck on the matter. As far as he knew, there weren't any cross country team members in this neighborhood, or else he would've sat out the storm or maybe bummed a ride home in the back of someone's truck.

If he pedaled fast enough, maybe he could get home before both his tires went completely flat and the storm hit. A snap of cold wind biting at his neck and a low rumble said otherwise. He could smell the rain coming.

A car was barreling down the middle of the narrow street ahead just as the rain started. Too fast for a residential street, that much he could tell.

A blur of movement caught his eye to the right. It was a dog, padding along. Same bushy tail and nondescript color as Fantasma.

The car kept coming. Still in the middle of the road. He searched in the dimming light for a driveway, so he could cross up onto the sidewalk and avoid the car. That was when he caught a glimpse of the dog again, ducking between two cars.

The stray had gone down an alley. He turned sharply to follow it, squeezing between two closely spaced garages, and saw only the flash of a tail as it disappeared underneath some bushes. The car whooshed past behind him. His bike was jostled hard as it bounced over potholes.

Afraid of damaging the tire rim, he slowed and got off, preparing to walk his bike until he reached the next street.

A door slammed to his left. Shook the house. A body thudded on wood.

Mateo froze at the edge of a garage. Whoever it was, they were just on the other side. If he went forward or retreated, they'd see him. No, his only choice was to stay where he was and hope they went back inside.

"Damn your lazy ass, kid! You think I'm here to make your life easy? Give you everything you need? Can't you do anything for yourself?"

Footsteps pounded. There was a grunt. A slap.

"Answer me!"

Whimpering.

Then... "Which question?"

"Huh?"

"Which question... do you want me to answer?"

Mateo had to keep his mouth closed. His heart was in his throat. The voice... It was Jed Delaney's.

"You know which one, smart-ass. Although you're not that smart, are you? The test. Who took the test for you?"

"Nobody, man."

"Like hell."

A heavy boot kicked at a piece of lawn furniture, sending it sideways with a clatter. Something heavier toppled over, banging.

"How did you get so damn stupid, huh? Do you even try? God, I'm ashamed of you. Think you can get by on being some pretty boy ball-tosser, so you pay some four-eyes kid to take a college test for you?"

"Pa, stop," Jed pleaded. "Please. Not here. The neighbors..."

"I don't give a damn about the neighbors." His speech was slurred, like he'd been drinking. "They can all see what a cheat and an idiot you are. Probably think you're one of those mentally challenged kids or something. Maybe I should just tell them you're not even mine."

"What? Are you saying—"

His laughter drowned Jed out. "Hell no. But... it would be easier to live with than the truth."

"Truth?"

"Yeah, truth is that your puny little brother was a mistake—and so were you. We weren't planning on kids after your sister. Your mom was almost five months along before she told me about you. Too friggin' late to do anything. She said it would all be okay, but look how you turned out. Sorry excuse for a human being. All you've ever done is fritter away our money and embarrass us."

Silence.

Jed's dad laughed some more.

"You're lying. Take it back," Jed growled.

"Don't you talk back to me. We all know *you're* the lying son of a—"

Jed's fist—at least Mateo assumed it was Jed's fist—slammed into his dad's gut. Someone stumbled, fell into the house, then slid to the rickety floorboards of the porch.

The heaving breaths of Jed's barely controlled rage resounded in the damp air of the otherwise quiet alley.

"I'll kill you for this," his father drawled.

Mateo rested his bike against the garage. He couldn't stand by and allow a murder to occur. Not even to Jed. Not even as much as he would've liked him gone from his life.

Frantic barking sounded from the yard diagonal to him, nearly stopping his heart. Mateo could only see the pointed snout of a short-haired black dog as it poked its nose through the part between two fence boards in the corner.

"Shut up!" Jed's dad hollered.

The dog only barked louder. A beer can sailed through the air. Droplets splashed on Mateo's arm as the can spiraled. It smacked against the boards of the fence and landed on gravel, its remaining contents gurgling as they spilled out.

In the end, it was the dog that saved them all. The neighbor opened her screen door and called the dog in. But the door didn't close right away. Whoever it was had heard the argument and was lingering.

Jed's dad stomped inside, muttering curses as the door banged shut behind him.

For several minutes more, Mateo waited for Jed to go inside. The neighbor's screen door creaked closed. The low rumble of thunder reached Mateo's ears. And then… a moan, a muffled sob, sniffling.

Lightning flickered, followed by the low rumble of thunder. On the tin roof of the garage next to him, rain pattered lightly. A cold rain.

Ping-ping-ping.

Mateo thought he heard the creak of the porch floorboards, the gentle closing of the door.

Soon, it became a downpour. Mateo shivered, but still he didn't move. Lightning flashed, more brightly this time, accompanied by the clap of thunder, its source hidden by the rows of rooftops all around.

He wasn't sure how long he stood there, shaking, getting drenched. His bicycle tire didn't look any worse. He had to get home.

So he wheeled his bike forward. Toward the house where the dog had barked. Past the bushes where the stray had disappeared. As rain obscured his vision and thunder rattled his bones, he hung onto the metal handlebars of his bicycle, thinking this was possibly the dumbest thing he had ever done.

Maybe he could find an open garage door, a tool shed, anywhere to wait out the storm. At any rate, he had to get away from here.

Mateo threw his leg over the bike, placed a foot on the pedal.

"That you, Sandoval?"

He should've pedaled like his life depended on it. It might have. Instead, he looked over his shoulder.

Barefoot at the edge of the porch, Jed stood in the deluge. "What are you doing here?"

"Going home from practice."

Jed shook his head, hair flat against his forehead. "No. What are you doing *here?*"

Mateo couldn't think of a decent alibi, so he told the truth. "The storm." He pointed overhead, then at his front wheel. "Tire's going flat, too. I took a shortcut. I didn't know you lived here."

Slowly, Jed stepped down from the porch and walked toward him. Peered at the tire. "Likely story. Not your lucky day, is it?"

The urge to throw his bike down and run like hell shot through Mateo. But Jed was too close already.

"If you give me a minute," Jed said, still coming, "I'll grab the keys to my sister's truck and take you home."

"Th-th-that's okay," Mateo stuttered. He was cold from the rain. Frightened, too. In the flashes of light, he could see the red rimming Jed's eyes.

"Really, it's no problem. Her scumbag boyfriend picked her up an hour ago. I'll be back before she ever knows. Besides, she owes me a tank of gas."

This was going from bad to worse. If he let Jed drive him to some obscure location that would be far worse than getting beat up in an alley. At least there were neighbors here—although he wasn't sure if any could've heard him getting slammed into the side of a garage over all the thunder and pouring rain.

He'd let Jed fetch the keys, then hide somewhere.

Mateo nodded. "Okay."

Through the steady pelt of rain, Mateo could see Jed's face clearly enough. For once, there was no sneer on his lips, his nostrils weren't flaring. He wasn't laughing at Mateo or hurling insults.

Lightning cracked dangerously close, the air searing with the unleashing of its power. Both boys flinched. Mateo gripped his bike harder. Afraid to hang on, afraid to let go.

"Wait, all right?" Jed backed up a few feet, as if he was sure the moment he took his eyes off Mateo, he'd bolt. "You can't go home on that in this. That would be really stupid."

It was true. It would be. But so would staying here or riding anywhere with Jed.

Jed didn't go inside, though. Something was keeping him there. Something he must've been wanting to say.

"What did..." Jed looked away. Into the darkness and rain. "Did you hear anything a few minutes ago?"

"Your dad, you mean?" There was no point in pretending he hadn't been there. They both knew he had. Although he could've lied. Then they could've both gone on their merry way, as if the incident had never occurred. But something told Mateo he held the upper hand. He'd seen the vulnerable part of Jed. Understood him better than anybody now. "Yeah, I did."

A window opened behind Jed. A woman's voice belted out, "Jed! Come in, baby. Why're you standing out in this mess? Get in here."

"Talking to a friend, Ma. He needs a ride home. Okay if I borrow Jessica's truck?"

"What friend, honey? I can't see you. Where are you?"

"Other side of the garage, Ma. It's Mateo Sandoval."

"Why do I know that name?"

Mateo stepped out into the alley and waved in her direction. He wasn't sure if she was an ally or not, but at least he had a witness now. In case anything happened to him.

"He's the star runner!" Jed shouted out.

"Oh, okay. The one in the newspaper all the time. Sure. I'll put the keys right here on the counter for you."

Something about her tone made Mateo trust her, at least. He'd let Jed take him home. If anything happened to him, Jed's mother would know.

A few minutes later, Jed had loaded Mateo's bike into the bed of the truck. His mother dashed out beneath an umbrella to toss blankets on the front seat—although from the stained, torn appearance of the upholstery, Mateo wasn't sure what she was trying to preserve. He thanked her anyway.

"Will you be home in time for our TV show?" Jed's mom asked as he climbed into the driver's seat. "It starts at eight tonight. Big finale."

"Sure, I'll try."

Jed shut the door and turned the key. The engine resisted turning over, but after a few more turns, it rumbled to life. He put it in reverse and backed as far as the end of the driveway before turning his head to stare at Mateo.

He looked like he was going to say something, which made Mateo horribly uncomfortable. A threat? A confession? An apology? Some reference to having asked Lou to homecoming?

"So are you going to drive?" Mateo finally prompted. Because he wanted to get home. This situation was beyond awkward. He could still get out and leave—with or without his bike. It wasn't too late yet.

Lightning ripped through the darkness, sending a shot of adrenaline through Mateo's veins. Okay, he'd let Jed drive him home. After all, it wasn't like this was going to become a regular thing.

"You have to let me know where you live, dufus," Jed replied. "I don't have ESP."

"Oh, right. Rockhill Road. Just head north up the main drag from here. I'll tell you where to turn when we get closer."

With a nod, Jed continued backing, then proceeded down the street.

Minutes went by in absolute silence. For which Mateo was grateful. He wasn't yet sure how to process what he'd witnessed. Except that it confirmed what Lou had told him. And then—

"He gets like that when he's out of work," Jed said flatly. Like it didn't faze him in the least.

"Oh." Mateo peered out the rain-smeared window to the side. The front window had two big spider web cracks in it where rocks had hit the windshield. Balled up clothes and fast-food wrappers littered the floor. The interior even smelled of cigarette smoke. "Does it happen often?"

"Does what? That he's out of work? I don't know. Sometimes it's a few months in between. Sometimes a couple of years."

"I'd imagine that's stressful—losing a job."

"It's not always his fault, you know. Sometimes he gets laid off. Low man on the totem pole always goes first."

"Oh, yeah. I suppose so."

It was almost like Jed was excusing his dad's behavior. At any rate, it didn't make it right. When his grandmother had lost her main source of income a few years ago, due to the motel she was working at closing down, she hadn't lashed out at Mateo. Instead, she prayed. Soon, another job came along. Then another. Until she was making more money than before.

Even as rough as it was with just the two of them, he was more grateful than ever in that moment for the stability his grandmother provided. He also pitied Jed. But he wasn't about to say so.

"Your mom," Mateo began, as he indicated for Jed to turn onto another road, "she seems nice."

"I guess." A muscle in Jed's jaw twitched.

"You don't think so?"

Jed shrugged. "She sees what she wants to see."

"What doesn't she see?"

The truck jounced over scattered potholes, unavoidable in the heavy rain, but Jed kept the truck steady. "You ask a lot of questions, Matty boy."

"I just wasn't sure what you meant. It's okay. You don't have to answer. I understand."

"Do you… really?"

Mateo kept his mouth closed. The fact that Jed was giving him a ride home without pulling over to beat the crap out of him and

279

leave him in a ditch... that *was* pretty much hell freezing over.

After a couple more turns and a long drive up curvy Rockhill Road with its narrow shoulder and steep ditches, they pulled into Mateo's driveway. Driveway was a figurative term. It was more a muddy path. At the end of it, close to the house, sat his grandmother's car, an older model economy car in a dull white finish— except for the front quarter panel, which was silver. She'd gotten a good deal on it and said it drove just as well as a car all the same color. Mateo could see her silhouette in the front window as she moved away from it. She'd been waiting for him.

"*This* is where you live?" Jed asked. "In that... house?"

Even though the neighborhood where Jed lived was an older one and the houses modest, they were easily three times the size of Mateo's. And they probably didn't have a tarp for a roof.

Scoffing, Mateo tried to make light of it. "Why else would I have you bring me here?" He jumped out of the truck, but before shutting the door, he leaned in. "I won't say anything... to anyone."

"Good." Jed held his gaze. "Don't even tell them I brought you home. Got it?"

Mateo nodded.

"Because that could be bad," Jed added, "for you."

He barely had his bike clear of the bumper and the tailgate back up before Jed peeled through the yard and left, leaving tire marks in the little patch of grass in front of the shack that was Mateo's home.

Mateo closed the front door softly behind him. His grandmother was no longer at the front window, but on the back porch. He could hear her talking to someone on the phone. Feeling a pang of hunger, he wandered to the refrigerator to see if she'd made anything for supper. He would've settled for a hunk of cheese or three-day-old leftovers at this point, though. He hadn't even opened the fridge when her voice pitched sharply.

"You call and ask for help *now*?" Ynez said lowly in Spanish as she stood in the back doorway, her small frame rigid. "Don't you think it's a bit late for that?"

Although he knew he shouldn't be listening, it was rare for his grandmother to receive personal calls. Rarer yet for her to use such a tone. Perhaps she had a client who was demanding her services when she was already booked.

"What do you want me to do about it? What?!" His grandmother clenched her free hand and shook it. "I did all that I could for you... and you ran away. You abandoned your son. What do you think I could possibly do for you?"

He could barely hear the voice on the other end, but he now knew whose it was. His stomach twisted into knots. Why would *she* be calling?

"I told you that man was no good, but no, you refused to listen to me. And now... No, I cannot help you, Anarosa. If they send you back, it is your own doing. You have chosen your own path—and I leave you to it."

chapter 24
Sooner

"Valentina Gutierrez—all the way from the teeming metropolis of Frankfort, Kentucky." Rex shook her hand heartily. "Pleased to meet you, ma'am."

"Thank you, Mr. Franzen." Her hair was black and her eyes brown, just like the Labrador we ran into at Tucker's feed store sometimes. Except she was prettier. And not as goofy. "But I would hardly call Frankfort a metropolis. It is a fine city, though."

I studied her carefully. Based on her fancy clothes, she looked more like one of the people who sometimes visited him from the 'court', whatever that was. I trotted up to her and sniffed the pockets of her blazer, just in case they were loaded with biscuits. Because why else would you have such big pockets if not for dog treats?

"What a beautiful dog." The lilt of her speech was a little like Ynez's, but not as obvious. She opened her palm to let me smell it. "Ohhh, poor thing. I didn't know you would be here or I would have saved a few pieces of chicken from my lunch today for you."

Chicken? I sat pretty, my paws crossed pleadingly in front of me.

"Sooner, come." Brandy patted her leg. I slunk to her desk, making sure she knew I was disappointed to not get any chicken from the nice new lady. "Sorry, Rex has made her into a terrible beggar."

"Hey, now," he said. "Maybe I find her tricks entertaining. She deserves a little reward every now and then."

Valentina glanced at the doorway to Rex's office. "The client— is he here already?"

"On his way," Brandy said. "He should be here any minute."

"Why don't we have a seat?" Rex ushered Valentina toward the back room. "I can fill you in on the situation until then. Would you like a drink? Water, soda, coffee?"

"Water's fine, thank you."

I almost followed them, but Brandy had latched onto my vest handle. "You stay here, nosy. Mateo's on his way."

I perked my ears. Boofed softly. *Mateo?*

"Yes, you heard right. He's coming. Sit tight."

She let go of me. I sat, then waited a couple of breaths before racing to the front door and pressing my nose to the glass. *Where is he? Are we going running?*

Every time I saw someone walking down the street in our direction, I got excited. There were five false alarms before he flew up on his bicycle and skidded to a halt on the sidewalk. I spun in circles, whining. Still in his running clothes, he always smelled like sweat, which was a glorious smell. I never understood why humans took so many baths when they could smell real, like sweat and dirt.

Run. I barked. *Let's run!*

"Sooner, hush!" Brandy wheeled up to the door and held it open. "They're waiting in the back for you," she told him.

"Is it okay if I bring my bike in here? I was running late and—"

"Sure, just put it over there. Your meeting with Ms. Gutierrez is the last today, so it won't be in the way anyway."

After placing his bicycle next to the chairs, he squatted down to greet me. I gave him my best 'I missed you', licking his face and curling around so he could scratch my hindquarters. It was the best butt scratch ever, because it went on and on and—

"Mateo." Brandy thumbed over her shoulder. "They're waiting."

"Right." His scratching faded, but didn't quite stop. "Is it okay if Sooner sits beside me? Unless you have somewhere to go, that is."

She scooped a stack of folders off the desk. "We're not going anywhere. Come on."

We followed her to the back room. After Rex introduced him to the new lady, Mateo shook hands with her and they all sat. I wedged myself between Brandy and Mateo and lay down.

"Let's begin," Valentina said. "I want you to understand that every case is highly individualized. It can also be a lengthy process, with no guarantees, no matter how spotless your record or promising your prospects. If you continue to excel at running that might help. That could make you what is termed a 'Person of Extraordinary Ability'. It is reserved for athletes of international caliber, certain artists and musicians, exceptional business leaders, scientists, and teachers. If you obtain your college degree, better yet an advanced one, and enter certain professions, that bodes even better. As for right now, you should look into community service. It shows you're willing to contribute to the betterment of society in some way. Your future sounds promising, so I want you to keep an eye on those things, all right? It can be an excruciatingly long process for anyone. It took me ten years to gain citizenship, during which I worked my way through college and law school, cognizant of the fact that I could earn a law degree here and still get sent back to the country I left at fifteen."

Mateo petted my head. "But you got it, yes?"

"I did. However… my older brother married and divorced a woman, an American, by the time he was twenty-one. He failed to file the proper documents to remain—and he was deported."

"That's all it took?"

"It was a little more complicated, but that was the primary

offense. So you see how important it is that we do everything correctly?"

Nodding, he stroked my head harder.

"Mateo, I want you to know all the possibilities, so we can set you up for the *best* outcome, yes?"

"I know. It's just…"

"What?" When he didn't respond, she added, "I'm here to answer any questions you may have and address your concerns. You're safe sharing here. It won't go beyond this room."

"Last night, I overhead my grandmother on the phone. She was talking to my mother. They… they're threatening to deport her, I think."

"Your mother?"

"Yes."

"She has someone to help her?"

"I don't know."

"Where is she?"

"Chicago, last I heard."

"I'm not sure what I can—"

"It's not my mother I'm worried about." He went quiet for a moment, his eyes fixed on mine. "It's my grandmother."

"That's Ynez," Brandy said. "She cleans here and also works at the motel by the interstate. She has multiple clients, including Rex. Can you do anything for her?"

"I assume she first came as an unskilled worker for a specific job?"

"Yes," Brandy said when he didn't answer, "that's right. The canning factory that used to be just off the interstate, but the place closed a long time ago. She told me about it once."

Valentina tapped her long fingernails on the table. "Hmm, all right. I'd be happy to help her, but I'll have to meet with her separately. It's important to know what jobs she's held since then.

It's a slightly different case than yours, Mateo, but since she's currently the primary provider for your household..." She paused, sitting back in her chair. "So much to take in, isn't it? It can feel overwhelming, I understand. I'll meet with her as soon as I can. For now, though, let's focus on you, okay?"

There was so much fear and worry and sadness in his face. I might've darted into the front room and taken my oldest, best tennis ball out of Brandy's tote bag and brought it to him if I'd thought it would help, but I didn't think a game of fetch would've made him even the tiniest bit happy right then.

So I did all I could. I sat there with him. In that dark place where the gloom and scariness lurked inside him, nudging his hand whenever he stopped petting me, leaning against his leg, gazing at him with the truest love in my heart.

"Now, as best as you can," Valentina said, "tell me your story. All of it. From as far back as you can recall."

Mateo looked down at me. The clock on the wall ticked loudly.

Finally, Valentina said, "Your life in Mexico. What do you remember?"

He began softly, sounding almost like a small boy. "Being hungry, mostly. Lots of noise. Sewage in the streets. No shoes. Wondering when my mother would come home..."

"What else? Anything more specific?"

"I'm sorry, that's all I remember. Only vague pictures. Some feelings. I don't remember any details of events that happened back then."

"Don't worry about it. You were very young then. You said you were five when you came here with your mother, yes?"

"I think my fifth birthday was when we were traveling with the coyotes through the desert."

"You remember that?"

"Some, yes. The memories of that are stronger."

"Tell me."

Brandy's pen scratched over paper as Mateo told his story.

"There was a dog. She followed us."

"Your dog?"

He paused. Looked at me again. "No. A stray. I called her Fantasma. It means ghost. She saved my life..."

chapter 25

Rex

Howdy. Rex here again. Pardon the interruption.

I've been trying my dangdest to let this story unfold on its own, but I owe you some explanation. Alrighty, not an explanation, maybe, just a dab more detail.

You see, you don't know what you don't know until you know it. Which means usually you have to figure it out on your own after having learned something. It's not good enough for someone to tell you how it is. Let me explain that.

This fine kid Mateo—and he was the most upstanding young person you'll ever meet—he's struggled a lot, fought hard to get where he was. Mostly by himself. A lot of what he knows about life is that he's better off not trusting folks from the get-go. It's not a bad way of being. Unless, that is, you always assume anybody who lends a helping hand must have some ulterior motive. Ain't true in every case. Not one whit in mine. So I had to set him straight.

We were in my pickup after our meeting with that whip-smart gal, Valentina Gutierrez. I'd offered him a ride to Mac Kendrick's auto lot, where he was due at work for the evening.

"Can I ask you something?" He was looking down at his lap when he finally spat out the question, which I figured had taken him a good ten minutes to work up to.

"Shoot."

"Why?"

One word. Why.

"Why mightn't I answer—or why help you?"

Still looking down like there was something intriguing to study on the floor mats, he nodded. "Help me, yes."

I turned the big truck onto the state highway heading out of town. "Why the heck not?"

He swung his head toward me and squinted questioningly.

"That's not good enough for you?" I said defensively. "A guy can't be altruistic, lend a hand where it's needed?"

"I just want to understand what you get from it, that's all. I don't have enough to pay—"

"Money's poor currency when it comes to showing your humanity."

"What exactly does that mean?"

"It means I took a chance on helping you for one simple reason, kid—I see promise in you. Now, could be you'll simply end up being some hardworking citizen who shows up to work every day, stays out of jail, and pays his bills on time—nothing more. But you've already shown you're not afraid of going the extra mile, no pun intended. Besides, I've noticed how you keep that copy of the Constitution snug in your back pocket like it's your best friend. I guarantee there's no other kid in your school who does that, is there?"

"Not that I know of."

"Right, that's my point. And why do you? Not because you have a test on it coming up, is it?"

"I... I suppose I want to understand it. To know it, word for word."

"Why—if I may ask *you* the million-dollar question?"

"Because someday, I want to do something that has to do with law."

"Cop?"

He shook his head. "Not law enforcement, no. I want to help interpret laws. Maybe even write them, someday."

"And why do you feel called to do that?"

"To help people. To make a difference. To make things... right."

"Guess that makes you more of an idealist than a pragmatist." We'd gotten sidetracked and it took me a few moments to remember what his original question was. "Anyway, life ain't worth much if you don't believe in the inherent good of other human beings. And most everyone has some good in them."

"I'm not so sure of that."

"Who is it makes you say that?"

"Jed Delaney."

"Uh-huh. And what is it about this Delaney kid that makes you think he doesn't have one speck of goodness in him?"

He didn't say anything right away. Just looked out the window. It took him some time to come up with something. "He's pushed me around. Called me things. Threatened to turn me into ICE."

"So you think he has power over you?"

"You don't know what it's like..."

"To be an immigrant? No, you're right. I don't. But I have ears and eyes and a heart—and an imagination. I listened to you tell your story today. I can only guess how difficult it's been for you since before you were able to read. Even more so now that you're older and people make assumptions about you. To be frank, I don't know where you find the courage to do what you do every day."

"Courage? I live in fear. I can barely remember what it was like where I came from. My grandmother has told me it was a terrible place to live. I don't know. Maybe it's not as bad as she says. Or maybe it's worse now. All I know is that this is the only place I've ever truly known. This land, the people… This is home. But every chance he gets, Jed reminds me I don't belong here. Tells me I should go back where I came from. Like only his ancestors had the right to come here, not mine. Like I'm going to take something from him just by being here."

"Are you?"

"No!"

"Look, son, one thing I figured out early on when I set up my practice here is that the people here, they only know what they know. And sadly, they don't know you all that well, let alone people like you. Which is unfortunate. Sometimes they think by being closed off from 'others' that they're protecting themselves and their way of life. But the truth is often more complicated than that. Just like you, even bullies have a story. So tell me what you know about this Delaney kid—his personal life, that is."

"My friend Lou… Louisa says he has ADHD. Although I don't understand why that would make him lash out at me."

"Now that you say that, everything makes a lot more sense. I can relate to that."

"What are you talking about?"

"Because that's me." The look he gave me was skeptical, but I couldn't help but laugh. "Ah, come on. Have you ever known me not to have something to say? My beloved tells me I talk too much and I ain't arguing with that. The words just pour out of me. Faster than my thoughts can keep up sometimes. I've been that way since I spoke my first word. And I could never sit still. My momma—God rest her soul—had the patience of a saint on tranquilizers. I was the youngest of four boys and she said that was a good thing, because if I'd been born first, I would've been the last. All through school, my teachers would send home notes that said, 'Rex is a bright child who needs to learn self-control'—or some version of that. By the time I got to high school, my folks were getting a tad discouraged. I came from a line

291

of academics—professors, a couple of doctors... heck, they even looked down on my uncle the chiropractor. It wasn't until I took a political science class as a filler my sophomore year in college that a fire lit inside me. Law books are full of words and there ain't nothing I love more than words."

"I still don't understand."

"Bear with me, son. My point is I had decent parents. They weren't perfect, but they were tolerant and determined. Most of all, they told me I just had to find my niche and whatever that was they were going to support me." Feeling I'd lost him by then, I gave him a good, long look—one eye on the road, of course. "Not everybody has that."

"So you're saying that maybe *I* should feel sorry for *him.*"

"Naw, you don't have to. But if you understand where a person's coming from, what made them the way they are, maybe even what they're afraid of, then it'll all make a little more sense."

"He's a big guy. I'm not sure what he'd be afraid of."

"Failure? Embarrassment? When someone's made to feel not good enough—not smart enough, strong enough, or successful enough—they find ways to compensate for those perceived shortcomings. Sometimes by making other people feel as cruddy about themselves as they do. I was lucky, having the parents I did. You are, too. Your grandmother may not make a lot of money, but she conducts herself with dignity. And she loves you. When you don't have that, well, life's not easy."

He sat with that a good minute before speaking again. "If I tell you something, can you keep it between us?"

"Confidentiality is one of my superpowers, Mateo. A lawyer who can't keep things private doesn't get much return business. What is it?"

"His dad is the same way. ADHD, I mean. Lou told me that. He can barely keep a job. I was riding by Jed's house one night and... I heard stuff. His dad called him names. Maybe even shoved him around a little."

There are times in your career that you ask yourself if you ought to get the police involved. Domestic abuse and child endangerment are both serious offenses. I've been involved in a few cases that darn near broke my heart, seeing how one person could treat another, especially defenseless dependents who don't know life's not supposed to be like that. But this was not one of those times. Mateo hadn't given me any details—and I didn't know anything beyond this one incident.

"Did he know you heard?" I asked.

"Yes."

"What happened then?"

"We talked a little. And he took me home. My bike had a flat."

"So he didn't beat you to a pulp?"

"No."

"And he did you a favor?"

He nodded. "Right, I know. So maybe he does have a little good in him—or maybe he was just afraid I might tell someone. I still don't trust him, though."

"Yep, I get that. Trust has to be earned. But he took a step, right?"

"I guess."

"Then that's a start." It was probably mighty hard for him to shift how he thought about the guy after his history with him, but then a thought occurred to me. "You know, what if all he needs is for someone to believe in him—and maybe that person... is you?"

Mateo gave me a sidelong glance like I'd just beamed down from a UFO. "What?"

"Let me tell you a story."

Because I love telling stories. Always have. A lot of times, they're even better than barraging folks with facts. Stories bring people into

293

other worlds, gradual like. Sometimes without them even noticing.

"When I was in elementary school, I got in trouble a lot. Not for being bad or having poor grades—I worked my tail off and was a polite Southern gentleman from the time I could buckle my own belt. Mostly, I got in trouble for talking. Sometimes for being late to class 'cause I helped the kid with the broken arm carry his books. Other times I'd get to asking the teacher questions, then she'd never get around to giving the lecture or explaining the homework. She said I did it on purpose, but really I was just curious—one question would lead to another, which would lead to another… So I'd get sent to the principal's office and Mr. Schneemann—yes indeed, that was his name—would say, 'What now, Reginald?' Then he'd hand me a stack of Nilla wafers and a carton of milk and I'd tell him my story. Mr. Schneemann was a good listener. Real good. Had a way of tilting his head and stroking his chin and saying 'Uh-huh, uh-huh. Do tell.' When I was done, he'd say, 'Reginald, you're not like the other kids, but that ain't entirely a bad thing. In fact, it just might be a really good thing.' I'd ask him, 'How so?' and he'd say, 'I don't rightly know, but you'll figure it out, someday. And likely the world will be better off for having had you in it.'"

I had to slow down and check traffic, which afforded enough pause for Mateo to pipe up.

"Sorry, but what does this have to do with Jed?"

"Fair question, son. You see, I learned two things much later on when I was all grown up. Probably close to forty, truth be told. I was speaking to Ms. LaCrosse about how my mind races like the engine on a souped up sports car flying downhill without brakes. She asked if I'd ever been tested for Attention Deficit Disorder. Now some folks might be offended if someone suggested that. But being the curious sort, I found a shrink who did assessments and lo and behold everything I'd ever struggled with made sense like never before. She said not to think of it as a disorder, but as being 'neurodiverse'. That's a polite way of saying not quite normal. I reckon this world is made up of all sorts of people, so it didn't bother me none.

"But you know what else I learned? That Mr. Schneemann said the same dang thing to every kid who walked into his office. No matter if they'd been caught sticking gum in the ponytail of the girl in front of them or cheating on a test. He wanted each of us to think we were unique or talented in some way. To believe in ourselves. Didn't matter how backward or ornery we were. He'd see that *one* thing and make it sound like something extraordinary. I often think how I might've ended up if I hadn't had someone like him in my life. So before you go writing off this Jed Delaney, consider how different things might be for him—and then subsequently for the people who cross his path—if someone were to tell him he wasn't so hopeless after all."

We pulled into a parking space at the auto lot where the kid worked on weekends. He didn't get out right away, though. Just sat there like the prospect of showing some empathy for a bully was too much to bear.

"So you're saying I should ignore what a terrible human being he is and pay him a... *compliment*—even if I have to lie?"

"Naw, you should always tell the truth. Just be selective about it. Leave out the bad parts. Find the one good."

He stared at me so long I was afraid I hadn't convinced him of anything. But then—

"It may take me a while to come up with something. But sure, I'll try."

"Trying never hurt none. You either succeed or you fail. But you sure as heck can't succeed if you never try at all."

"Coach Tervo said something like that to me once."

"Tervo was a sharp man."

Thanking me for the ride, he got out. Shut the door. Retrieved his bicycle from the bed. Opened the door again real quick. "If you can wait, I have the money I owe you for my bike in my locker here. It'll only take a minute for—"

"Hang onto it."

"Oh, okay. I can pay you next time I'm—"

"No, I mean indefinitely. Until someone else you run across needs it."

He blinked at me, so I elaborated.

"When you're in a better position in life and you see someone in need, help them out."

"I don't understand. I said I'd pay you back."

"I don't need the money. You do... or did. So I helped you out. Someone did it for me once, so I'm just carrying on the tradition. It's called paying it forward. Keep it going, son. Now shut the door and get to work."

He did, but even as I backed out and pulled away, he was standing there, like he was still turning it over in his mind. Sometimes it takes folks a while for things to sink in, especially if it's the first time they've ever heard something.

Wisdom is one thing you can't force on people. It comes in its own time and its own way. If it comes at all.

chapter 26
Mateo

While Mateo and Lou saw each other at cross country practice every day, their time there was too structured and occupied, and their chance at being alone next to impossible. So during the school day, they would walk to class together every chance they got and linger at their lockers until the last possible moment.

They were on their way to sixth period that day when the halls seemed particularly empty. Lou opened her locker door to serve as a privacy screen, then pressed her back to the locker next to hers.

"My cousin is letting me borrow her old homecoming dress," she said quietly but excitedly. "She only wore it the one time. We're the exact same size, except she's a couple inches shorter. My mom's going to let down the hem for me. I'm not much of a dress person— actually, I *hate* the things"—she broke her gaze, looking off at the floor tiles somewhere—"but I wanted to look nice just this once. For you."

Mateo had a hard time imagining her dressed up in a gown fit for a red carpet event, but he liked how excited she was about it.

"You'd look pretty no matter what."

He'd meant to say something more, well, poetic, but it hadn't come out that way.

Still, she blushed. "Thanks."

He moved closer. As close as he dared. He couldn't wait until that night, either. To spend hours holding her close, swaying to the music, staring into her eyes. And then—

"Have you thought about what you're going to wear?" She looked at him then. "It doesn't have to match. Really, I don't care. A lot of couples go to extra lengths to coordinate their outfits, down to the flowers and the guy's pocket handkerchief or tie…" Her forehead furrowed suddenly. "Oh, do you like bow ties or do you think they're dorky?"

All he could think of in that moment was how much a suit would cost. He didn't even know where to rent one. Or if Goodwill had any to sell. How would he even know what to pick out if they did?

She must've seen the apprehension on his face, because she quickly added, "I can ask my cousin if her date had a suit he doesn't need anymore. He looks your size. They're still together, two years after they graduated, can you believe that? Want me to ask?"

He nodded. "Yeah, sure. That'd be nice."

"Seriously, there's no sense going out and buying something brand-new if you're only going to wear it once or twice. I'll ask her and let you know."

Even as accommodating as she was, Mateo couldn't help but feel embarrassed. He had money from his job, but he was saving it. All of it. Except for when he bought the two of them root beer floats from The Kone King, a walk-up ice cream cone place a block from Founder's Park. He'd heard the guys on the team last year talk about going out to dinner at fancy restaurants before the big dance. How much would that cost him? He didn't have a clue.

And how was he supposed to take her *to* the dance? On his bike?

Lou had her driver's permit. Would she be able to drive them? Should he even ask her? His grandmother hadn't had time in her day to do the supervised driving with him for a permit. Forget ever being able to afford the fees for a driving class or the extra insurance for him.

More and more, the idea of taking her to a formal dance seemed beyond his means. He was starting to wonder if he should back out of—

"Don't worry," Lou said with an understanding smile, "we'll work out the details later."

It was like she knew what he was thinking without him ever having to say a thing.

Then, she grabbed the front of his shirt and yanked him to her. The thrill of his chest pressed against hers temporarily overpowered the panic of potentially being caught. He leaned into her. The warmth of her breath was a magnet to him, beckoning his mouth to hers. They brushed lips. Kissed more deeply.

Somewhere farther down the hallway, rumbling laughter ricocheted off metal lockers, startling them back to awareness.

Reluctantly, Mateo pushed himself back from her, allowing her the space to slip past him as she shut her locker door.

"See you at practice." She hurried into the classroom next door, the long ruddy locks of her hair an untamable glorious mess.

Mateo stared at the door through which she'd gone, trying to hold onto the sensations he'd just experienced. Last year, he'd thought that winning state was the culmination of his existence—a triumph of athleticism and hard work. That the only thing which might one day eclipse the exhilaration of standing atop the podium there would be repeating it on the bigger world stage at the Olympics.

He'd been wrong. So wrong.

—oO0o—

"I'm not going to say that's wrong, Jed, but..." Mr. Sutherland shifted on his stool and clicked the overhead display off. "Let's just say I don't recall that in the textbook. You did read the chapter, right?"

The government teacher had been reviewing the subject for tomorrow's test when he'd called on Jed, who'd been busy tossing paper wads at the waste basket. Mr. Sutherland didn't cut anyone slack. Not even the star tight end.

Even though Mateo had dreaded having class with Jed at the beginning of the year, he'd come to look forward to Mr. Sutherland's scrutiny of his nemesis. It was especially satisfying when he called on Mateo to provide the answers Jed couldn't.

Slumped in his chair, Jed flipped through the pages of his open book. "I thought you said to read Chapter Twelve."

"We've been on Chapter Eleven all week, Jed. It says so on your syllabus. We haven't moved on yet."

Avoiding eye contact, Jed muttered, "I could've sworn I heard you say read Chapter Twelve yesterday."

"Well, you'll be ahead of the game next week then. Don't forget your test tomorrow, everyone."

Half the class groaned.

"Better be on Chapter Twelve." Jed snickered.

"It wouldn't matter either way for some of you, I'm betting." Mr. Sutherland retrieved a stack of papers from his paper tray and began passing them out to each row. "Since we have a little time left today, I'll let you get started on these."

Vivi glanced at her paper and immediately raised her hand. "You're giving us group projects? Do we get to pick our partners?"

Her best friend Mikaela shot her an excited look. They did a silent clap together.

"I am. And no," Sutherland replied flatly. "Your partner's name, which has been randomly assigned, is written alongside yours in the upper right. Presentations will be the last week of grading period—and before anyone asks, yes, you will be graded on them."

Another groan.

Vivi raised her hand again. "Can we—"

"No, you can't swap partners or topics. You'll each select one of the listed subtopics and present your portion. There should be some natural overlap, but you needn't consult each other on how you choose to present it."

When Mateo got his paper, he was sure he'd read it wrong. But no matter how many times he blinked and refocused his eyes, it didn't change: *Mateo/Jed, 1) List three reasons that would motivate someone to immigrate to a certain country and one reason why they might do so 'illegally', 2) Give three examples of immigrants who have made major contributions to the U.S. in the last twenty years.*

"Go ahead and pair up. You have fifteen minutes left in this period. Soon as you've decided who has which topic, let me know, but it has to be before the bell rings."

More groans and mumbling.

Stunned, Mateo considered going to the principal to protest. This entire scenario had been cooked up by Mr. Sutherland on purpose. Not to enlighten Jed, but to embarrass Mateo. There was no way it had been randomly assigned.

As the rest of the class paired up, Jed remained slumped down in his seat, tapping his pen on his notebook like he had no inclination of participating or even moving. Mateo went up to Mr. Sutherland's desk as the teacher sat down behind it.

"Excuse me, Mr. Sutherland?"

The teacher raised his eyebrows. "Question?"

"More of a request."

"The answer is no."

"What?"

"No, you can't change partners—or topics."

As much as he wanted to tell Mr. Sutherland he'd just subjected him to a special kind of hell, he couldn't. Not in front of everybody.

"Just make sure you both do your share of work," Mr. Sutherland said.

How was he supposed to do that?

"While you're here…"

Mateo couldn't venture to guess what he was going to say next.

"Starting today, I'd like you to tutor Jed during your study hall period. I'll get you a pass to the library. You can help him prepare for tests there."

Study hall was Mateo's last period. He normally spent it in the library anyway, rather than the cafeteria. When he didn't have homework, Mrs. Gebhart let him put books back or deliver media equipment to classrooms. If he had to tutor Jed, that was going to eat up all his time.

After glancing at where Jed sat to make sure he wasn't paying attention, Mateo lowered his voice. "Do I get a choice in this?"

"Sorry, dude. Football coach asked me to make sure he passed this grading period and you're the best candidate here. It'll be good for both of you." He checked his watch. "Better get to work on your project. You have ten minutes."

Until today, Mr. Sutherland *had* been Mateo's favorite teacher. He wondered if this could at least count toward the volunteer hours Rex had said he'd need. He couldn't remember. All the same, he'd rather pick up trash.

Grudgingly, he complied. Which amounted to him walking up to Jed and Jed saying, "I'll do the first one, since I already have an opinion on the matter. Sounds like the second one would require"—he pretended to retch—"research."

Meeting over, Mateo resumed his seat and opened his textbook to the chapter on immigration. The textbook was woefully out of date. He'd have to do his research online.

As the bell rang, Mr. Sutherland announced, "As a reminder, your grade will be determined by your *joint* presentation. Each of you is responsible for talking about half the material for five full minutes, after which you'll be open to questions. Meanwhile, don't forget tomorrow's test." Then, as Jed passed his desk, he handed him a hall pass. "Library next period. Mateo will review the chapter with you."

"I don't need this, man." Jed flipped the paper back onto his desk.

"Actually, you do. If you get below seventy percent, you won't be eligible to play next week. I checked." He pounded him on the upper arm. "Now, beat the tar out of Somerset, okay?"

Sneering in disgust, Jed picked the paper up and stormed out of the room.

—o00o—

When Mateo arrived at the library, Jed was already seated at a small round table tucked in the far corner. It was where kids went if they wanted to take a nap or whisper rumors to each other.

Mateo stopped at the counter to see the librarian.

Mrs. Gebhart's face lit up as she pushed a rolling cart stacked with books forward. "Mateo! Just who I was looking for."

"I'm sorry." He slipped off his backpack and took out his government book. "I have to help Jed study."

She looked confused. "Really? Well, that's an even bigger surprise than him showing up here in the first place. Have at it, though. Just keep it down to a dull roar."

With each step, the knot in Mateo's stomach tightened. When he reached the table, he waited a moment for Jed to tell him to leave. Finally—

"You want an engraved invitation or something? Sit."

Mateo did as ordered. He opened the book. "What do you need

303

help with?"

Jed rolled his head back to gaze up at the ceiling tiles. "Everything."

"Legislative or executive branch? Or maybe judicial?"

"You don't get it, do you?" Jed lowered his gaze. "It's not as easy for me as it is for you."

Although unexpected, Mateo understood the statement. But Jed didn't know he knew, so he asked, "What do you mean?"

"Learning. Studying." Leaning forward, Jed planted his elbows on the table. "My mind... it kind of leaps around. I get bored easily. So by the time a teacher's done talking about whatever, I have no idea how they got there. Can't remember what they said. Reading's no better. I have to stop and start so many times... Drives me nuts, you know? If they break it down, real small, I understand. But they try to cram so much in. I just can't stay focused that long."

"So it's not a vision problem?"

"More like a brain problem. But I'm not stupid like my dad says. I'm not!" He thumped the heel of his hand on the table, but surprisingly no one looked. Not even Mrs. Gebhart. "I can take an engine apart and put it back together in an afternoon. That car I drive? I built it myself. From pieces, for frick's sake. Know anyone else who can do that?"

"No."

"Meanwhile, you sit there in class like a sponge and repeat it all back the first time. I can't do that. No matter how hard I try. School stuff, it bores me. Last year, I took one of those tests so you can get into college. It lasted *all* day. My score was really bad. So I"— he glanced around—"I 'retook' it. Or maybe someone who looked like me took it. But you have to understand the pressure I'm under. That night you came by, my dad read some letter that said they suspected I hadn't actually taken the test and wanted me to do it again. I told my dad I wanted to go to trade school instead of college.

Become a mechanic. Maybe open my own business someday so I can be my own boss. He went off on me. Told me I needed to go to college so I could play football or baseball. That if I tried I could become a pro. I don't know about that. It's hard to go pro. Even if you do, an injury could end your career before it barely starts—and then what? I love cars, man. Cars. Football's just something I do. Helps get girls. Except... Lou."

The mention of Lou's name ignited a spark of protectiveness in Mateo. "Were you ever *really* interested in her?"

"Buddy, I'm interested in all girls. Not that I need to prove anything. But she's the only one who turns her nose up at me."

"Maybe you're just not her type." It was the nice way of saying Lou didn't find anything redeemable about Jed. Anyway, he didn't want to dwell on it, so he changed the topic. "I thought we came here so I could help you prep for the government test tomorrow. Why are you telling me all this?"

"'Cause, my whole life, I've been called stupid. Maybe not outright, but people made me feel that way. Teachers mostly. The other kids stopped when I started lifting weights and got big enough to threaten to beat their brains out."

"Have you ever done that?"

"Beat someone's brains out? Naw. Shoved a few kids around, maybe. Called them names and made them cry."

"And that"—Mateo met Jed's eyes—"makes you feel better."

He snorted. "No, but it makes them feel as bad as I do."

"Again, why are you telling *me*?" Because actually, he wanted him to stop. Being strong-armed into tutoring him was torture enough. He didn't need to become his therapist, too.

"Because I don't want you to think I'm stupid, too."

So he kept saying. Which made Mateo wonder—"What does it matter what I think about you?"

"Because you know *things* about me." At that, Jed looked down at his clasped hands. Then, shrugging, he ruffled the hair at the back of his head. "Never mind. I just thought you might understand."

"I do. I understand what it's like to be thought of as stupid. To be judged by looks alone."

"Ow!" Jed clutched a fist to his chest. "Touché, Zorro."

For close to a minute, they were silent—Mateo copying his notes and Jed staring absentmindedly at a bookcase as if the knowledge contained there might seep into his brain by some sort of osmosis.

"What about you?" Jed asked.

"Me?" Mateo looked around, then at Jed. "What about me what?"

"Yeah, you. What are you gonna do with your life when you get outta here? Pick vegetables? Clear tables? Push a broom at the hardware store?"

Mateo couldn't figure out if he was serious or kidding. "Coach Tervo said I could get a full scholarship. I plan to study law."

He wasn't sure why he'd told Jed Delaney that. He shared his dreams with precious few people. Maybe it was because he wanted to remind Jed he was a better student than him.

"Law, huh? Makes sense why you like Sutherland's class so much. Me? I don't see much use for it. Boring as hell, too."

"Your dad ever draw an unemployment check?"

A shrug. "I don't know. Maybe."

"Your parents pay taxes? Drive on the interstate? Stand in line at the BMV to renew their licenses? Go to public school? Have you ever seen a segment on the news about guys who've been busted and are standing in front of the judge for arraignment or sentencing?"

Jed yawned. "Your point?"

"Government touches your life every day. Laws give us all rules to live by. You should care about how they work. Everyone should."

The moment the words were out of his mouth, Mateo could tell Jed had shut his ears and mind to it all. Saying any more would only be wasting breath. It saddened him so many people knew so little about the subject.

A trio of girls paraded by, one of them smiling at Jed. She brushed her hand over his shoulders as she passed and he winked at her, which brought a round of giggles from the bunch of them.

As Mrs. Gebhart glanced at the boys, Jed flipped his book open to a dog-eared page and ran his finger down it. Then, loud enough for her to hear, he said, "Sooo, explain the legislative branch to me. I've got less than twenty-three hours to ace this test."

"I'm afraid I can't perform miracles."

"Ha-ha. Okay, dude, I need an eighty-five, or seventy-five. Or something like that. Can you manage that?"

"I can. Can you?"

Jed smiled wryly. "You're a regular comedian. Now are you gonna help me or what?"

For the remainder of the period, Mateo explained both houses of Congress, then had Jed summarize them back. When Jed stumbled over specific terms or names, he helped him remember them by teaching him mnemonic devices. He made a copy of his own notes and highlighted certain phrases.

"If you have trouble remembering anything in particular," Mateo told him, "write it out by hand as you say it out loud. At least ten times. The act of speaking and writing the words works much better than simply reading the same thing over and over."

"What if I put eye of newt and kitty whiskers in a boiling pot, then utter the names of my enemies over it three times backward—will that work?"

Mateo put down his pen. Stared at him blankly. Part of him wanted to chastise Jed for not taking this seriously. School was important. To him, anyway.

Then, he reminded himself of something. He was not Jed—and Jed was not him. "If it does, let me know. I could use the extra help on my ACT exam next month."

"I won't even charge you for the tip." Jed winked. "Consider it payment for your services."

As awkward as the last two hours had been, his view of Jed had shifted ever so slightly. Which still left room for questions. "So if you do well on this test... bring your grades up, maybe get the chance to play college ball—will you? If college isn't what you want to do, will you go just because your father wants you to?"

The humor fled from Jed's face. "I haven't decided yet." He closed his book and stuffed his folder in his backpack. "Right now, I just need to keep the gorilla off my back."

As the bell rang and they rose to leave, Jed grabbed Mateo's elbow. "By the way, Mateo... thanks for not telling anybody. Because if you did... I'd find out."

Mateo rolled his eyes. All this time, he'd assumed Jed's threats were real. In truth, they were only a shield. And yet Jed continued to toss thinly veiled innuendos. As if Mateo still believed him.

In reality, Jed was probably too afraid to actually beat someone up. He didn't have the guts, because inside, he was just a scared little boy, wounded by his father's words. Realizing that made Mateo a tiny bit braver than he'd been only a few hours before.

"Do you want to talk about our project tomorrow after the test?" Mateo asked as they stepped into the crowded hallway.

"What for? You do your part, I'll do mine."

That was hardly reassuring, considering Mateo already knew what Jed's opinion was on people like him.

chapter 27
Sooner

Except for the furniture that had been there when we first moved in, Brandy's apartment was empty. To make sure I hadn't left any toys behind, I sniffed around the bed, behind the couch, and beneath the dinette table and chairs.

"Sooner"— a box on his hip, Grayson pushed the front door of the apartment open wider—"come on, girl. We checked. Nothing left behind, I promise. I have all your things here—toys, bones, balls…" He rattled the box. "Yep, stuffed full. Let's go."

I cast one last glance around, then trotted after him. Somehow I knew we would never come back here. But I also knew that life could only get better from this day forward.

In one of the parking spaces in front of Brandy's apartment, Tucker loaded Brandy's small work desk into the cab of his truck. The bed was covered with a tarp, under which were more boxes containing Brandy's remaining belongings.

After stopping at the main office to drop off the keys, we followed Tucker to the feed store.

"You'll need these to keep you busy while we're unpacking,"

Grayson said as he put three basted bones in the cart.

Tucker already had two bags of kibble at the counter where one of his coworkers rung us up. Then we put all that in the SUV and drove out together to the farm, where Gertie met us. Once inside the house, she gave me some special biscuits that tasted extra yummy.

"Like those, girl?" Gertie said. Then to Brandy, "I baked them myself. Special recipe. All natural."

"Really?" Brandy ripped the tape off a box and pulled out some trophies of ours from our competitive days that she'd had on a shelf in the apartment. I'd never quite understood what their purpose was, but they seemed to hold some special meaning for her. "I've never seen her snarf anything down quite that fast. What's in them?"

"Organic carrots, blueberries, and cranberries to make it tasty. Fish oil for a shiny coat, various herbs for nutritional benefit, probiotics for digestion... You don't think I went overboard, do you?"

"Sounds like you could corner the Faderville market on healthy dog treats. Are you going to sell them at your shop?"

"I'm working on it. It's a whole new production line. Right now I'm in the testing phase, though." She held out another biscuit. I sat pretty and she popped it in my mouth. "It was Tucker's idea. He said he could get me a special display in the center aisle if I wanted to sell them at the feed store, too."

"I'd say you two make a great team." Brandy placed our biggest award on the sideboard behind the couch. It was a big plate with pictures of dogs painted on it and a lot of scribbles.

"My ears were on fire." Tucker carried in the last box and set it next to the stairs where Brandy's lift chair was. I'd seen her go up and down on the thing a few times. Between that and the other adjustments Grayson had done around the house, she didn't seem to rely on him as much now. For some reason, though, her walker was still at Rex's office. Tucker came over and took a biscuit from

Gertie's paper bag and fed me another. "That plate there looks mighty special. You two win that?"

"Yes, we did," Brandy said. "Second place in rally excellent at the national specialty. She was more than halfway to her trial championship when…" She didn't finish the sentence. A sadness fell over her briefly, then she glanced at me. "I've since learned that dogs don't care about ribbons and titles. I think she's even happier now than she was then. Look at all the wonderful people who've come into our lives since we moved to Faderville."

Brandy's laptop case in hand, Grayson came in the front door. "Want me to put this upstairs or in the office?"

"Office." Brandy set the box with the rest of the awards on her lap and wheeled toward the hallway. "Since you said it was okay to put these in there, I thought maybe you could help me decide where's best."

"Sure." He followed her through the living room and down the hallway.

Gertie and Tucker stood toe to toe.

He pecked her on the lips. "Pick you up at eight?"

"Eight?" Gertie patted her middle. "You expect a girl to wait until eight to be fed?"

"I don't get off until six. Plus, chores."

She scowled at him.

"Fine, darlin'. Seven then?"

"Just don't be late." She poked at his belly. "I get hangry when my blood sugar gets low."

"Yes, ma'am." He grabbed her then and kissed her harder. They did that for a long time. I was starting to wonder if they could both breathe. "Catch you two lovebirds later," he hollered back the hallway.

"Bye!" Grayson said.

"And thanks!" Brandy added.

Tucker marched out the door with more energy than I'd ever seen from him before. He was different somehow. His steps lighter. His eyes brighter.

Song broke out behind me. Gertie, her head stuck in the fridge as she put Brandy's groceries from the apartment in there, was singing a song.

"*Never know how much I love you. Never know how much I care.*" Wagging her behind, she slid the milk jug to the back to make room for the juice cartons. Next, she began to place cans of food in the pantry. "*When you put your arms around me—*"

Eyes closed, Gertie began to hum the tune as Grayson and Brandy came out of the office, but she couldn't stop swaying to the music. Her hands drifted wide, then her eyes flew open and she pointed at me.

"*You give me* fever, *when you kiss me...*"

It looked like fun, so I joined her. Gertie caught my paws and we danced around the kitchen floor together, her singing and laughing, me trying my best to stay upright.

Grayson cleared his throat. He and Brandy were standing in the kitchen doorway.

Gertie froze. But only for a second. She bounced from side to side. "*What a lovely way to burn. What a lovely way to burn.*"

Then she twirled me around and let go of my paws. I remained on my hind legs for one more turn before landing on all four and letting out two excited barks. *More! More!*

Brandy clapped and Grayson whistled with his fingers.

"Encore!" Brandy shouted. "Encore!"

Throwing her head back in laughter, Gertie leaned against the counter and pressed a hand to her chest as she caught her breath. "Why, thank you. Little known fact—I played the part of Eliza Doolittle in my high school production of *My Fair Lady*. Don't ask what year."

"I'm sure you played to sold out crowds," Brandy said.

"Indeed I did." Gertie flipped me another of her special biscuits. "But it was a small gymnasium."

Brandy and Grayson joined us in the kitchen.

"Do you know there's a community theater group in Somerset?" Brandy said.

Gertie put the last of the cans away. "There is?"

"Yes. They do a musical every spring. I hear they're casting for *Oklahoma* this year."

Pulling herself up to the table, Brandy took my bone out of the bag from the feed store. I rushed to her and placed my chin on her armrest, waiting. Meanwhile, Grayson was heating up some soup and making sandwiches.

"You don't say." Gertie sat across from her at the big table. "I could start taking voice lessons again. Work my way up from the chorus to a feature role."

"You sound chipper today, Gertie." Grayson set a plate and bowl in front of her. "Special plans tonight?" He winked at Brandy.

"Maybe." Gertie took a bite of her sandwich. "What've you heard?"

He shrugged. "Oh, nothing. Just asking."

"You're a terrible liar, Grayson." Handing me the bone, Brandy leaned forward. I dived under the table with it and went to work. "I may have told him about you and... you know who."

"No keeping secrets in this town," Gertie said. "Just as well. The other ladies need to know he's off the market."

"Sounds serious." Grayson sat and began to eat.

"Serious enough. Let's leave it there, okay? If it doesn't work out, it doesn't. But if it does... well, lucky us. Thanks to you, Brandy."

"Me?"

"I know you sent him over to my shop that day. I'm grateful. I really am."

313

They talked for a long time, spoons clinking, laughter bubbling. I was busy with my bone. I didn't stop gnawing on it until Gertie got up to leave.

I followed her to the door and did my best sit. *Biscuits?*

"Sorry, girl. Cookies are all gone." Gertie patted me on the head. "But if I come up with any new recipes, you can be my first taste-tester, okay?"

Okay! I barked and spun around twice to let her know how enthusiastic I was about treats.

After she left, Grayson and Brandy took me on a walk down the lane where Grayson whistled to the horses. One by one they turned and moseyed toward the barn with us. While Grayson pushed Brandy along, I ran wide circles around them, checking out every fence post and rabbit hole and scent on the property.

Inside the barn, Felicity watched me smugly from the rafters, her gold eyes glinting in the evening shadows. At the base of the hay bales, I kept vigil. I didn't trust that shifty creature. The one time I'd tried to sniff her up close just to get to know her, she'd sliced me with those claws of hers and made my nose bleed. I didn't want her to do that to my people. Not even to the horses. So I guarded the stacks and kept her up high where she belonged. Meanwhile, Grayson fed each of the horses some flakes of hay while Brandy checked on the water in the troughs.

I must've dozed off, because next thing I knew that cat was weaving in front of Brandy's wheelchair. Horror-stricken, I leaped to my feet and rushed forward.

"What's the matter, Felicity?" Brandy reached over the side of her wheelchair and scooped the fanged one into her lap. "Are you starving for attention?"

As I skidded to a halt before them, every muscle in my body shivered with barely contained terror. A low growl rumbled in my throat. *Be careful, Brandy.*

Brandy clutched Felicity to her chest. "Sooner, no! She's not hurting anything."

For a torturously long time, Brandy sat with the sharp-clawed creature in her lap, petting the deplorable thing and fussing over her like a human baby. A sense of danger gradually gave way to jealousy. Why was the cat getting all the attention? What did she do besides catch mice for her own entertainment, sometimes leaving their mutilated little corpses at the front door? She guarded nothing. She didn't take walks with Grayson and Brandy. Didn't sleep in their bed or play ball with them or... Didn't even take the visiting kids on rides like the horses did.

Useless thing.

She was curled up in a ball in Brandy's lap now, her eyes shut. Cautious, I leaned forward, sniffed her. She smelled of hay and old wood and dusty earth. Her eyes opened and I pulled my nose back. She stretched a paw toward me, but her claws didn't come out. I sniffed the top of her head and her eyes drifted shut once more as Brandy stroked her fur. It was short and soft and had so many glorious smells. Curious, I sniffed her all over.

Unlike me, Felicity was permitted to roam wherever she pleased. Not only in the high places of the barn, but up the branches of trees, under fences, along the creek, and far, far out into the pastures and even the woods. It would have been wondrous to follow her on an adventure someday, to see what she saw and go where she went.

"See, Sooner? She's not so bad after all." Gently, Brandy lifted her and set her on the ground. Arching her back, Felicity yawned. "You might even like her if you gave her a chance."

"Ready for supper?" Grayson dusted bits of hay from his shirt as he walked toward us.

"Sure am. It's been a long day."

"Why don't you leave the rest of the unpacking until tomorrow? A good meal and a good night's rest... I think we could both use it."

Grayson pushed her through the open barn doors and out into the dusky glow.

I was still sitting in the barn close to Felicity, watching her in my peripheral vision. She was making that rumbling noise Loretta called purring. But it wasn't a growl, more of a contented sound.

She hadn't scratched me yet. Hadn't even hissed. We just had to get to know each other. Maybe someday we could even hang out together. Go on an adventure. As long as we stayed within sight of the farm. Maybe.

As a peace offering, I gave her a quick lick on the head, then trotted off after my people. Being a cat, she didn't follow us. Figured. No loyalty.

Just as well. Let her stay outside, arrogantly independent. Felicity could come and go all she wanted, answering to no one. But that life, as tempting as it sounded, wasn't for me.

I was going in the house. My home. To be with *my* family.

And if I never had anything else—no bones or balls or Frisbees—it would be enough.

chapter 28
Mateo

Tell me something." Jed leaned back against the bricks of the wall just outside the gymnasium. Studied Mateo long and hard. "You used to be afraid of me. What changed?"

Mateo thought about it and shrugged. "Got to know you, I guess."

It was Thursday, two days before the homecoming dance. School had just let out. Jed was suited up for football practice and Mateo was on his way out to the track for an easy five-mile run before the weekend's regional meet.

"Huh. You like me then?"

"Like is probably too strong a word." Mateo sank down on the sidewalk to pull on his socks and running shoes. Today the autumn sky was a cloudless blue, the sun a spotlight of teasing warmth. Somehow, without either of them knowing exactly when, the tension between them had dissipated, like a storm that had loomed but never broken. In its place was something oddly... comfortable. "It's more that I stopped asking myself, 'What *if* he beats me up?'"

"I could." Jed tilted his head back. "You know it's true."

"That's the thing, see. You could—but you haven't."

"Good thing, huh?"

"Right." Shoes laced, Mateo stood. "Good for you. Being in jail makes it hard to get football scholarships."

Jed gave him a sidelong glance. "Funny."

They walked toward the track together. In no hurry.

The football team was gathering on the practice field a couple of hundred yards to the west, but Jed obviously had more to say.

Ignoring him, Mateo did some drills to loosen up.

Jed propped himself against the gate to the track. "Why?"

"Why what?"

"Why haven't you told anyone about... you know?"

Mateo paused in his high stepping. "Your dad?"

Jed nodded.

"I could, you know," Mateo said, echoing Jed's earlier threat.

Jed pushed away from the gate post. Took two steps toward Mateo. "If you tell anyone—"

"If I tell, then what? What'll you do?"

He almost asked if Jed would call the authorities on him or his grandmother. But that was the one thing he *was* afraid of. Would always be. He didn't want to put any ideas in Jed's head. Still didn't trust him entirely.

Jed was silent so long Mateo almost took off running. Not to run from him, but to join the rest of the team on the other side of the track. Then Jed looked away, like he was working up more words but couldn't quite wrestle them into submission.

"It's harder to hate someone when you know them, isn't it?" Mateo said. "In the same way I don't utterly hate you anymore. And do you know why?"

No answer.

"Because I feel sorry for you. Just a little bit. Enough to care. Enough to know you're not the monster you appear to be."

Without replying, Jed started to walk away.

"You really want to know why I haven't told anyone, Jed?"

Jed's steps slowed, but he kept going.

"Because I get you. I understand. Everything about you."

At that, Jed turned around. "Oh, yeah? What d'you understand?"

Mateo closed the distance between them so no one would overhear. He didn't want to embarrass him. "That words hurt just as much as getting hit. Worse, in a way. Because you hear them so often you start to think… maybe they're true."

For a few moments, Jed stared at him. "My dad's a loser. I don't believe anything he says about me."

"Then why does it bother you?"

"Because it's not right, what he does."

"So you want him to stop, huh? But you can't make him stop. If you speak up in your own defense, he could make things worse. You can't leave, either. You're not even eighteen yet. Where would you go? How would you live? No, you're stuck hearing it *every* day."

"Not every day," Jed objected. "Some days he's…"

He didn't finish. Because there wasn't much to say in defense of his dad.

"It may not be right, but it still hurts—and you're powerless to do anything about it. That's what sucks." Mateo gave that some time to sink in. He'd peeled back the crusty outer layers to expose the tender spot in Jed's soul. Discovered the humanness in him. But he wasn't going to back off until Jed saw it, too. "So you put up with it, thinking one day success will be your revenge. That's how I deal with people like you. It's how you cope with your dad. I figure someday, if I ignore you long enough, maybe I'll go to college and become *somebody*. You figure you'll eventually get out on your own and maybe start your own business doing something you're good at. So see, we're not so different. We're just alike in ways that aren't obvious. Besides all that, why do you suppose it is I haven't told anyone?"

319

"You're so smart—you tell me."

"Because... because I thought—where does it end? I bet your dad's dad beat him or called him names. So he does the same to you. Then you do it to me. When does it stop? What if instead, *I* showed *you* kindness? What if you learned the power of *that*?"

"That all sounds pretty holier-than-thou. You want a trophy or something?"

"Maybe there's some truth to what I said."

Jed's jaw twitched. "You know what I really hate about you?"

"The color of my skin?"

"It's that once you get on your high horse you don't know when to shut up. I just wanted to..." He shook his head, studied the ground. "You know what? Never mind. Maybe you're the one who needs to let your defenses down."

Shame flooded Mateo's chest. He'd gone after Jed. Made him out to be weak. He hadn't meant to be so harsh. "I'm sorry, I—"

"Forget it."

"No, I *am* sorry. I shouldn't have been that—"

"Honest?"

A pause. It was all true. Still, it didn't make it right to tear him down that way. "Yeah."

"Okay."

Mateo guessed that was his way of accepting his apology.

"Hey, what race is this Saturday?" Jed asked abruptly, evidently done with the personal nature of their conversation.

"Regional meet."

"You gonna win?"

"I guess. Toughest competition in the state is in another region. I'll see them at state next week."

"So, what if I want to come and watch you race *next* Saturday? Provided you make it. Where, when—that kind of thing?"

The question was an unexpected olive branch. But maybe it was

320

Jed's way of making things right. "It's at the Kentucky Horse Park. I think it's the second race, but I'll have to get back with you on the time."

"Thanks." Jed started to leave again. Stopped. "My last government test... I got an eighty-nine. With your help. Maybe I'm not so hopeless after all, huh?"

"You never were, Jed. You're a lot smarter than most people realize."

"Think so?"

"Yeah, man. I couldn't put an engine back together. I can't even change the oil."

Laughing, Jed walked away. "Dude, you ride a bike. You don't even know how to drive."

"Thanks for the reminder."

"Anytime."

—o0Oo—

It wasn't that Mateo minded Lou picking him up for the homecoming dance. She was a few months older, anyway. Plus, her family owned more than one car, which meant they had a spare for occasions like tonight.

It was that he had to sit in the back seat. Because her mom was riding shotgun.

"Only twenty-two hours to go before she can take her driver's license test," her mom said. "She's such a careful driver. Only one chipmunk fatality so far."

"Mom!" Lou growled. "It was an accident, okay?"

"I know, sweetheart." She patted her shoulder. "Those rodents are like tiny kamikazes."

Blinking nervously, Lou peered at him in the rearview mirror. "Hey."

He noticed her eyelashes, long with mascara. Noticed how her hair was carefully French braided along the sides and curled into long ringlets at the back. A corduroy jacket lay draped over her shoulders, so he couldn't see her dress at all. She'd kept it a secret. He didn't quite think that was fair, since she knew what his suit looked like, but that was girls for you.

"Hey," he said back. Then to her mom, "Hi, Mrs. Abrams."

"Hello, Mateo—and call me Carrie." Her hair was scooped up in a loose ponytail and she wore a worn gray hoodie that made her look like she'd just gotten done working in the yard. There was a casualness about her that made the whole situation less awkward. Until, "You look devilishly handsome. Like a movie star."

The heat rose so fast up from his chest that he felt his face redden. "Thank you… ma'am." It was a distinctly Southern word he normally didn't use.

Carrie's eyebrows lifted. "Manners. I like that. But please, it's Carrie. Not ma'am or Mrs. Abrams. That makes me feel old."

He wasn't sure he could bring himself to do that. So he just smiled and nodded.

Lou carefully checked her mirrors, then backed out onto the road.

"Such a gorgeous place to live," Lou's mom said. "The hills, the woods. Nature all around. And the trees right now— breathtaking. All that amber and crimson. I'm jealous of your setting. If I look out my kitchen window, all I see is the backside of my neighbor's roof over the top of a rickety privacy fence."

She'd said it so genuinely that Mateo didn't doubt her for a second. It even gave him pause to consider for a moment how fortunate he was to live on remote Rockhill Road where he could listen to the rustle of leaves on a breezy day and watch the colors change in the fall.

Ten minutes ago, Mateo had felt so nervous about the

homecoming dance that he could hardly eat. On account of their races ending late that afternoon, they'd decided to forego a fancy dinner. Although relieved, it only gave him more time to worry about what he would say to Lou and how the evening would go. Even whether or not he'd feel out of place at the dance. He was achingly aware that the pants he'd borrowed from Lou's cousin's boyfriend were an inch too long and the suit jacket slightly big on his lean frame. He'd found the shoes at the local discount store and bought them with the money he'd earned from cleaning cars at Mac's. They were black and plain and in the dark of the gymnasium he hoped no one would notice they were a little scuffed.

Several times, he found himself adjusting his bow tie. He'd never worn one before. Hoped he wouldn't have to again anytime soon. His running clothes were like a second skin. This suit, while it marked a special occasion, made him feel like he was pretending to be something he wasn't. Not yet, anyway.

Lou's mom tried valiantly to ask questions to fill the quiet as Lou drove carefully. All Mateo could come up with were short answers. Yes, the regional meet went as expected. Yes, he planned to go to college. No, he wasn't sure yet what he was going to study. It was almost like she was interviewing a prospective groom for her daughter. When they stopped at a light, just outside of town, Lou glanced apologetically in the mirror. Mateo smiled back to let her know it was okay, he understood.

Funny how they could read each other with a mere look, a shrug, a smile, or an arched brow. From the first time he'd ever spoken to her, he'd felt like that.

When they finally arrived at school, the parking lot was full. A dozen other cars were streaming into the drop-off loop, which made Mateo thankful there were others like them who needed the assistance of parents or older siblings to chauffeur them to the dance.

When Lou pulled up to door, she paused, waiting. "Well, here we are."

It took a few seconds for it to register. He hopped out, opened her door, and held out his hand to her. As she placed her hand in his, he was only vaguely aware of Carrie standing beside them, snapping pictures with her phone.

Not wanting to openly gawk at Lou's dress, he stole quick glances as she shed her jacket for the impromptu photo shoot. Everything about her dress was modest and simple: pale blue, without embellishment, the hemline ending at mid-thigh. Other girls wore skin-tight, very short dresses in shimmery colors, or off-the-shoulder gowns with lacy layers of skirt, but it was as if they had to don their beauty, rather than allow what was already there to stand out.

"Mateo, Lou," Carrie said, the car engine still running, "would you mind standing by the wall so I can get your photo next to the school sign?"

Her back to her mother, Lou rolled her eyes, then pasted on a smile and spun about to oblige. Mateo stood rigidly beside her, still awed by her metamorphosis. A few clicks later, Lou grabbed Mateo by the elbow and started toward the school entrance.

"Whoa, hold up. I'm not done," Carrie protested. "Put your arm around her, Mateo. Where's the corsage?"

He and Lou looked at each other. Mateo had never been to any kind of dance with a girl before, let alone a formal one.

Lou squeezed his hand before slipping under his arm. "I told him I didn't want one, Mom. They're itchy."

"Oh, okay." She snapped away, changing angles before pausing at the end to clutch her phone to her breast. "My little girl... So grown up."

Dashing away a tear, she rushed in to kiss her daughter on the cheek. "Have fun, you two. Call me fifteen minutes before—"

"Got it, Mom." She pulled Mateo away. "See you later."

"Thanks for the ride," Mateo added.

The night was a whirlwind. For days, Mateo had fretted how it would go—whether he would step on her toes or fall on his butt. He'd studied videos feverishly, practicing his dance moves in front of the cracked mirror on the back of his bedroom door, thankful his grandmother's recent uptick of extra cleaning jobs had at last afforded them enough money for wireless internet on their phones. His fears were eased when he noticed how some of his teammates appeared even less graceful than him on the dance floor. Lou made it all more fun, laughing about her own awkward moves and chatting with him to take his mind off things. He even forgot about paying attention to the popular kids, the ones who'd shunned and made fun of him for so many years.

Metallic streamers dangled from the rafters, catching rays of dancing beams from the strobe light as it spun from a wire in the center of the high ceiling. There was a certain anonymity in being surrounded by so much noise and motion. They were like two bees on the fringes of a buzzing colony.

As moments melted into minutes, which became one hour, then two, Mateo was ever more aware of her. The intoxicating nearness of her. Her slim waist and smooth back beneath his hands when they danced slow and close. The contagious excitement of her energy when she danced fast. The tickle of her whisper in his ear.

He wondered if he could feel this way about her a year or a decade from now. Would they grow closer... or would they discover annoying flaws about each other that would drive them apart?

Either way, he was sure there was so much more about her that he would find magical. For now, she was just enough of a mystery he would lose himself in the discovery of her. She had the power to make him forget his fears. To make him feel like he belonged. Here. Now. With her. Perhaps always.

As the hands on the big gym clock crept toward eleven, he seized every moment. Breathed it in. Let the beating of his own heart impress itself upon his ribs like a memory of what it was to be alive. Until—

"Oh." Glancing at the clock, Lou frowned. "I suppose it's about that time. I should—"

Mateo silenced her with a brief kiss. Even though Mr. Sutherland was barely twenty feet away, leaning against the railing of the stands, stifling a yawn with his hand. She'd been about to break the spell. He didn't want to let her.

Prying herself away, she looked around. It was the first time Mateo noticed anyone looking at them. As if questioning whether they belonged there together.

"I'm going to grab my jacket out of my locker." She rubbed her arms vigorously. "I'll call my mom. Meet me by the band room door?"

"In the back?" There would be fewer people there. A place for those who wanted to steal a few minutes alone before parting ways.

Her smile revealed a teasing promise. "Sure. Give me five… no, ten. I need to hit the little girls' room."

"Okay," he agreed as she scurried off.

As if on cue to her departure, the music ended. Ms. LaCrosse's weary voice came over the PA system. "Thanks for attending this year's Faderville Harvest Homecoming. Drive safely. Get your homework done. The real world resumes Monday morning at seven-thirty sharp."

An elbow bumped his. A couple, arm in arm, strolled past. Somewhere, a ring of boys laughed raucously. He thought they were laughing at him, but when he located them, they were already walking away. He drifted into the commons, still abuzz with the night's excitement, then hooked a right and went down a long, less crowded hallway.

Once out of the building, he tucked himself in a corner between the outside of the band room and the tech room where he could easily see Lou when she emerged. Which seemed to take forever.

After a few minutes, he wondered if he'd missed her. He went around the corner and was met by a couple making out heavily. They didn't even stop when he nearly ran into them. Did the chaperones not know about this place? Embarrassed, he slipped back to his hiding spot. Checked his phone. Nothing.

Maybe he should go back inside. Find Dusty or Bucket to talk to until Lou was ready.

He stepped up onto the sidewalk. Reached for the door handle.

The door blasted open. He barely jumped out of the way before two hulking forms stomped through. One of them he recognized as a member of the football team. A guy named Brogan. He didn't remember his last name. But the other guy... Mateo couldn't recall ever seeing him before.

"This the dude?" The ogre—all six-and-a-half feet of him—loomed over him, grinding a fist into his palm. "The one fixing to hook up with that girl?"

"Yup." Brogan spat at the ground. "That's the sleeze, Cash."

Stepping backward until he met the wall, Mateo held his hands up. "Hey, I'm just waiting for a ride."

Brogan looked around and behind him, where a recess between two walls led to a garage door for equipment storage. "Right. Looks to me like you're waiting for *her*, to, you know... get her alone."

A car pulled up just around the corner. Two doors slammed as the makeout couple got in. The car drove away. Leaving Mateo alone. With the two thugs. Beyond the cone of light shed by the security lights.

"I'm going inside." Mateo lowered his gaze. Made to move past them. "My friends are waiting for—"

Cash clamped onto Mateo's arm. His breath, reeking of beer, steamed in Mateo's face. "You ain't got no friends around here,

327

Poncho."

Calmly, clearly, he said, "My name is Mateo." Then, in hope of escape, he drove his shoulder between the rough brick wall and Cash's chest.

The next thing he felt were the bricks scraping at his back through his borrowed suit. The world flipped sideways. Asphalt smashed against his cheek. A calloused hand drove down on his jaw. He tasted bits of gravel and dirt in his mouth. Blood on his tongue. Felt a boot impact with his ribs. The wind bellowed from his lungs in a visceral grunt.

Reflexively, he hugged himself in a ball. Covered his head with his arms. Tensed for the next blow. Readied himself for the beating he'd known for years would be coming.

Heard a body hit the concrete of the sidewalk. But not *his* body.

Trembling, Mateo peeked between his forearms. Cash lay on the sidewalk, rubbing his wrist.

"Crap!" Cash cried. "You broke it! I'm gonna sue your ass."

At first, Mateo couldn't understand. Had Brogan shoved Cash aside? But as monochromatic shapes took form in the shadows, Mateo noticed Brogan backing away.

"Dude!" Brogan looked down at Cash, then up. "What was that for?"

Fists clenching and unclenching, chest heaving, Jed swayed above Cash.

For a moment, Mateo thought it would all end there, that Jed's dominance, both physical and social, would dissuade either bully from acting further.

"You two jerks," Jed growled, "need to leave my friend alone."
Brogan scoffed. "What'd you say?"

"You heard me." Jed pulled his shoulders back, stood tall. Very tall. "Leave. Him. Alone."

"No, the other part. What did you call him?"

His breathing was audible. That of barely contained violence. "My friend, you mean?"

Brogan laughed. A hollow, sardonic laugh.

Shoes scraping over cement, Brogan barreled at Jed. Clumsily, drunkenly. They collided in a percussive flurry of fists. Twirling sideways, Jed rammed an elbow into Brogan's gut. He doubled over, gasping.

By now, Cash had pulled himself onto his hands and knees. His face contorted in a grimace. Slowly, he stood, leaning against the wall for support, one forearm cradled to his chest.

Sensing Cash's eyes upon him, Mateo scrambled to his feet. He was a runner, not a fighter. Had never understood the compulsion to throttle or hammer another human being. Until now.

If Jed could stand up to these losers, so could he.

Blood thrummed in Mateo's ears. The caution that had served him so well all these years was lost. Gone. Overcome by the rage of injustice.

Mateo curled his fingers into anvils and squeezed them painfully tight. He focused on Cash, only because he was closer than Brogan. Assessed how easy it would be to grab that injured arm and twist it behind his back, then slam him to the ground. Thought about how he could pummel his blocky head against the wall, just like he'd been shoved to the ground. Asked himself if the revenge would be worth it.

He wasn't sure.

Because he didn't want to be like them.

"Mateo?" The voice had floated so softly on the cool brittle air, it took him a moment to figure out where it had come from. "I heard something—"

Lou stood huddled at the outside corner of the building, her jacket clutched tight across her. She glanced at Cash, at Brogan, and lastly at Jed. Then to Mateo, "Are you okay?"

He nodded, aware how bad the scene must've looked to her.

"Mom... Mom's in the drop-off circle already. Maybe... we could go back through the school. Give you a minute. I'll just tell her I had to look around for you."

They joined hands, but Mateo stalled, waiting for Jed. "Come on."

With barely a pause, Jed shuffled after them.

After the doors had closed behind them and there was no indication the two boys were following them, Lou raised her fingers to brush the bruise on Mateo's cheek. "Sorry it took me so long. What happened?"

Other kids were still milling about in the hallway.

"Long story. I'll text you," Mateo told her. As he went to put his right hand in his suit coat pocket, he noticed the pocket was ripped. And the back of his hand was scraped raw and bleeding. He tucked his hand in what was left of his pocket, grateful he'd be sitting in the back seat so Lou's mom wouldn't see. He'd repair the pocket himself before returning the suit to Lou—hoping it wasn't damaged more. As they were about to head out the main doors, he turned to Jed. "Thanks, man."

Jed shrugged. "No problem. I owe you."

"For what?"

"For not blabbing about... you know. And for helping me. You're all right."

Then Mateo put his arm around Lou and walked back outside with her. Into the cold night. And the rest of their lives.

chapter 29
Mateo

Mateo's legs were restless. Like he could've climbed every flight of stairs to the top of the Empire State building. Something about tapering week always left him feeling cagey. Even more so this season than normal. Grayson's training methods and race advice had differed considerably from Tervo's. Despite his doubts, Mateo had decided to place his trust in him. Not everyone on the team had been as compliant.

At the conference meet three weeks ago, Cruz had busted to the front of the pack and built a commanding lead by the half-mile mark, despite the fact that Coach Grayson had clearly told him to hang back behind Mateo. He was still ahead at the halfway point in the race when the refrigerator landed on his back. Cruz finished as the team's fifth man in, more than a minute behind Dusty that day, their second man.

At the end of the finish chute, Cruz had collapsed to his knees, then rolled over onto his back. Mateo grabbed a cup of water and began toward him, but the coach had already beaten him to it.

Grayson stood over Cruz. "I see you decided to make a bold

move today. Hit your first mile split twenty seconds ahead of target. How'd that work out for you?"

Still prostate, Cruz stared up at the sky. "Not very well."

Nodding, Grayson offered him a hand. Cruz clasped it, then staggered to his feet.

The coach gave him the cup of water. "You learned something valuable today. Remember it."

That was Grayson. Simple, direct, calm. It had taken time, but Mateo had come to appreciate him in more ways than he could've ever imagined.

They'd won the meet by a mere five points—a much closer margin than anyone had anticipated. The blessing was that it taught them not to take their past successes for granted. And that each one of them was critical.

This week at practice had been lighthearted and easy. A last-minute grasp at how close they were to the season being over with. Which was a sobering prospect. As much as they'd wanted to get to this point, they also didn't want it to end. Many of them were seniors. These days, this team, would soon be a thing of the past.

Since the girls hadn't qualified for the state meet, their season had concluded the previous week. But every day, Lou would wait after school just to wave bye to Mateo before her mom picked her up. He was still thinking of her when practice ended that Wednesday.

Even though all the other guys had left, Mateo lingered to retrieve the safety cones marking their workout loop that started out in an open grassy area at the park and went partway through a patch of woods. He skillfully collected them without breaking stride, dipping into a crouch and scooping the next one up wherever they marked a gentle curve. Sooner had stayed behind with Grayson, peering at him sadly through the bars of her crate as he'd gone off without her. She'd somehow split a pad earlier and had been despondent over having to be sidelined for the entire practice today.

332

Hugging the cones to his chest, he took the trail into the woods to fetch the last of them. There were only two left. Once he had those, he could give them to the coach before heading home. He didn't have to work that night, just had plans for studying—which meant he'd continue debating with himself whether to ask Lou to the movies next or to the sandwich shop in town. It would mean splurging, but she was worth it. He didn't mind asking her to drive, since she had her license now, if it meant they got to spend—

Footsteps crashed behind him. He turned, but heavy hands knocked him to the ground. The impact bellowed the air from his lungs. Cones scattered in all directions. Miraculously, he'd landed in a flattened pushup position. More mentally stunned than physically harmed, he gulped in air. Before he could flop over onto his back to see who it was, a length of cold metal pressed against his cheek. A knife's point glimmered just beyond his right eye. If he moved an inch—

"Did you think you'd get away with it?"

Brogan.

Dropping to his knees, Brogan knelt over him. "Nobody's gonna miss a cockroach like you."

The knife pinched Mateo's flesh. He flattened his palms against the earth, as if he could push his way into it and somehow disappear. Holding his breath, he listened for sounds. Heard nothing but Brogan's ragged breathing and his own heart pounding.

If he did nothing, he was at Brogan's cruel mercy. If he fought back, there was a chance. But Brogan was nearly twice his weight. Strong in ways he was not. And thirsty for revenge.

From the edges of his memory, Mateo heard a familiar voice. *Breathe, Sandoval, breathe. Everyone thinks the secret to coming out on top is about fighting harder. It's not! The secret is in conserving every ounce of energy you possess. Save it for the final stretch.*

This *was* the final stretch. He might very well be dead in a minute.

333

Use the last of it when it counts most, but not until then. Give up too much too soon and you're as good as gone.

Then he remembered Coach Grayson. If he didn't come back with the cones soon, he'd begin to wonder where he was. He could scream for help—but no, he was too far away by now for the coach to hear him. His pleas for help would die in his throat as Brogan laughed.

"Who's gonna help you now, Mariachi Boy?" Brogan's cackle morphed into a heinous growl. "Nobody, that's who."

Brogan spat at Mateo's face. The glob clung to the ridge of his cheekbone a few moments before sliding to his jawline, then oozing down his neck toward his Adam's apple.

"One thing's fer sure—you done danced your last dance, Bean Eater."

There was only one choice.

Fight.

For three heartbeats, maybe four, Mateo focused. He estimated Brogan's body position, his center of gravity, how quickly he might react. But no matter how he weighed it, the odds were not in his favor.

You haven't lost until you have. Don't decide the race before it's run.

With a backward thrust of his elbow, Mateo twisted sideways. He jabbed again. Hard. The point of his elbow found the soft of Brogan's belly, forcing a grunt. With a magnitude of force born only of adrenaline, Mateo threw his body backward, heedless of where the knife was. It was just enough of a surprise to throw Brogan off-balance.

But not long enough.

Before Mateo could scramble to his feet and take flight, Brogan slammed his fist into the ground and reversed his momentum to torpedo at him. His blocky head rammed into Mateo's thigh, sending him crashing to the ground onto his hip. Mateo rolled under Brogan's weight, sticks cracking beneath them, stems and leaves lashing at them as they tumbled into the underbrush.

It was only Brogan's flannel shirt snagging on the branches of a thorny bramble that bought Mateo a moment. He planted one knee into the earth and launched upward.

Brogan flung himself forward, cloth ripping. The blade flashed in a beam of light as it arced through the air.

Sidestepping, Mateo avoided being slashed. Barely. His knees buckled with the momentum. He stumbled. Caught himself on a bent sapling. As he ducked under the tree, Brogan staggered into a stand. Mateo cleared two more low branches before he realized he'd wedged himself into a dead end. Before him was a cliff. On either side was a thick tangle of brush. He glanced up. The rock leaned overhead. There was no way out. He whirled around.

Somewhere behind Brogan, a low furtive form flew over the leafy ground. A rabbit or fox stirred up by the skirmish, perhaps. Mateo shut it out and focused on the threat in front of him. There was no one there to save him. There was so much for him yet to do and become. He refused to have gone through all that he had for nothing.

"When they find your body," Brogan said, "I'm going to tell them you attacked me and it was self-defense."

Mateo didn't respond. He was saving his energy for the moment that mattered.

Because unlike Jed, whose taunts were merely a shield for his own insecurity, Brogan *would* kill him. If he could. There was no soul in him. No compassion.

Blood ran from a gash near Brogan's temple. Somehow during the scuffle, he'd hit his head on a branch or a stone. His free hand wandered to his wound. He drew a fingertip over the blood, looked at it. "You're going to be sorry for what you did."

"No"—Mateo said calmly—"you are."

With crazed eyes, Brogan threw his head back and laughed. In an instant, his laughter became a howl of pain. Teeth had pierced his calf. He spun around, flailing the knife, but he could not shake the dog that had latched onto his leg.

Sooner shook her head ferociously, ripping Brogan's jeans, tearing at his skin. Almost in slow motion, he crashed to his knees and then went face down like a giant tree felled by a tiny ax. Somehow, he rotated his cumbersome bulk and stabbed at the air.

But Sooner's reactions were lightning quick. She'd let go of his leg to avoid going down with him and was waiting for the arm that held the knife. The moment he flung it in her direction, she turned her head sideways and clamped onto his forearm so tight the knife fell from his grasp and clattered over a log. He yelled out in pain. Threatened her. Still, the dog did not let go.

Transfixed by the mortal battle before him, Mateo slowly became aware of his surroundings. To his right was an opening between the bushes. Arms before him to clear the way, he charged through. Fifty feet away, he turned to look. As fierce as any Schutzhund dog, Sooner held Brogan to the ground by his arm.

"Let go! Let goooo!!!" Brogan screamed in terror. If not for the thickness of his shirt protecting him, it would've been a bloody scene.

Mateo knew he had to run—but he didn't want to leave the dog behind.

"Sooner." Walking backward, he clapped his hands. "Sooner, come!"

He couldn't leave without her. If Brogan killed her...

Somehow, Brogan raised himself up on his other elbow and located the knife. He reached for it, but his fingers fell inches short.

Sooner was beginning to tire. Her legs shook. Her cheeks puffed out as she gasped for air between her teeth. Brogan's arm slid free. Undeterred, Sooner lunged in for another bite.

Darting forward, Mateo snatched up the closest stick he could and beat it at the nearest tree.

"Let's go, Sooner!" he cried. It was the phrase he so often used at the beginnings of their runs.

Her head popped up. She turned toward him. Just as Brogan staggered to his feet.

Mateo didn't wait to see what Brogan would do. He took off. Faster than he'd run to win his last race. He thought he heard Sooner's footsteps behind him, rustling the leaves. Hoped he had.

And he ran, and ran, and ran.

Trusting she was there. Yet never truly knowing.

chapter 30
Sooner

I'd known from the moment I first saw him that Mateo would need my protection. Someday, somewhere, somehow. Although I didn't know then that I knew. It was like a memory that was already there. A sense. A calling. A duty.

Brandy and Grayson were my family, but Mateo would *need* me.

When I woke up that morning, it was with a feeling of... I'm not sure. Not worry or dread, but alertness, maybe. Like my nerves were raw. I'd felt that way the day Mateo and I had gone running alone on the trail and he'd wanted to show me what he called 'the bluff'. Maybe it was the storm blowing in, but I'd felt the danger long before the first rumble of thunder. Turned out it was me who needed looking after that day.

This morning, Grayson had let me out to potty and I'd run laps around the house looking for something or somebody without any indication there was anything to be concerned about. In my burst of energy, I'd stepped on a flake of stone that had cut my pad and come in limping. Brandy had cleaned the cut and put ointment on it that she warned me not to lick. Throughout the day it got better, but when

I'd first run up to Mateo at practice, the cut had opened again, making me limp back to Grayson just enough that he confined me to my crate.

No matter how much I whined or pawed at the crate door, Grayson wouldn't let me out.

"No, Sooner," he'd said. "Brandy would have my hide if that cut got infected or torn open more. You stay right there. You'll be fine— in a couple of days."

When Mateo disappeared into the woods alone, I started to howl.

Earlier, I'd seen the man-boy. Still young, like Mateo and his teammates, but bigger. He'd lurked at the edge of the woods while the others were running, watching them, waiting.

There were often other people at the park. That was nothing new. But this man-boy... he didn't belong there. Somehow, I knew.

As Mateo moved along the loop, plucking up the cones, I'd lost sight of the stranger. So when Mateo disappeared into the woods, I fussed even more.

"All right, all right." Grayson abandoned his notebook at the picnic table and let me out of the crate. "Go potty. Hurry up."

I'd no sooner hit the ground than I took off running.

"Sooner, get back here."

But I ran. Straight toward the trail. Even as Grayson shouted after me, "Sooner, come! Soooooonerrr!"

I didn't know what I was racing to, but I had to get there *fast!*

So I just ran. And ran. And ran. Searching for Mateo.

My muscles knew these trails—all their turns and dips and rises, the fallen logs and the biggest trees. My nose and ears led me. The scent of crushed leaves and the snap of branches.

Then, I saw a hulking form looming before Mateo. I left the trail and crashed through the brush, flying low, barkless.

I dived for the man-boy's leg. Opened my jaws wide. Snapped

them shut. Hung on, even as he screamed and tried to shake me.

I couldn't let him hurt my friend. I had to protect Mateo. Even if it meant my life.

It was so hard to do. Not just physically. My jaws tired. I could barely hold on as he kicked at me. I'd fought another dog once, but I'd never bitten a human. My conscience told me not to. That hurting people was bad. I was meant to guard and comfort them, never to harm.

But this stranger had come to kill Mateo. I'd sensed that. The feeling was somehow familiar. And I could not let it happen.

It came as a surprise when he fell to the ground. But I wasn't done with him. Mateo wasn't safe yet. I hadn't even seen the knife until he stabbed at me. Ducking sideways, I bit his wrist and held on. The knife fell from his grasp. Still, I didn't dare let go. It was not my own life I feared for, but Mateo's.

His way clear now, Mateo ran past. He may have been calling for me, I'm not sure. All I could think was that I couldn't let this man-boy get up and pursue Mateo. I had to keep him where he was. On the ground. In pain. Powerless.

The memory came hurtling at me then. A memory not even mine. A memory from a dream when I awoke at Doc Hunter's office.

Of the man named Caesar. The gunshot. The stabbing pain in my chest. The smell of sulfur and iron, of sandy earth and nervous sweat. The fiery glare of the sun while my body went cold.

Mateo in his mother's arms...

And then—

"Let's go, Sooner!"

—o00o—

"What happened?" Grayson's chest heaved as he sucked in air. He'd met us just past the trail's head. "I heard screaming, but it didn't sound like you."

Mateo had finally stopped running. He looked at Grayson, then back at me, before sinking to his knees and opening his arms wide. I rushed into his embrace, curling my body against his chest and licking his face.

"You're okay, you're okay." Mateo wrapped his arms around me, but only briefly. He let go and shot to his feet. Farther down the trail, the man-boy ran toward us—if what he was doing could be called running. More like weaving, one arm clutched to his chest.

"Who's that?" Grayson asked. "And what happened back there?"

"Brogan," Mateo uttered with contempt.

"Brogan who?"

Mateo shook his head. "I don't remember his last name. But he and some guy named Cash tried to beat me up after the dance. Jed Delaney saved me."

"And he showed up here to finish what he started?"

"I guess." Mateo came to stand next to Grayson. I went behind and wedged myself between them. "But it was Sooner who finished it."

They both glanced at me then, but Brogan was still coming at us, mumbling curses. Growling, I took two steps toward him.

"Sooner, stay." Grayson went forward, his hand held up. "Stop there!"

Brogan staggered to a stop, his face still twisted in pain. "I'm going to call the sheriff on that dog! He's vicious. They'll gas him."

"You don't need to call the sheriff."

"He almost killed me!"

"First of all, it's a she. Secondly, I think you tried to kill her—and Mateo, here."

Brogan scoffed. "I was just taking a walk in the woods and that damn dog came out of nowhere." He raised a bloodied hand to point

341

at Mateo. "He sicced him on me!"

"The knife you dropped back there"—Mateo nodded toward the trail from where he'd come—"the one with your fingerprints on it, will prove otherwise."

The wail of a siren ripped through the air. Shock fell across Brogan's face.

"I already called the sheriff," Grayson said. "Feel free to tell them your version of events. We'll see who they believe, given the evidence."

The sirens grew louder. They were coming down the road. Turning into the parking lot. Tires squealed. Car doors banged shut. Feet pounded on pavement, then earth.

Brogan spun around and started back down the trail, dragging the leg I'd bitten.

I took off after him, swung past, skidded to a halt. Stood square on four feet.

Stay! I barked. *I'll bite you!*

He took one step at me. I dove at his ankles, teeth snapping.

"Sooner, no!" Grayson said. "Come here, girl. Come!"

As Brogan broke to the side to crash through the bare undergrowth, I heeded Grayson. Brogan stumbled, fell, got up again, went in another direction.

Two men and a woman in black jackets and tan pants came running down the path then. The men—one of them young and fast—headed straight for him as he wove through the brush. Brogan was lame and disoriented, though. The faster officer cleared two fallen logs in quick succession and caught up with him easily, tackling him to the ground where he held him until the other arrived to put metal rings on Brogan's wrists behind his back.

The woman officer trotted up to Grayson and Mateo. "My partner and I just happened to be on the state highway headed this way when the call from the dispatcher came in. Deputy Miller there, the fast one, was investigating a littering violation at another one of the park's entrances when he heard the call for backup. He was a national runner-up in the hurdles while he was at Morehead State."

Brogan was yelling at the officers, but his words were muffled by the fallen leaves against which his face was pressed.

"Who is he, anyway?" the officer asked as they hauled Brogan to his feet.

As briefly as he could, Mateo explained his run-in with him and Cash after homecoming, then Brogan's ambush out on the trail. The officer jotted it all down in a notebook, asking simple questions while the other two officers hauled a surly Brogan to his feet and read him his rights.

"Brogan goes to my school, but he's two grades behind me. Flunked at least one, maybe both." Mateo explained.

"So this guy jumped you on the trail just now, no one else? Threatened you with a knife?"

"That's right."

"What did you say the other guy's name was—the one from the other night?"

"First name is Cash. Never seen him before, though."

"Cash Weisenberger, by chance?"

"I don't know his last name, either. There wasn't time for introductions."

"Big guy? About the same age."

"Yeah, really big. Why?"

"I think we know where to find him. He's a dropout from Somerset. Those two have been in trouble before. Vandalism, trespassing. They were accused of assaulting a Korean kid a couple months ago, but got off with a slap on the wrist. If this Jed Delaney backs your story up, we can charge them both this time. Should be some security footage from the school." She looked Mateo over. "Forgive me—I should've asked. Are you okay? Did he hurt you?"

343

"Just scratched up, but thanks, I'm fine." Mateo sank down beside me and put his arms around me. It was the best feeling in the world.

"Thank you for watching over me," he whispered into my ear. "It's almost like you're my guardian angel—there exactly when I needed you."

chapter 31
Mateo

Mateo wanted it over with. Desperately.

"Any questions?" Mr. Sutherland barely paused. "Ah, no. Thank you, ladies." Pushing back a yawn, he leaned back in his swivel chair before motioning to Jed and Mateo. "Now, last but not least."

Vivi Arvin and Mikaela Ransdell had just gone eight minutes over time—Vivi on term limits in Congress and Mikaela on the divisions of duties between the Senate and the House of Representatives. Intent on maintaining their honor roll standings, they'd included every mundane detail garnered from their online searches. Even Mr. Sutherland had nearly fallen asleep.

"Now what were your topics, Jed and Mateo?" As they rose from their seats and went to the front of the room, Mr. Sutherland drew a paper from his desk drawer. "Ah, yes. *List three reasons that would motivate someone to immigrate to a certain country and one reason why they might do so 'illegally', 2) Give three examples of immigrants who have made major contributions to the U.S. in the last twenty years.*" He tossed the paper back in its place and folded his arms. "Your turn, gentlemen."

"You first," Jed told Mateo without hesitation. As if he'd

planned it all along.

Right. Jed was just hoping Mateo would take up too much time. Probably hadn't started until last night. Meanwhile, Mateo had put dozens of hours into the project. By himself. Checked and double-checked his sources. Gone down countless rabbit holes. The hard part had been limiting himself to just three people. In the end, he chose not the ones that meant the most to him, but the ones he thought his classmates might actually recognize.

"Imagine it's your first day of school—and you can't understand a thing anyone is saying. Imagine that despite that, you one day become known to millions. Yet you began with nothing. You worked harder than anyone. And you achieved the American Dream." He looked from face to face, wondering if this was what it was like to address a jury. "When this immigrant's parents moved to Los Angeles from Ukraine, they had seven children and only two hundred and fifty dollars. She began elementary school, as I said, unable to speak English."

Mateo paused there, his thoughts drifting to his own first day of kindergarten in Faderville. He'd been terrified. Unable to eat. He'd wanted to run all the way home, but his mother had told him to stay until she returned to get him. In every glance, he'd felt the burn of judgment. Above all, he was aware he did not look like any of them. The teachers had guided him from room to room, placed papers in front of him full of words he didn't know, repeated phrases over and over. He'd felt so out of place. So... dumb.

Yet he'd shown up day after day, drifting silently from room to room, surrounded by children he desperately wanted to play with, but couldn't even talk to. Every time he heard laughter he was certain it was him they were making fun of.

Back at his grandmother's house, the TV had been his only friend. Cartoons and *Sesame Street* filled his hours beyond school. Two months into that first year, a boy named Oliver had befriended him.

Oliver was *gordo*, as his *abuela* would say—plump. He had a round face and a round body and smelled of cigarettes because both his parents were chain smokers. Oliver wasn't popular. In the hierarchy of students, he was barely one rung above Mateo. But he was kind and goofy and helped Mateo learn words. At lunch he taught him 'milk', 'cheeseburger', and 'pizza'. When the first day of school rolled around the following year, Oliver was nowhere to be found. One of the teachers finally told Mateo he'd moved to California with his father. By then, though, Mateo had learned enough words to get by. Still, he struggled. He didn't like feeling stupid or lost, so when he wasn't outside exploring the woods around his home, he watched TV. One of the shows he watched was *That '70s Show* with Mila Kunis. It wasn't until much later that he learned her story. She was the child from Ukraine.

Then he told his class about Sergey Brin who came from Russia at the age of six and later co-founded Google. Next, he told them about Steve Chen from Taiwan who, together with Jawed Karim from Germany, started YouTube.

"Soooo"—Vivi twirled a ringlet of blond hair around her finger—"the guy who started Google and Mila Kunis are both from Russia?"

"Mila Kunis is from Ukraine," Mateo gently corrected.

She rolled her eyes. "Isn't that part of Russia?"

"They were both once part of the Soviet Union, but no, Ukraine is not part of Russia."

Hands went up with more questions.

"You're saying Google was started in a garage by a couple of college guys?" Bucket asked. "No way."

"Yes."

"And because this Karim guy's dad was from Bangladesh, people in Germany were giving them a hard time, so they moved to... *Minnesota*?" Half the class laughed. As if Kentucky were a more sophisticated place to live.

"Yes."

Bucket looked truly perplexed. Mateo wanted so badly to explain to him, to all of his class, how it felt to not be invited to birthday parties or asked to sit at a lunch table with others. Or to be watched at the convenience store as if shoplifting were a foregone conclusion. More generally, how it felt to be judged and excluded and blamed for things not your fault.

"As informative as that was, Mateo," Mr. Sutherland interrupted, "we need to move on to Jed so we don't run out of time. Well done. Thank you."

Mateo stepped back and waited. Fifteen seconds ticked by on the clock as Jed unfolded the paper he'd written his presentation on.

"Three reasons..." Jed's voice quavered. His hands were shaking. He put the paper back in his rear pocket. Shoved his hands in his front ones. He rocked on the balls of his feet a few seconds more. "Let me get real. I, uh, had a hard time with this. At first, anyway. I'd never really thought of it from the other side. Gotta protect your own interests, as my dad would say, and to hell with those 'others'. Sorry"—he shot Mr. Sutherland an apologetic look—"just quoting the old man. Didn't mean for it to slip out. Anyway, I need this grade, so... so I asked myself the question: What would make me leave the place where I was born and grew up? What would make me leave *here*? Well, first thing I thought of was to get a better job. Maybe just *any* job. Like, what if I couldn't make enough to move out of my parents' house or put gas in the car or feed my family? Which made me think of the second thing—food. What if food was super expensive where you lived or it was even hard to get any because the stores were empty or you had to go a long way to get it? Why stay?

"And then I saw something on the news last week. There was a story about how some dudes my age down in countries like El

Salvador, Guatemala, and Honduras were pressured to join gangs. They didn't do it because they thought it was cool, but because they were afraid. It's either join up or someone gets hurt. Like you or someone in your family. Maybe even killed. Hard to imagine living somewhere like that. Somewhere you didn't feel safe.

"I'd sure want to move from a place like that. Maybe even to another country. But it's not as easy as you think. I looked it up, see. And if you lived in a place like I described, you'd want to get the heck out of there as soon as you could. You wouldn't want to wait. Not years and years, anyway. So you'd leave. Taking only what you could carry. Because you don't have thousands of dollars to rent a moving van. You'd probably take your kids, too. I mean, you wouldn't want to leave them behind, would you? And once you got someplace else, like here, you'd be willing to take any job, just to have a chance for a better life."

The class waited for him to go on, to say more.

Jed shifted on his feet. "I'm not so sure about the term 'illegal' anymore, though. How can a person be illegal? You can do an illegal thing, maybe even cross a border just so you can, you know... live. But what does that make you?" He shrugged. "Desperate? Hopeful? I don't know. Maybe brave is a better word. I'm not sure I'd have the guts to do it. But I think anyone willing to take a risk like that, well, they deserve a chance."

349

chapter 32
Sooner

To humans, different clothes meant different activities. To a dog, this was nonsense. Our fur was appropriate no matter what we did. But I did appreciate knowing ahead of time what my humans' plans were.

On the days Grayson put on his long tan pants, the ones he called khakis, that meant he was working in his home office at his uncle's old desk. Sometimes people he referred to as clients came and sat in the room with him. They would pass papers back and forth and look at the computer screen together to talk about things like taxes or investments or retirement savings. I found this all very boring and would try to liven up the meetings by bringing out my ball, because clearly those people needed to play. Whenever I dropped my slobbery ball in a client's lap that would get me banished to the kitchen. Once I even carried one of Grayson's running shoes around, hoping he'd get the hint. That earned me crate time. Not what I was going for, but it was a good opportunity for a nap.

The meetings, I figured, were basically excuses to sit and talk with other human beings. Okay, so sometimes humans just wanted to be with other humans—no dogs allowed. Seemed like a sad existence to me.

When Grayson did put on his running shoes along with a pair of shorts or sweats and a T-shirt, I knew we were going running. This was my favorite thing to do—next to playing ball, going for car rides, snuggling on the couch or bed with Brandy and Grayson, napping, chasing Felicity the cat, digging holes, greeting new people at Rex's office, and… and… I was forgetting something.

Anyway, when Brandy put on comfy clothes, I knew we were either staying home or doing something together with Grayson. When she put on her best clothes—zip-up pants and a fancy blouse or sweater—I knew it was a workday.

Then there were Grayson's coaching clothes—a pair of dark sweatpants with deep pockets, a zip-up jacket with words stitched across the back, his best running shoes, and his big wristwatch. Those were the days I stayed home with Brandy while he went off to a race with Mateo and the others.

All of these told me what my job would be that day—whether it was to go running, to clean up food when it fell on the floor, to chase the squirrels back up in the trees where they'd be safer, to remind people it was just as important to play and relax as it was to work, or maybe just to be there if anyone needed me. For anything. If my humans were happy, I was happy.

So I was very confused the morning Grayson was all fitted out in his coaching clothes and Brandy had put on a nice sweater, pants, and was getting ready to go out. Maybe Grayson was going to drop us off somewhere on his way to school to catch the bus.

"Grayson?" Brandy called out. "What time did you say Rex would be here?"

His own jacket in hand, Grayson came flying down the stairs. He stopped abruptly at the bottom step. "Oh, Sooner has her vest on already."

"Yes, I couldn't remember what time you said he'd be here to pick me up and I didn't want to make him wait."

He turned his wrist to check his watch. Their obsession with time was another thing I didn't understand about humans. To me, there was only 'now' and 'not now'.

"Not for another hour. No sense in you getting there too far ahead of time. There are two races before ours, so…"

"You say that like you don't want me there early. Maybe I'd like to see all the races. It builds the excitement. Plus, I get to visit with people. I was thinking maybe in the future, I'd go to more of them."

"Oh… sure." His eyebrows suddenly lifted. With a look of panic, he patted all his pockets, then relaxed. "Um, say, want me to take Sooner's vest off, since he won't be here for a bit? You can put it back on her when you get to the race."

"She's fine."

Last year, Brandy had put this vest on me, telling me it let other people know I was working. Sounded like an excuse to force me to wear clothes. I tried not to fuss about it, because I really didn't like calling attention to the thing. Better than that time she put a costume on me at the dog club for some Halloween party. Now *that* was embarrassing!

As he came nearer, Grayson bent toward me. "No sense in her wearing the thing for an extra couple of hours if—"

Brandy touched his forearm. "Grayson… she's fine, really. She doesn't even seem to notice when she has it on. I swear, sometimes it keeps her calmer, like she knows she's on duty. That's not a bad thing around Rex, you know. He can be a whirlwind and if he knows Sooner's going to be around, he stuffs his pockets with biscuits and runs her through her repertoire of tricks for his own entertainment."

"Okay, whatever. Just thought she might be more comfortable." He glanced around the living room. "Do you know where my Faderville jacket is?"

"In your hand?"

"No, this is just one of my regular zip-ups. I need the embroidered one. It *is* the state meet today."

"Last I saw, it was on the back of your office chair."

"Could you grab it for me? I can take Sooner out really quick for you."

"Ooookay." Shrugging, she wheeled toward the office.

Grayson and I went outside. Not just into the front yard, but around to the side and behind the biggest tree. Not my usual spot, but he seemed insistent. The second I was done with my pee, he squatted and called me to him. Must've been time for our morning hug.

I trotted to him, but before I could put my paws up on his shoulders, he grabbed the side zipper on my vest and stuffed a little pouch inside the pocket there.

"Whatever you do"—he tapped his finger on my nose, then pointed at me—"do... *not*... lose that. I'm going to need it today. Got it?"

I licked his face really good. It tasted like lavender soap. Brandy's soap. I snuffled his hair. Coconut. Brandy's shampoo. I liked those reminders of all of us being together all the time. I wanted it to be this way forever.

Grayson's arms went around me. Tight.

"Thank you, Sooner," he said into my fur, "for bringing us all together. But no more scares, okay? No more getting lost or sick or struck by lightning. You've given us more than our fair share of heart attacks. Please, let the next few years, the next ten, be peaceful, all right? I can't stand seeing Brandy worry about you. Heck, *I* can't stand worrying about you. I just want us all to be happy. No more drama. No more. Just... love."

I licked him some more, so hard he fell backward onto the ground. He welcomed me into his arms and we lay there on the dewy, cool ground while fog drifted around us and a watery sun peeked above the eastern hills.

"Grayson?" Brandy called from inside. The front screen door creaked open. "Where are you?"

Gently, he pushed me off him. "Over on the side."

She rolled to the side of the porch and stretched her neck to peer over the top of the rail. "Ah, I see you now. Found your jacket. It's chilly out this morning. What on earth are you doing on the ground?"

Standing, he brushed the dirt from his pants. "Playing with the dog."

"I thought you had to leave."

I followed him up onto the porch as he helped Brandy back inside and closed the door. "Yeah, I should. I'll catch up with you at the meet, okay?"

They shared a kiss. I started to follow him to the door, just in case he decided to take me with him—it was always worth a try—but Brandy had her hand firmly latched onto my vest handle.

Grayson was halfway through the door when he stepped back inside and gazed at Brandy.

"Forget something?" Brandy said.

He shook his head.

"You look like you're about to say something."

A few moments later, he said, "Just remembering how incredibly lucky I am."

Nodding, she laughed. "In that case, it's a good day to be going to the biggest meet of the year."

—o00o—

There were people everywhere! Some running to see who was the fastest, some cheering them on. I wanted to find Mateo and run with him, but this wasn't like practice. In certain areas, there were ropes strung from poles and only those racing were allowed on the other

354

side. People were gathered in rows and clumps outside the ropes, whistling and clapping.

Aside from that, the place looked a little like Grayson's farm, with painted board fences and horses grazing behind them among the grassy hills. Here, though, there were more barns, many more, and so *many* horses in the faraway pastures. I searched the crowd, but I couldn't yet pick anyone out.

After parking in a special lot closer to the race, Rex had pushed Brandy along a paved path that crested a short mound and then onto the grass for a better view. There, the crowd wasn't so thick and he'd promptly charmed a group of high school girls to give up their front row spot for us.

"Last time I was at an event like this, a colleague of mine was running a half marathon in Cincinnati. Bunch of lunatics, up at O'dark hundred, running thirteen miles in their skivvies for no good reason. I see now they start them young." He tipped his cowboy hat back and looked out over the rolling hills. "Good thing it hasn't rained this week or you'd be sunk in mud. The grass is pretty trampled in some places. Looks like a herd of wildebeest has been on the stampede, as is."

Wiggling my shoulders so the vest sat comfortably on my back, I settled in on Brandy's left. Even as much as I hated the thing, I have to admit it made me feel… important.

"You texted Ynez about how to find us?" Brandy asked Rex.

"I did."

Brandy scrunched her face up. "You haven't told Grayson, have you, Rex?"

"Now that would spoil the surprise if I had, wouldn't it? No, dear heart, I haven't so much as hinted about it. I'm a man of honor. Do you know how many confessions I've heard over the years? Hundreds, I reckon. So not to worry—your secret is safe with me, Brandy. I haven't revealed it to a soul." He winked at her. "Except maybe the dog, but I don't believe she counts."

Cool air brushed my whiskers and I inhaled the scent of horse hair, nervous sweat, and crushed grass. Clouds hung low in the sky, but they were the kind of gray clouds that carried no rain and moved slowly.

"There she is." Brandy stretched her arm high and waved. "Ynez, over here!"

I peered past the wheelchair. Ynez was pushing the walker up a short hill. Why did Ynez have Brandy's walker?

"Sorry, I am late... *I'm* late." Ynez positioned the walker to Brandy's left and squeezed in beside me. "So much... many cars."

"No worries, Ynez," Brandy said. "We didn't account for the traffic jam getting off the highway, either. Thanks for swinging by the office and picking up my walker. I'm so nervous for Grayson and the boys. I'm expecting my knees to buckle."

"No problem. It was... on the way. You will do good."

Rex unzipped his jacket partway. "Ynez, do I detect a trace of Southern accent in your speech? Your English is sounding mighty fine these days. Brandy here tells me you two have been teaching each other. I'd ask for lessons myself, but"—he tapped at his temple— "the gray matter is getting kind of rusty and since my mouth works faster than my brain, who knows how I'd mangle your beautiful language."

Ynez gave Brandy a questioning glance.

"He says your English is good," Brandy interpreted, "and he's too lazy to learn Spanish."

Rex crossed his arms. "That is *not* what I said."

"True, but it's what you meant."

"Why do women think they know what I mean? My beloved is constantly reinterpreting what I say. I swear, they ought to—"

The murmur of voices rose, then broke into a roar as a gun cracked in the distance. I saw them then—the great swarm of runners as they sped across an open expanse. The girls next to us jumped up and down and shouted. Even Ynez was clapping her hands and calling out Mateo's name. Gradually, some of the runners pulled ahead and the hoard funneled into a narrower swath. They raced along a fence, then swung toward us. I looked for Mateo, but they were still all too closely packed and too far away. Then, just as Brandy had done many times at physical therapy and lately at the office, she raised herself up to stand behind the walker.

Closer and closer they came. Feet stomped. Legs churned. Arms thrust back and forth. So much motion! Even as the leaders came near, I wasn't sure which one was Mateo. I looked for dark hair, but there were several. Then, a short way behind the leaders a familiar stride caught my eye. It was the uneven arm swing that gave him away. And like that, they all shot past us—a blur of bare limbs and uniforms of every color.

"He's behind," Brandy said to Rex. "Is that bad?"

"Naw. They're only coming up on the mile mark now. Two more to go. Mateo's a smart kid. He knows what he's doing."

"I hope you're right."

Her hands clasped to her heart as the runners descended the other side of the hill, Ynez rattled off something in her different words.

"What did she say?" Rex asked.

"That he's running his own race. He knows every one of the other runners and what their best times are. He figured they'd go out too fast, trying to shake him, and that if he stayed behind, they'd get overconfident and exhaust themselves in the second mile. His strategy is to sit tight until the last mile."

Rex cocked an eyebrow. "And then?"

Brandy asked Ynez. She turned back to Rex. "He didn't tell her that part. If you'll excuse me, I need to sit now." She folded amazingly gracefully back into her chair as the lead runners disappeared over a distant hill.

Sometimes when I was feeling full of energy and exploring the farm with Grayson, I'd run as fast as I could for as long as I could, just to feel the wind in my face. There was never any destination. I did it because I could, knowing one day I might not be able to. I never had anyone to race—except for Felicity, and she was always up a tree or in the barn rafters before I could close the gap between us. She probably knew she'd lose, that's why.

It seemed like such a long time we waited for Mateo. Every once in a while, I could see motion in the distance as the race went off in another direction. Some of the crowd ran from place to place to get a better view.

When it became clear the runners were headed toward us once again, the excitement grew even more. Rex put his fingers together and let out a shrill whistle. Again, Brandy raised herself up. Two runners were far ahead of the others. One of them... was Mateo!

"Mateo! Mateo!" Ynez shouted, bouncing up and down. "*Ve rápido*, Mateo!"

They blew past us, side by side, their strides matched. Mateo never slowed. Just kept going faster and faster, shoulders relaxed even as the one arm stayed tucked more tightly to his chest, his eyes set on the finish line.

I remembered all our time spent together. How he sometimes jogged slowly with Lou and stood with her after practices under the big trees, talking softly, looking down at the ground and stealing glances at her, his confidence growing. The day we went up to the overlook and he stumbled and then the lightning ripped through me. When he pressed himself against the wall at Doc Hunter's clinic as I lay on the cold, hard table, my insides still buzzing.

She saved me, he'd said as he knelt next to me. *I'm here.*

And then, not long ago, when Brogan had attacked him in the woods after practice.

I'd never understood why I felt drawn to Mateo. My life was full enough with Grayson and Brandy in it. It was just a sense that he needed someone to watch over him. A sense that we already, somehow, knew each other. I was aware of it, especially when I looked into his eyes and imagined him as a young boy, with so much life yet ahead of him, and then as a young man, forging forward into a world that was not always friendly or kind. It wasn't so hard to think of him as an older man, too, content and fulfilling his own purpose in the world—whatever that might be.

Now, as I watched him sprinting the final stretch, the other boy matching his speed, I saw them carried on the waves of the crowd's energy, until at last they reached a narrow line painted across the grass. Mateo stumbled and fell forward, depleted. The other boy staggered, slowed, and twisted around to look at the giant sign flashing numbers behind them.

Eyes closed, Ynez uttered prayers into her clasped hands. Rex tipped his hat back, speechless for once.

"Did he win?" Brandy said to no one in particular. "The clock's too far away. I can't tell."

No one answered.

For several minutes more, Brandy stood resolutely, as Cruz, Dusty, and Keen ran past. Finally, she sank back down. Two more Faderville runners went by.

When Bucket finally ran toward the finish line, I could see Grayson jogging on the far side of the roped off area yelling, "Go, Bucket! Go, go, go! All the way. Don't let up now. Two more spots, right ahead of you. Don't quit now. Every point counts!"

In response, Bucket picked up speed. I'd never seen him go so fast. He passed one boy, then two more, then another—all in a very short distance. When he crossed the line, he took one more step and collapsed. Keen and Dusty ducked under the ropes and scooped him up by the arms to escort him down the chute on wobbly legs. I thought I saw Mateo standing close by, a cup of water in his hands, but he was soon obscured by more runners and by officials urging them along.

In time, the runners became fewer and farther between. The shouts had dimmed. Most of the crowd by now was drifting past the finish toward the end of the chute where they joined up with the runners, some happy, some nervous, others spent or heartbroken.

Then, a familiar face came jogging toward us. A happy face.

Mateo! I barked. *Let's go!*

chapter 33
Brandy

"Sooner, shhh, no barking," Brandy said, although she found it hard to admonish the dog, given the circumstances. Mateo was jogging toward them, looking less exhausted than she felt. By now, she was sitting in her wheelchair again. She hadn't meant to stand so long, but it was easier to see and the drama of the race had mesmerized her and filled her with an energy she hadn't known since her agility competition days with Sooner.

"Son"—Rex reached over the rope cordoning off the course to clasp Mateo's hand—"you about gave this old man a heart attack, taking it all the way to the line like that. I was just about to look the results up on my phone, but why don't you fill us in. Looked like a photo finish from here. Did you wallop him in the dive or not?"

Mateo squeezed his eyes shut. Then, blowing out a long breath, he looked at the sky. "I knew he'd challenge me, but... I wasn't expecting that."

Ynez blew him kisses, even as she frowned.

Leaning out farther, Rex pulled him into a brief, manly sort of embrace. "As long as you didn't hold anything back. We're still proud of you, young man. That was a heckuva race."

After Rex let go, he added, "I heard someone behind us say those were the fastest two times *ever* at a state meet. You can hold your head high, son. Those college coaches are still going to be pounding on your door, begging you to—"

"Yo, Speedy!"

A boy Brandy didn't know ducked under the ropes and gave Mateo a high five. His shoulders were freakishly broad, which led Brandy to guess he was probably a football player.

"Way to kick it in, Mateo. You were a total beast."

"Thanks, Jed," Mateo said humbly.

"Results say you nicked him by six-one-hundredths of a second. Six-one-hundredths! Do they have instant replays in this sport? Because I'm betting the other dude contested that call."

"It's chip-timed *and* they have it on camera, so yes," Mateo said softly, "I won."

At that, Ynez clapped her hands and erupted in tears of joy.

"Awesome! Guess we can call you champ now. Hey, I brought the team along." Jed pointed to a group of guys wearing Faderville jackets and hoodies about fifty yards down the ropes. They hooted and hollered, some raising posters up in the air with sayings like '*Run, Mateo, run!*'

"The whole team?" Mateo said in disbelief.

"Well, minus Brogan. They wouldn't let him out of juvie. Not that we'd want him here. But yeah, all the rest came along. This is pretty wild. I had no idea it was this exciting watching a bunch of skinny dudes slop through the mud. How'd the team do?"

"I don't know yet. The last few runners were coming in when I came to look for *mi abuela*." Mateo worked his way down the line to hug his grandmother. She clung to him, speaking rapidly in Spanish, and kissed him several times on both cheeks before he was able to unlatch himself.

"Hey." Jed bent down to pet Sooner. "This the dog that brought Brogan down?"

"That's her."

"Wow, cool. Doesn't look that scary up close. Must have a pretty fierce bite." He yanked his hand away. "Am I allowed to pet her? Should I, even? Is she a guard dog, too?"

Brandy chuckled. "She's not trained to be, but it is her instinct to be protective when she needs to. And thanks for asking about petting her. Sometimes I need her to focus, but right now it's okay."

"You have to come to the awards stand now, *abuela*," Mateo said, then looked directly at Brandy. "All of you."

Brandy's stomach flopped. "Did you—"

"Yes, don't worry." Mateo smiled at her. "There's a place for you right up front."

Mr. Sutherland shouted at Mateo from the other side of the course alley. "Mateo, that was spectacular! Great job!"

"Thank you," Mateo called back. Ms. LaCrosse was there, too, wearing sneakers and a puffy jacket. He waved to her.

Bending down, Mateo took Sooner's face in his hands and kissed her muzzle. "I couldn't have done this without you. Actually, I wouldn't even be here, if it weren't for you."

Sooner kissed him back—big, sloppy licks that made him laugh.

"Ynez," Brandy said, "will you take my walker for me?" Then to Mateo, "Where's Grayson? We saw him a few minutes ago when Beckett was coming in."

"With the team. This way." Standing, Mateo motioned them toward the finish line.

"Go on ahead." Rex unlocked the brakes on Brandy's chair and positioned himself behind her. "We'll be there in a few. Might have to take the long way. Gonna be a might bit tough maneuvering through the crowd, but Ynez here'll plow us a path." He whistled through his teeth, then gently pushed as he shouted, "Pardon us!

Coming through! Pardon! Pardon!"

It took some time, but their little group made their way to the awards area. Somehow, in the midst of a sea of faces in the stands, Brandy saw Mac Kendrick waving from the midsection of the stands. Jed and the football team were cheering in the top row now, doing the wave. Off to the side of the stage in a section reserved for the top teams, the Faderville boys' team stood clustered in their matching sweats. Last year, if Brandy recalled what Grayson had told her, they'd been just out of the medals and although they'd worked hard all year, Tervo's death had initially dealt their spirits a blow. It had taken half the season, he'd said, to restore their determination. While she often missed Grayson's presence at home on meet days, she could see his investment had paid off. She'd always been proud of him, but she hadn't known until today how important it was not just to him, but to his athletes, as well.

What Brandy noticed the most in all the celebration was the energy and the abiding sense of community in this lesser known sport of cross country, where resolute athletes poured heart and soul into preparing for this single day, running mile after mile, sometimes alone, in blazing heat and bitter cold. Here, there was no ball or bat, no hoop or goalpost, no timeouts or substitutions. Every competitor ran the same course under the same conditions at the same time. And although hundreds would rocket from the starting line at the firing of the gun, only one would be the fastest.

Today, that one was Mateo Sandoval, the soft-spoken young man who wanted only to care for his grandmother. How easy it would've been, Brandy mused, for him to merely put his head down and accept 'good enough'. But more than anyone, Mateo understood what sacrifice meant.

As she watched Mateo and his teammates drift toward the awards stand, Brandy wondered what it would feel like if the fruits of her own struggles were recognized in a ceremony like this. Society, however, didn't celebrate a handicapped person overcoming their daily tribulations. That was done in private with loved ones. If at all.

Yet, she'd come so far in this last year, after having fallen so far down. Most of her battles had been fought alone or with just her physical therapists as witnesses. Nothing like this. In the last few months, after having reached a plateau in her progress, she'd pushed herself even harder, toward a goal she once thought impossible. And now today... *finally*... she was going to share her triumph with Grayson.

Along the way, she'd learned others had fought their own private battles behind shields of anger and walls of resignation. She wasn't the only one. Sometimes, all a person needed was someone to listen. To care. Compassion had become her purpose. She felt more needed and appreciated now than she ever had before. And that brought its own kind of satisfaction. One that could not be measured in medals or ribbons or dollars.

To make a difference in the life of another, for the better, mattered. *She* mattered.

All she needed to be... was kind. And in that one simple gesture, she'd found a way to both belong and have purpose.

Before the accident Brandy had kept herself busy with dog sports. She'd never really spoken to her dog friends about deeply personal issues. While she was close with her brother and dad, there were some things she wasn't comfortable sharing with them—like how long it had been since she'd gone on a date. The busyness of the dog sports was really just a cover for the loneliness she felt. It wasn't until she met Grayson that she experienced a profound connection with another human being. And now over the past few months, her other connections had grown exponentially. Just by reaching out with a kind word. By listening. If she'd only been brave and selfless enough years ago to ask the first question of others...

Sooner rested her chin on Brandy's knee and gazed at her. She'd been so good today, despite the crowd and noise. Even when the voice came over the loud speaker, announcing that awards were starting, Sooner hadn't flinched. Amazing how she'd transitioned from a high energy performance dog in her younger days to such an even-keeled service dog.

"I don't know how people without dogs get through some days, girl." Brandy rubbed Sooner's ear. "We're both survivors, aren't we?"

Sooner yawned.

"Right. Just doing your job, huh?"

"It is… it's starting." Ynez pumped her fist in the air. "Mateo, Mateo, Mateeeo!"

The top placers were being lined up to the side of the stage. Noticing that Sooner's vest had shifted a little sideways, as it sometimes did, Brandy reached over the dog's back to reposition it. As she gripped the left edge to the front of where a zippered pocket was, she felt a lump inside. Had she placed something in the pocket yesterday at work? She couldn't remember what, if she had. Just as her fingers found the zipper tab, her attention was diverted by the approach of a man in the black outfit of a race official.

"Miss Anders?" he said. "Would you mind coming with me?"

"Me?" Brandy pointed to herself. "Why? What for?"

"Your presence was requested." He had a gentle face and soothing voice. She had no reason to distrust him. Still…

"Presence where?"

"If it will help, Coach Grayson Darling wanted you to have the best seat in the house."

Brandy glanced at Rex. "Do you know what this is about?"

He shrugged and held his hands wide. "Sounds like your beau just wants to give you a better view. Go on."

Suspicious, she narrowed her eyes at him. From where she was in the front row now, she could see just fine. Something was up, but it didn't look like there was a graceful way out of it.

"All right." She unlocked her brakes. "I'm going to need a little help, though."

"No problem-o," Rex said. "Right on your tail."

Brandy was certain they were just going to allow them to observe even closer, down in the empty area with just the photographers, but then the official motioned Rex to a ramp toward the rear and he wheeled Brandy up it to the far side of the stage, Ynez toting the walker close behind. There was a long row of chairs to the front and she could see the boys' individual placers lined up at the base of the stairs.

How irritating that she was watching them from the side rather than straight on, Brandy thought at first, but after a while she came to appreciate being able to look out at the crowd. Where was Grayson, though? She couldn't find him, no matter where she looked.

As the top runners filed across the stage, Mateo waved at his grandmother, a huge grin on his face. They started with fifteenth place and worked their way up. When the second place finisher received his medal, Mateo shook his hand, then embraced him. The same official who'd fetched Brandy to the stage placed the medal over Mateo's head as his name echoed over the speaker system. Applause erupted when his new state record was announced.

Next, the team placements were announced and they began calling the teams up in reverse order. Faderville had defeated the runner-up by a mere two points and it occurred to Brandy that Bucket—although he'd been the seventh of Faderville's runners to cross the line—had beaten four runners in the final stretch, displacing one of the top five scorers for the contending team. Cross country was like golf, Brandy remembered, in that you wanted the lowest score possible.

Just as the last medal was hung over the last neck, Grayson crept up the stairs to appear at the far corner of the stage. The official who'd escorted them onto the stage brought forth the team championship trophy and presented it to the Faderville boys.

Brandy tapped Rex on the leg. "Are they going to take Grayson's picture with the team? Suppose it will be in the newspaper tomorrow?"

"Could be." Rex smiled down at her.

Then, just as Brandy had guessed, they called Grayson over and, with the boys arrayed in two rows—one standing, one kneeling—the photographer snapped pictures. The day would be immortalized in the annals of Faderville High School. These kids would forever look back on this day with pride.

While life, Brandy mused, could be captured in snapshots of glorious high points like this, those moments were often determined in the quiet hours alone, sweating, cursing, struggling, sure of failing in ignominy—when no one was watching. The win hadn't defined them; the daily struggle had and Grayson had laid out the path for them.

Brandy was surprised when they placed a microphone on a stand in front of Grayson. Maybe it was tradition for the winning coach to give a speech.

"Thank you for coming out today, everyone." His voice had the hint of a nervous tremor to it. While Brandy had given many presentations to total strangers in her previous career, as a numbers guy, speaking to large numbers of people was clearly not something Grayson relished. "As many of you know, I took this program over after the sudden passing of Coach Tervo Heikkinen, who'd over decades built a worthy program at Faderville High School. It was crushing. Never underestimate the influence a good coach can have not only on a team's record, but in shaping the individual characters of his or her runners. This crew had their doubts about me starting out—and rightly so. I even had to beg some of them to come back out. But I wouldn't be standing here without them having put in the work."

His head lowered, he went quiet for several seconds. Then he gazed at Brandy. "But I might not be standing here at all today without the love and support of a very special person and her amazing dog, who both came into my life a year ago."

He nodded at Rex. Some sort of pre-planned signal, Brandy was sure. Rex began to wheel her forward, but Brandy held up her hand. She wasn't about to be upstaged.

She grabbed Ynez's wrist. "Remember what we talked about."

Ynez nodded vigorously. Then her brow crimped. "Now?"

"Yes, now."

Ynez positioned the walker before her. Not so gracefully, Brandy hoisted herself into a stand. She gripped the bars of the walker and waited until her lightheadedness ebbed away. The very same energy she'd felt as the race was ending surged through her.

The look on Grayson's face as she walked toward him with Sooner heeling beside her was one she knew she'd never forget. He dashed the tears from his eyes with his jacket sleeve.

The crowd cheered. People took pictures. She wondered if this would be in the paper or on YouTube. Before she knew it, she was standing before Grayson in the middle of the stage.

"Grayson," she began quietly so only he could hear, "I have—"

He silenced her with a kiss on the lips to hoots and applause. Then he held up a hand to speak.

A little more insistently, she began, "Grayson, will—"

"Give me a minute, honey. Just... one minute." He turned back to the crowd and spoke into the mic. "This incredible woman, Brandy Anders, was gravely injured in an auto accident last year. Her dog here, Sooner, was thrown from her van and lost for weeks. When this dog was on her final leg, I found her—or she found me, I'm not sure which. You see, I was in a dark place that day. I'd lost everything that meant anything to me. But this dog, she made me get up every day and have something to live for. Imagine my fortune when I took her back to meet her owner and found this gorgeous lady. If it hadn't been for Sooner, I wouldn't have met Brandy, and if it hadn't been for Brandy, I probably wouldn't have gotten this coaching job. She seemed to know what I needed even when I didn't know it myself."

Brandy had nearly forgotten her plan, he was speaking so lovingly. Her heart felt like a chocolate bar that had been left in the sun and gone all gooey. For all those times she'd questioned whether she was worthy of being loved as she was—heck, even before the accident—she was now overcome with a feeling of connection so powerful it left her without words. So she just took it all in. Let it fill her spirit.

"I can't imagine going through the rest of my life without her. So on that note"—Grayson returned the mic to the stand and called Sooner to him. He unzipped a pocket on the dog's vest and took out a small velvet bag. Fingers trembling, he undid the string on it and took something out, then knelt before her as he reached for her hand—"Brandy, my love, will you—"

"Stop," Brandy whispered urgently. Then more firmly, "Just stop... okay?"

"What?" Mouth open, he stared at her. Confusion, then disappointment and fear crept into his features. "W-w-why?"

"You're spoiling my moment. I had this all planned. I've been working on it for weeks." Glancing out over the crowd, she leaned forward and spoke so only he could hear. "Okay, maybe not... *this*, but I was going to ask you something after the race, when we were alone, and here you had to go surprise me. Damn it, just... I was going to..." Her gaze slid to the stage floor for a few moments as she tried to regroup. "The only thing I couldn't work out was how *I* was going to kneel. I mean, if I did, I wouldn't be able to get back up and that would be awkward. So I was going to do this. Walk to you and ask... the question. Just lay it all out there. Take the biggest risk of my life. Because… what is life if you don't live it fully? Why not be as happy as we can be—together? Forever."

His hand now clenched to his chest, Grayson's frown was slowly replaced by a smile. "Sooo… do you want me to stand or…?"

Suddenly, she was aware that no one—*no one* anywhere was making a sound but them. And that she'd actually been speaking much louder than she intended. "I think the best way to salvage this would be if we said it together, don't you?"

"Okay, but"—he pointed down, then up—"kneeling or standing?"

"Stay there." She pinched her lip between her teeth and nodded. "On three? One… two… three."

Together, they said, "Will you—"

Brandy inhaled sharply. Her lungs felt like a sudden frigid wind had snatched her breath away.

Hesitantly, Grayson pushed the next word out. "—marry…?"

As if hearing the singleness of his own voice made him doubtful, he left it hanging.

The crowd waited.

"Yes!" Brandy shouted. "Yes, I'll marry you, Grayson Darling! Yes, yes, yes!"

He slipped the ring on her finger and stood to kiss her. Cheers enveloped them. Their kiss lingering, Brandy peered out into the audience and saw dozens of camera phones being held high, preserving the moment to share with the world. Embarrassment tried to grab hold of her, but she ignored it and leaned into buoyant joy for as long as she could, knowing such moments were rare. Her heart had wings. Her soul was soaring. She sensed not only Grayson's love and Sooner's, but that of every person there. Which made her wonder what it could be like if everyone paused more often to notice all that was right in the world, rather than all that was wrong.

Soon, someone would interrupt, motion to clear the stage.

People, eager to head home, would begin to drift off. But Brandy held onto the moment for as long as she could. Hugged it hard. Threw herself into the depth and breadth of all the emotions overtaking her. Until at last, her body protested.

Leaning her forehead against his, Brandy said lowly, "If you don't mind, my arms are tired. I need to sit now."

"Oh, sure." He motioned to Rex, who scooted the wheelchair forward. They helped ease her back into it. As he pushed her across the stage and down the ramp, they waved to the crowd.

Joining them, Rex couldn't hide his grin.

With an accusing squint, Brandy pointed at him. "You knew?"

He shrugged. "Sorry, but I keep my secrets."

"Oh, come on, Rex," Grayson coaxed. "Might as well take credit." He leaned closer to Brandy. "He helped me write the proposal speech. The flowery bits were his. He has a way with words."

"So I've noticed." Brandy shifted her focus to Ynez, who'd slipped in just behind them. "And you? Were you in on this, too?"

After glancing at Rex, Ynez blinked several times before gazing off into the crowd. "Maybe... maybe not." She was dragging the walker behind her over the rough ground. Then, as if she could no longer conceal the truth, she blurted out, "You two—you were... meant to be together. But you were acting... afraid."

"Afraid? Of what? I don't understand."

Rex groaned. "Ah for Pete's sake, Brandy. Yes, afraid. Ynez and I get that Grayson here's been married before and maybe he messed that up and that you, Brandy, have been through a mess this last year, but holy cow, it was like you were both expecting the worst—that if either one of you went all in, the other would run away. Problem is, if you live your life that way, you never—"

"Never get to fully experience all it has to offer," Brandy finished. Sooner ambled along beside them, her cheeks bunched into a smile, as if even she'd been in on the conspiracy. "Believe me, I understand that part now."

Brandy glanced up at Grayson as he maneuvered her wheelchair out into the fragmenting crowd and toward the parking lot.

"I suppose we both needed a nudge," he admitted. "At least I did."

At that point, Rex and Ynez drifted off to talk to the boys and their parents. So much celebration. So much happiness.

Sooner nuzzled her hand—the hand with the opal engagement ring surrounded by tiny diamonds in a starburst pattern—as they bumped along over the trodden grass.

It was as if the dog was trying to tell her, *See, I knew all along. It all turned out exactly like it was meant to—you, me, Grayson. Together. Happy.*

From this day forward, Brandy vowed to live life more like her dog, unafraid to love with all her heart.

chapter 34
Mateo

The cadence of Mateo's heart was only now beginning to slow. The night before the race, he'd barely slept and that morning he'd awoken to a sense of expectation—that today was a day of beginnings and endings. A bridge from the past to the future. From the foggy gloom of fear to sun-bright glimmers of hope.

Although he knew there would always be matters beyond his control, there was so much he *could* do. He could choose to believe the worst inevitably would happen—or he could choose to live as if the best possible outcome was within his reach.

Maybe it was the day's excitement finally catching up with him, the months and years of having worked so hard, but fatigue was now setting in. His feet seemed glued to the ground, his body a hundred pounds heavier. He'd returned to where their team's camp had been to retrieve his gym bag and the distance back to the school bus might as well have been a marathon. The rest of the team was waiting on the bus for him. Waiting to go back to Faderville.

He knew he should head back, yet he hesitated. Turned around to take it all in one last time—the trampled grass and muddy paths, the rows of drooping pennants, the clumps of spectators and teams straggling off to their vehicles, the horses in their distant pastures grazing unconcerned. Hours before, the place had been filled with the collective energy of thousands. With expectation and excitement. Hopes and dreams.

Above the memory of the crowd's roar, an old familiar voice echoed:

Remember, Sandoval, that you have to take the risk. You have to dare to be great. Don't shy away from success. Be afraid of giving up in the final stretch, of never stepping up to the line. Just don't be afraid of failing. Very few people who succeeded in the end never failed at all.

When he'd first heard those words, he hadn't understood them. Now he did.

Dusty jogged up to him, his team jacket zipped up to his neck. "You coming? Coach says you've got five minutes or he's leaving without you—and I think he means it, state championship or not."

Until then, Mateo hadn't noticed how the wind had picked up and the temperature was dropping. "On my way. Just... you know, remembering everything."

"Gotcha. But hurry up. It's a long jog back home." Dusty flipped his hood over his head and trotted toward the bus.

Hoisting his gym bag over his shoulder, Mateo began walking that way, his gaze sweeping over the scene, a movie of the race playing in his mind. Exhilaration trickled through his veins, lightening his steps.

Halfway there, he stopped dead. A woman stood in his path. Not just any woman—his mother.

He blinked. Stared harder. She looked older than he remembered. More worn. But also, more subdued. As if the fiery restlessness in her had somehow been doused.

"Mateo..." Anarosa shifted the strap of her purse. She attempted a smile, but her nerves were apparent. "I was *so* proud of you today."

It was her face, her voice, but the reality of it hadn't quite caught up with his senses. Still, she was the last person he'd expected to see today. He would've been less surprised if the ghost of Tervo had dropped down from the sky to crush him in a sentimental hug.

"*¿Madre?*" He tried to swallow, but his mouth had suddenly gone dry. Finally, he managed, "I didn't know you were back in Kentucky. How long will you—"

"Only for as long," she rushed to say, "as you and your grandmother wish me to stay." Anarosa glanced to her right, where another woman stood waiting by a food truck, sipping from a cup of coffee. Valentina Gutierrez waved at him. He was about to wave back when his mother spoke again.

"Ms. Gutierrez and Mr. Franzen... they came to see me this week in Chicago. The police were questioning me and they—"

Mateo narrowed his eyes reflexively.

"No, I did nothing wrong, Mateo. Please believe me. My man... the man I had been staying with, Caesar... He is... was... How do I explain?" She gripped her purse strap, her knuckles whitening. A lock of hair fell across her eyes like a wispy veil, but she made no move to push it back. "There were other women besides me. One of them, Lia... she shot him. They are not sure if he will live. I had to give a statement. Of how I had been treated. The things I had seen. Of the fight I heard between this Lia and him the night before the gunshot woke me from my sleep." As she searched his face for a reaction, her speech became more rapid, more insistent. "It *is* the truth. Ms. Gutierrez and Mr. Franzen will tell you so."

She seemed so desperate for him to believe her. He had no reason not to. Still, it was all so surreal. He wasn't sure what to feel or think.

Yet in that moment, he chose compassion over rejection. He set his gym bag on the ground. Drew in a breath. "That must've been horrible."

Nodding, she shuddered. A tear slid down her cheek. She swiped at it. Pulled her shoulders back. "The past ten years have been... hard. I'm sorry, Mateo. So sorry. Your grandmother warned me, but I was too stubborn to... It is very complicated." More tears sprang to her eyes. Head lowered, she covered her face with her hands. The purse slid from her shoulder, the strap catching in the crook of her elbow.

He went to her. Placed the strap back up on her shoulder. Circled her in his arms. "Stay, *madre*. As long as you need to."

"Your grandmother... She won't—"

"I'll talk to her." He remembered the conversation he'd overheard. It wouldn't be easy, but starting over never was. "Don't worry."

She looked up at him. He was much taller than the last time they'd been together. "There are things I need to tell you, to explain..."

"I know. But not now. Later. There will be plenty of time to talk later. And to listen."

epilogue

Rex

You get it now? Here you reckoned I was just some puffed up blowhard, rambling pointlessly. Just in case you didn't, though, let me spell it out for you. We think we know folks when most of the time we don't.

Remember—everyone has a story. Everyone has their share of problems, too. Think a little more kindly about others before you form an opinion.

On the whole, I've found dogs are better judges of character than most people. If a dog likes you, it'll let you know. If it doesn't, well, shouldn't assume it's the dog who has issues.

Dogs protect and comfort us. Think about that—you're getting a bouncer and a shrink for the price of a bag of kibble and a few tennis balls.

They also remind us that a day spent doing nothing is never wasted if you're with those you love. Point being, slow the heck down. Live in the moment.

Most importantly, dogs understand it doesn't matter where you came from or what you look like. They love you—for being you.

And ain't that what we all want?

author's note

Fiction has the ability to inject us into worlds we might never have discovered otherwise. Other Faderville Novels have dealt with a homeless veteran, substance addiction, animal neglect, aging and death, the loneliness of having a spouse with dementia, survivor's guilt, the challenges of raising an autistic child, depression and suicidal thoughts, overcoming acute trauma, and living with a physical disability. Life can be rough and, let's face it, most of us have been through some messes we'd rather we hadn't. My intention isn't to put readers through an emotional wringer. It's to show that even in the worst of circumstances there are lessons to be learned, challenges to be met, that there is value in pain and grief, and... there is always hope.

When I first conjured up the idea of continuing Sooner's story, I knew that a young immigrant named Mateo would be a pivotal character. I hesitated about how in-depth to delve into his history, aware it could be viewed with a political slant. But I also knew that if I didn't share his full story, the heart of it, then there was no point in telling it at all.

about the author

N. Gemini Sasson is a serial remodeler, intrepid gardener, dog lover, and Boston Marathon qualifier. She lives in rural Ohio with her husband and an ever-changing number of animals.

Long after writing about Robert the Bruce and Queen Isabella, Sasson learned she is a descendant of both historical figures.

If you enjoyed this book, please spread the word by sharing it on social media or leaving a review at your favorite online retailer or book lovers' site.

For more details about N. Gemini Sasson and her books, go to:
www.ngeminisasson.com

Or become a 'fan' at:
www.facebook.com/NGeminiSasson

Made in the USA
Las Vegas, NV
01 December 2021

35784859R00225